Yet more !!!!

[signature]

The Journals
of An
Invisible
Woman

1

Hello Reader, I find myself sat in Exeter in the Boston Tea Party, chatting to the lovely Emma Jardine, who wants to be a Nursery Teacher, assistant manager and friend of Sir John, although when I show him his picture, she laughs and smiles saying, "Oh Fred, he was here last week."

Sorry Reader, I guess you are wondering who I am, well if you read my mentors journals you will of known me as Suzie Johnson; the CIA agent that killed Sir John. I have been on the run sort of, but more importantly I have become an Invisible. I read the journals he wrote and felt it helps me write down my stories. I had written one almost, but escaping Serbian crime boss it got destroyed in a paper mill shredder.

Anyway, always found that Sir John, Art Cable or Fred spent time coming back here so thought would come see if this place gives me space to think. I had romantically hoped he would walk in with a steamer with half a shot of coffee and yet I see why he came here.

Emma is amazing and then announced 'Fred' had offered her a week in New York on him and she can take a friend. She was so excited and scared and happy to meet another woman that knew her generous customer.

Emma was just full of joy, funny and writing the journal helps with clarity and you see what is around you as you look to describe. I see two Tony Berger paintings on the wall and suddenly realise the people in the journals we read were real.

Little Flo is actually back in Honiton serving coffee at the Boston Tea Party there. Clara is now travelling after her exams at Exeter University and suddenly I feel relaxed. I still look around as even here the Serbs are looking for me. I have a picture I need to recover of me as if they find it I am dead.

I feel a tap on my shoulder and jump a little startled and see this kind face smiling at me. I recognise him, but I do not.

"Hello Suzie," he says, "a mutual friend asked me to pop over and give you this."

I looked at him and he smiled.

"It's OK I am Jimmy, yes that Jimmy," he said smiling. "I followed you here from a small town in Serbia."

I looked at him confused and he sat down opposite me. Emma comes back in full swing and hands me my coffee starts to laugh and then disappears.

"A friend I owe more than a favour to has asked me to hand you this and see if you wanted to travel back to New York?"

I looked at Jimmy wondering if Sir John was watching.

"Art is not here. Listen, the Serbs are at this moment following him thinking it is you to St Petersburg. Long story just don't ask. In the envelope are a beauty spot and a USB. It is what we all use now, well I do not use beauty spot, more a mole guy myself. Anyway, inside are instructions on a new identity and how to Bluetooth that identity to the spot and whenever you go through customs that is whom they see. New identity and even first class ticket to New York, with a transfer to LA and time you got your old identity back. Listen in New York invisibles will be in touch and relax the Serbian job was truly beautiful. All of us are talking about it and the new Invisible we call Jaguar. Felt that this was an apt name as deadly, stealth like and not to be messed with. Now enjoy your coffee and if ever in Venice, well I will know you are there, just arrive and the wife and I would be more than happy to have you stay."

And with this, Jimmy got up and disappeared.

I sat there looking around me in wonder as the Invisibles have a network where they know of each ones movements and support without being seen, and once you have carried out a few successes yourself, then they say hello. I guess to stop infiltration from groups that would prove harmful.

Listening to a table behind me discussing how the government in the UK had taken 20,000 policemen off the streets and removed 7,000 armed response officers many were feeling scared of attacks. I turn to smile and find myself involved in the conversation and highlight that the scaremongering is coming from the Tory Party led press in a move to control what you talk about. The depletion of resources, the fact the 'terror attacks' were not terrorist, but mentally ill people thrown onto the streets from more cut backs, and that means they all focus on the wrong issues. They seemed to understand until one, a devout Tory, chipped in that the opposition leader was a terrorist sympathiser. Then conversation returned to attacking him for his views rather than look at the route of the problem.

As I exit with my envelope from Jimmy I remember chatting to Sir John in New York just before I disappeared. His words ring true as he told me that as invisibles we could only hold a light up to the problem, but in the end it is the people who have to make the change. Change scares so many, but I feel change in the UK and throughout Europe is needed, and needed fast.

I bump into Emma on the stairs and ask when she was going to New York and I knew from the way she bounced up the stairs smiling it was soon.

"Next week with Emily, other waitress from here. She's a singer, never been to New York either."

"Well Emma," I said, "it seems that I will be seeing you there."

"OK," she replied and rushed up the stairs with poached eggs on toast for a customer.

I exited and as I was staying at an air bnb in Exeter and felt time to read up on my beauty spot. I felt proud, as this was the first step to feeling I was being accepted into the Invisibles ranks.

Walking down Queen Street into the crowd I enjoyed disappearing and becoming invisible.

Back in my room I see an Australian passport needing name and picture and the tickets, first class, not too shabby as Roseanna would say, friend from college that is, and also details of a room rented for me in Queens. To have lunch at the St Regis and ask for Penny, and also five thousand dollars travelling money.

Now, I laugh as Sir John is thorough, but he knew I was broke, as the money from my contact did not turn up after the Serbs mission. Looking at my beauty spot I marvel at how I could become someone new and within seconds have the identity uploaded to all American security systems. Who was I to be? I sat on the bed in my room and giggled.

2 Walking through customs at JFK I walk up to the customs booth as an Australian actress, Stephanie Dubois. I know, help me Reader, I stood in front of a mirror and decided that it sounded good.

The customs officer looks at me and places the passport under a scanner and all the usual things and then looks to me and without any facial expression says, "G'day Miss. Steph Dubois."

I smile and look to see my new identity on the screen and he hands me back my passport. Smiling back I realise I could not do an Aussie accent. He winks at me and I walk through back into my beloved America.

Well still we have this total asshole in charge with his family running amok, but it was my country and I loved it no matter what. Driving in the news of Yerno marrying the President's daughter is rife. Unifying two major households and a power broker deal more than a love match. I mean to say that he is no catch, a ruthless, nasty piece of work, and I know the things she has done for her father in the name of commerce. Well less said the better. The news is that the 'golden couple' are now behind the POTUS as advisors. Corruption is the new dance and all falling under its spell.

The driver remarked that they were known as the golden couple and then laughed. I asked, "Why such laughter?"

Giggling he replied that it was a phrase that seemed apt as her father enjoyed a golden shower or two. I laughed with him and realised that the Russian Prostitutes to having the

POTUS know he got people to pee on his enemies beds for revenge, of course Reader I refused when asked once on a mission to a democrat lawyers, but my fellow agent was more than happy to oblige. He now works for the White House, cushy job and no responsibility. Even acts as a caddy now and again, helping screw up visiting heads of state's games as they play the bloated POTUS at golf.

Traffic was, well New York is New York. And as I sat smiling to be home the cab took me to a bar with rooms in Queens. Seems Sir John knows it well. I was in Room 22 and as I sat on the bed there was a knock at the door. In walked Deloris, a large breasted girl from New Jersey. In her Jersey accent she said, after looking me up and down, "Hey Babe, this is for you."

At which point she hands me an envelope and I thank her.

"Names Delores, I own this place, well with my new husband. He owned it before." And with that she exited the room and a waft of cheap perfume lingered in the air.

I open the envelope and it is a small itinerary and on it details of lunch I am to have at St Regis Hotel today. After reading the Journals of Sir John I realise I am walking in his footsteps. Was I to meet him again? My heart quickened and I looked at myself in the mirror.

"Jesus Christ Suzie, I mean Stephanie!" I heard myself said to myself. "You were once one of the elite CIA and now an Invisible," but in my heart I was about to possibly re-meet the man who changed my whole life.

Don't get me wrong Reader I still am in awe, but this is just a business partner status. Mind you what if he fancies me? OK, OK, got to stop this Reader, and why am I writing this, and why am I writing this writing this? I am a woman and just as strong and as capable as any man. I was the top of my class in the department, ran more missions, successful missions and was in charge of thousands of operatives when based in Miami. I was, I was, and all right Readers I am in awe of Sir John. I never met anyone who had the resolve and confidence to stay calm like he did, out thinking Sherlock Holmes with the sophistication and charm of Cary Grant, younger readers that a larger than life sort of George Clooney. I realise I have nothing to wear and see a note in the envelope. I take it out and it reads 'Open the closet and outfit for tonight inside.'

Whoever set this up was smoother than a baby's bottom. I am writing all this Reader as this journal has become a bit like testing that a microphone works at a do and then unable to talk to anyone unless you are on the mic. My God this internal monologue is a worry, but then again I have poetic licence and can safely write that once in the dress in the closet I looked great. I had the sexiest curves and great ass, well if Reader's are looking for visuals, you'll have to indulge me. Being in room 22 if I was here all those years ago I reckon JFK would of push Munroe out of the bed for me. OK, OK! I am starting to enjoy writing. It is now eleven o'clock and meeting is at twelve and so that means I have to travel across New York in lunch hour. My newfound benefactor has a great sense of humour as the shoes for this dress are magnificent, but not for walking. I look back at the closet and see a small shoebox with a smiley face on it. As I open it I see a smart pair of sneakers and a note that reads, wear this to the hotel.

As I exit I see Delores coming out of another room and looks at me as if to challenge me to say something. Real Jersey girl. As I walk past the open room door I see a young muscle boy, Jersey too I figure, pulling up his trousers. She married for the money and not for the sobriety I guess.

On the subway to Manhattan I realised nothing to do with me, but felt that sometime Delores and I would have a chat. I mean, no one looks me up and down, especially not a cheap tramp from Jersey and gets to walk away superior. I smiled as I walk up to the streets of Manhattan from the subway as dropped a couple of eye drops into Delores' drink she left on the bar.

At the bar in the St Regis I order an orange juice and look around. A pretty young girl comes over and smiles from the restaurant.

"Hi, I am Jenna, I believe you may be here to meet one of the Knights?"

My heart sank and smiled calmly, "Yes, you're an actress aren't you Jenna?"

"Well yes I am next month doing a film in New England, but today I am Jenna, waitress and your guide to the function." And with that I found myself following Jenna through the restaurant and into a side suite where standing with his back to me was the Ex-President of the United States.

"Hello, sorry for the cloak and dagger, and Jenna can you tell the wife we are almost ready to eat?"

"Certainly, Mr. President," smiled Jenna who then literally skipped out of the room.

I realise that we are the only ones in the room.

"We are eating in here today if that is OK with you... sorry, I gather you have no idea of why you are here and I actually do not know your new name Suzie."

I just looked in dumbstruck hopelessness and held out my hand, "Steph, Stephanie Dubois Mr. President, but feel tomorrow I will have a new name."

He is just amazing. He laughed put me at my ease and we sat at the table made up for six. The door opens and in walks the First Lady and their two daughters with another man who smiles and says that he apologises that Arthur is running late, but we should start without him. He says that Arthur intended to skip starters and makes to leave room.

"He'll be here for dessert," say both the President and his wife and laugh.

"Will Guinevere be coming later this week?" asked the President's wife.

"I hope so as she is so much better organising things than me." He smiles and goes to leave.

"Henry, please join us, Arthur's loss is your gain," say the President and we all sit to eat.

The President's wife gives me a hug and sits me next to her and her oldest daughter.

The youngest asks, "What is your name?" I look to the President about to give the stupid reply of a name I hate when he interrupts.

"OK. I want you to guess. She likes to give names to people we see sat at other tables and sometimes they are very close. Come on. Look at this young lady and tell me if you can guess her name?"

"Dad! You are being naughty," says the older daughter.

"No please name me," I reply.

I stand and give a little twirl as she looks as if guessing and blurts out, "Susannah."

All look at me and I reply, "Yes, that is correct. Susannah Lovejoy." All clap and the President smiles. Then I realise I must practice my name choosing, 'Lovejoy'?

Then the door flies open and in walks Arthur. He stops looks at me and I offer my hand.

"Hello, I am....." yes Reader I had frozen as he looks at me and then The President's family.

"She is Susannah Lovejoy, I guessed her name," came a small voice.

"Susannah, delighted to meet you, and yes young lady we have met before," said Arthur and I remember him helping me escape Willis and shooting Sir John and…. "Yes, you like Suzie do you not?"

"Of course Arthur, and is Sir John with you?" I asked.

"I am not sure he just set this meeting up as we thought we would like to welcome you back to America and say that we all were happy to hear you concluded the Serbian escapade unscathed. Sir John has told my wife I am here and although she cannot join us, she did say that she hopes you can help me avoid dessert." All laugh at Arthur and he places his hand on my shoulder and leads me to the table where he gallantly takes out my chair for me to sit and then I see the ex-President follow suit with his wife and then they both follow up for the daughters. Arthur has Henry stay and fetches a chair for himself.

"By the way Mr. President, Sir John wondered that as you are now the Commander-In-Chief for the Guardians that as an honorary members of the Knights we have a name for you so when referring to the President confusion does not rein."

"So tell me Arthur, what would you have us be?" asked the ex-first lady.

"Well, El Cid, I know a little Spanish and Sofia. Thought of you both being knights that will cause a little confusion in the name with intelligence that could work in our favour."

"Sophia, I quite like that."

Both smile and the door opens as in walks Jenna and begins to take orders.

"Hello Jenna, how is the acting?" asks Arthur.

"Well have month off in Canada acting in film with Dominic, a lead role too." Jenna is really excited, "Oh and Clint has Wentworth play the lead in his first feature he is directing. Anyway, today for you lovely people I am your waitress, so who would like to choose first?"

"Sophia," says El Cid, "Why do you not choose for us and Suzie you can choose for Arthur and Henry."

I look at the menu and see a really nice salmon and salad and then look to desserts. Sophia chosen all then look to me. I look up and smile.

"Right, I am ravenous so the steak for me and Henry, the poached salmon on new potatoes for Arthur," and Arthur smiles, "Oh and Jenna," I ask, "Can the salmon come with one of your lemon meringues on the side, but served after the main?"

"Good call," says Jenna and looks at Arthur, "So no one tell Guinevere and shall I cancel the order of Lemon Merengue you made on the way in Arthur?"

"No, I will have that one," says El Cid, "Well now officially a knight I am going to need to keep up my strength." All laugh and we enjoyed a really relaxed and fun lunch. I mean no holds barred, no standing on protocol just a really lovely family get together with funny Uncle Arthur and the new crazy, me, well had not thought who I was in this scenario, but just feeling so gifted to be here.

As we finished eating Sophia stood and said to the girls that they needed to go shopping and after polite hugs and kisses all round they left. So there I am now with El Cid, Arthur and Henry. Surreal.

"Suzie, Sir John wants you to know he is about and that the Serbs met a difficult end dealing with explaining to the Russians why they were in the country without passports. Seems they had followed and flown into Russia without even knowing and now enjoying life in the north of Russia breaking rocks, so you have no one chasing you."

"And I had a visit to an old friend of mine at the Pentagon and sorry to say had your profile wiped so that you are a ghost, but you are still Suzie Johnson and have all family connections just no CIA. I have here for you your passport. I also would like it if you could watch over my girls and Sophia as Arthur and I are off to New Orleans to check on the rebuild of Guardians land down there. That is if that is OK with you?"

Gobsmacked I looked at both men and smiled as El Cid offered me the passport.

"I would be delighted to sir."

Both men smile and they stand to leave, then turning looking at me they tell me that I am now booked into the hotel and that everything I need is in my room. Then they left like schoolboys giggling off to a frat party as if they had time off.

In walks Jenna and Arthur walks back in after her, "Sorry Jenna we forgot to pay." He hands her hundred dollar bills and gives her a hug, "Thanks for dessert."

And with that he waves rushing back out the room.

I sit there for a few seconds as the rest of the staff come in and clear. They all dart round me in silence and it is as if I am invisible. Then there I am in a private dining suite, alone at an empty table I decide to leave and go chat to reception.

As I walk towards it a manager walks up to me, "Miss. Johnson I have your room ready and all your bags in your room with your clothes put away as asked."

"Oh you have, well that was kind of you," I replied.

Looking at his watch Jenna appears and he smiles, "Miss. Johnson.."

"Call me Suzie."

"Jenna, will you take Suzie to see Tracey in the spa and then arrange time for the hair stylist to be ready?"

"Certainly sir," says Jenna then turns and asks, "can I show Suzie her suite first in case she wants something and then the spa?"

"Jenna, as always you are right, what would I do without you, what am I going to do without you when you're making that film. I hope you do not take this the wrong way Jenna, but I hope the filming bores you and you run back here to stay. I

17

will alert Tracey." And Jenna and I watch him mince off to the salon.

In my room I find a letter for me and in that the code to the safe in the room and in that the most beautiful necklace in a case and letter from Sir John. It read:

> At the event tonight you will
> officially be Mair Clause and girls
> companion and eyes open as
> intelligence has it something
> is up. Enjoy dresses, spa and
> relax as all is going to be fun.

I look at Jenna who has a robe for me and I put it on before we take the lift to the spa. I look around as Jenna leaves and see a whole itinerary has been sorted for my afternoon. Even my pieces from room 22 in Queens were now in my room. I decide to relax and felt that after a month on the run I should enjoy this moment.

Washed, buffed, manicured, massaged and hair done I stand in my room looking at myself in the mirror. I am naked and think, 'not bad', before seeing that it was now five o'clock. Better put some clothes on Reader or my invisibility may be compromised.

3

So there I am standing in my room looking at myself, hair done, nails done, and in a dress that leaves nothing to the imagination. Sir John I feel knows how to dress a woman. I smile as the dress is low cut, a one off by Elizabeth Emmanuel, stunning and the note pinned on it said 'Just the dress for a woman as beautiful as you and ideal to stay invisible; everyone's eyes will be diverted to not look at your face' and a smiley drawn.

I open my clutch bag also left with the dress and in it money and my new business cards, Mair Clause, Nanny and confident to young ladies. I laugh as I have never had children, I do love them Reader, but my life led me elsewhere.

As I walk into the lobby El Cid meets me. He is ridiculously charming and I am literally spellbound by this incredible person who is so humble, yet has be a man of great stature and a true statesman. My favourite President by far, well the country is still in the hands of the idiot savant waiting to be impeached.

I hear calls from my new wards, "Suzie, Suzie?"

I turn and smile as the youngest gives me a hug and the older smiles and is just all grace and manners. We smile at each other and then for no reason either of us can fathom we both curtsey and fall into laughter. Sophia arrives and is just stunning.

In walks El Cid's security, his name is Albert, and is obviously gay, but hides it. He looks at me and smiles, "Miss. Clause, my name is Albert, nice to have you on board."

"Albert, I think we have our work cut out tonight, four beautiful women."

"Yes sir, I agree, ladies you look stunning," says Albert.

"And thank you for the tip on my dress it was definitely the right colour," says Sophia, "Mair, if you want to know anything about fashion Albert is your man, he actually choose that dress for you tonight."

I look at Albert looking humbled and reserved. I walk over to him and offer my hand and as he takes it I give him a hug by surprise. As I hug him I feel his gun inside his jacket and whisper, "Please call me Mair," and then recoiling back slowly, "Albert, I look forward to many days and nights educating me on all I obviously need to know."

"Car is waiting folks so shall we go see this musical, and Arthur has already called ahead to say he and Guinevere are already there backstage with the star who has become a friend."

"Thanks Albert, Ladies shall we?"

And with that we all move to the street and are whisked away and to a Broadway show first night. I am still wondering like you Reader what is happening and to be honest nothing is except I am having the time of my life.

As we drive up to the entrance there is a small flurry of secret service and as the car slows I start to exit as if part of the security team. Albert does the same as we time the exit of the limo perfectly as it stops to hold the doors open.

Suddenly crowds see who it is and start cheering and clapping. There are luvvies all around who also stop on the red carpet to clap and cheer. El Cid and Sophia enter with the girls arm in arm with me behind. I am invisible, but my boobs are not. I have never worn such a sexy dress before, but I like it.

Looking around I see a face, and then look again and he is gone. He looked out of place and inside the room for the boxes in the theatre we are sat in I calmly walk over to Albert.

"Albert," I whisper, "did you see the face in the crowd, the guy with the scar on his left cheek?"

Albert looks at me, and smiles, then looks concerned, "I heard you were good, but tomorrow was going to go shopping with you to bring you up to speed. I will have team know to keep vigilant. Talk in interval."

I smile as the girls come over to me and insist I sit with them.

"You seem to be a hit Mair, it is Welsh for Mary is it not?" said Sophia.

"It is? I mean, yes it is. And thank you for being so wonderful the girls are lovely."

"Mair, I know Albert is bringing you up to date and Sir John and Arthur highly recommended you, but please any time you need anything just ask." And with that Sophia looked to the door to see Arthur arrive with Guinevere and all hug.

Guinevere walks over to me and introduces herself again and I remember how kind her eyes are. The British have a nobility that we in America will never be able to replicate, but Sophia and El Cid are certainly close to nobility as I watch everyone interact.

"Just been backstage with Jonny and Glyn, Johnny Barr and Glyn Kerslake the stars of the show. We are all going to the after party if the girls don't mind staying up," says Arthur.

"Oh Uncle Arthur you are funny, but up to Mummy," says the little one.

"Not up to Daddy then?" asks Arthur.

"Oh Uncle Arthur, you know Mummy always decides on things that matter," she replies and all fall about laughing, "but she does so knowing Daddy agrees, he knows Mummy is wise, he told me."

We take our seats and the theatre is packed. The show is called Mr. Newley and all about a guy trapped in a high-rise block under rubble with just a fireman to talk to hoping to save them both. The connection between the two men is that they are both fans of Anthony Newley and the musical is brilliant. I was in floods of tears as was everyone else, even El Cid had a tear in his ear and stood to give Johnny and Glyn with cast a standing ovation.

The story has the audience thinking that the explosion was a terrorist attack and has you on a rollercoaster of highs and lows, but the crowning glory is that in the end the explosion had nothing to do with what we thought and you left the auditorium feeling and thinking how we must never knee jerk to any conclusions.

As we gather to leave I see in the front row Emma, you know Emma Jardine from the Boston Tea Party in Exeter. She looks up and sees me and we wave. With her is Emily, who is also from the Boston Tea Party and they smile.

Albert standing beside me asks who they are and I explain and within seconds he is on his earpiece and mic and two security men greet them and bring them to the box.

I loved the look on their faces as they walked into the room and see El Cid and Arthur and then in walks the stars of the show and we are all chatting and drinking champagne. Emma is just lovely and she keeps saying things then apologising for thinking she is being too forward or facetious. Arthur hugs her and El Cid hugs Emily and says that they should travel with us in the limos to the party. All laugh as Emma says out loud that they would love to, but do not have passes to the party.

Johnny steps forward and gives her a hug saying, "I don't have one either, but I am sure you will get in with this crowd." All laugh as Glyn and Johnny wave goodbye to freshen up and say that they will meet us there.

I then am arm in arm with the girls and interlinked with Emma and Emily as well.

Guinevere looks to Emily and asks, "Boston Tea Party Exeter, friends of a friend of ours I am sure?"

Emma bursts out excitedly, "You know Fred?"

Guinevere looks to me and I nods and smile 'yes'.

"Yes, we know Fred, but he is also know as Sir John I believe," smiles Guinevere.
"Funny that as the folks in the house where we are staying says he is known as Walter Mitty," says a confused Emily.

"Yes that sounds the same Fred, Walter Mitty," laughs El Cid and we all exit.

At the party there is just everyone who is anyone in theatre, film and stage. As the stars from America try to sidle up to say hello to El Cid and Sophia he starts to enjoy seeing Emma and Emily completely star struck. Now Reader El Cid has a wicked sense of humour and he makes sure that Emily and Emma are next to him. One by one he asks whether the stars would pose for selfies and include his best friends pointing to the two girls from Exeter. Emma soon is loving the night and getting slightly drunk and Emily more reserved, but after all said that they were churchgoers like her she relaxed and managed to get drunk quicker than anyone else. My favourite moment is when El Cid was chatting to Brad Pitt and George Clooney and I watched as they walked over to Albert and Glyn dancing with the girls and asked to butt in. The looks on the girls' faces were priceless.

Albert walks back to join us, and laughs, "I could have sworn Pitt was hoping to dance with me." Albert and I share a joke and then I see the man with the scar again exit via a waiter's service door.

I manage to get Albert to see and he looked alarmed and is on his control mic. Two security guards follow through the same service door and after a few seconds return to nod no one there.

"I think I need to bring you up to speed later, you up for coffee after we get this lot to bed tonight?" asked Albert.

"Sure," I replied and looked around to see Emily take the mic on stage. Johnny Barr is with her and grabs everyone's attention.

"Folks, thank you all for coming to the show and drinking so much with us all here tonight. I have my new friend here from Exeter, Emily, who sings with her band and I think that tonight we should give her her American debut." All Cheer Johnny.

"My great friend and quite frankly most talented bastard I have ever known, Mr. Glyn Kerslake is going to play piano and we are going to accompany Emily sing Adele's Turning Tables"

Everyone applauds and Johnny holds Emily's hand as she suddenly realises the enormity of the audience and where she is so as Glyn starts to play Johnny sings along the first few lines with her and then steps back as Emily completely lets rip. My God Reader, what a voice! The audience are spellbound as she finishes the song there is a huge cheer and applause over which we can hear Emma shouting, "Go Emily."

Then the doors open as waiters arrive with the papers, the reviews. Glyn is by the mic and says, "Folks the reviews, whatever they say I have to say that this has been the second most incredible night of my life, sorry third. Well birth of little one number one, meeting and marrying my wife number two."

"What about me?" asks Johnny and Glyn hugs him and on the mic, "Of course Johnny my friendship with you is up there as well, well at least in most memorable moment number forty-seven." All laugh and then a voice cries out, "It's a hit, it's a hit!" I look to see the voice cheering is Jenna who is also a guest.

The reviews are amazing and the room is just one of the most amazing experiences I have ever witnessed and see Albert cheering with a tear in his eye. The show has a huge gay theme of strong men and I think he identified with a lot of the show.

One of the security team appears and he comes back to earth and nods in agreement. El Cid automatically knows what is going on and rallies Sophia and girls and I have a tired little one in my arms. We make our goodbyes and soon back in the limos and off to our beds, well all except me, Albert and Big Tony our other security guard as we have coffee in the hotel lobby.

Sat alone and in a poorly lit corner it feels like we are in a Noir film as Big Tony goes to fetch some biscuits. The reason he is called Big Tony, well at six foot seven and weighing in a hefty three hundred and fifty pounds it seemed apt.

"We have Intel that the President, the idiot in the White House, is furious that whatever he does is never as good as El Cid. Whether it is twitter followers or numbers that turn out to see him. But now El Cid is 'Commander-In-Chief of the Guardians here in America it has driven him bats. He wants to hurt El Cid and realises killing him is out of the question, but the girls or Sophia may be something he would try. He has a huge revenge problem. The Russian deal is being screwed as an enquiry lingers and he is firing staff left right and centre to stay in power to ensure he is not impeached and in power to get it through. We were told to have you with us to be with the girls as Nanny, confident, lady-in-waiting as Arthur calls it, and after tonight I realise you are just what we need. There was a report that a terrorist attack was going to be made on the family, but the reports came from a source we traced back to the CIA and a group run by Yerno."

"Yerno, but he is all loved up marrying the President's daughter."

Albert throws a look at me, and then Big Tony as if about to drop a bomb, "There are rumours that the President has dementia, terrified of losing power or getting the Russian oil deal through before he is impeached was a worry for them, but trying to keep his illness quiet is another. It seems Boss Hog and Yerno formed a pact with the daughter, she is the smiling assassin behind all the shit storms lately and it seems she is in charge. Well Daddy does whatever his Princess tells him to do. The marriage is a power pact and they even feel that they will be the golden couple that inherit the crown. Yerno is terrified Sophia may stand and to weaken her hand the word is that Yerno, who has no boundaries, is willing to hurt the daughters in order to make sure Sophia knows her place."

I sat horrified and listened as Big Tony then hands me a folder and in it is a picture of the man I saw with the scar, but he looked different. As they updated me on suspect hitman they think has been hired I take Albert's glasses and use as a magnifying glass and then I see it.

"He has a mole!"

"What?!" Albert asks me.

"There on the side of his nose, a mole. You took a photo when he never knew it, but the mole on the side of his nose is a Russian developed personal cloaking system."

"What?" asked Big Tony.

"Here I have one...never mind it was from the Knights. All I have to do is upload a new identity onto my computer and then load info into the mole. When you go through customs, whatever your identity you have created will come up on the data scanner at passport control, security cameras, CCTV etc. He changes his identity and enters completely invisible."

"So how do we find him?" asks Big Tony.

"Cross check every name on list of guests that we know and those we do not check them out," says Albert. "Well this has been a successful night, the kids are safe and tomorrow you are to accompany them to a music show with Tony. Keep eyes peeled and I am sure that nothing will happen in such a high level event as too risky, so bed and see you in lobby at 11:30am to brief for the concert."

And with that Albert and Big Tony stood and left. I shook their hands and watched them depart. As an invisible I knew that the concert was possibly the best moment to make a move. I did not inform Albert or Big Tony, just so funny that I am working with a guy called Big Tony Reader, but I thought I would send message on Knights email pages to say having great time and at concert if anyone about wants to come say hi. Crude code for Sir John or Jimmy if they are about. Cannot say had an easy sleep that night.

4 I overslept. This was the first time in years I woke in bed and the light streaming into the room. I sit up in bed and look around the room. It is like a room out of a Grace Kelly movie, you know Reader the old classics where glamour was the thing. And the bed was the most comfortable bed I have ever slept in. I realise that this type of room was always out of my price range.

I get up and check my emails. I see an email from someone called Robert saying that the concert sounds fun. Hoped I enjoy and relax, as it will be attended by thousands of fans. I felt that Robert was saying others were there, but not sure. Dressed in jeans and tee shirt of Bring Me The Horizon logo, I put on my sneakers and New York baseball cap whilst grabbing my leather jacket, I leave the room only to return to remember to collect my wallet. I know Reader we all make mistakes, forget things. Which is a reminder of just how I need to be on top of my game today and for as long as the girls are in danger.

I meet Albert in the reception and Big Tony waves as he exits the hotel.

"Hi, Tony is off to do a sweep of the concert hall. You sleep well?" asks Albert.

"Yes. Overslept believe it or not. So what have we got today?"

Albert sees Jenna arrive with coffee and toasted teacakes. I take a double look and he smiles, "Loved them in UK and got hooked. Want one?"

"Sure and coffee be great Jenna." Jenna smiles and pours me an orange juice.

"I will get you a cup or would you rather a latte or something?"

"No just a cup of Joe and thanks I think I will need the OJ."

Jenna smiles and turns to go fetch another coffee cup.

"All staff have been checked out at concert tonight and also we have a list of names not sure of, only six so hopefully Tony will return with face ID's from driving licences."

"Unless he has changed name to fit new scanned face."

Albert looks at me and then smiles, "All suspects will have photos to be checked upon arrival and any discrepancies will be dealt with at entry point."

"How many entry points are there?" I ask.

Albert looks quizzically at me, and then hands me the service entrances and a schematic of the venue, " I forgot you were CIA. So how would you get in?"

Albert smiled as Jenna returns with the cup and Albert pours me a coffee from coffee jug. Looking at the map I see four possible entrance points that are ducts and facilities entrances shared by adjoining buildings. I show Albert and he raises an eyebrow thinking that would be highly improbable, but as I explain that is why I would use he realises there is a chink in the security blanket armour. Talking into his mic in his sleeve Albert communicates with Big Tony to check them out and sends pictures from his mobile to look at.

Drinking coffee and eating teacakes Albert tells me how during the LGBT days where being gay was discriminated against, it was Sophia who personally employed him from the ranks of lowly staff. She never stated it was because he was gay, but on one Presidential trip she had found out his boyfriend was fixated by Italy and she invited him to accompany them all on the visit. Albert laughed as the President and she just did everything as matter of fact, and even sent them on fact-finding missions to test restaurants and attractions to visit in case they wanted to go. Albert knew it was just a free holiday all paid for on the State for them, but never forgot the generosity and is possibly why everyone is so loyal to the ex-President and his family still as they treated everyone with respect. Albert laughs as the new President is hated by all his staff; and they leave carpet tacks on the floor in the bedroom hoping he will step on them as he walks barefoot to the bathroom.

Big Tony interrupts saying that all secure and that they have placed vibration and light circuits so if anyone did enter an alarm would go off.

"So what else does she think?" asks Big Tony and I smile as Albert has already handed me my set of earphone and mic.

"Well, I think that I may not make an attempt until the girls either are travelling to or from the concert. Just check any new road works started in past two days. And Big Tony, or shall I just call you Mr. Big? Thanks and I will be with the girls and feel a few Knights will be around too."

"I love this family so whatever we need to do will do it and yes, quite like the name Mr. Big, Albert you hear that, I am now Mr. Big." You can hear Tony laughing on the other end.

"Ok Mr. Big, will call you later and meet up as planned. Seems you have made a few friends and can see why. I will be in town with El Cid and Sophia, I really am enjoying calling them that as it is causing huge problems for the White House secretly tracking us as they have no idea what it means. Well when I say tracking us in truth we are tracking them tracking us as many still loyal to the President."

"So what is my agenda exactly?"

"You are to meet girls at their house, address in file and also enjoy the concert. The girls are completely unaware of situation and like to keep it that way. Tony will be at concert to join you and be with girls. They want to be in crowd so you will have to sort out Mr. Big from upsetting anyone stood behind him. Listen, they are expecting you in a few hours, but relax, look at file and anything you feel would help call in and will have done for you and I am really glad to have you with us. We all love the girls so no pressure." And with that Albert left and saying to Jenna in my earshot to charge breakfast to my room. He then turned and grinned as he waved goodbye.

I sat looking over the file and then looked at my watch. I saw Jenna look to greet a young black girl and her little sister she had in tow. Jenna came to clear my table as they waited in the reception.

"Friends?" I asked.

"Yes, one of the actresses in film I am meant to be filming next month and her sister who is fourteen."

"What are you all doing tonight?"

"Well, having girlie night in at my place, you want to join us?"

"No," I said, "you *want* to join me?"

I called the girls over and we had drinks together and then asked them to meet me in an hour as they were coming to a concert with me and friends and then all out after for pizzas and milkshakes, all on me of course.

The girls were called Melissa and Juliet. They were just really nice American girls from Chicago. They were staying with Jenna and Jenna was ending her shift in ten minutes so they could meet me in an hour in Greenwich. We agreed where to meet and then they went off. I told them that the day was to be a surprise.

I told Mr. Big and Albert my idea and Mr. Big was to meet me in Greenwich Village. I then found out we were to see new movie band The Lone Wolves. It was a concert for their Because We Can charity. I knew nothing about it, but looking forward to the experience.

5 Well in a coffee shop in a hippy part of Greenwich Village and looking at the trendy clothes as Jenna with Melissa and Juliet came over. At the same time Mr. Big arrived. I saw a series of tee shirts with wolves on them howling and bought the girls all one each as well as El Cid's girls.

The girls were giggling and Mr. Big looked at me as if to say he was totally out of place and then Juliet found a huge shirt with a pack of wolves on it and said that he should wear it. He looked at me as if to say 'Really?', but I could see he liked it. We went into another shop and bought him jeans and new sneakers and a really awesome leather jacket. All the time he was laughing and I saw we needed to get to the house. Mr. Big had it covered and I realised just how good he was as he had been joining in and yet watching everything around us at the same time. Outside the shop came the limo and so in his new get up he entered the limo with the girls and I as we travelled to the house of the ex-President of the United Sates.

The girls were enjoying the limo so much when we arrived it was wonderful to see their faces as the gates opened to let us in. Suddenly Big Tony looked at his clothes and a worried look came across his face. The door to the house opened and Sophia was there to welcome us. As Big Tony stepped out of the car sheepishly she said is a jocular manner, "So this is the new Mr. Big? I like it. Come on in Tony and you must be Jenna's friends Melissa and Juliet."

Stammering Melissa looks around at me and everyone, "But you are..you are..aren't you?"

"I was the last time I looked, come on in even El Cid is here looking forward to meeting you and Mr. Big he is going to love your effort for the girls." With that Sophia turns and we all walk into the house.

In the main room Melissa and Juliet still stand in disbelief, well can you blame them Reader, as El Cid arrives shakes their hand and introduces them to his daughters. The girls all get on famously. Sat having drinks and pizza Melissa looks to me, and mouths about the family, 'they are so nice'. I smile back and go into room with Mr. Big and El Cid.

"Sir my plan is that the girls join us and act as decoys if needs be at the concert. We have leather jackets and identical shirts for your daughters. Mr. Big you will be with Melissa and Juliet, as no one would ever think you would leave the girls, and I will be with your daughters sir. We have seating so looks as if all just met and this way the girls can feel more incognito than before. We have had all buildings adjacent secured and I feel that on the way or leaving driving back will be the moment of attack."

"I don't like it and I know you will be there, but I wish they would stay home," said El Cid.

"Extra security since that Ariana Grande concert so we will be fine and I like the way she operates Sir," says Big Tony.

"Me too," interrupts Sophia, "but I too wish they would stay home. We, well the girls know too that we are always going to be a target."

I looked at my watch and saw it was time to leave. Smiling we all walked in on the girls all getting on famously. It was like the perfect mix of personalities and Juliet was singing to a karaoke song on the TV.

"Right you lot, time to go and please listen to what Tony and Mair, yes Suzie is Mair and will be your companion for a while. Well no need to say I love you, but quick hug before you go?"

We all laugh as Melissa rushes over and gives El Cid a huge hug.

It's on. We are in the limo and on our way to the concert. Blood pumping, adrenalin kicking in and suddenly I see the traffic ahead and look for those driving past who others cannot see.

The car pulls up and Tony exits and looks around. He does not notice that I am already out and as the girls climb out of limo he looks inside to see where I am. He looks to see I am next to the girls and smiles. We are ushered really fast into the theatre and realise we have caught the attention of a few as we pulled up in a limo. We are whisked into a green room with stars behind the stage and then I relax, as Tony seems to know many of those present. Seems the past President's popularity is still thousand times bigger than the latest incumbent.

All the girls are given goodie bags and Tony offers to look after them, but he then hands to another security guard who takes them to the limo outside parked.

The concert is being filmed and it is a huge event. Over ten thousand people crammed in, and a stage full of equipment as well as a celebs pit etc. The girls look to see the front spot and then Tony looks at me and asks if we can all be in the crowd. He feels we will be better hidden as well as he can see anyone trying to approach easier. It is actually a smart idea and soon the concert starts and I am with the girls in the crowd, Tony slightly off to one side so he does not block others view, but he can see everything. I put in earplugs to soften the sound and see Tony does the same.

The concert was amazing. The Notting Hill Sound Machine presented the Lone Wolves and then everyone who was anyone was on stage singing David Bowie songs as all played tribute to the man many of us were there to celebrate. I see Tony watching his iPhone and then see he is watching us from a drone he controls in the roof area. Tony has skills Reader.

The girls are all loving the concert and after the first hour realise that we were not going to be attacked here. Then my gut tells me differently. I see in the special dignitaries seats Yerno and his entourage. No wife, the President's daughter is obviously seeing to her father's needs as his wife is away screwing her new chief of security she hand picked herself. I then see a young lad with baseball hat leave their room and signal to Tony to watch him as he comes through the side door to the main auditorium. Tony grins as he has him on the drone then he looks concerned as Yerno and his complete entourage leave, not just the VIP room, but also the building.

The boy has a backpack and makes his way to the main auditorium. Yerno was going to have the girls and many others killed by what would be seen as suicide bomber. President and staff want to get bans on Muslims and I realise Yerno feels he can kill two birds with one stone. I motion to Tony to get her fast and for a big man can he move fast. Next to me we see on his drone the lad with backpack walking into the crowd.

"Move girls away I will meet our friend."

Tony looks at me and calls in situation as he and the girls dancing are moved sideways without realising. The whole stadium starts dancing and everyone is on the move. The lead singer crowd surfs and I see my chance to grab the guy with the backpack. He has taken it off and was about to leave it next to a group of kids screaming at the band.

I grab the bag and open it. Inside was a bomb on a timer, but also antennas so Yerno could even push the button, as he would happily double cross his accomplice, and kill everyone. But Yerno is an idiot and there is an off button as I click and then disconnect the mobile phone link. Tony is now next to me wanting to take the bomb out himself, to save the girls.

I look at his drone to see young backpack bomber exiting via the VIP door and rush to connect. Chasing him up the stairs I shout for him to get out of the way as I need a toilet. Another good ploy if chasing someone is not to shout 'Police. Stop!' why give them a heads up?

As he stands aside I hit him hard to the head and he hits the railing knocking himself unconscious. I see two police men and ask them to detain him until I get back, flash them my card saying Nanny to the President's children and they salute me as I exit.

The concert is coming to an end and I see Tony and tell him to have the guy collected and taken to a safe house to be questioned. The second half is under way and I am back with the girls. That was scary; Yerno and the President would murder thousands of innocent Americans in order to get some dreadful executive order through. No doubt a huge arms deal also would have been then done that they would personally profit from as weapons of mass destruction they make sold to retaliate against extremists.

I am a little shaken and the girls are none the wiser as the concert ends I manage to get Tony to get us passes through the backstage to exit.

Little did I know that Yerno was in a limo close by hitting the send button on his mobile furious that the bomb had not gone off and sent two of his goons back to see why.

As they re-entered the building via the VIP area Tony saw them and managed to grab the still unconscious backpacker and get him out via the front exit as if he was carrying a drunk from the premises. Tony even commandeers Yerno's goon's car and drives it off to meet another member of El Cid's personal team and exchange before dumping the car in the middle of Times Square where it was ticketed and then towed away.

The girls are alive, bubbling with energy and I decide that with Yerno's goons in hot pursuit best we saw the band another time. I told the girls we should all go for a pizza in Greenwich Village and it was not long before I realised we were being tailed. I called Tony and he was too far away.

As we ran into the darkly lit empty streets I found myself at the back of a series of houses with garages and suddenly the door opens and out steps Emma. Yes Reader, Emma from Exeter.

"Hi, this way, just got a call to say come out to open door for you guys."

She seemed completely unfazed and we all trundled in as I shut the door I could hear the goons run past. Walking through some flats and into a garden then up into a kitchen I met this amazing black lady who was making food.

"Hi, I am Mrs. Hudson. He said you would be coming by and hungry about half an hour ago."

"Who?" I asked.

"Fred," said Emma and I looked at Mrs. Hudson.

"Well it seems 'Fred' has many names but this is his house. He will be here in a minute. Like some coffee or I can open nice bottle of wine?"

It was amazing, but Sir John, Art Cable, my mentor was about and been also invisibly looking after me, and the girls. A stunning woman enters and I recognise her face. It was Marjorie, but only saw her for a second and she did a double take then whispered in my ear, "Please tell me you haven't come to shoot him again?" She laughed and looked at Mrs. Hudson, "Mrs. Hudson I think a glass of wine for all three of us ladies would be in order." Jenna walks in.

"What an amazing concert, we were wondering if we could eat in our flat?" I look at Jenna and see she too has a place here.

The door opens and in walks Walter Mitty, OK Sir John and he has a big smile on face.

"Jenna how was the concert?" he asks as he brushes past me to try to taste what Mrs. Hudson is cooking. Mrs. Hudson smacks his hand and he laughs.

"Well is there enough for me?"

There is another ring at the door and a big man wearing a trench coat and hat enters. I am a little dazed and realise it is Tony. Tony smiles and winks at me then calling out to the front room, "Pizza arriving in fifteen ladies then home when eaten."

The President's daughters and the others rush and hug Tony shouting his name.

"Go On Jenna take the girls to yours and I will bring pizza up when it arrives," I say and make out I am back in control, but to be honest Reader after tonight, I felt a little out of my depth.

The girls go, the pizza arrives, then Mrs. Hudson takes hers and her husband Ernie's to their flat and suddenly as Marjorie went to bed just Tony, Sir John and me eating some of the best soul food chicken I have ever eaten.

It seems Jimmy was also at the concert and both he and Sir John missed the boy with the backpack. Big Tony agreed to not tell the President until the morning and that the girls could have a sleep over with their new friends. Tony called through and it was agreed.

Trying to sift through the mega headfuck presented to us tonight there is a knock at the front door. Sir John raises his hand to say relax and opens to allow Albert to enter. Albert is really agitated.

As Sir John walks into the kitchen he offers Albert a gin and tonic. Albert looks startled at how he thinks Sir John is acting and Sir John raises a smile and says, "I knew it was Albert at the door, he is the only one who knocks, everyone else rings the bell, and of course Jimmy is watching. Listen Albert the girls are safe, no thanks to me or Jimmy, but Suzie and Tony saw the problem and acted fast."

"Where are the girls?" asked Albert.

"Eating pizza and laughing with new friends in the flat at the rear. In fact if we all calm down this has been a fantastic result for us all."

I looked at Sir John as he smiled and continued.

"We have the backpack bomber, singing like a canary. We have the bomb and it will be handed back to Yerno tomorrow morning as a package for his wife to collect. Yerno will know we know and we will hold this card to be used much later. Yerno will be ours from now on or risk facing an electric chair for treason. And we now know that the President is capable of anything as revenge, as this is what he thrives on, revenge. Albert girls fine and safe will of course inform El Cid here with friends. Returning them in the morning. I will accompany you all to return girls and have the chat we need to have then. But must say Suzie you were magnificent."

"She was. But you Sir John are shit," says Albert, "You offer a guy a gin and tonic and then fail to pour it!"

The brevity made us all laugh a little and relax. But the enormity of what this new administration running America would do for self gain was more frightening Reader than anything any of us had ever encountered.

Albert looks at Big Tony in his wolf tee-shirt and leather jacket, "So who is your tailor?"

"Suzie," replied Tony.

"Well I must say I like the jacket."

Sir John gave Albert a Gin and Tonic and then called Jimmy all was good. "I feel everyone must stay the night and Mrs. Hudson has made up rooms for you all, and no Tony you have your own room, I would not have the audacity to make you have to share with Suzie." He laughs and then makes his excuses and makes his way to bed. "See you all about 10 tomorrow morning, the girls will be up all night watching films I reckon."

I am sat in my room at Sir John's in Greenwich Village and writing up these events Reader and it seems like everything that has happened is just a blur. As I passed Big Tony's room could hear him snoring and then as I went to get undressed a very pretty silk nightie was laid out on the bed for me and I saw my work clothes hanging on the wardrobe. Sir John was invisible all right and I lie here in bed in awe, but then secretly grinning inside as yes it was me that saw the bomber.

It was this last thought that made me stop grinning. Yerno and the President's daughter happy to murder innocent Americans and all to sell a billion dollars worth of their own companies weapons to the United States to drop on innocent victims in an Arab state somewhere, with the American people behind it not knowing the truth, and enable the President to get his stupid travel ban on Muslims through a dodgy right wing court.

Reader, we invisibles report the truth and then it is up to you to act. Act with your vote, democratically, peacefully, but do not sit idle.

6

The morning came and I was awake at seven. I wake at seven roughly every morning, even if I went to bed at six o'clock an hour earlier. Habit I guess. Well I smelt coffee and bacon so that was enough to draw me downstairs. Mrs. Hudson and Marjorie were chatting and making breakfast with Ernie getting ready to go to work.

"Morning," said Mrs. Hudson, "Please call me Evangelina, Mrs. Hudson is what Walter calls me, and Walter is what I call his Lordship as it seems you all have different names for him. New girls call him Fred. Bacon and eggs Suzie?"

I laugh and smile, "That would be perfect Evangelina and you are Marjorie who I met…."

"Lovely to meet you Suzie and yes it has been a while since New Orleans."

Marjorie gave me a smile and a hug and then handed me a plate, "Self service here," she says and I am soon sat chatting with them at the table as Albert arrives and Big Tony.

"So who are these two brutes?" asks Evangelina.

"Evangelina Hudson, it is my pleasure to introduce you to Albert and this big brute and gentle giant is Big Tony."

Mrs. Hudson looks at me as if unimpressed and smiles then orders them to sit down and she will make them breakfast.

"I had better check on the girls.." says Tony only to be interrupted by Mrs. Hudson, "You leave them well alone, they is fast asleep and I will call the girls down at nine for breakfast earliest. Now stop fussing and coffee in the jug, water, orange juice, cranberry if flushing out your system....OK? So Albert, Big Tony, here you have bacon and eggs and full English as the many named fool calls it upstairs."

Albert smiles and looks to me as if to say who is the many named fool? Strangely we all eat in silence to hear footsteps above. Big Tony moves and Mrs. Hudson standing behind him places her hands on his shoulders to sit, "That'll be many named fool upstairs, Marjorie darling would you see if his Lordship would like to ordain us with his presence?"

"Of course Evangelina," says Marjorie and smiles as she exits bumping into Sir John. With a smile he enters in jeans and a tee-shirt with CND emblem on it.

"The many named fool or his Lordship would love a full English, Mrs. Hudson and extra mushrooms if possible? Albert, Big Tony, we are all up before the girls it seems. Their mum and dad will call about ten as told them the girls were having a lie in."

"Will I be needing to save breakfast food for them and if so, you ain't getting extra mushrooms," quips Mrs. Hudson.

Sat in the kitchen washing dishes all together we literally walk about in silence. We are all reflecting on the fact Yerno would suicide bomb an American concert to hurt the ex-President as well as start war with Muslims. As we finish dishes we walk into the front room and the news is on. All

47

quiet and pictures of El Cid and Sophia enjoying guest of honour status in New York with all the President Elects arch enemies. I look to Sir John and he looks to see Mrs. Hudson enter the room.

"Ah will you just look at those two, aren't they wonderful. Shame they ain't still in White House instead of that dementia-riddled idiot we now have. Oh and by the way folks, do not make a mess if we have company of those nice girls parents coming. I ain't cleaning twice." And with this exits the room.

"She is the boss folks," says Sir John, "now last night we saw how depraved Yerno and the President's daughter are. We have no Intel to link them to the plot as our young backpacker had no knowledge of them it seems, BUT, Yerno does not know and we will do nothing."

I look to Albert perplexed and say, "Do nothing; achieve everything." Sir John smiles.

"Exactly Suzie. Yerno and that streetwalking first daughter, well I have to say holding back my anger is hard as personally be good to deliver the backpack back to them, and this is what I think we should do."

"What?!!! That'll have same reaction as what they wanted except war without them making the money, but war anyway."

"I know Big Tony, I love calling you that. Listen Albert, call your guys who have the backpacker and get a nice photo of him taken last night sent over as a 10 x 8. Yes I was there, but never saw him; thanks to Suzie all is good. Get me print before El Cid arrives and he is still unaware of last night's charade. Now the deactivated backpack bomb should be hand delivered to Yerno's house at twelve noon, he is out as have his diary here, but wifey, who is his boss it seems will be at home. She will find package, no explosives, but detonators and picture so they know we know. A brief note saying that if ever anything happens to El Cid or his family then bomber and explosives will be found, and part of new public investigation on US arms dealers trying to commit atrocities to sell arms. Basically we will have them in our back pocket as this potentially could bring the whole country into civil war and the end of America as a peace loving nation and never to be trusted in the western world again. Oh and some info in from friend in Venice tells me that he met President's doctor who later was found dead in a road accident that informed him the President is suffering from dementia. I feel Yerno married President's daughter and they hold the keys to the seat of power whilst the fat buffoon plays golf and tweets stupidity keeping the press looking in the wrong direction."

"Why we never hired you is a mystery to me," says Albert, and I laugh and look to the kitchen as I hear the girls loudly chatting in the kitchen, giggling and talking about the concert.

"Go say hi," say Albert, "and remember this happy morning is all thanks to you, it will not go unnoticed."

I walk into the kitchen feeling really great and the girls hug me and can see Evangelina is loving having all the youngsters there.

"Now come on girls sit down, this is my kitchen and you will do as I say. Good now please help yourself to juice as I have a feeling that wine was taken last night and you know I don't want the law broken in my house." All look surprised and a bit sheepish as they sit quietly. "Now don't worry secrets safe with me and glad to of met you young ladies and that you are friends with my friends and neighbours, but your parents coming soon so better eat as not having anyone leave her with an empty stomach."

Jenna walks to Evangelina and gives her a big hug, "Ladies, this is the Evangelina Hudson, wife to Ernie and the most wonderful woman you could ever hope to meet, she is also an amazing cook and can I have one of the Lordships Full English's please?"

"Of course, everybody can, now sit down and relax we are all family."

The youngest daughter stands and hugs Evangelina and smiles as her older sister stands and more formally thanks her for her hospitality and confidence.

"My, my, you girls are well mannered. You must have some fancy parents and I will tell them so myself now sit down and sort out juice and what you want." Evangelina turns and laughs to herself as she cooks.

As I enter Marjorie re-enters with a cup to wash and places it in the dishwasher, "Ladies, do tell me, how was the concert?"

"It was awesome. Thanks to Suzie we escaped the box and were in the crowd for the first time and then after meeting all the stars we came home, well here on the subway. Never done that before."

Evangelina looks to the girls as if to say 'What? Where you been living?' as the doorbell goes.

"It'll be Marielle, my daughter, can someone get the door?" Marjorie goes and soon enters and joins in having a pancake made for her and as she realises who the two girls are I look to Marjorie and she in turn looks to Marielle to say sush, and all chat on happily as Evangelina cooks.

As the hall grandfather clock strikes 9:30 the doorbell rings and Marielle says that Julius is meeting her here and goes to answer. At the door is a secret serviceman and Albert takes the envelope he has to hand over and exits. Marielle stands looking confused and as Albert shuts the door and introduces himself. Marielle then walks back to the kitchen to eat her pancakes as the doorbell rings again.

"Sit down, it'll be Julius, I'll get it," and with that Evangelina walks and opens the door to see El Cid and Sophia standing there. There is a few seconds delay as realising who they were Evangelina in shock asks, "Can I help you?" I am behind Evangelina and shake El Cid's hand and invite them in. Evangelina then realising to do so also ushers them in and in the hallway stands dumbfounded.

"The girls are having a late breakfast, and this is Evangelina, the head of the household and wonderful cook."

El Cid shakes Evangelina's hand and asks if can have a coffee and she still stands there speechless.

"Honey the boys seem to be in the front room, Morning Albert," says Sophia, "how was the concert Big Tony?"

"A great success and really liked the band. I trust you had a good evening?" replied Tony.

"Coffee, yes coffee, coming up, gentlemen, more coffee?" stammers Evangelina.

"I will give you a hand Evangelina and trust my girls behaved themselves?" asks Sophia.

"Your girls? Oh yes, your girls are a credit to you. You are who I think you are?"

"I hope that is a good thing. Come on hubby smells bacon and he is meant to be on a diet. Kitchen this way?" And with that Reader Sophia and Evangelina join the girls as I joined the boys with El Cid.

Well reader the next few minutes was a heated discussion and I have never seen El Cid even when President become this angry. As the story unfolds and my part is told El Cid stands and hugs me like a father would his own daughter and a tear in his eye just as Sophia enters with coffee and a bacon sandwich.

"To think while I am in the kitchen he is with other women." she laughs and he hugs her as she places the tray on the table. As the enormity of the previous night unfolds she sits and literally is in a state of shock. I return from the kitchen with an orange juice with brandy in it. Sophia takes it and drinks. As the brandy hits she smiles and looks to me places down the glass and hugs me.

She then adjusts herself and straightens to offer the rest of the brandy and orange juice to El Cid, "Darling the rest of this is for you."

El Cid smiles and downs the drink in one without knowing about the brandy either, "WOW, where did you get your oranges from?" he quips and all try to relax. Sir John's idea is agreed, but El Cid wants to hand the backpack over himself. And an hour later that is exactly what he did.

El Cid drove to Yerno's house, walked up the steps to the door, rang the bell, waited for the President's daughter, Yerno's wife to meet him there, handed her the backpack, said, "I believe this is your husbands, returning it and please let him know. Oh it is safe and a little something inside for you both." With this he turns on his heels walks down the steps, gets into his car and as he drives away Sophia gives a look from the back seat up at the First Daughter, as she so hideously refers to herself, standing in shock and scared she has a bomb in her hands. The window on the car slowly goes up as El Cid and his security drive away.

I am on the corner in a car watching as she rushes inside and slams the door. Within seconds a team of bomb experts arrive and we take photos. I thought be good as a second wave of press that Yerno should receive qualifying we know he was behind then attempted attack as they slowly approach the backpack that had been dropped by the door and left as a terrified and evil woman ran to save herself inside.

It was Albert who visited the White House to meet Yerno, who first acted furiously how we had scared his wife and was looking to press charges, but was being magnanimous and thought best it was all dropped, then sat ashen faced as Albert read out a note from El Cid that he and his families utmost security was to be given top priority and that should anything happen to him or any member of his family or household would result in exposure. Albert then handed the photos of bomb disposal experts with the backpack retrieving the photo from within stating that this was enough evidence as well as the testimony of the bomber of their involvement and that it was El Cid, who on behalf of the country was magnanimously letting this unfortunate incident slide.

Albert laughed later to me how Yerno was fuming inside and did ask after the bomber's whereabouts to which Albert replied that he and his family are all well and enjoying a new life, and that the last thing Yerno would want is him to resurface dead or alive. Albert then said he stood and walked out without another word being said.

I was rewarded with a trip to a paradise island with the girls, accompanied with their newfound friends, and even Evangelina came as friend and cook with Ernie on the holiday as guests, Evangelina would need to be doing something and happy to see Ernie try to sit idle as she ribs him he should be doing something where at one point he remarked, "I am. Tonight I am playing gin with the President," and walked off grinning. I think it was the first time ever he had had the last word and left his wife speechless.

7

I flew back to London and accompanied Emma and Emily back to Exeter after the trip and was there to enjoy hearing their tales of the times they had. I was introduced as the special nanny of the President's daughters and was there to say that the girls loved her and Emily as well as possibly when she is ready, a job full time as assistant to the girls.

Emily also got a call from the Notting Hill Sound Machine to come see them perform at the Roundhouse in Chalk Farm for the charity Guardians Help. They even asked what song she would like to sing as they perform a tribute to David Bowie.

I managed a few days on the south coast of Devon in Budleigh Salterton. The red cliffs and stunning scenery was the blue skies shone gave me time to relax. I had a call from Albert to say hi and that all was well and that anytime in New York to call. A couple introduced by Walter Mitty called Stanley and Javier is redesigning his apartment. A gay couple that have now become good friends, and they have been enjoying dinners out, and a new social life has opened for him.

It seems things are easier as although the incumbent President tweets displeasure at all his previous President stands for, his daughter and son-in-law, Yerno, do everything in their powers to protect him and his family.

I sit writing up my journal and reflect on how life has changed for me when my phone rings and it is Arthur and the Knights. He wonders as I am still in UK if I would come to Parliament to meet up, as there are major concerns with President as he now decides to deny climate change and his dementia and senility is undeniable. I agree and decide to catch the train to

London from Exeter St Davids. I manage to get a first class ticket to Paddington for just £33, and smile as I stand on the platform thinking how I love London. As I enter the station I see two men in a Range Rover watching the entrance and one gets out.

As I nonchalantly enter the building I pop into the WHSmith and look to buy a paper. The man enters and from other shop exit can see the Range Rover drive off. The man has gone into Starbucks and is looking around for someone. I realise he is looking for me. He cannot see me as I have managed to join a group of school kids going through the gates causing a commotion. He looks past them and past me as I enter the platforms. I put on a floppy blue sun hat I have and make it conspicuous so it can be seen.

Standing waiting for my train I see another man on a mobile smile at me then look away. A few moments later the man from the Range Rover enters, looks to the man on the mobile and then as if unseen rushes to my platform as my train begins to pull in. The hat has made me visible.

Luckily the kids from moments earlier swarm onto the platform as they too are on the train. I make sure the man on mobile sees me enter a waiting room with only one door kids are exiting. He looks to the other man and nods acknowledging that I am in the waiting room, but this is the thing you learn as an invisible is in the split second he looks to his accomplice you change direction and exit among the crowd.

I am on the train watching unseen as they slowly enter the waiting room to see the hat on a leaflet carousel and rush out as the train pulls out. I stand out of view and then once out of the station I take my seat in first class. I look out of the window as we go over the road crossing to see the Range Rover waiting and guy in the car shouting furiously on the phone.

I decide to sit and relax and collect myself. I order a drink and try to think what all that happened before was about. As the waiter brings me a complimentary prosecco I decide to call the Knights.

Henry answers and I ask if he has a moment to chat and he offers to call me back. This is our way of saying call on secure line with scrambler as something has happened.

It is Arthur and Henry together as the mobile rings I answer it, "Huge apologies Suzie, I rang from home to come here and it seems someone is tapping my phones. Not sure what is happening only to say when you get to Paddington there will be an ambulance on the forecourt, fake an arm bleeding injury, get in ambulance and we will meet you when you arrive. Sorry again and train stops at Reading only so we will also have friends jump on as whoever this is will also possibly put two and two together and board train to see where you went. Say no more and see you later."

Then the line went dead as I entered a tunnel. I decide to sit tight and see that the meals on board are chicken in red wine sauce and steak. I joke with the waiter whether the steak is the vegetarian option. He laughs and says that the steak is done separately when heated up and therefore vegetarian option is the steak meal without the steak, but in future if I wanted a vegetarian meal then to order in advance. He was really sweet and in fact up to Reading became a friendly face bringing me more prosecco and I realise coming into reading I was quite pissed.

Sorry Reader, but it seems that we Americans love bubbles, especially when free and served by a hunk in tight trousers. His name was Olek and he was polish. Incredible manners, and have to say that the polish service on British trains is second to none.

As I manage to refuse another glass of bubbles my mobile rings, it is Henry.

"Hi Suzie, Henry here. Seems we have interest from Russia and they are furious, as woman they think is you had them wipe out a Serbian group that was actually working for them. Now not to worry, the wife will be getting on with some info for you and be nice to have new blood for you to talk to. Got to go, except her name is Chastity."

With that he hangs up and the train starts to slow as we enter Reading. Being in the front compartment I watch as we pull into the platform to see if I can see anything Russian. The train stops and people start to get on. Nothing and then suddenly there is a lull. The train is held up as a large woman with a trunk, yes an old style trunk people took on voyages on Atlantic liners finds it too big for the doors. Guards rush to carry it to the luggage carriage and struggle, as it weighs a ton. The large woman screams at them in an eastern European accent to be careful. She enters first class and sits in the seating diagonal to me. As she sits a very pretty girl breaks my eye line and sits opposite me.

"Hi, Chastity, Henry said we'd meet on here."

I smile and suddenly look to the lady with the trunk who has decided to sexually harass my prosecco waiter. He smiles at her as she crudely flirts with him and licks her lips and turns to smile embarrassed towards me.

"Oh and a glass of water too please young man as I have more than a thirst that needs quenching," she calls as he grimaces looking at me. I then see the trunk woman adjusting her huge boobs and look to see me looking at her, then smiles. "Valeria Kuznetsov, I am appearing at the ENO next month. Obviously you recognise me, as does the handsome waiter. You love opera, yes?"

"Lovely to meet you Miss. Kusnetsov. This is my friend Chastity from London, and I am Suzie from LA," I reply.

"I'm sorry, but are you playing Cleopatra in Handel's Giulio Cesare?" asks Chastity.

"Yes, you a fan?"

"Of all the female roles it is a favourite as Cleopatra is a real hero and wins the day out smarting the men. It is such a powerful piece do you not think?" asks Chastity.

"It is indeed and that is why they demanded I play the beauty Cleopatra," says Valeria who thinks she is a sexy young thing rather than the forty five year old woman whose age has not been kind to her looks.

"Please excuse me I say," and go to the steward or waiters area. Anyway my polish friend is there preparing the steak and drinks for Valeria.

He looks to me and laughs, "I think she is not just wanting to eat the steak, I think she wants to devour me too."

"Let me take her the water and I will tell her food is on its way."

"No, you are, I must do…." He insists but I have the water already in my hand and exit as he cooks the steak.

"Your steak is being lovingly cooked for you so as I passed bought you your water," and with this handed Valeria a bottle of sealed water and a glass.

Valeria sees the bottle is not opened, "Honestly, this is not even opened, never mind I am sure I can manage," and with that twists the top off and empties the water into the glass.

"Wish I had ordered food ahead as starving," says Chastity.

"Trust me," I say with a smile, "your steak will arrive shortly and I watch Valeria gulp down the water in one. Now the bottle was unopened but I had placed a few droplets of eye drop formula into the glass Valeria had not noticed and within thirty seconds it had started to work.

I know it is naughty Reader, but Valeria was just too pompous and the waiter too nice to be subjected to her leering and bum grabbing hands. I could see the contortion of her face as her stomach start to gurgle and then the look of terrified realisation that she might actually shit herself.

Like a gazelle weighing nothing she makes a dash to the toilet and screams for everyone to make way. I laugh and Chastity looks at me to say, "Did I miss something?"

The noise from the toilet cannot be muffled and our waiter arrives with the steak and places it at Valeria's table. He walks to the toilet door and politely knocks and announces that the steak is ready. Valeria screams from the toilet, "Take it away I don't want your steak," to which I stand and remove it and say to our waiter, "Not to worry my friend will love it and can we get her some bubbles?"

It doesn't take long to arrive in Paddington and Valeria has not left the toilet. I fear she is too embarrassed and as we exit Chastity and I see the ambulance.

Chastity opens her bag, pours fake blood on my arm and rushes me to the ambulance through the ticket attendants and into the waiting arms of the paramedic who looks incredibly like Jimmy. As I jump I see the Range Rover draw up on the concourse from Exeter. I point it out to Jimmy who smiles and closes the door.

"Welcome to London Suzie." I look at Jimmy and give him a hug. "OK Chastity, Henry says off to yours as this is your new house guest."

"Oh fab!" says Chastity and we speed off in the ambulance to sunny Notting Hill.

8

Sat in Chastity and Henry's house I see photos of all the knights and their trips but no pictures of Jimmy or Sir John. I see Arthur and Guinevere at the wedding and see pictures of them in LA with stars for the opening of new centre with Wentworth and Dominic, as well as standing in Africa at an opening of a hospital built by the Guardians as I hear someone walk into the room and say hi. It is Art Cable. Well Reader to honest I have no idea who this man is anymore except a true friend and mentor. We hug and then sit on the two sofas facing each other.

"Well, no need to say you look well, just let's get straight up to speed. Since your Serbian adventure the Russians are smarting after realising they helped you escape with their enemies and killed their allies in error. You then are centre of attention as plot to silence another big enemy of theirs is ruined by you as El Cid now has gained power in America. Their puppet is now a liability and they are trying to run America with New Order via their new puppets the daughter and her husband Yerno, but of course that is now compromised and you seem to of become enemy number one. So you are now a magnificent beauty of the nail world called Emma Beauchamp. Emma has businesses based out of Tamworth and is currently working on a project in Birmingham and is a good friend of Albert's, who she met in Las Vegas. I love telling you this as you try to write it all down. I have a file for you here."

I look through the file and see Emma is away on a trip to Las Vegas and is on a paid holiday by the knights whilst we sort this out. Emma was previously a policewoman, but after the sad passing of her best friend she decided to do works that meant she could help others. I think I like Emma and hope to one day meet her, but am worried that Russians may get confused and she end up in the crossfire. But Arthur says that they have a breakdown of me and Emma is beautiful too, he diplomatically tells me, but bigger bust and thoroughly British so if they did chase down they would have her down as same name wrong person.

The Russians realised their mistake as the Serbs were working on getting support, by hostile force, by threatening other states into voting against climate change policies. Sadly, Yerno has been working with the Russians with King Tiller and President on getting sanctions lifted as they want to make their oil deal. With Yerno under pressure from El Cid things stalling and now Arthur and Knights see how the New Order in cahoots too so this is bigger than anyone realises.

Yerno and the 'First Daughter' running things on behalf of incoherent Daddy want to release climate change and with the UK appointing the idiot from ruining schools to Minister for Environment, PM has her perfect fall guy as well as a guy that thinks climate change is a hoax.

Amazing Reader that the New Order and American Press that are run by the big corporations that run the companies and governments continually put out fake news that climate change is a hoax and employ idiots to do as told in the face of mounting evidence daily of how real the threat is. As an Invisible we can but show you, hopefully reading these journals you will know the truth and see the dangers ahead and vote the criminal governments out.

In order to down play their collusion Yerno attack Russia on its record for poor emissions and lack of care in extracting fossil fuels both then came together to agree climate change was a hoax, as if a joint investigation, as in reality with environmental guidelines they could not find cheap ways to exploit profits for their businesses.

Whilst in a summit with other world leaders the Russian Premier, who basically could not care less what anyone else thinks, was embarrassed as Yerno did not back him up on their climate change agreement and instead of bolstering their union, enabling opening trade deals, the climate change dispute took centre stage and all deals were again on hold. Russia then looked to Serbian ally to apply pressure to discover that they had in fact wiped them out in an operation where I duped them.

You see, the Russians rigged the US election in order to lift sanctions imposed by El Cid during his time, and then systematically remove climate change in order to make huge profits on their huge fossil fuel reserves.

Reading the paper I see the ex-head of the CIA is in talks with NATO and I used to be under his command, and in fact worked closely on a situation in Bolivia years ago as a rookie gaining his acknowledgement. I remained in contact and was often at functions where he was always nice to me. I decided that I wanted Arthur to get me to the meetings with NATO and help me get to him to let him know about Yerno and wife, with Boss Hog and Tiller really running things.

I was quite surprised as Arthur thought it was a good idea and immediately organised a massive party for the Knights with all the countries there to come as a huge thank you, and felt he could get my ex-boss there. A day later I hear that El Cid will be guest of honour although he will be surprise guest and be there to talk about the project in New Orleans and the many new hospitals and clinics being built in the USA by Guardians Help USA.

I watched with joy, as Arthur gets excited getting a plan together. I met all the Knights and was going stir crazy at Henry and Chastity's so put on my mole, new identity as Emma Beauchamp, I walked out to tea at the Ritz with an old friend I met in Cannes. He never knew who I was and joked that he could guess and joked I was a female wrestler, and I said correct so often he would meet me in London as wealthy female wrestling star. Go figure.

With my Knight's credit card I decide the Ritz for tea would be perfect and soon there having the time of my life. I was able to be me again; well me being a wrestler I never was, being a person called Emma I am not, meeting a friend discussing a job I am not doing, but anyway, in among all the bullshit was me, relaxed joking like me.

I noticed on the table down from ours a woman alone that seemed sad. I do not know why, but wanted to see if she wanted company and join us. As I reached her table I was too late to recoil back as she turned, saw me and smiled. It was Valeria Kuznetsov, the opera singer from the train. I asked her to join us and she took one look at my companion, asked if we were an item, I said no, then jumped and said that she would love to join us.

It turned into a wonderful afternoon and evening as there had been technical difficulties so rehearsals cut for the day and she realised she had no one in London to meet. She was a really wonderful character and sang for orphanages in Russia raising millions and once sang at an oligarch daughter's wedding giving her fee to help three hundred orphans go on a trip to Disneyland. She even had a few photos on her phone as she accompanied them as also was to sing in Miami.

You cannot judge a book by the cover Reader; you cannot judge a book by the cover. I decided that we must take in a musical and rang Arthur who rang Sir John and then I get a call from John Barr saying his friends were doing Follies at the Royal Albert Hall. He had mentioned the Knights and Valeria Kuznetsov and the next thing is we have twenty VIP seats.

So the Knights, Valeria and me and my friend, plus a handsome waiter Valeria had her eye on called Jeff, who was a huge opera fan and of Valeria, plus Arthur and Sir Lancelot and wives, plus a surprise visit from El Cid and Sophia, I mean suddenly this was huge. When we all arrived and walked among the other audience El Cid was gracious as was Sophia, shaking hands and selfie's, as was Arthur and it was a major coop for the concert.

The Producer came to see me as friend of Johnny, and even then I faked it, asked if OK that my guests could be filmed as raising money for children's charity. I said to him to wait for a second, but I felt a moment coming and soon we were all backstage with the cast. Taking photos, doing interviews as briefed El Cid, Arthur and all about charity concert was for and curtain delayed fifteen minutes as major news stations drove to make sure that got coverage.

Then El Cid said that if the Producer wanted he would join him as he made his speech to the audience know about how he threw the concert to help the charity and help awareness.

The audience start to get twitchy. The press trying to get in, and Henry and Robert marshalling then to the sides of the stage. This made the audience even more excited and the atmosphere was electric.

"Listen sir," said El Cid to the Producer, "as we have the world press now set up would you like me to introduce you?"

At this moment the poor man almost fainted. Sophia grabs his arm and smiles saying she would walk him on. Arthur and the Knights decide they too will also join forces and it would be fun as the cost of the production was over £150,000 and ticket sales were only 75% sold out. I could see Arthur with a twinkle in his eye and then Guinevere whisper in his ear. He nodded at her even more excitedly and made sure Sir Lancelot and Elaine were in on it too, as no one person takes the credit with the Knights of the Round Table, and El Cid looks at me and smiles.

"Emma, will you take my arm? Help me on stage, well the wife has another man so I should at least have another young lady?"

"Sir, may I suggest Valeria be your date on stage."

I needed to remain invisible and this was the tonic that would be just what Valeria needed, apart from ravishing her fan from the Ritz waiting staff later.

Sophia steps forward and smiles saying, "Miss. Kuznetsov if you would not mind accompanying my husband on stage?" Valeria Kuznetsov smiles as if in a trance, "then I think we need to get going as the audience awaits."

"Do not worry Valeria my wife is always in charge, please allow me." And with that El Cid leads Valeria onstage and the audience erupts and all in front of the worlds press.

Standing centre stage El Cid takes the microphone, "Please everyone I know your standing ovation is for my fellow guest the wonderful Opera star Valeria Kuznetsov."

The audience applaud and cheers and Valeria is a woman at home, on stage and a smile that radiates beyond happiness.

"Now I see my friends the Knights from UK here also and please join us as we firstly want to pay tribute to Russia and their generosity and that of one of their brightest stars, the wonderful Valeria Kuznetsov who has given millions to orphans across the Soviet Union." The audience applauds even louder and Arthur steps forward to the microphone.

"Friends, this is an amazing night that will be remembered and hopefully the DVD of the concert will sell to raise even more funds for the children's charity benefitting tonight. But many of you may of noticed that my friend from America is minus his Commander In Chief and ask the former First Lady to join us for a speech from the man that made all this possible, the producer of the show, Mr. John Brant."

There is another round of applause as John steps up and talks about the charity. He thanks his cast and team for working for nothing, although expenses often can be as much as a night's pay, and hopes that the audience enjoys the show.

I see El Cid and Arthur discussing something with their wives as the producer thanks everyone on stage for their profiles they bought to the evening and Arthur raises his hand and walks up to the microphone again. Sorry folks, the three most important decision makers in our organisation have an announcement.

Everyone looks at each other in the audience as Guinevere steps forward with Elaine and Sophia.

"Friends, as everyone is a friend to the Knights and we just want to say in honour of Valeria Kuznetsov and all that Russia does to help their children. So in our new dear friend Valeria Kuznetsov's name we from the Knights UK and USA would like to donate the costs to hire Royal Albert Hall, all fees incurred so all the money you paid goes to the charity. And of course we will be at the box office during the interval as we booked seats and have to pay for those as well. Now finally, lets get set to enjoy one of our favourite shows 'Follies' written by one of America's greats and performed by Britain's finest stars of the West End."

Huge applause as we exit the stage to our seats as the audience applauds until we are all ready to sit. Funniest moment for me was when Valeria passed me completely fazed and mumbling, as she cannot believe what just happened. And during the interval camera filmed Arthur and El Cid trying to pay for their seats and in the end Elaine stepped forward and offered her Knight's card and with one look the tickets were bought for double the price.

Members of the public chatting to Sophia, feeling safe as security was low, but everyone was in great spirits. With his arm around Valeria, El Cid and Arthur with Sir Lancelot on camera saying that the Russian people were an example for the world as seen by the huge work done by one of its own, Valeria Kuznetsov.

Valeria for her part was humble and hanging on to her Ritz waiters arm as he enjoyed being part of the entourage.

As we walked back into the main hall to take our seats Valeria pulled on my arm and with a tear in her eye smiled and said that today was the greatest feeling she has ever known. We hugged and this formidable woman was humble and beautiful. I never forget as she said to me, "Emma Beauchamp will always be known as the most wonderful woman in the world."

I smiled and after reading about the real Emma Beauchamp whose generosity I was humbled by myself Reader, I felt good that her name would be so revered. I hope I meet her one-day, so you know how much what you think is nothing changes lives. I was proud to be called Emma today.

I have now experienced the unbelievable force that is the Knights of the Round Table and Guardians Help. I have seen how the leaders operate without trying to upstage anyone else, include everyone and can only think I know exactly who has made this all possible. His stamp may be invisible, but his presence is everywhere.

9

I woke up at Henry and Chastity's and decided to pop out for a coffee. Sat in the Costa I see all the papers for customers to read are full of the headlines about the concert. Sponsors and donations flooded in after the news coverage as Robert on camera made sure they put up the text to donate number, which doubled the amount the night raised. I enjoyed thinking how my mentor would have been so pleased as I look at all the papers and not one photo of me. I laugh to myself Reader, but it is hard not to see anyone know what you do as an invisible.

Page four of the Sun, a really worthless paper, has a seedy article on Valeria going back to her hotel with the young waiter. And then the Daily Mail, a well known nasty piece of right wing, racist, homophobic and truly crass newspaper runs articles on how did the Knights have the right to give money in the name of a Russian and the that Lancelot is a communist happy to make Russia look better than Britain. Some nonsense in another paper called the Express had more right wing angles on Lancelot selling Anglo-American triumph to Russia. Not sure what they watched but the main stories and three times threads in articles belie their true nature.

Climate change the big hoax. Yes Reader, papers like these try to brainwash you to their agenda. Remember Brexit? Well all the owners of these papers make billions from currency changes if Brexit goes through. All the lies were filtered through these papers and can see how they work as an invisible looking into what is happening with climate change it becomes more visible. The New Order and its right wing agenda or corporate profit at any cost to human lives or that of the planet is very visible and this is my new mission.

I receive a call from Henry asking if I was OK and close by as wanted me to come in to Parliament with him and Chastity. Something was happening and also we had all been offered first night tickets to Valeria's opera.

So there I am in the infamous Knight's office in the British Houses of Parliament. Sat in the boardroom having tea served to me by Arthur. Most of the team are there, Robert, Henry, Chastity, and others, but all of us wait for one missing element; one of the team is not there, Quetty.

The door opens and in walks this tall vision of beauty. I am taken aback by her breath-taking beauty, and she stands erect, a powerful woman.

"That rancid old cow, I just love winding her up. Thanks Arthur you know how I enjoy seeing the wicked witch," she says then turns to me and offers her hand, "Quetty, you must be Emma. Sorry late, but Arthur loves me going to see the Prime Minister as it winds her up having to wait for me with updates on how Knights are doing, well I am black and she is a racist who is in agony trying to not show it. All here, well you were right Robert, something is brewing and now that other useless tosser is moved to Minister for the Environment she has shown her cards. She really is inept." Quetty throws a file on the table.

I look around the room and Arthur smiles at me as we all sit or perch on furniture for a briefing. All look at Quetty who looks and shrugs her shoulders as if to say 'what?'

Arthur speaks, "Well thank you for this Quetty, you stole this file without them even noticing? Emma, Quetty is a formidable woman and we all love that the Prime Minister demands to see me and sadly I am indisposed and we send Quetty or someone else instead. It is just one of the perks of the job annoying the Head of the UK New Order. Our PM is looking at shifting power and up to something, but what it is I fear the New Order is massing a new strategy."

"My Intel is climate change," I say and all look at me, "but that is just a ruse for what is really happening. A few weeks ago we stabilised a situation that could of started World War Three as our President, who we are reliably informed has dementia, so the country being run by Yerno and his daughter behind closed doors. Now this is a President and children bred to win at any cost and care little of anyone they come up against. Revenge is their weakness and also our trump card. We have Yerno in a truly difficult situation and can control, but the daughter, his wife is still arrogant and headstrong, well she promotes how they will make America a great nation again and yet all their industries use foreign sweatshops to make their 'luxury goods'. We see a war over climate change coming. It will dominate the news. But it is a front for something else going on behind, and we need to find out what that is. I fear that file is about US leaving the Paris Agreement and a letter from the PM, or email, saying she will also suddenly bring the UK out as well."

"Not bad. Not bad at all Emma, I like you, but what is the New Order up to?" asks Quetty.

I look at Arthur and then smile, "No fecking idea as my Irish friend always says. That is what we need to be listening for. Anything the New Order discusses as mere small talk, look at that and delve, but delve carefully as I have a feeling from my latest run in that the Russians are finally ready to make their move."

"There is one thing I heard," says Caitlyn. "Well, Michael and I were in Ghana and had three days with Joseph and Chenguang. Whilst there Chenguang told me her father was annoyed as a Russian group had met people from America, sounded like Yerno and Hogg. Well there is a land deal going down and a special payment being made to an account in Cayman Islands. It seems the money is for the deal and from Russians to themselves as America to buy the land to replace the money the New Order in Russia have syphoned from their country. Her father was furious as they openly flaunted their contempt for the work we are doing as if they had bigger concerns."

"Can you find out if the money deal has been done?" I ask the room.

"I can," says Robert and makes a call on his mobile, then hangs up. The phone in the office rings and he picks it up in the boardroom extension and answers, "That was quick, yes thank you for your time sir, I trust the weather is good, yes Arthur is well and sends his best. I want to ask a sensitive question? Do you know if the money transfer from the Russians has been made? Yes we are annoyed too. They intend to meet again at the hotel and do it in front of everyone, well so we know next week. Thanks for the Intel, Yes Arthur would love a word, one second please Aiguo, he is coming now."

"My good friend, I believe congratulations are in order as you are to be a grandfather, yes, Caitlyn and Michael had a wonderful time with your daughter. Be grateful if you can keep eye on what is happening and are you about next week and can spare a few days in Brussels as another bit of fun to be had, as well as good business. Be nice to see that lovely daughter of yours too. Sorry, can Michael come cook for you if you come? Well not up to me have to ask Caitlyn, but if Chenguang and Joseph come then it will be agreed I am sure. Yes and please come, be seen as good that we are all seen elsewhere as got a feeling that deal is about to go bad for the Russians. I thought that would make you smile. Oh course I will bring my wife, I am shackled to the woman," Arthur laughs and then says goodbye and hangs up. "Robert, I think we should have you and Quetty run the country, smart move. So you heard everyone we are all off to Brussels next week. Chastity, can you and Caitlyn liaise on travel documents, accommodation etc. and Emma would you care to join me for lunch as love to have a chat?"

I agreed of course and we sat in the main parliamentary restaurant in plain view. We talked about life and his love of his country, but mainly about how I should go visit Ghana and meet the President as an envoy for the Knights.

That night at Chastity and Henry's all were really excited and they bought me back a large folder to go through papers. A lovely girl from the Knight's office called Clara joined us as she was doing nothing and they invited her home.

Everything was so civilised in Britain. That is why it is called Great Britain as Arthur said proudly, as the way you guys react and deal with situations is mind-boggling. In the States if there is a crisis, people have no idea how to hide the fact they are in meltdown. Here a cup of tea and stiff upper lip, well I am learning the first Invisibles were all British.

Clara was an absolute joy and she was a little down as life was boring as no boyfriend, not really much to do at work, and missing family from Spain. I smiled as I listened to everyone drinking wine and then we all played scrabble. Clara thrashed us all and realised what a lovely young girl she was, which made me think of her hero, she said she missed seeing, Sir John. And then I thought to myself, what would Sir John do.

Not sleeping too well so read the file and basically it was names and information of Ghanaian President and family, the hotel, a guy called Nelson and two women Ntombi and Stephanie. I was to be meeting them and they would sort me out place to stay and keep me company as a Knight visiting them.

It was five am and I woke suddenly. I heard a noise downstairs. I grabbed my dressing gown and put it on. I also grabbed a baseball bat next to the bed; well I do not have a gun Reader so a girl has to sleep with some protection.

I creep downstairs and see the fridge door open and the light coming from it outlining Chastity's incredible figure. She turns and sees me.

"Sorry, did I wake you?" she asks.

"No I was up. You're up early or just got the munchies?" I asked.

"Just thinking of what Clara was saying about Sir John." Chastity looked wistfully away and I saw that there was more than a small infatuation for Sir John. "He literally has changed everyone of our lives, and now I meet you, it seems when you go to Ghana you will realise he changed a lot of people's lives there too."

"And in America," I quipped.

"He's alive," Chastity whispered.

"I know," I said, "it was me that shot him." There is a sudden silence and we both laugh.

"He even gets us to kill him and thus keep him alive. I do wish I could see him again soon."

"I am sure you will Chastity, I am sure you will. He has a habit of turning up. Listen didn't Clara say it was her parents twenty-fifth wedding anniversary next week?"

Chastity nods her head and then looks at me to say 'why?'

"Think you and Henry will get to twenty-five, you know years married?"

"Oh God yes," she says without hesitating, "Unless of course I don't shoot him first. Goodnight." And with that wandered back to bed.

"Yes, good morning," I replied as looking at the kitchen digital clock it was 5:35am. There I was in a kitchen in the dark with a baseball bat watching a woman with the most sexiest arse go back to her man and thought, may be I need to look around and settle down.

10

As I trundled to bed a little plan hatched in my head and realised it was the perfect plan for this mission. Reader tomorrow, what am I saying, writing, 'Today' is going to be a good day.'

I lay in bed jotting down notes of plans and soon it was clear, I have three days to make a plan, get agreed and touchdown in Ghana. I was about to take on a seriously dangerous mission and foil my hit with moments of pure joy.

I managed to email a friend in old firm before hearing Henry pass my door to the bathroom.

Sat having a coffee with Arthur in the Savoy American Bar was quite surreal. I told him my plan and he said that we were to meet someone in their suite who I knew very well. I was intrigued, but relaxed and smiled as I trust this British fella and thought somehow I knew who was waiting to say hello.

Arthur walked to the reception where the front desk greeted him warmly and they made a call for him. I watched them call and then hang up as Arthur walked away.

As Arthur returned behind him I saw two old CIA agents walk into the lobby and take the lift. Arthur was looking at me and smiled, "seen a ghost?" he said. I was about to say that two CIA agents just went in a lift when he continued, "It's Ok only we know they are here."

The receptionist came to where we were seating and said that our friend was ready for us in the Presidential Suite. Now I am confused, but still cannot wait to nonchalantly walk in the door and say, "Good morning Sir John."

In the lift Arthur was talking about the fact that tonight we were all going to the opening night of Valeria at the English National Opera. I suddenly thought, Presidential Suite, El Cid, Sophia, as the doors to the lift opened and there were my two old colleagues from the CIA. They smiled and opened the suite door as we walked closer.

I walk into the room with Arthur gallantly as always offering after you. As I walked in another CIA guy smiled and says, "Welcome, sorry to of kept you waiting."

"Not at all, nice to get out of the office doing real work," replied Arthur and then a voice I recognised from the other room laughs and calls back, "When have you British ever done a good days work?" and into the room walks my ex-boss, the recently sacked Head of the CIA.

"I got your email Suzie and I concur with the Knights it is a great plan although risky for you. I am not sure I can sanction."

"Sir, it is an honour to see you, but had no idea you were in London..."

"I am now in Brussels according to one of Sir John's moles." And with this he gave out an almighty roar of laughter. "Now I am retired I finally get out in the field."

"Well, you should know sir that my name is now Emma, Emma Beauchamp, and I no longer work for the CIA. I am working with the Knights and also for El Cid as a nanny of sorts."

"Yes, the bomber and Yerno. We have only just learnt of this and it gives us even more concerns about this idiot we have let the people install in the White House. But El Cid, I love his name as the whole of the service are rushing round to find out who El Cid is in these messages from the Knights."

"So if I may be so bold sir, who are you working for if not CIA?" I asked and Arthur stepped forward.

"Emma, may I introduce Hugues de Payens, first Grand Master of the Knights Templar. Well we decided to have a little extra help to ease the strain off the Invisible Men and Women. At this moment the POTUS offices are trying to find a new French force and what their plans are. Hughes has even set about this charade himself from within the Pentagon. In Brussels when the world is watching we will announce the Knights Templar will be a new group of Knights from around the world accessing security from all nations to provide transparent security for individuals. When the eyes of the world and the POTUS are on El Cid and Hughes de Payens standing together at your party in Brussels we expect him to have his eye off what we are really doing. Your African venture is bold and not expected and with this distraction will provide the opportunity for the plan to work as Yerno and Hogg will feel we are not watching them."

"This is Robbins and Nichols. They are also now Knights as came with me when I sort of left. They are going to travel with you to Ghana. They will act, as part of the American party looking to set up deal and you will be the banker they have come to meet. I like your idea and they are the only additions and please no arguments as if anything happens to you El Cid and Sophia would not be pleased with me. You three go have fun in the Knights Templars office we have set up and good luck. See you in ten days in, actually feel we should meet in LA. Let's call the guys at the clinic as they have a breakthrough for Hepatitis C and believe one of the doctors is in Mumbai now doing a deal on production. Anyway, that is something we can discuss in Brussels with El Cid," Hugues laughs, "I love this whole Knight naming and it is going to confuse the hell out of that moron in the White House. Listen just be careful and you are family all three of you and I have been proud to work with you all, so make sure you make the party in Malibu, OK?"

"Yes sir," says Robbins as Nichols nods his head.

"I have the Chinese and Family also ready to make sure you will be safe, but make sure you take steps to ensure you watch your backs." I looked at Arthur who seemed concerned as he said this.

"Can I ask for a steak at the party medium rare?" asks Nichols and we all smile.

"Come on let's get to work," says Robbins and the three of us exit. I look back and see Hugues smile and wink at me. I feel that the being part of the Knights is truly infectious.

I am back at Chastity and Henry's with Robbins and Nichols. Funny thing Reader is in the CIA or many of the American institutions we rarely use our first names or even know what they are. I think Robbins and Nichols have been answering to their surnames for so long even they cannot remember their first names.

I hear the door go and in walks Chastity. She stops upon seeing us, and smiles. The two men stand and Chastity takes off her jacket and I can hear the two men gulp as she walks towards them with her huge bosom tugging at the shirt buttons and erect nipples. No idea why I mention the nipples, but the poor boys could not know where to look and were completely disarmed.

"Hi, I am Chastity, Arthur said you may be here and we have two spare rooms in the attic made up for you guys, Robbins and Nichols, yes?" The two men look and me then Chastity and just nod.

Suddenly Nichols moves forward to shake Chastity's hand as she lunges forward and he strokes her breast. "God, I am sorry, I mean, hi Nichols, this is Robbins."

"Well glad that's sorted," said Chastity, "would have been embarrassing if this were two more men Emma had collected on her way home. Well you guys could have been Ben and Jerry." Chastity laughs and asks if any of us wants tea, iced tea as has a can when Robbins steps up.

"Hi Ma'am. You took us by surprise there. Met Henry a year ago with Arthur and he told me about his lovely wife."

Robbins offers his hand and Chastity shakes it and laughs, "Damn you guys know I am married. You're not are you Emma?"

I looked at her mischievous grin and smiled back at Chastity, "Well as you are offering maid service I would love an iced tea."

"I have some cans in the fridge," she replies and Nichols steps forward.

"Miss. Chastity, would it be OK if I made some real iced tea, you have an ice machine dispenser I see and it would be no trouble, no trouble at all."

Nichols had this really beautiful softly spoken southern drawl and seemed sexier by the minute. It took Chastity by surprise and she was for once speechless.

"Chastity, why don't you slip into something more comfortable and we'll have tea ready for you to join us. You know get out of work clothes and you were in Ghana so bit of local knowledge would be good," I said smiling and she grabbed her jacket and walked upstairs to get changed.

There was a second of silence then I laughed, "It's OK boys, they are magnificent tits, I think that is what the British call a big pair of tits."

Nichols laughed and opened the fridge as Robbins searched for a glass jug. As Nichols struggled to find a jug Chastity returned in a tee shirt and shorts.

Nichols turns to ask, "Excuse me Chastity, do you have a couple of large jugs?" Both Robbins and I burst out in a fit of laughter. Chastity gives a grin to me and I am fully aware of her flirtatious nature as she opens up a drawer bending over in front of Nichols and pulls out two large glass jugs.

"Here you go Nichols, please fill my jugs up and if you can make extra for later as feel it will be really hot tonight. You're American right? Of course so will get Henry to bring home some steaks and we can have a barbeque in the garden. Quetty and Robert will pop by too and a few of the other Knights. Seems Emma Beauchamp has a secret event we all have to help with. Tell me Emma do you think I will need to get more of my jugs out?" And with that the doorbell went and Chastity exits to answer.

"Well guys going to be a fun evening I gather," I said.

"We'll be fine, we watched loads of Benny Hill on the flight over so in sync with the Brits," says Robbins.

"We can quiz them for info on Ghana and.." starts Nichols.

"No," I quickly jump in, "You guys need to relax and take a night to savour your new roles. Listen it took me a while and once you get into the flow all you need to know will be clear. I believe two new girls are coming as well as I asked them when chatting to Quetty."

"Quetty, when did you chat to Quetty?" asks Nichols.

"Oh I forgot, you're guys, can't multitask. Listen I work for nobody, but work with lots of people. Just note that you will have friends from, well from a certain family to trust, organisations sympathetic to our causes, and it is a different world of black and white. Quetty said that she has three friends coming over that she thought would be nice to meet and so they'll be coming..." and as I start to say this in walks Chastity with three stunning girls in their twenties.

"Ladies, this is Emma, she's American, but don't let that fool you she is as smart as us and ladies these two young men standing to attention, are Nichols and Robbins. Gentlemen and lady, this is Sylvia, Chantel and Mandy. They are new to the office as I believe we all are to each other so let's relax and enjoy a good night getting acquainted as heard from Arthur we are all going to be working together. Is anyone Jewish, vegetarian? No one, Ok any allergies?"

"I have a nut allergy," says Nichols.

"Me too says Mandy," and smiles.

"Well stay away from the satay as Henry loves his sauces and guess you already seem to have something in common."

"I love Americans, sorry love your accent," says Chantel. Robbins smiles and Sylvia looks to me, "I like people, I am Polish, we are great at everything."

"Oh Henry is going to love you. Do you cook?" asks Chastity.

"I too love making traditional sauces from Poland."

"OK," says Chastity as she dials on her mobile then holding up her hand as she hears Henry answer, "Honey, you need to get food for barbeque for about fifteen as think neighbours will be home, also handing phone to Sylvia who will needs some ingredients as going to have you and her in the kitchen on

86

sauces and feel you may have a challenge." Chastity then hands the phone to Sylvia, "Tell him what you need and I promise he will come with it."

Sylvia gingerly takes the mobile and we can see her nervously ask for something and Henry's response then triggers a smile as we hear her say 'you know it' and then the pair chat over a recipe she and he will make together.

Chastity looks at me and laughs, "Henry will be in seventh heaven. He once took me to a cookery class with him and it was a disaster. I think he wants a cooking buddy in fact let's put those two on catering duty in Brussels for the party with Michael, you know Caitlyn's fella?"

"Drinks! I forgot drinks!" exclaims Chastity.

"Please let us if you show us where to go we will do the drinks as our part," says Robbins.

"There is an off licence around the corner we use, we can take you," says Chantel and Mandy nods in agreement.

"Listen this is a Knights event and so here Mandy take my Knight's card and use for the drinks. I feel a prosecco and a good red would be nice. The pin is these four digits of the sort code." Nichols looks to protest and I smile, "Gentlemen you are our guests and the only thing is don't go over twenty-five thousand."

"Twenty-five thousand!" exclaims Chantel.

"Just get what we need plus extra as hate to think we run out of beers and wine. And Mandy, you're in charge, Nichols you choose the beers, and Robbins I suspect you may just have some knowledge on red wines. Take a taxi back as no need to pull a muscle before the party starts."

Mandy gives me a hug, "I knew somehow you were going to be fun. Listen if you think of anything else call my cell," and hands me her new Knight's card.

"Or me, I got cards today too," says Chantel.

The doorbell rings and it is Robert and Quetty. As they pile in the guys exit and Quetty asks for a bottle of gin and slim line tonics to the list. A scotch or single malt for me shouts Robert and all wave as they exit.

"They seem nice," says Robert.

"They are a couple of gooduns I agree and think this is perfect to relax them into Knight's ways from the CIA style," I say.

"They were CIA?" says Quetty as she looks at me then back at the door.

"Well if they were they probably know exactly what we all drink and have files on us all so no need to worry about small talk," laughs Robert. "Where's Henry?"

"Hello Rob, I am here and can you help me unload the car. I even got some traditional American pies," says Henry as he enters with bags. Chastity looks as if to say impressed as

Henry admits, "You must be Sylvia, we never really met at the office, but it was Sylvia's idea the key lime pie and Polish Cheese cake. Thanks and look forward to cooking with you. I got all you asked for." And with, that a quick handshake, and Henry exits to the car to retrieve the rest of the shopping with Robert.

Chastity gives Sylvia a hug and smiles, "You have no idea how much that man is going to love cooking with someone tonight, but do not worry I have a friend of mine coming who is from Hungary that works for a piano company. He is a huge boy and I think you will enjoy his company. He is a body builder and saw that on your file this morning so he lifts pianos on his own. Please do not feel bashful, just take this as lesson one in being a Knight, do things for others because you can, and we alert to things about to happen. Emma is a specialist so watch her to learn, I learnt from her mentor too and hope you will meet him soon as well. Ladies can you help me set up the garden looks like it will be a perfect evening for being outside."

I smile at Sylvia and we follow into the garden with Chastity who as we exits gives a wave and a 'yahoo' to the neighbour and invites them to pop over if they are free. Chastity is a force of nature and I wonder why she hasn't lined me up with any men? She hasn't even lined me up with a woman so obviously doesn't think I am gay either.

I laugh to myself Reader, but looking back on the night I am filled with joy, warmth and love, and grateful for the life I now have.

I get a call from Hugues that takes me a back a little and asks if I could forward the UK nannies that went to the concert with us in New York and stayed at Sir John's. It seems El Cid is going to Brussels and will be an excellent cover for the Russians and our dodgy POTUS and Yerno to feel that they can do their deal without anyone seeing.

Robbins once saved Hugues life in an attack in Istanbul and Nichols saved five members of the previous administration singlehandedly in Rome on a tour where the New Order had made a move to flex their muscles and tried to blame the family. It seems this is their main objective to cause chaos and attribute blame to their enemies.

I told him that Nichols and Robbins had settled in well, had a night off and relaxed enjoying time before we disappear. Hugues thanked me and told me they were like his sons and ended that I was now officially his favourite daughter. He was a great family man who loved all his men and they all loved him. Loyalty and honesty, even when dishonestly working due to situations needed in the past, never sat well with Hugues, who I feel now he operates as a Knight Templar suits him much better.

He sends me two photos of contacts the Russians have been given to deliver the money to, it is a woman called Jenna Smith. This was whom they were to meet and hand over the transfer to. The disguise was simple and I saw pictures of the men coming and also now knew that the Knights Templar were intercepting via the Pentagon from the White House directives and all messages sent were being intercepted and then changed by Hugues and his team.

This was not going to be simple, but in two days we fly. The reality of knowing the danger suddenly hits me and I realise that the life of an Invisible is never turned off.

The night was a huge success and friendships were made. The event in Brussels will be awesome and as it happens we will be looking to make a major sting on the Russians New Order and lay it at the feet of Yerno.

11

Things are moving fast Reader on this mission and have been given two missions as another needs handling while we are there waiting for the Russians. I am now travelling on a flight to Accra. I am to all intense purposes three identities. So all I can say is hang on to your knickers Readers, as this may be a bumpy ride.

Robbins and Nichols are with me as Robbins and Nichols as we have Knights Templar and Knights of the Round Table wearing moles so it looks as if they are with Hugues as his security. I have a sneaky suspicion Jimmy and his wife are there, as 'mole wearers' and I know that at the celebration Jimmy will be honoured.

The meeting we had prior to departure was great. Really fun and I am so sad not to be there. Funny thing is I will be Reader, as Clara is wearing a mole and registering on camera as me, Miss. Margo Leadbetter. I told you this would be confusing, but I wish I was in Brussels as the event and surprise lined up are incredible and just wish I was there. I feel Sir John would be proud and I got a message from someone in New York saying that the idea was worthy of a great 'Invisible' and 'proud to see how I have developed into one of the greats as well as a beautiful person'. It may be hard to understand Reader, but only two years ago I was CIA hunting a man for a psychopath that we should have been protecting, then killing him, albeit faking his death to save myself, and now same person takes time to say he is pleased with me.

Arthur remarked before we left this morning that he is still pissed that he should of thought of the event and how is it we Invisibles always know the passive aggressive move best? I smiled and replied, "Because we can," and he hugged me and gave me another package that I have opened just now. It is a beautiful watch. Yes I know Reader, loving Bond movies I thought it possibly had a rocket launcher, lasers or something, but no, it was just a perfectly beautiful watch. Inside the box was a note from Arthur saying,

'Please accept this watch as a gift from us to remind you how much we think of you, and when looking at the time remember to enjoy the time.'

I smiled and sent him a message saying,

'Thank you for my watch and think you just did an Invisible act. I love it. And yes enjoying my time as you and all the Knights are now my family.'

A message came back from Arthur saying,

'I thank you for this message, but the wife was responsible for the choice of watch.'

Typical Knight, always giving credit to those around rather than taking it for themselves. Then my mind wonders to the man that made us all aware and looked at Robbins in the window seat fast asleep. Nichols looked at me and smiled. This was the first time I noticed his smile, it was warm and inviting and found myself flirting. Nichols takes my hand and looks at my watch.

"From someone special?" he asks.

"Yes, the Knights. I have no one special in that way."

"Get some rest as I feel we are going to need it," Nichols replies, "and I am sure there is someone for you soon. You are a beautiful woman."

I was taken aback and Nichols rests his head back and closed his eyes. I realised he was still holding my hand. We sat there like this for about half an hour until the Captain announced we were coming into land.

I felt my mole in place and laughed, as I was about to become Margo Leadbetter, who was a character chosen for me by Arthur and from a British sitcom called the Good Life. Irony is big with the Knights.

I made sure I had Margo's passport and not Jenna Smith's in hand and departed the plane. Walking to the customs area Nichols smiled and Robbins put on his sunglasses.

"You look CIA," I said.

"Good," says Robbins we need the Russians to think we are.

We sign into our hotel and have a cabana close to the club where I am to meet a guy called Nelson and Stephanie his girlfriend. Also Joseph and Ben were to meet tonight and have folder for them.

It is a four bedroom cabana and we each take a room and make sure Nichols has the main pool view room as he will be watching as I make contact. Robbins decides he will be my escort.

Robbins makes contact with colleague in CIA and they confirm that their identities have been given with mine to leak at Yerno's office to give to Russians. The Russians are dispatched to meet us and are on their way and with us in two days if all goes well. We all look to each other and I smile as I say that time to relax and be seen. We need the Russian spies to know we are here.

Nichols looking at the window looks to Robbins, "Hey Robbins, remember Carmichael?"

"What? Of course he..." starts Robbins.

"Is here."

"What?" says Robbins. Both look out the window as I join them.

"Who is Carmichael?" I ask.

"Only the greatest ever Navy Seal." Says Nichols and Robbins walk into the main room from Nichols bedroom. I follow and then see a tearful Robbins look to me.

"The reason Nichols and I were honoured and alive to be honest is because of that guy. We were all on a mission for the CIA that went tits up. A group of seals led by Carmichael came to our rescue and we were all cornered, about to be blown out of the house, literally, by Afghani tank commandeered from Russian's previous battles, when

Carmichael appears in a house to the other side and starts shooting. The Afghanis think they have the wrong house as Carmichael draws heavy fire. We all escape and run to pick up point. Carmichael did not make it. But a week later a submarine offshore at Arabian Sea not far from Mumbai meets him. He had secured the guns to wires and they fired as he fled in opposite direction to us at back of his house and as the rocket hit the building all went quiet. We heard the Taliban cheer and wanted to go back, but the Seals said that he did it because he needed us to escape. He saved his whole team and four of us. He is one of the most decorated officers in the history of the services."

"So he knows you, but why is he here. Is he CIA?" I ask.

"God no!" says Robbins, "this is a hero not a covert like we were."

"We went to Hugues to say we were ashamed of what we were doing and he too was seriously concerned what the new administration wanted doing. He assigned us to him full time and Robbins even took a bullet for Hugues in a bizarre attack we thought was set up by new POTUS."

"Listen guys, everything is coincidence until we know different. Give me a second I have a new costume and feel it may get me Carmichael's attention. I will be back in a minute."

Both look at me and Nichols opens the fridge to see drinks, "Beer Robbins?"

"Sure, why not?"

I return in my new bright yellow bikini and say to Nichols to keep an eye out. Robbins laughs and looks to me, "In that you'll probably take his eye out."

I laugh with them and tell them that to work for the Knights, Round Table or Templar, that rule one is enjoy your day. With this I exit and make my way to the bar where a stunning ex-Navy Seal, Carmichael is sat. I look over to the cabana and see both Nichols and Robbins watching intensely.

"Hello, I am Leadbetter, Margo Leadbetter," I say as Carmichael politely looks at me, and smiles. He has an incredibly toned torso and a six-pack I think even my two friends watching from the cabana would love to have.

"Hello," he replies, "I am Iain." He offers his hand and I shake it.

"Well Mr. Carmichael it is an honour to meet you." Carmichael suddenly looks at me as I use his surname not given.

"Yes, I know who you are, but may be start by saying who I am. My name is Margo for now and I was wondering why you were here. Now I believe in coincidence first meeting, but then look to see why America's most decorated seal is here in Ghana just as something big is going down."

"What are you on about? I am on holiday, left the seals last year and nothing to do with saving you crooks at CIA. So if you don't mind, walk away." He gives me a stern stare and I stand.

"Sorry to hear you no longer care about your country," I say as Carmichaels grips my wrist and pulls me close.

"Listen Margo, if that is really your name, I love my country, I still love my country, but I do not love the idiots in charge, OK?"

"Thank God for that." Carmichael stares at me in confusion. "Can we start again?" I smile and tell him I am actually here to screw over the governments of both Russia and America. Now this may seem a dangerous thing to do, but my gut feeling tells me I have a friend.

"I am now an operative for the Knights of the Round Table. Listen let me buy you a drink and tell you how you may be able to help and if not interested walk away." Carmichael still looks at me, and laughs.

"You CIA lot really are the pits, you think you can con me, well forget it and not interested."

"OK," I reply, "So would you like a beer with me and listen anyway as love to know what really brings you here."

Carmichael looks at me and then asks, "Will the two stiffs in the cabana be joining us?"

"I knew you would be just the man love to talk to. I will tell them to be less stiff and join us. One of them you saved his life."

As I walk away I turn to look back as I rocked the new bikini and saw Carmichael totally uninterested. Now I have to find his story. I enter the villa and tell the guys to put on bathing trunks and join us at the pool. Nichols and Robbins look as if to say I could of compromised the mission, but I say 'not yet' and they both agree to change.

Walking out of his room Nichols looks at me concerned and says, "Carmichael has gone."

Robbins appears in his trunks and seems concerned.

"Right gentlemen, relax we should enjoy the pool, Carmichael is not here for any other reason that to decide something in his mind that has nothing to do with the mission or us. He is a real patriot as you say, I sense that, but he seems disillusioned and to say he thinks even less than the incumbent in the White House is an understatement."
"You gathered all that from saying hello I am Margo?"

We all look to the front door as in from the shadows steps Carmichael. Robbins is first to move, "Sir, it is an honour to meet you." Carmichael looks even more confused.

"OK, OK what is going on?" asks Carmichael.

"Hi, I am Nichols and this is Robbins and yes we were some of those idiots at CIA you saved, we work for Hugues de Payens, the Knight's Templar, the ex-head of the CIA as safety now for the Knights of the Round Table. Listen I feel we need to tell you everything and trust Jenna, yes here she is Margo, and this is us high jacking a CIA new White House mission for the greater good I believe. Sorry, can I shake your hand I really have always wanted to say thanks and we never met?"

Carmichael still looks wary and steps forward and shakes both Robbins and Nichols hand.

"Listen, we have a meeting with Nelson at his club on other side of pool, it involves chatting, laughing and eating, and I am starving. Please join us Iain and promise no lies, just getting to know each other." Carmichael looks at me and smiles and we all stand there in our swimming costumes.

"It is completely casual so may be a shirt guys and I have a wrap, so let's go."

"Great I am starving. Iain, can I call you Iain? Listen we will tell you anything you want to know, just please have lunch with us, it would be an honour," says Robbins.

"OK," says Carmichael and together we walk past the bar where Carmichael pays his bar tab and a truly stunning, petite black girls walks towards us.

"I hope the cabana is OK for you? Hi I am Stephanie, Nelson is just inside sorting out our table."

"Stephanie, I am Margo and this is Nichols and Robbins and our new friend Iain Carmichael who will be joining us."

Stephanie smiles, "Well gentlemen follow me and Margo I like the company you keep." I see Robbins grin as he watches Stephanie's pert bottom move as we follow.

Inside a busy restaurant is Nelson and he sees Carmichael and quickly organises another setting. The waitress is busy sorting as we arrive at the table.

"Hi, I am Nelson, and Sir John told me to expect one of his favourite colleagues and my guessing is it is you Margo?" He laughs and we all introduce as the waitress asks if we want to order from the specials there is only three swordfish steaks left. "Thanks Carmen, give us a few seconds and bring us the drinks list first. OK, sit everyone."

It was a wonderful lunch and we all just chatted about common interests and Nelson offered to take Nichols and Robbins to a great fishing spot as all loved to fish. Carmichael was really into design and colours. He offered Stephanie advice on to help bring shade in the restaurant to tables possible put up coloured cloths cut like sails and stretched out causing shadows, but also bringing more colour into the restaurant itself. I think we were all impressed and who would of thought a Navy Seal was such a fashionista. Carmichael started to relax and had a moment when all laughing he stopped as if off guard and caught my eye. I smiled and suggested we chat later after a swim.

Nelson had organised an office space via Sir John for us to meet and use and that was about the extent of our meeting on the mission and it was all Nelson knew, and we want to keep it that way.

Nelson asked if Carmichael would mind modelling his new shirt range designed by Stephanie and Ntombi as they were having a photo-shoot tomorrow. In fact we all agreed and as the waitress Carmen returned I asked if she was busy tomorrow.

"Would you like me to be person server on shoot?" she asked.

"Good God No!" I exclaimed, "you are to be model too and feel Iain could help style shoot with Stephanie and get Nelson in shot, as well as Nelson will join me as personal server."

Carmichael laughed and agreed to be part of the shoot then stood took Carmen's hands in his and looked her up and down, "I would die for your cheekbones you are exquisite and lets get some fabric that would be used in restaurant as have an idea."

Stephanie laughed, "I love it, spontaneous, Ntombi will be here tonight to discuss and yes as long as you pose in the shorts topless, we already saw you rack."

Nelson spurted out his drink, "Stephanie! What did I tell you about being less direct, but great idea as long as I don't have to stand next to you, I have a one pack that wants to be a six pack."

All laugh and we part for the pool, "Laters," I call back as we exit and take Carmichael's hand. He reacts surprised and I grip it tight. "Come on you, few lengths of the pool and let us have that chat."

Carmichael smiles and agrees. Nelson hands Nichols keys and he and Robbins go to look over the offices.

As we head to the pool Nelson catches us up and hands Carmichael his sunglasses he left behind, "Oh you left these and Margo, what is it with you guys you always make the right moves. Carmen is an orphan we adopted at the club, wants to model, but like Stephanie too short for catwalk, anyway that was inspired and came from you guys not me so she is even happier. Thank you."

And with this Nelson walks back to his club.

"You guys? So tell me what you are doing and I will tell you everything afterwards. But first I need a swim." With this Carmichael places his glasses on a sun lounger, takes off his shirt and dives in the pool. I place my wrap on the sun lounger next to his and dive in. We swim and laugh and as we exit the pool Carmen walks over with four beautiful towels and gives Carmichael a hug. He hugs her back like a loving father and I think that as we work as Invisibles we must always leave a trail of happiness and joy, building futures rather than the old CIA days of leaving amid mass destruction.

"You have a fan," I say and Carmichael smiles.

"Carmen are you free tonight?" asks Carmichael.

"Yes I finish in half an hour."

"Good then tonight as main model of shoot you must join us for the meeting and I want you to contribute, not be a mouse, any ideas bring it on, OK?"

"OK. I will." And with that a literally exploding waitress soon to be models runs back to Nelson's club and gives him a hug and then rushes back to work. I see Nelson look to Carmichael and me and smile shaking his head and disappear.

12

Sat, sipping drinks with this Adonis of a man I smile, and think that being an Invisible Woman Reader is just the best job in the world. I get to travel the world, do good and let people decide whether they want change, happy knowing they have all the facts, and if not we also help save many innocents caught up in the crossfire of the politicians illegal games they play.

Once dry and relaxed sat on my lounger facing Carmichael I tell him that the new POTUS has dementia and his inner council of Yerno and daughter trying to run things as well as Boss Hog and King Tiller at loggerheads trying to get things the way they want them.

"Tomorrow the Knights will introduce the Knight's Templar, with ex-CIA chief in charge now know as Hugues de Payens, and they will be seen all in Brussels. The mission for us is to intercept a huge trade of money and start a major disagreement between the Russian New Order and American New Order with all our key figures seen to be miles away and nothing to do with what happens here. We will intercept a five hundred million payment in bonds stolen from Russia without them knowing by Russian New Order and placed into a bank account in the Cayman Islands. Then the Americans will buy rights in a joint venture for five hundred million to the Russians. This money will replace the Russian money and a few months later the stolen money divided by those involved. As the deal is for no money as it will be for the oil rights shared that is a joint production where America pays to drill at their cost the Russians are not expecting any payment. Thus the New Order gets five hundred million to use to move people into power for the new coming of power trying to sweep through Europe, America and now Russian and Eastern Block. The Knight's Templar with the Knights of the Round Table has been covertly screwing them up for years. This we look to have fun with as bonds are non existent to all parties, I had an idea we would donate the money to Mexico to start building clinics and schools much needed with better housing, and the Guardians would then go help build and start building stronger communities."

"Sorry, I am with you, but confused. Why tell me?" asks Carmichael.

"Well, why are you here?"

Carmichael looks at me then looks at the ground. I feel what he is about to tell me is something he has wanted to tell someone for a long time, but I may be the first person to hear it.

"Well I love my country, but no lover of this new administration. I served my country though thick and thin for over twenty-five years. But....." he hesitated and then looked around, "Oh Fuck it! You've trusted me, I have always wanted to be a woman."

Well Reader this is not what I expected to hear and I instinctively held his hand. I smiled after a pause and said, "To be honest being a woman is not all it's cracked up to be." We both laughed and asked, "So why come to Ghana?"

"In all my years in the service this is one place I had never been," he said. "I was leaving as thinking of transgender options and many of my fellow seals are also transgender and needed to get away somewhere with no memories to decide. Truth is the real dilemma is I love sex with a woman, do not necessarily want to loose my friend below, but feel I am a woman. Fucked up I know."

"To be honest there is not many things that compete as a difference from perceptions from meeting you, but I have met many people far worse than you that think they are normal. Sorry not meaning normal as in you are not... my Dad told me, as did another dear friend, that the truth is what you see through your eyes. I was bought up by my father, mother ran out on us all and not as unusual as people may think, but when people say I did not have a normal upbringing I would reply that it was normal for me as I knew no different. For me being bought up by my Dad was the norm, just as being a woman in a man's body is the norm for you. So what's next?"

"Well the rise of hatred for LGBT due to this POTUS is on the rise, America is nowhere near the land of the free as I feel there is more repression from the elite on the poor, and the poor and different paying the price for the rich follies. The transgender ruling for all service personnel who placed their lives on the line when this bogus, fake President, and all his family dodged signing up, have the nerve to dishonour these brave people I knew it was time to leave. Sadly, it is costly to have operations, press would hound me once word got out, and the pension I get is good if I want a small house in a deadwood part of a backwater and enjoy getting drunk until I die. I am ashamed of how this ignorant POTUS has degraded America and a country I love, made us no longer proud Leaders of the Free World, but seen as what we truly are underneath, a racist, divided nation, easily scared into unthinkable acts through fear of losing something we don't even have."

"Great. So this is why I knew you would have a new life with us."

Carmichael looked at me as if to say 'what?' I smiled and looked at my watch. "OK here is the deal, I was banking on you being disgruntled and this is what we are looking to do. I trust you to help us screw this latest US White House fakery and in return earn five million dollars, enough for operations and new life, a further trip to Mexico and give the money to Mexican President as new identity, I know the op is not instant, but as a man that CIA will hunt not realising it was a woman they need to find, and hand to Hugues, the ex-CIA boss in Switzerland five hundred million dollars in bonds that will be deposited into Russian New Order's account. I want you to be the man the Russians meet, me your assistant, and Nichols and Robbins security. So this way you get your dilemma solved as you want as you will have options, screw this POTUS out of a dodgy deal, and his family controlling deal, as well as they tried to kill ex-President's children and blame ISIS, but we thwarted, long story another time, and know that you will be a member of the Knight's Templar guarding the wonderful projects doing good around the world."

Carmichael just looked at me for a second and then smiled, "So what have we to do?"

"Tonight enjoy a night here visibly seen as a production company with models to shoot, you organise the styling with

Stephanie and another girl we are to meet called Ntombi, who is now married to a local politician of note, one we love as an honorary Knight as well, tomorrow the shoot which will be fun, wait for Russians to make contact and take the bonds in a transfer in office boys are checking out, then disappear and I have a few things to help that happen."

"And you decided I would say yes when you saw me across the pool earlier today?"

"Iain, the boys spoke of you before I saw you as they spied you first. Hearing what they said I knew there was a good chance... well I was right and really glad. The whole transgender part is up to you, but you will always have friends with the Knights."

I hear Carmen come rushing over to us and waving. I wave back and smile, "Your new best friend needs you."

Carmichael smiles, "Carmen, you are my lucky charm so let's start with getting you a drink and decide on what we are shooting and where."

"I am so happy. Stephanie wanted me to be part of this too and I would love at least one shot with her and Nelson if we can. They are like a mum and dad to me, but not actually old enough, anyway I would love a picture of us three."

"Something tells me this will happen, and please Carmen call me Iain, Margo will be also with us...."

"Not in front of camera," I jump in as last thing an invisible wants is photos of them in circulation.

"But you are so pretty," says Carmen, "she is, isn't she Iain? And very sexy no?"

"All of the above and very wise," Carmichael replies, "Now let's get us all fresh drinks."

Carmichael starts to go to the bar and Carmen follows him. She holds his hand. It was a strange and touching moment as he looked down on her and smiled back.

Reader, plans as an Invisible change and adapt, but feel that this is the best change I have ever been part of. We are building people's lives for the better, helping fight disease as have file from Arthur for Joseph, and the only people we hurt are those that feel they are above the law.

So Reader, you now know the POTUS and his family are corrupt and despicable, they have no regard for the American people, their country or the safety of the world. Just saying so that next opportunity to vote them out it is up to you.

I see Robbins walking towards me and then talking on his mobile is Nichols. Both come join us and Robbins gives me the thumbs up to say all OK. Carmichael sees them and motions from the bar 'two beers' they nod yes and Carmen rushes over to give them the beers.

Suddenly I have a stunning black girl tap me on my shoulder. As I turn she smiles and introduces herself, "Hi, I am Ntombi. You are Margo? Of course you are, Nelson said that you were a sexy blonde with great tits."

Carmichael laughs as he hears the last part, "Iain, this is your shoot partner in crime, Ntombi. Ntombi this is Iain who has some styling ideas as well as will be in shots as well."

"I am doing shoot too, Ntombi," says an excited Carmen.

"I know and I asked Nelson earlier as thought we need all looks and ages, but this man will be in some shots with me," she says seductively moving towards Carmichael to shake hands. As they are up close Ntombi adds, "My husband will also look forward to meeting you all. He come tonight with Joseph and Chenguang."

"Excellent. Where are we all meeting?" I ask.

"Nelson thought we should meet at Ben's as Joseph will be there working. He lives in the house with Chenguang now and they are married. Anyway, Carmen what are you drinking?"

Carmen laughs, "I saw you coming and got you a glass of bubbles." Carmen hands Ntombi a glass of prosecco and she takes a sip then sees Robbins and Nichols.

"Oh my Margo, get you girl you can come again, look at all these men you and your boobs have bought to the party." Nichols looks embarrassed and shakes Ntombi's hand, and then Robbins, "I will ask my husband if he has two girlfriends that would like to join us tonight as the temptation will be too much and I love my Abraham. He is Ambassador for Overseas Development."

"It all sounds like it will be a full on evening, I think I may go have a little rest if OK?" says Nichols and smiles at me.

"He got hots for you, you do realise don't you? I tell Abraham just one girl to come. And may be my friend Paulina, a drag queen, very funny. It party is it not?" And with that Ntombi sits and sips her drink waving at Nelson clearing a table.

"Well she is a whirlwind," whispers Carmichael to me, "do you think she got the drag queen for me?"

We both laugh and Ntombi looks over and smiles, "You can have him for tonight, but tomorrow he is in shots with me." She laughs and Robbins joins us and asks if all is OK? "Great," I say and Carmichael shakes Robbins hand.

"Tonight we relax and enjoy the African hospitality, tomorrow we can set up the mission," says Carmichael, "but I feel that our friend here has already sorted out a plan so she can tell us tomorrow."

I smile at them both and to be honest Reader I had half a plan, but tonight wanted to go check out the office as wanted to make an Invisible inspection.

It is 3am in the morning as I creep back into the cabana. I have been out sourcing routes out in case of mission suddenly going out of shape. As I close the door quietly Nichols opens his room door.

"I can't sleep. You OK?" he asked.

"Yes, just sorting out exit strategies. The office is perfect as behind filing cabinet is an old laundry shute and found out it was a laundry, then laundering cash for drug dealers, and big enough to slide down into a set of mattresses in a small shed at the rear. I think once deal done we should have tapes done of us talking in the office using phones and exit that way, so if Russians are watching or looking to double deal they will be waiting for us to come out, no doubt monitoring our movements."

"Really, Robbins and I never saw it."

"Did you move any furniture? Well must be a female thing."

"I feel I want to learn from you this Invisible 'thing', somehow now we are Knights Templar we should be looking to source all avenues if we are to keep the guardians safe."

"I will look forward to showing you what I know," I said flirtatiously.
"I will look forward to more time with you too," Nichols replied. "Goodnight," he said and went back into his room, but left the door open.

I stood there for a second and then saw the light go out. Nichols, what am I thinking Reader, Nichols? Sat here writing this in my room I cannot but wonder if his bedroom door is still open. He has a great frame, tall, handsome even and a real gentleman. When he smiles he makes everyone relaxed and now writing this I realise that it has been a while since I had a man in my life and yet remember I am an Invisible Woman; we cannot afford to get others hurt in our crossfire. But this was Nichols, he's a Knights Templar, part of the gang........ Sorry Reader not sure where I am going with this but chatting to you has helped. I often find the reason for the journal is to talk, we all need to talk.

Nichols, I bet he, sorry Reader forgot you are still there, but I think I really fancy him. At Chastity's, Robbins was straight in for the kill with the new girls, but Nichols joined in, but remained distant.

Well as you are still here Reader, what would you do, ladies mainly this question goes to. Would you walk straight through that open door and into a handsome man's bed or wait for the right moment? Is this the right moment?

OK back to the mission. Tomorrow a shoot for Nelson and Stephanie, who has some other photos she needs taken, and in Brussels the first part of the plan unfolds.

14

Arthur, El Cid, Hugues de Payens and all the women will be on television making huge announcement, showing all focus is there, we are all there united and therefore giving Yerno and Russians confidence to meet down here as they planned.

Going to leave the open door to Nichol's bed open for now, but God help me, he is my type, well he is a hunk, that is my type Reader.

It is now 9am and a few hours sleep as we all gather eating breakfast in Nelson's club. Stephanie has a beautiful set of Louis Vuitton suitcases, a present from Sir John and Arthur for her to use when visiting them in London with Nelson. They have been so busy with Little Feet and the club that two years have passed and they have not had a day to themselves.

Nelson is fussing around with Gabriele, a lovely middle-aged woman, who Nelson is leaving in charge as he is coming on the shoot. Gabriele has a truly infectious laugh and to all of Nelson's worries she reassures him like she is his mother, 'I know, it'll all be here when you get back' or 'of course, just enjoy your day'.

Stephanie walks in and smiles, she sees Nelson and winks at me, "Just a second, can you watch my luggage please Margo?" and walks over to Nelson. Nelson sees Stephanie and gives her a hug. Stephanie then gives Gabriele a hug.

"So Gabriele, let me recap shall I? Whilst Nelson is away having a day off you will promise to burn the club down, but not before upsetting all the members and framing Nelson for murder?"

"Well I was hoping you'd be gone by now as there is going to be a busy day and so many customers to insult you are all holding me back," replies Gabriele.

"OK OK Very Funny, listen don't forget the President's wife has just booked and needs her table"

"Don't worry, she is the first person I will insult, honestly Stephanie I do not know how you survive with this man, but I do love him. Now listen to me Nelson, I have the bookings, we have more than capable staff, you need to start looking after this one here as there are a few hunky looking fellas that may just catch her eye. Go! Come on I will not tell you twice, Go!" and with this Stephanie walks Nelson to greet all of us.

Cars arrive and we all go to depart as Gabriele walks over to the table and hugs Nelson, "Relax, enjoy the day you deserve it. I will look after your baby while you are gone."

"I know you will, I am sorry," replies Nelson and looks at me, "Oh Gabriele, this is Margo, she is a friend of Sir John and.."

"Sir John, my that man has stamina, so many beautiful women, well Margo Sir John and I managed only one dance, but tell him to pop back anytime he wants to have another twirl around the dance floor or any floor for that matter," and with this Gabriele gave me a big hug, "Now Margo I am leaving this one in your safe hands and please if he looks as if he is fretting over the club slap his ass from me."

And with this she walks off and cuddles Carmen who then grabs mine, and Nelson's arms and walks us to the cars. At the car Nichols smiles and shows me his phone with live feed that the world's press are in Brussels.

"Wishing you were there, well tough luck, we need your naked body here for photo shoot," I smile.

"Naked?"

"Nichols, please, for America, for the Knights Templar, today you take one for the team." And with this I get in the car leaving Nichols to shut the door laughing and smiling. Robbins gets in to drive and starts to laugh then gets out as the driver looks confused, "Sorry force of habit."

"You know where we are going?" asks the driver.

"No actually," replies Robbins.

"Well good that I am driving as I do." And with this Robbins stands outside the car and looks dumbfounded. "Well, get in American gentleman, other side," he continues.

As Robbins rushes round to get into passenger seat driver turns to look back at Nelson, "He's model is he? Explains a lot."

We all laugh as an embarrassed Robbins gets in the car and then a convoy of three cars trundles off to the shoot destination. On the radio is David Bowie singing 'Heroes' and I look at Carmen and give her a little hug. I was feeling all maternal and looked at the car ahead where Nichols sat in-between Ntombi and Stephanie. Both incredible flirts, and in the front seat another model looking back adoringly. I felt sorry for him then thought I should be in that car and then Reader I realised I fancied Nichols. Carmen nudged me to ask what I was thinking and I smiled saying nothing, but hoping Nichols door is left ajar tonight.

It was now 10am and we were already at the location. A really colonial style small house, and next to the river, secluded and stunning in its simplicity. As we all stood there admiring the views Nelson took his two suitcases and started to unpack in the kitchen as he had bought a huge picnic.

"Iain, you and I must see models in tee shirts and also lingerie and dress sets, come on let's get started," says Stephanie. Carmichael smiled and helped her with luggage, as did Robbins with the new model, and I helped Nelson in the kitchen.

"This is going to be heaven," exclaimed Nelson, "my beloved has a new man to order round and I get a day off."

I smiled at Nelson and we chatted about the club and Sir John, how he is totally in love with Stephanie and how he really wants to take her to Paris. I hear another car pull up and it is a stunning Bentley and in it Nelson shouts out 'Earl!'

Rushing out the car pulls up and out gets Earl, Ben, Chenguang, and Joseph. Nichols appears in a pair of tight shorts and Earl sees him and offers a camp hand to say hello. Introductions done and Stephanie appears with Carmen all made up in the club tee shirts.

"Chenguang! And Ben you came!" Stephanie hugs them both as out walks Carmichael and Earl's mouth drops. Ben steps forward and offers his hand, "Hi, I am Ben, my partner Earl and this is Chenguang and Joseph."

"Hi, call me Iain. Wow, love the car."

"It is Bentley electric car, only one of a few in the world," said Earl, "Chenguang and I thought it may be good for the shoot and as Nelson was doing a picnic we thought we'd stay and help."

"You are geniuses and Iain what do you think?" asked Stephanie.

"Would you park it just by the trees there and already have an idea," says Carmichael.

"Sure," says Ben, "Earl I sure will help, he looks like he has ideas flashing through his mind too. Earl, if I can prize you away can you guide me in?"

"Guiding you in sir," says Ben and then looks to Stephanie, "twice in one day lucky me."

In no time at all Iain has models draped in and around the car, even has Ben at the wheel in a few shots, and Earl has joined in as a model. The shoot is going really well and my favourite shot is of Nelson and Stephanie laying out the picnic cloth with Carmen helping. Then the shots of the three of them are sensational. Within four hours the shots in the chalet, which is part of White Sands hotel, and by the car, are done. Nelson kept us all going with snacks and then we all stopped for lunch sat by the car and in the garden area shaded by a beautiful tree.

Nelson had done a deal with the hotel as a joint promotion as he wants to extend his club memberships. All was working perfectly. I notice Nichols pop into the chalet as other chatted and laughed. I followed him in and soon Robbins joined us.

"All going really well in Brussels, they are two hours ahead and uploading the video of the event that Hugues has just had sent. Message is all eyes watching here and huge success and that we will receive a message in the next hour."

Carmen joins us, "What you guys up to?"

"Friends, the Knights have sent video of event we are missing so just downloading as signal better in chalet than outside," says Robbins. "How about we all join everyone else again as almost downloaded and sure they will be wanting to know where their main star of the shoot has got to?"

"I like you Robbins, but I am not a star," laughs Carmen.

"I was talking about me," Robbins replies and we all laugh.

Carmen squeezes Robbins hand and whispers, "I think Candy fancies you."

I smile and as we walk back into the garden area Candy pats the blanket next to her and waggles her finger beckoning Robbins. Like a lamb to the slaughter Robbins walks over and sits down. I hear a ping and it is Robbins mobile and the video has downloaded. Looking it is a report from the BBC so knows it will be safe for all to view.

"Video downloaded so we can watch later," he says.

"Count me in," says Candy.

As we relaxed Carmichael was fixing tight triangular pieces of vivid coloured fabric to the tree and inside the chalet. Then with tin trays he bounced extra light into the room. He was a natural and became totally engrossed in his role as set designer. Lifting Stephanie in one arm and positioning her in different positions and then standing back and framing shots. To say she loved the attention was an understatement and then watching Robbins lifting Candy in the air for a 'Dirty Dancing' style shot in lingerie was breath-taking. Bouncing light he even had Earl as driver with scantily clad models in Stephanie's new lingerie range in the car, with the colours of the fabrics and light just right it was truly a sight to behold.

I secretly had a mission I wanted to achieve without notice and managed to do it without Nelson seeing. Nelson was also incorporated into the shots and with an open shirt holding a limp, lifeless Stephanie in his arms made an amazing shot. As he finished the pose he looked to see me in the kitchen area.

"Oi! What are you up to?" he shouted.

"Too late," I shouted back, "dishes all done."

"No dishes! Hooray, I love you Margo Leadbetter," shouted Carmen.

Giving her a hug Nichols looked at me and smiled, "I think we all appreciate Miss. Leadbetter."

Sat in the chalet Robbins used his mobile to somehow use the Internet TV to play the video on the TV from Brussels. It was twelve minutes of absolute joy watching something I had suggested happen in front of my eyes. Candy was now happily sat on Robbins lap as we all watched.

Joseph and Chenguang were sat outside and I handed Joseph a folder on Guanabana fruit in Brazil and that we were looking to have them go source out with scientists there having incredible results fighting cancer. They both looked excited and Chenguang said that it would be wonderful to see Rio and I realised these are two people totally in love.

"Well you have made them happy and gather there is a chance for them to travel to research. No doubt our mutual friend is behind this. They need a holiday and I feel they will. Been nice meeting you Margo and if OK with you going to take those two and Earl as need to get some rest."

"Yes, it has been a wonderful day Ben and we loved meeting you."

15

Sat watching the video again with just Nichols, Robbins and Carmichael messages came in from Hugues. He was full of joy, I know Reader, ex-head of CIA chatting and described as 'full of joy'. The whole day had been an amazing success. I was delighted to be mentioned in dispatches and the boys were replying how much fun they were having. Arthur interjected with a few lines about the Knights always look to make events fun and to highlight the way things should be and then on Skype we all laughed as Carmichael stood bolt right up to attention when El Cid and Sophia joined us online.

"Carmichael is that you?" asked El Cid.

"Yes sir," barked Carmichael.

"We have commandeered him for the mission sir," I replied.

"Then great to see you there my friend," said El Cid.

"You remember me sir?"

"Iain Carmichael, one of America's greatest sons, you kidding? Now I know I am no longer your President, but I am sure a man of your calibre can note the delicacy of the situations we face and happy to make sure you are up to speed, as events have happened. To be honest this whole Guardians Help and Knights is just the best thing I have ever become part of and we are still dancing so must go and dance with Clara's mother so Hugues will fill you all in."

"Sorry to drag him off," says Sophia, "but we do not want friends overseas noticing we have all left the room."

"No worries Sophia," I say and with that they are gone.

"Did you see the BBC report?" says Hugues, "just one of thousands, I mean everyone was watching. The British PM was completely pissed, Yerno looked smug so he has taken the bait and we already intercepted his call and you should hear about the meeting shortly. Just be careful, and Carmichael, great to have you with us son. Now Yerno and Russians seemed happy to see everyone here. In fact I sense that the Russians are not the Russians Yerno is dealing with, just a gut feeling. So be careful, be wary of who you are dealing with and remember you work for Tranvapumi Holdings. Now we have met again Carmichaels I will have our friend in the house make sure that you will be lead negotiator with the boys as security and Margo, you as Intel doing all paperwork. 'The little woman' as they say but not me" and Hugues laughs as he says it. "Seriously, guys, be careful and happy landings and want to see you all here as soon as done."

With that Hugues gives a wave and signs off.

Sorry Reader, never explained the Brussels event. We needed an event to show all, I mean everyone was seen in Brussels so that Yerno would feel now was his time to move and do his transaction. We still have not got completely what he is up to, but it involves the oil fields.

Today in Brussels Arthur had flown in Clara's parents and all their family without even Clara knowing. The parents came as they all thought they had won a trip on a competition none of them remembered entering. The icing on the cake was the Spanish King had called to tell them he would meet them in Brussels and to bring everyone they had in their family. A family of forty-two made the journey by plane and arrived at the hotel and came to the announcement from the Knights as guests.

Arthur stood up and announced that there were two huge reasons to celebrate today. One is that we now have a new Knights Templar, men who will work around the world protecting the innocent and helping Guardians build new communities in safety. They will be charged to looking after the Knights of the Round Table and we have Knights Templar being added from all our members from America to Russia to African countries to Europe, the UK and well just every country. The man coordinating everything is here, and Hugues was applauded as he took the stage. The media went mad and then to calm them down, Sophia walked on stage and asked Guinevere if she had seen her husband? He joked and ran on stage saying did I miss anything? And then he invited the Russian Ambassador to join him and they joked about how it was also thanks to the Russians affecting the outcome of the resulting new power of the Knights Templar, many journalists laughed as it was a direct hit at the POTUS, who was possibly in the White House fuming, as El Cid invited the Russian Ambassador to announce the special guest for the day. The Russian Ambassador beamed as he introduced the King and Queen of Spain.

The King walked onto the stage and with his wife stood next to him he looked lovingly into her eyes and gave her a kiss.

"My friends, we are all friends here to celebrate the work the Knights have done, are doing, the Guardians Help program, the Go Build Communities Ambassador Partnerships, all looking to help build communities and build global communities around the world. My wife and I," a huge cheer goes up from the audience as if it was a wedding. "Actually I would like my wife to announce the more important news of today." With this he stepped back and her majesty stepped forward and smiled.

"Thank you to my darling husband who has given me a wonderful life being married to him is a joy," the crowd go berserk and in the front is all of Clara's family who are completely aghast that they are there.

"For today we have a wonderful day to celebrate with wonderful people from Spain. Today we are gathered here to celebrate the marriages between countries in the resolve to do good, as a man in a party in New York, a Knight explained, 'we do it because we can'. But this is a marriage where all the people become equal and so today we will be hosting, and you are all invited, to a party to celebrate a great marriage." The crowd cheer.

"My friends, young Clara I see in the front, and I believe with your mother and father. I have to tell them that I am so proud to be Spanish and produce such incredible young people like your daughter." Clara looks to her parents and her mother hugs her. The flash from cameras of the world press almost blinds them.

"Clara, would you please invite your mother and father to the stage?" and the Queen starts to clap, as do all on stage. A completely over awed Clara and her parents walk towards the Queen, shaking hands with Presidents and Ambassadors, with Knights and then their King.

"The big celebration today we are announcing is your Ruby wedding Anniversary."

The whole crowd applaud and again cameras flash and all of Clara's family scream and cheer. The King hugs Clara's mother and then Arthur steps up to the microphone.

"Yes friends all, our big party will be in honour not just of the work the Knights have achieved, but a party to celebrate the marriage of this incredible couple, who produced this incredible young lady we are proud to call a knight, and we want to share our joy and wish them a further forty years." Arthur steps back and soon the world press have their new headlines, 'All the World Leaders Converge to Celebrate a Ruby Wedding'.

The only people to leave the party were Yerno and his entourage. The Russians stayed and partied on with their Ambassador dancing with Clara's mother and doing vodka shots with her father. He even invited them as special guests to Moscow.

I saw all the Knights hugging an emotional Clara who then rushed to Elaine and Guinevere and hugged them where Guinevere told her that sadly I was not there to say congratulations, but that I was behind the whole day. Again selfishly handing the accolades forthcoming making sure they were given to the right people. Seeing her in tears of joy was an emotional moment and I saw Nichols also have a tear in his eye.

Suddenly the cabana phone ringing interrupted us. I answered it and it was a call from the Pentagon. We were to meet a Russian delegate and receive the package for delivery. They then hung up. Carmichael laughed and asked if we could go through what he was to do. All worked out we knew it would be straight forward, but a knock at the door to the cabana and there was Nelson.

"A package arrived for you Margo at the club."

"Thanks and are the pictures all OK?" asked Carmichael.

"They are incredible, seriously Iain you should do that full time you have a real eye for detail. Stephanie and Ntombi are over the moon and been told by Carmen and Candy to make sure you guys come and join us at the club."

"Love to, can we get just a few minutes?" I asked.

"Listen I will walk back with you," said Robbins and Carmichael looked at me and Nichols, "Yes I will join you too, when you've done with the package will you too join us?" he asked with a wry smile.

"Of course, yes sure," I said.

"Sure thing buddy, I will stay and escort Margo when she is ready," said Nichols and then suddenly we were in the cabana alone. We heard the men giggle as they left and Nichols and I looked at each other.

"Sorry, I am not shy," said Nichols and walked straight over to me and kissed me, "I have wanted to do that all day."

"Well have to say kind of wanted it myself," I replied and it was an hour before we joined the others. Readers I cannot tell you exciting that moment was. Nichols was just incredible and as we left the cabana he joked 'what happens in the cabana, stays in the cabana' and tapped my ass as we exited.

In the restaurant Carmen came over and took my hand, "The guys said you were not feeling well and were not sure you would make dinner. I told them we must wait and so we are now ready to sit, will you sit with me?"

I looked at Robbins and Carmichael who smiled and said nothing. Gabriele comes over and laughs, "Seems I never burned the place down, follow me I will take you to your table."

During the meal we all laughed and Gabriele was told to join us and we pulled up an extra chair. During the desserts Nelson stood to say a few words.

"Friends, today was a great day. The pictures are looking amazing, the models and car, again Ben and Earl, too much, but today I saw my stunning wife with other men in her underwear and it made me realise I should pay more attention." Everyone laughed.

"Gabriele, you are my rock, I may never give you the credit you deserve, or thank you enough at the right times, but today you showed me, although this time I truly saw, that you can manage this club without me any day of the week. I guess my fear is you'll run it better than me. What I am saying is would you do me the greatest honour of being the clubs first ever General Manager, and before you ask yes we will discuss money. I have decided that that beautiful luggage my wife has needs to be used and I will be away for the next month with her in Paris and a few other destinations as we feel we want. My darling Stephanie, now that Gabriele has finally beaten it into me that she does know better than me, would you please come away with me, and enjoy a holiday I feel we both deserve?"

Stephanie hugs Nelson and we all raise our glasses, "To Nelson and Stephanie" only to hear Carmichael stand and say, "No. To Gabriele." All turn and look at Gabriele and say 'To Gabriele'.

Gabriele stands and we all sit. She gathers her thoughts and looks to Carmen who hugs her.

"Well if I am to be General Manager please note that my first duty will be to ask..... who's paying the bill?"

Everybody laughs and Carmichael stands, "Please allow me to take care of this." He looks to all of us and laughs as if reading a bill, "Right who had the steak? I have two swordfish here, who had the swordfish?"

"I am afraid to say the Knights Templar actually ordered everything, can you put it on my card?" says Nichols, "I can claim it back at the office." Everyone laughs and as Nelson says on the house Nichols forces it on Gabriele to charge. He then takes out a roll of Ghanaian Cedi. "And please can you put this in the tips for the staff."

Taking the money and the card Gabriele looks at Nelson, "You see only five minutes into the job and as General Manager I am making the club more than you do."

Everyone laughs as Nichols sits and throws a smile at me. I was sat next to Ntombi who squeezed my hand, "I do not know what you did to him in that cabana, but boy oh boy would I love to know your technique."

I was slightly taken aback and then laughed as I realised that for the first time in ages I had connected with someone I could see being someone more than a passing stranger in the night.

Oh the package Reader, what was in the package? Well seems Hugues was chatting to Robbins and the package contained all information regarding Carmichael's new identity. He was to be Arnold Swagger, one of Yerno's right hand men, and was on a fishing trip in the Gulf of Mexico. Fake ID's and tickets to Switzerland for us all, but it seemed a private jet paid for by Yerno. All this done by Hugues and El Cid as they had fun planning with their contacts. In fact all sorted with just two calls and interception of Yerno's calls to Pentagon made it possible nobody apart from us knew what was afoot.

Call came in and we were to meet at the office the Russians and do an exchange as we had the details to the bank in the Cayman Islands where Yerno had intended the money to go.

16

This morning I woke in my room with Nichols spooning me. It was a truly sensual night. This was a hardened CIA operative who showed that he has a loving gentle side, and was possibly one of the most considerate lovers I have ever had. As I laughed he opened his eye and smiled.

"Laughing? Have you just seen my friend Wilson?" he said referring to his manhood.

I smiled and said, "It was more than adequate."

"Adequate?! Oh well you weren't much yourself."

I looked at him in sudden shock and he suddenly pulled out his mobile and took a picture. "Sorry your look was just too good."

I was in confused shock, I was laughing to myself thinking he was so good in bed may be the CIA had trained the male operatives. Females never had any such training as I guessed females all are better in bed than men. Not that I have had a woman Reader! No, one second there, not that I have anything against women and women, I am now laughing as this journal takes over and I seem to write everything.

"You were incredible," he said and that sat up and held my face in his hands and kissed me. I was already fallen under his spell again, but we had a mission. "Sorry to of laughed at your friend Wilson, and why Wilson? Actually not laughing at in as was going to say I thought the CIA must of given you training in bed."

"You were just, listen we've got a mission, you're right, let's er um, sorry who's room are we in?"

"Yours Nichols," we hear Robbins cry out. "Listen just taking Candy to the taxi and see you both in twenty."

"See you guys again soon," we hear Candy cry.

"Oh and he calls his Johnson, Wilson, as he once referred to it in a drunken stupor as his Wilson the little rocket. Laters," and with that we heard the door shut and Robbins exit with Candy.

I started to laugh and Nichols laughed too.

"I remember Candy starting off with a drinking game and then the rest of the evening is a little blurry. I know they went to bed and we played on, but, I remember the sex, but no idea why we ended up in my room," said Nichols.

"I think that was me instigating as you were being too much of a gentleman."

"Apologies, won't happen again," he smiled.

"Oh yes it will, but be a gentleman and this will happen again."

With that I jumped up and walked out of my room across the lounge naked to my room to see Carmichael sat on the sofa.

"Hi, I made coffee and thanks for letting me have your bed last night. I went out like a light."

"No worries pleasure," I said thoroughly embarrassed. I then heard Carmichael call out to Nichols, "Hey, Nichols, heads up I am in the lounge so if you would mind making sure Wilson is not on view there is coffee and bread in kitchen."

Jumping in the shower the mortification transcended in to uncontrollable laughter. Not since I was a college graduate had I done anything remotely this spontaneous, in fact the CIA was my life, no relationships, no family, just work. As the shower washed over my face and cascaded down my body I felt alive. So this is what I had been missing, right, got to get ready for the mission.

The cabana phone rang and Carmichael took it and we all listened.

"Yes it is me Arnold Swagger and I am here to over see the deal. Sorry, you have untraceable bonds. No that is fine. You have been sent our details? OK then we meet at seven tonight when the other offices will be closed. Yes that is right, just to let you know we are expecting you, two of your men and no one else. Anyone else we see other than you three we will kill. Yes, it will be a pleasure doing business with you too." And with that Carmichael hangs up.

"Blimey you are good, I mean you were born for this," I heard Nichols say as I walked into the room looking for my shoes.

"I thought the three inch blue heels would be best with that outfit," says Carmichael.

I stop and look at him and then resign myself that he is probably right, and go change shoes. Walking back out

133

Carmichaels smiles. "You see, slight lift accentuates your butt and arches your back giving more curvature to your rack. Coffee?"

"You are a man of many skills," I reply, "and yes coffee would be good."

"When in the meeting doing the computer part Margo, undo two buttons to your blouse. From the conversation on the phone I feel we are dealing not with the Russian government, but another fraction altogether."

Nichols looks at Carmichael then at me, "Yes seeing you like that makes me need a coffee to."

"You are a lucky man, Nichols. In or out of clothing this woman is good to look at," says Carmichael.

Nichols gets a little defensive and remarks that hopefully we can be professional and may be that will be the last such remark.

Carmichael stands and walks to Nichols, "I said that to see your reaction. Margo is the brains, and we need to hide her so they see her tits and not her face. We also need to realise that the type of person we are meeting are going to be watching us. You react to a crude remark that Margo means anything to you we are undone. I am happy to be here, I have placed my life on the line for people I do not care about, and you have no competition from me for the ladies affections, but I am in a unique position today as for once I am actually excited in the mission as it has purpose, and because I care about the people I am working with. Nothing personal."

"Nothing taken except my thanks," says Nichols graciously.

The cabana door opens and Robbins enters looking flustered, "OK everyone here as it seems things are not what we thought."

I walk in with two coffees and Robbins takes one and Nichols looks to take the other and then looks to Carmichael, "Iain, I mean Arnold, can I get you a coffee?" Carmichael nods yes and Robbins is on his phone.

Nichols returns with two coffees and we all sit at the table off the kitchen.

"I think these are not the Russians we thought, they are not from Russian government," says Robbins holding up a picture on his mobile. "I just took this and this is Vladimir Roskov, hitman for crime outfit in St Petersburg once had a run with years ago. We never met, but he was on our radar and the other guy here (showing another picture) is Peter, we just knew him as Peter."

"Peter was the contact for the Russian politician we had in the frame for a mafia bust where the head of crime lords was killed, no retaliation and all quietened down after," said Nichols.

"Guys, I think Yerno and his loons at the White House are doing deals that are going to cause major wars within Russia and if these powers manage to take power, well then the peace in what was the cold war will return and who knows what. The guy I spoke to was representing Mikaei Kowlowski, the second in command to the President, and if he is involved with this New Order you told me of then there may be a coup brewing with Kowlowski working with the Russian Mafia."

"No worries, as good to know as really was a little concerned with lack of info, but if Kowlowski arrives with untraceable bonds and we sign for them to them have them taken from us by Roskov and Peter there would be a huge international incident. But as we are ripping off Russians in a secret deal with Yerno and White House no one will say anything and if they cannot find source to us then there will be even bigger grief trying to sort anyway for our New Order friends. OK, now it is not happening until seven and we know we are being watched I suggest we pack everything up and I mean everything. Nichols let Hugues know what is happening and have jet ready to go as from eight tonight. Iain, you are to relax by the pool today and enjoy having me act as bimbo secretary in bikini whilst sadly you two get to run errands as if CIA. You can take everything we need to airport first and load on plane as well as visit the office and set up my laptop ready for meeting. Keep coming back here as if reporting in and have lunch at the club. I will tell Nelson and team to be distant and we will eat at the restaurant paying cash so no credit cards or traceable links to us. In my case is enough cash for us to enjoy a wonderful last day here and lastly, Robbins, what is Candy up to?"

Robbins looks to me and said that Candy was off modelling in Abidjan tomorrow so there for a week. I smile and then smile, "Right let's get out of these clothes and Iain which do you think? The bright yellow costume or the blue one piece?" I hold up the two options.

"Nichols, what do you think?"

Nichols looks at Carmichael and smiles, "The yellow bikini, we do not want people looking at your face now do we?"

We all laugh and Carmichael grins, "Good choice, I concur, but may be suggest if on a break with Nichols the blue is better so he can concentrate."

"I concur with that as well," says Nichols and we all laugh.

"Right, will go scout the pool as if checking for you and make a space for you. Lucky you are a hero of mine as would not do this for anyone else," says Robbins and leaves.

"I have some swimming shorts and a polo shirt that'll fit boss." Carmichael looks at Nichols and goes to change. "I will join Robbins and do a sweep of the bar then get car to load up at back of cabana out of sight when our femme fatale has the Russians attention." With that Nichols exits and I walk into the lounge with Carmichael walking in smiling. He hands he a big floppy hat he found in Nichols room and tells me to wear it as it also hides the face from the sun.

I look at Carmichael and he has an incredible physique. He has a short-sleeved shirt on that is totally unbuttoned. "Blimey, you look amazing," he said, "Mind you do not fall out of the top."

I do have large breasts and the cups on the bikini were struggling to contain then Carmichael walks over adjusts a strap and then slides his hand inside the bra and adjusts my breasts. Afterwards it all fits like a dream. Speechless he kisses me on the cheek and whispers, "May be I could have that outfit for after my op?"

We both laugh and I see this Adonis, the perfect male specimen looking to become a woman, go figure Reader.

"Ready Miss. Leadbetter? Time for you to take a letter later, now I may need sun cream duties."

"Happily Arnold Swagger, where would you like it first?"

"Well let you make it up as we go along and try not to tease Nichols I think he will have a cardiac arrest seeing you like that."

"Cannot believe you are a woman inside that body? Are you sure about this op?"

"Listen I am a woman trapped in a man's body, last night you were a woman with a man's body trapped inside you; wasn't all that bad was it?" and with that Carmichael opens the door and off we went to the pool.

Nelson had managed to put a completely different team on at the club so we would not be bothered as I told him we were doing something Invisible, which he understands, and at the pool see Nichols and Robbins. Robbins walks over to meet us and directs us to the sun loungers.

"Well no one is going to remember any of us, I think the bikini is like an excorcet missile exploding in the Russian friends at two o'clock faces. That is them, Nichols will go behind them and introduce himself and them bring them over to say hello, just so they know we know who they are."

"Make sure I am face down and Margo is applying the lotion and her face is looking down at my back. Seems we all think alike, I am feeling alive and loving this, you guys may see more of me after this as feel I may want to sign up."

Robbins looks to Carmichael and agrees and nods at Nichols who is in position unseen by the Russians. "May I suggest you bend over for the lotion on the floor when they arrive, nothing personal, but be good test for Nichols too, and they will remember nothing after that."

"Robbins you are such a naughty boy, but good idea, come on Arnold lie down it is part one of the sting." I smile at Robbins who then stands as if on attention by the sun lounger and notes Nichols has casually walked up behind the Russians.

"Peter, Vladamir, how nice to see you."

Both Russians looked worried and turn quickly to see Nichols every inch CIA.

"We are meeting tonight, but as you are here already thought we'd say a quick hello now, break the ice so to say. Please follow me, Mr. Swagger looks forward to meeting you."

With this Nichols walks towards us, and the confused Russians, who thought that they were under cover, follow. As Nichols arrives he winks at me, and smiles, then back in character he speaks to Carmichael face down.

"Mr. Swagger, please may I introduce Vladimir Roskov and Peter, sorry Peter I do not know your last name?"

"Jones, Peter Jones," he replies worried that we do know who he is.

"Mr. Kowlowski not with you gentlemen? Never mind," says Carmichael as I turn to pick up the lotion bottle and they both get a good look at my backside. Nichols doesn't flinch. Flustered both look away nervous and Carmichael stands and he towers above them both. He stands with the sun behind him so the sunlight directly in their eyes he offers his hand to shake.

"Mr. Swagger, Mr. Kowlowski will see you tonight," says Peter and Carmichael returns to the sun lounger and lays on his front as I start to run sun lotion into his back and shoulders.

"Gentlemen, if you would like to join us please do or if busy may be later tonight we can conclude business and have a drink afterwards."

"Thank you Mr. Swagger, but we must get going," says Peter and pushes Roskov to move who is eyeing up me rubbing on lotion. "Vladimir, I feel we should not take up any more of these good people's time." And with that they doff their panama hats and exit. Robbins standing guard watches as they leave the hotel and Nichols slinks off to see they have indeed driving off.

Nichols returns, "They have left the hotel, but been thinking, now if Kowlowski arrives with two other goons we know they intend to hit us, if he turns up with those two we won't know. I think you will all be fine here, if all OK will take first car load to airport to put on jet that Hugues says is already in situ."

"I will be seen being seen and then I think make a few trips myself to see where our friends are staying. As he brushed passed leaving managed to get a tracker on his jacket."

"Robbins, brains and beauty," I joke.

"Well someone has to take the lead," he replies and Carmichael laughs.

"Be careful guys and all back in Cabana at five tonight. Now Miss. Leadbetter, will you please finish putting lotion on my legs and Robbins order me a vodka martini, shaken not stirred. Be fun if after we disappear Russians only lead is a man who drinks vodka martinis, shaken not stirred."

"To think, wasted all that time in the CIA when I could have been doing this, one drink on its way."

And with that Robbins and Nichols left. Suddenly Robbins returns and I look as if what is the matter. "Sorry Margo, what did you want to drink?"

"Robbins I like you more every minute, just a glass of chenin blanc, please."

"And by the way, Nichols never flinched when you picked up the lotion. I fear he may of gone gay," laughs Robbins.

"Don't worry Robbins, I will endeavour to bring him back to the straight side later tonight. Now I feel you have drinks to fetch," I grin

"Oh I love it when you are so direct," says Carmichael and waves his leg as if to put on lotion.

17

It is now 5:30pm, early evening and a wind blows through the streets as we walk to the office. I see Peter and Roskov parked in a car around the corner. As Robbins opens the office door for me he whispers, "Yes, saw them too."

Inside we set up the office. I am sat at a front desk with computer, Robbins standing by my side, obscuring view of Carmichael at the rear desk and Nichols stands by the filing cabinets on the opposite wall. We all wait now for Kowlowski, and who he will turn up with. If our new friends Roskov and Peter 'Jones' do not come with Kowlowski well then we know they have other plans to double deal on Yerno.

Carmichael smiles as I turn to see he is alright, "You know Margo you are a clever woman and would never underestimate you. Seems once Kowlowski enters and with whom, playing his cards, we know his hand and all will be fine."

"We have the car at the back ready and made a tape of us talking as if on the phone to Yerno saying that we will wait for him to call where to meet," say Nichols.

"Should give us time to get to airport before they get curious wondering when we will leave," I laugh. "So we double cross Yerno, who is looking to double cross the POTUS, who is being double crossed by the Russian New Order, as they have double crossed their President, who may know nothing of what is going on, and they also wish to double cross Yerno and kill us stealing the bonds for themselves making out Yerno's men, us, had stolen them and this really is a little does he know

143

that we know that he knows that we know he is two timing him."

Nichol's mobile rings and he answers, "One second," and then takes the phone to Carmichael mouthing 'Kowlowski'.

"Why Mr. Kowlowski, Mikaei, you are early, well we are here, you have the package...no transfer all in bonds, I see, no that is not a problem and wise on your part as no trace. Yes we are all here and ready to confirm drop made. Yes please do Mikaei, be happy to see you earlier as we all fancy having a drink back at the hotel before we fly out tomorrow. And Mikaei, please make sure you come in person as we then know we are in safe hands, yes I agree it will be great to meet you." Carmichael's hangs up.

"Right I have one more thing for us to do," I said, "I have two motion sensor cameras here so one facing the door and only get those coming in and out and one for just here where it is over your shoulder, but we are not in frame. Little insurance with the Russians in case their President is involved."

Just as I set up the second camera the door buzzer goes and we all get ready as Nichols lets them in with the door entry system. The door opens and two new Russian Secret Servicemen walk in followed by Mikaei Kowlowski. He sees me, and smiles, and then turns to see Carmichael obscured by Robbins. Carmichael stands and in a different voice welcomes them in without rising.

"Mikaei, how wonderful to see you, I trust the heat is not giving you trouble."

"Mr. Swagger, I am pleased to meet. Now I will need a signature for the bonds and also note that instructions have been sent to your Mr. Yerno for execution. I need nothing else as Mr. Yerno knows the deal."

Carmichael signs the form with a pen I hand him and Kowlowski looks at my cleavage. He then takes the signed form and exits. We all stay in position and I motion no body move as I skirt along the floor between the two desks to then turn off both cameras I had set up.

"Well I expect someone will be waiting for us with a sock full of coins, usual Russian weapon to knock people out," says Nichols. Robbins plays the recorded message.

"OK guys Yerno here do exactly as I say, go to front and check all clear outside and then wait for my next call in thirty minutes and give you drop off point." The message ends and Robbins motions placing his finger on his lip to be quiet. He exits and opens the office door to the street slightly and closes it, so if anyone were to take a photo they would not get one of him. Robbins returns and smiles and motions the filing cabinets and Carmichael and Nichols lift it away exposing the exit shute.

I go first and land on mattresses placed there earlier. Then Nichols who passes me and opens up the car in the siding by the door to the rear. As Carmichael follows I get in the car, Carmichael next to me in rear and Nichols gets in the passenger seat. Soon Robbins is getting in the front seat to drive and we begin to exit the office rear lot and as we pull out our exit is obscured from the view as Roskov and Jones are watching the front door. They too are waiting to make their move.

"Slight change of plan as the Knights stayed an extra day as meetings with Brazil over the new cancer treatment fruit so we fly to Brussels and are seen at that meeting exiting with Hugues and El Cid. Carmichael, you will be getting another award in a public way, although no one will see your face and I believe you will meet the Mexican President who will enjoy meeting you again in Switzerland. All we need is on the jet at the airport. Everyone OK? Great and it has been fun boys, real fun," I say and put on my big floppy sun hat so no one, no traffic camera can see passengers or drivers of the car.

At the lights before turning into the airport a large SUV pulls up alongside. The window is down and Robbins looks in and talks to the driver, "I wish we had one of those, some of the roads out here are to be believed."

"You know it," says the Driver, "you got a cigarette?"

"Sure, here keep the packet," and as the lights change Robbins tosses a packet of cigarettes into the car and drives off waving his hand out the window as the Driver looks to find the cigarette packet and then waves back thank you.

We arrive at the airport, whisked through customs to our jet and within an hour we are heading out of African airspace.

Carmichael is sat pensively in his seat as I decide to join him. I hand him a single malt, which I know he likes, and I have a can of lemonade.

"Could not of done this without you Iain."

"I don't know Margo, or who are you now?"

"Suzie, Suzie Johnson, and yes that is my real name. El Cid and Hugues managed to have my former life ghosted out. You ready for the op? I mean you have ten million dollars that should cover costs."

Carmichael looks at me and says that he is still worried, "I am definitely a woman in a man's body, but not sure I want to be the woman I dreamed of being. I have to put on loads of weight at first, then the drugs, then the new drugs to change my body shape, then the implants and then the extraction that has me wincing."

"When we get to Brussels would you let me help you?"

Carmichael smiled and sipped on his malt. Robbins came and sat with us as Nichols was talking to Hugues.

"Seems Yerno is really pleased with himself according to Hugues, I think tomorrow may be a different story. Well here's to the Knights and Knights Templar, and to you Carmichael as it has been an honour to see you and not feel ashamed." Robbins raises his glass and Nichols walks up and clinks his too.

"Hugues is mystified why there was no bank transfer, but in bonds, and so there is no way to really trace. So we take everything with us from this jet, but Hugues did ask if there was a tracking device on the bonds and in the light of everything I forgot to check. Did anyone else?"

Robbins looks at me and Carmichael then laughs, "Yep it had a trace on it and placed it in that pick up at the lights in Accra. Roskov and Jones will be tailing that SUV all over the place."

Landing in Brussels we are all exhausted. It is the early hours of the morning as we arrive at our hotel. I open my room to find it filled with cards and flowers. They were from Clara and her family as Arthur had let slip I was the person that orchestrated the party for her parents.

I hear a second knock on my door and thought may be Carmichael needed to chat. As I opened it Carmichael was not standing in the hall, Nichols was.

"Nichols?" I said.

"Just thought it should be me instigating things first as I do not want you having the impression I am easy." And will this he walked in, lifted me off my feet and took me to the bed.

Reader, I was tired, happy and within seconds extremely aroused by my man. He kissed my neck and in the true tradition of the Invisibles, it was incredible, but we never kiss and tell.

The next morning I woke to realise I was in deep trouble. I had completely fallen for Nichols and yet today he returned to Hugues and I was to be seen as a person that was at the party, but finding out what was to be done from our mission just finished.

I heard Nichols turning on the shower and walk back into the room naked, "Listen there may not be enough hot water for two so think you should join me." This man was now truly taking the initiative. I was impressed, I was impressed, with what I saw standing there, and scared. The kind of scared you get when you know you are falling in love. Nichols held out his hand and I happily followed him into the shower.

18

It is now eleven o'clock in the morning and the four of us are in a meeting with Arthur, El Cid and Hugues. Also there was Jimmy, he was the first to give me a hug. Jimmy was never introduced and Carmichael was the only one slightly confused by his presence.

El Cid shook Nichols and Robbins hand and then walked over to Carmichael, who was standing there feeling out of place. Carmichael sort of bowed as El Cid walked up to him and said, "Mr. President."

El Cid hearty grabs Carmichael's hand and then pulls him in for a hearty hug, Carmichael, you saved the day according to their report and they call me El Cid for some 'Knight' reason. I just want to say thank you personally and also fully support actions you wish to undertake to make yourself happy."

There is a slightly awkward silence and then El Cid laughs and Arthur also shakes Carmichael's hand, "They call me Arthur and what El Cid was saying was we are extremely grateful. We want you to meet the Mexican President in about fifteen minutes and be part of the last part of this operation or mission as we call them. We too are dismayed at the slur LGBT service men and women have been victimised by your POTUS, but although I cannot say I understand your current situation, please note that if you truly wish to become a women then we, and I mean all of us, fully support you."

"Thank you sir, I mean Arthur? I have been struggling whether to or not and the recent events back home victimising colleagues by a group of draft dodgers like our President made me want to make a statement."

"A Statement? Well hopefully as you become aware of the true consequences of the actions of the past few days in Ghana you will come to realise you already have made an incredible statement," laughs Hugues who also shakes Carmichael's hand.

"The Mexican President is in the foyer sir, shall I go to meet them," asks Robbins.

"Yes, both of you, Nichols as well. Guys be seen and even hug the miserable bastard, sorry but he has been a misery all weekend as our new leader keeps phoning him late at night, and do me a favour, make sure you take ten minutes to get them here as Iain, it is Iain isn't it?" Carmichael nods, "yes, great, so I can make sure Iain is happy with the final part."

And with that Robbins starts to leave and then he returns to shake Carmichael's hand as does Nichols and they exit.

"Iain," says El Cid, "we want you to meet with the Mexican President in Switzerland and deposit the money in a bank there, they will cash the bonds without question, got to love the Swiss, and then you are to open another account in your name and deposit the ten million to fund your op or whatever you wish to do with it and please do not argue, your country owes you a great deal more."

"Iain, heard about your improvising skills so here is the thing. Going to introduce you as benefactor and that you will deposit the money for the Mexican President to start clinics and hospitals for the poor in his country," says Arthur.

"Oh and enjoy telling him that you redirected this money from the President and his White House team looking to line their own pockets," says Hugues.

"Showtime gentlemen," I say as all turn and I open the door to have Robbins and Nichols enter with Mexican security and then the President himself. As he walks in he realises who is in the room and seems a little confused as was asked to meet by El Cid in private. I walk up to him and shake his hand, which makes him even more confused and see he is looking at my boobs and not my face, Jimmy is in the shadows, and then El Cid walks over and embraces the President.

"Beinvenido," says El Cid.

"Please in English, you are most gracious," he replies. "I need to better my English."

"Just as well Mr. President as I think that was the full extent of my Mexican," laughs Arthur.

"Gentlemen shall we have a seat?" says Hugues and everyone sits as Robbins and Nichols offer the security men a drink.

"Mr. President, please let me introduce you to one of our most decorated servicemen, Iain Carmichael. Now Iain has something for you that he has procured on behalf of the Knights. Iain if you would?" says El Cid.

"Thank you sir, El Cid," says Carmichael.

"El Cid, you are El Cid? We have seen messages that El Cid would be in Brussels, but no one knew who El Cid was," said the delighted President.

"Well sir," continues Carmichael, "Although you may of intercepted some classified Intel you probably were unaware that our President's team were doing a deal over some land and placing four hundred and ninety million dollars to each other to seal the deal. I am proud to say that the Knights Templar with friends managed to intercept the money and want to have you accept the money, in secret, to start a new series of clinics in Mexico, small enough for lots of villages, where the people can receive real medical help. We know that this is something close to your heart and also would enjoy laughing every time you saw our stupid White House team knowing that they have no idea you received the money. Now the only way to ensure the safety of the lives of those that did this is to make sure you never tell anyone."

"What? You bring me here to meet you in Switzerland and you deposit four hundred and ninety million into a secret account for me to use to help my people, and no one must know about it? I am speechless, emotional too as my wife would be overjoyed, but she talk so not tell here all details, just I have found money for clinics. Gentlemen, we in Mexico watch and are in awe of the work the Knights do, but this is just too much. So what do you need me to do?"

"Well in Knight's tradition, would you like to name the new clinics after your wife?" says Arthur.

"I go one better, after my daughter, she is new Mexico, she is new future, and she is our joy. I can start a rumour a wealthy

Prince donated the money as a rouse to woo her. I am already too excited and I want my country to also help the Knights. What can I do, what can we do for you?"

"Sir, Mr. President. Just knowing the good this money will do is enough and we know you are a good man so we trust you. In fact we will invest in new housing with the Guardians to build and we will build the clinics as well, by funding the work through our war chest it will be wonderful to show us working together and helping each other.." says El Cid only to be interrupted by the President, "Because we can."

All laugh and shaking hands becomes embracing and then Carmichael steps forward, "Sir, please no announcements, see you in a few days time in Switzerland, where you must bring your wife and daughter to attend a meeting with Arthur to then see that this can be announced then that together you are building homes and clinics with the Guardians collective. Until then even your wife must be surprised on the day, I am sure you will understand?"

"Sir, I cannot thank you enough," and with this kisses Carmichael on both cheeks and exits. " I will announce to the press today that we meet in few days in Switzerland to announce new joint venture, good?"

"It will be an honour sir," says Carmichael and the Mexican President and his entire entourage exit. There is a lot of press already outside and Arthur smiles, "I let slip to a friend we were meeting."

"Well we will go out with Robbins and Nichols. You guys need to be seen and then Carmichael and Suzie, best you slip out without being seen," and with that Hugues look round to see Jimmy has gone, "well seems our friend has gone already, but he wants you invisible Suzie, but turn up with El Cid when he leaves as Sophia wants to give you something as not seen you since New York."

"Be good if you can be in Switzerland as well in the background as feel I want to monitor any Russians," says Arthur. "Let's catch up tonight we need to go, and by the way this is for you," says Arthur and with that they left.

Carmichael looks at me and does a double take and removes a stick-it-note on my back, "You did us proud again, and door at back leads to restaurant. Go have coffee together talk soon, J. Who is J?"

"Just another invisible, one of the best, he was in the room just now."

"I don't remember seeing anyone..... an invisible, I understand I think. What did Arthur give you?"

I had forgotten and opened the envelope. Inside was a picture of me, the one the Serbs had and underneath another picture, the same as the top photo, but I had been removed. I knew that they had found the photo and eradicated me from the picture.

"I don't understand," says Carmichael.

"It means I am Invisible again."

Carmichael and I disappear out the exit Jimmy had told us of and we found ourselves back in London having coffee with Tasha Danvers who was staying with her son at another of Sir John's houses in Notting Hill.

She was an incredible character and we all got on like a house on fire. Arthur had told us to go here after we left Brussels as the Mexican President would be delayed a few days. Also word from the White House was Yerno was trying to find his men that collected the bonds in Ghana; it seems that they and disappeared and he was extremely concerned. With no routes to us, and even Swagger on the CIA, records being reported missing, as he was a real person created that never existed years ago, Yerno was chasing a ghost. More to the point he was now five hundred million short and suspected the Russians foul play.

Hugues heard that Yerno had done research as to where we all were and all checked out as being in Brussels, but somehow the recording of the jet landing from Africa had been high lighted somehow. We were not known as being on the flight or who was actually on it, but Yerno was not far from starting nuclear war to find out.

Main Intel we came to realise was that this was Yerno and his wife acting alone on their own mission. The Russian, Mikalei Kowlowski was also acting without Russian Prime Minister knowing and has taken party funds thinking they will be repaid and he will benefit from the five hundred million exchanges with Yerno. Well he needs Yerno to give him the five hundred million he has for land deal and does not know Yerno has not got five hundred million as his men were enable to steal in double cross. It gets complicated as now the Russians have shown their hand as in a meeting in Brussels with the British PM it appears that Kowlowski is new head for the Russian New Order. Together they hope to embarrass the leader and bring an embarrassing coup with Kowlowski taking over and they can access huge funds for the New Order.

Our delay has only heightened problems as if the Mexican President meets us in Switzerland someone will see and once funds may get known as exchange the Serbs will be the least of my worries.

Sat in the Groucho Club with Carmichael we stick out like sore thumbs being two American tourists and we are there to meet a member Arthur said would be fun to talk to and has info on the Swiss Banking boys.

In walks Conchita Rodriquez, a stunning Mexican actress and assistant to a Producer that makes films in Hollywood. I rise to meet her, as even though we are loud Americans she cannot see us for all the other bright colourful characters from film and television parading the floors.

"Conchita, hi I am Suzie and this is my friend who will be helping with the transfer," I say and Carmichael stands and shakes her hand. He then sits Conchita to a chair with us, and sits and calls to the waitress with his hand, he never speaks. The waitress comes and he motions to Conchita who orders a margarita. Carmichael motions we are fine and hands the waitress twenty pounds.

"Well nice to meet you both and I will be with my producer boss in Switzerland day after tomorrow. I also will be organising a venue for the bank and you to meet the President in complete secrecy as banks have many ways in and out of them, from revolving walls in adjoining buildings to secret passages from nearby hotels. I have had to move a few dubious characters depositing money for my boss's films on a few occasions and pay-outs in similar fashion. I do these dodgy deal transactions, get parts in films and not have to sleep with anyone."

"Sounds like a plan," I said.

"I have here a list of hotels and routes to the bank. Call me on this number an hour before meet time which route you are taking so to safeguard you as well as me. The President will be at the bank for one fifteen until one thirty and will be meeting my boss on the idea he will be given access to film in Mexico. Of course my boss is an idiot who knows nothing and will not be at meeting until one thirty giving us the fifteen minutes needed to trade and go. The press will be all over my boss for info and he will refuse to say anything, but we expect him to accidently stroke his own ego and let slip he met about a huge film deal. This will immediately quell any interest in the story of the Mexican President being there and you can exit through any one of the exits I just handed to you."

The waitress returns with the drink and we all toast as Carmichael motions to the waitress to keep the change. She smiles and dips as she places tray with the change on the table. Carmichael catches her hand and stops her from leaving. She looks a little concerned and he slowly lifts the tray of change and hands it to her and winks. She smiles and graciously accepts the tip and walks off.

"I like your style, you could be great lover in one of my bosses movies, we do sex scene real intense. I always say no when in script, but for you I think may be fun," says Conchita and she looks at her watch, "I have to go as catching flight tonight to sort out bank and I have a man there who attends to me. I have you as my guests Mr. and Mrs. Flintstone so stay as long as you like, it is fun here." With this Conchita stands and kisses me on the cheek and as Carmichael makes to stand she manages to catch him full on the lips. She then smiles, and exits.

As we watched Conchita sashay out of the club we both smiled and Carmichael orders two more cosmopolitans for us and we decide to relax for a while and I decide to see where Carmichael's head is at.

"So Iain, in two days you will have ten million in a Swiss Bank Account and the ability to have the ops and change you want to become the woman you feel inside."

"Funny, I have always fought what I thought was my feelings and now finally able to change and seems this last fortnight has changed me again. I was going for the full op as a result of our ignorant POTUS and now, well now I feel I better sit this through properly. Read up on that Jenner guy and he went for it, courted fame and now not a happy person it seems in a report read on the plane over here. You see if I do this, my options after are limited, but would it make me happy? I love women; I am not gay, just screwed in the head. I thought I would just embarrass that idiot racist in the White House, but once gesture done I realise it is just a gesture. I guess what I am saying is I feel I am not woman enough to go through with it all." Carmichael sits back and looks concerned.

"Iain, whatever you decide at least it will be your decision, but I have an idea that may be fun. In America made a friend who is rehearsing for her show in London and has people that may be fun to hang with. Let's down these and we have two days so let us enjoy London and all it has to offer."

Carmichael smiles and we finish our drinks. I see the waitress Carmichael tipped grabbing her coat and looking to end her shift. I call her over and she comes with her coat and as she is explaining she is just finished I ask her if she can help us get to Fred's Bar in Soho and she smiles saying she would love to sing there one day.

"Well my lovely friend and I are going to meet a friend I met recently on my travels who has come over from Australia to perform in her cabaret show with the infamous Priscilla Drag Boys. Join us if free."

"Really? Oh my God, I would love to, are you sure it is OK?" she asks.

"Of course," I reply, "on one condition, you tell us your name."

"Katie, Katie Raban."

"Well Katie I am Suzie and this is Iain, lead on as I think this will be a fun night out."

19

As we exit Iain and Katie are chatting and I am on my mobile calling Erin, she answers and tells us to come so we can see part of the show they have been rehearsing. I tell her we will be there in five and have a cunning plan, well reader we Invisibles always think we have a cunning plan.

Walking the Soho streets there is always a buzz and excitement from the people that gather there. Often maligned as a sex trade or drug den of iniquity, but as a sex centre goes it is not really that in any way and drugs are taken by the POTUS family in the White House.

The way this New Order running the Government of the UK are operating is all the prime real estate is being politically used to gain for their own financial benefit. Soho has always been the home of the troubled, the artist, the lost and the outcast; a place where you can find hope and a home. Now if the PM of the UK has her way it will be a sanitised shopping area with cheap shop outlets that monopolise the rest of the country with their boredom and boring shop fronts.

There are many opposed to this change and a group fights to keep loyal to Soho, but it seems futile, as even the Invisibles are impervious to beating such corporate corruption. We arrive at the new drag show venue called Fred's Bar, a stone's throw from the old Madam JoJo's. Excitement as anti establishment folks manages to secure and rip from the developer's hands.

Inside as we enter past Leonard the stage doorman, an ex-stage door Johnny who would hang outside stage doors desperate for autographs that he became part of the area's folklore and when was found down and out in Soho, Soho picked him up and looked after him as it looks after all its own and he found he was the new stage doorman for Fred's.

We heard Erin belting out a Queen number, 'Killer Queen', and a series of incredibly fit male dancers twirling round her. Some with backpacks on, as they will be in full drag. A backpack Reader is a frame they wear which has the huge headdresses and outfits seen in Rio carnival and such.

As Erin finishes she sees me and screams with delight and as she sees Carmichael she rushes over and laughs, "Place is wall to wall homosexuality darling, we are never going to find a date here, but I love it. Who is this?"

"Iain, my name is Iain and you I feel must be Erin. This is Katie and also sings we believe."

Erin looks at Katie, "You believe? Hello Iain be with you in a minute, but Katie, do you sing? Do you want to sing? I feel that is why Suzie has dragged you along. Seriously wanna sing with the boys, show is still not finalised and we all just have a ball. Do you know... what do you sing?"

"My own stuff and have a tape here, as well as backing tape," says Katie.

"She has a backing tape," says Erin laughing, "Tony can you play this for us and fellas gather round Katie here is going to sing for us."

Katie looks at Carmichael and then me and walks to the stage. I did feel as if we had led the lamb to the slaughter as Katie looked as if she had not said a thing. We had walked into the room as Erin was in full flow belting out to perfection each note and now Katie had to follow.

The backing track starts and it is a slow ballad and then Reader the most incredible thing happened; Katie started to sing. A sexy, husky voice and effortlessly she glided across the stage and all the drag queens started to cheers along with Erin. Confidence growing Katie starts to perform to her new audience and by the end of the song everyone was on their feet cheering. Tony walked over to Katie and gave her her backing CD, "That was awesome," he said.

All the queens looked to Erin and grinned as Erin looked at Katie, "Well we all loved that, but sadly no room in the show for you," as the guys all groaned and cried 'what?' "You expect me to have to compete every night on stage with that talent? She is going to make me look bad," laughed Erin, "but what the heck, we fecking love you, you wanna come tour with us?"

"Really?" I said and then everyone looked at me. "I mean really, that's wonderful, not really as in.."

"Oh hush Suzie, you knew she was good," said Erin and all laughed and hugged Katie. "What's your name?" asked Erin.

"Katie, Katie Rabin."

"OK we'll just put you up as Katie Rabin, one Katie is enough," laughs Erin.

Suddenly all the attention is on Carmichael.

"Erin, gentlemen, this is Iain."

"WOW, in heels he'd been even bigger," screamed one queen.

"Oh and I think baby blue would be his colour, especially with those green eyes," said another.

"Iain, have you ever dressed as a woman?" I asked knowing probably wore his mother's clothes in secret as a child. "Let's have fun. Boys we have an additional singer why not take Iain backstage and dress him up as additional star of show, for one night only of course."

Iain looked at me and laughed, "OK. But what will you be doing?"

"Well special promotions manager of course." And with that pushed Iain into the boys and they marched him backstage. Katie watched and then looked at Erin and me.

"So Katie, you need clothes or what have you got?" asked Erin.

"I have a few nice dresses and outfits," Katie replied.

"Well bring them tomorrow and we'll go through them as we start the show in three weeks."

Katie looked a little nervous and Erin turned back to look at her, and in that incredibly generous Erin Cornell way, Erin smiled and said once again that she would be stunning in anything she bought and not to sweat it. I then opened my bag and pulled out a chilled bottle of prosecco.

"Bubbles!" screamed Erin, "I'll get the glasses."

I held Katie's hand and she was trembling, "Listen you will love Erin, everybody loves Erin, and soon everybody will love you too. I will be back in a moment," I said as I quickly popped out of the building. I saw an ATM and my Knight's card. I drew out two and a half thousand pounds then turned and took out another two and a half thousand. As I returned to the rehearsal space Katie and Erin were already good friends.

"Where the bloody hell you disappear to?" asks Erin, "there is bubbles here."

"Just went to check something and was wondering what your budget for costumes was and marketing?"

"Listen beautiful, we are hoping to be a success so we can pay ourselves at this point," says Erin.

"OK so this is what I am thinking. Here is £2,500 for costumes for you two and here is £2,500 for publicity posters etc. Now, don't stop me I am in full flow. When is press night? Three weeks you said so that will be a mainly freebie night and press, with after party."

"You're nuts. We cannot possibly take this and we have some press coming, but we have a low budget opening as cannot afford what you thinking of even with using all this lovely cash injection," Erin is interrupted as Carmichael returns with the boys in full drag, "Jesus Christ Iain you look amazing, boys you have outdone yourselves. Listen this crazy woman has given us cash for costumes and press night." All cheer.

"No I have not!" I said and all looked confused. "I have given you two money to go shopping for incredible dresses as it looks as if the boys are already outshining you two. I have given other half for publicity and a few pounds towards the boys having treats. What I am going to do as your new special promotions manager is organise the first night party and tickets."

"Honey that will be a fortune have you seen Erin drink." All laugh and then a wonderful thing happens. Carmichael raises his hand.

"If I can have everybody's attention. It will not cost Suzie a thing. I will pay for that, we have also I am guessing from the look on Suzie's face people to invite that will make everyone in town want to be here, and I will also cover the rent for the theatre space and all production on the agreement that if I ever do come again you guys will drag me up and tell no one."

"What?!" shouts Erin. "Listen we know Suzie is something crazy, but are you one of those Knights too? Seriously that would be about £20,000 for the run and.."

"No it will be a budget of £100,000 and you will all have to keep this a secret as way to repay. Seriously, you need better digs I am sure, hire a seamstress and possible designer as well, I may keep this dress so this would have to be replaced..." and then suddenly everyone rushes Carmichael and hugs and kisses flow.

In walks the Landlord, a small man, who looks at Carmichael in drag and asks, "Who's this?"

Holding out his hand Carmichael steps forward and says, "Sir I am the show's backer, can we settle rents up front and also if paid in cash a reduction as well as we want your licence for the bar to cover us to sell and we will give you 10% on profits."

Shaking Carmichael's hand the landlord laughs, "Hey Erin, I like this guy. I came to say did you want extra month, but seems this guy will be sorting yes?"

"Hey Uncle Mike, have you a few bottles we can open to celebrate?" shouts Erin.

"I had a case of bubbles for the launch night as a present."

"That'll do, fellas relieve Uncle Mike of the bubbles," says Erin and they follow to the bar and out of the fridge bring six bottles of prosecco.

"Uncle Mike?" I ask.

"Yes, we all call him Uncle Mike. Nicest guy in theatreland, he is always helping out new faces and shows and met him a few years back doing a show with Johnny, Johnny Barr. If it wasn't for Uncle Mike we would of all been homeless as we crash in the rooms upstairs." Erin looks emotional and vulnerable then sees the bottles being opened and again jumps back to being Erin Cornell the girl that can not only lead a party, but also take it to a place you've never been before.

Carmichael returns and I see Katie offer him a glass of prosecco, "Are you gay?" she asks.

"No, but I could get used to wearing these dresses." And with that laughs out loud as I join them and we all go back to the Ivy where we manage to gain a table for everyone, plus Chastity and Henry join us and then Arthur and Guinevere. After a very boisterous meal we get up to go, Arthur pays the bill and then is informed that the press are outside. The manager asks if Arthur would rather slip out unnoticed than be photographed with the ladyboys.

"Oh no tell them we will be out in a second," says Arthur then turns to me, and Carmichael. "You two possible meet me tomorrow before flight and take exit as all are watching us, and you were going to have us come to the show's first night were you not?" I nod. "Good then the wife will be making an announcement. Katie, Erin and Boys, please all get ready to greet the press, wife is going to say a few words to press so Erin can you tell her dates etc. when prompted etc.? Yes folks, this is ShowTime." And as Arthur said it the entire restaurant laughed and applauded as they all exit the Ivy.

Carmichael and I ducked out the back and were able to watch the show unseen. Literally a row three deep of reporters and police holding back crowds as Arthur introduces Guinevere. She raises her hand and with Erin and Katie by her side, the boys all behind like a chorus line then bunched together, light bulbs flashing, Arthur even had a feather bower round his neck, Guinevere raises her hand. The whole street went silent.

With majesty and style Guinevere announced how much Arthur and she would be looking forward to the opening night of the show, introduced Erin, Katie and the boys, and saying that she hoped all the press would come to see this amazing show. Then a few seconds' later cabs arrived and Arthur told them all to get in. The cars had been sorted by Iain it seems who did a deal with Arthur earlier. Confused, but all drunk and well fed the cast jumped into the cabs and were whisked to a huge house in Pall Mall that is a secret residence used by Heads of State, thirty-two bedrooms and all been made ready for the gang to live there.

We arrived a little later and I saw Katie hug Carmichael who saw me watching and smiled and mouthed thank you.

20

Later that night in my room at Chastity's again I had a knock on my room door. I opened it to see Nichols. He smiled and walked in. All I remember is he kissed me, and it was the next morning.

It was later in the afternoon on the flight to Geneva that Carmichael turned to me and spoke. We had been to the briefing, we knew the times and where we would meet to hand over the bonds, and we knew that moments after Carmichael would disappear and start his hormone treatments and become a woman.

Now Reader this all may be strange and hard to take in, but today it all seemed normal. On the plane Carmichael held my hand and squeezed it as he turned to look me in the eye.

"So how much of last night did you know would happen?" he asked.

"Well Nichols visit was a shocker."

"Suzie, yesterday in the dress and with the boys and my night with Katie,"
"You were with Katie?" I asked, as I was a little surprised.

"Yes, it was weird, I wanted to be a woman, want to be a woman, but will always be a man. Katie understood totally. I was shocked and soon she laughed that it was a shame I was so tall as otherwise being with me meant she would double her wardrobe."

We both laughed. "So the op, you are thinking….?" I asked.

"Keep the money. I am who I am and I feel a little transvestism will go a long way," he replied.

"No keep the money, I have a feeling your taste in dresses will soon use up the money, plus getting heels in your size is going to be expensive." We both laughed and he kissed my cheek.

"No thank you Suzie Johnson, you have changed my life. Plus after chat with Nichols I have been offered employment as a Knight's Templar, so you will see more of me."

The plane was coming into land and we had two cases with the bonds in and were travelling as diplomats so straight through customs. Into cars and then at the hotel to then have a knock at our door and the fabulous Conchita Rodriquez enters. She is in a black trouser suit and hands me an envelope with the details to entrance and exits of the bank. Looking at the plans she smiles, "It is bank next door. Listen see you both at 1:15 later today." And then as fast as she came she left.

Sat in our room Carmichael decided we should stretch our legs and have breakfast. I agreed and soon we walked from the lift to the hotel dinning area. We took a table in the corner close to the exit and ordered full English breakfasts. We both laughed as both starving and spent a few minutes deciding initially on melon and toast or poached eggs or scrambled egg and smoked salmon. Then in unison smiled and simultaneously said two full English please.

As the food arrived I saw a familiar face. It was a Serb from my old mission, but he was in a prison in Siberia. I alerted Carmichael who then saw Kowlowski. Moments later Boss Hogg entered another lift and all three lifts went up simultaneously to floor 23 and stopped.

I took out my mobile and called Hugues. The phone rang, but did not answer. I looked at Carmichael who seemed as always to be incredibly calm.

"Whatever they are meeting about will take some time and we both need the breakfast. Relax and eat as here it comes." And with that the waitress bought us two full English breakfasts. "Can we get some orange juice as well please miss?"

"Certainly sir," said the waitress and then Carmichael smiled at me, "we can see the lifts as soon as one stops at 23 to come down we know were they are. Eat and what do you think is going on?"

"No idea," I replied and that is exactly what I had Reader, no idea. Then my mobile buzzed. I answered; it was Hugues.

"Hello sir, just a quick update Kowlowski, Boss Hogg and Serb from a previous mission who is meant to be in a prison in Russia are all on the 23rd floor."

"Right, we have Robbins and Nichols on route to you and you will drive out of Switzerland to Germany. It seems Yerno went ballistic at Kowlowski when money never arrived or did his men and Kowlowski was furious thinking Yerno had double crossed him as they were tracking the money. Coincidence that they met where you are, not a good one I grant you, but we have to continue with plan, but be careful. The Mexicans are unaware and the Russians are also unaware as seems Kowlowski is doing deals behind his President's back. Yerno also acted with Hogg without White House knowledge. This POTUS and family team are the worst crooks we have ever surveyed. Low profile, do the exchange then get to the Parc des Bastions. You will see a chess game being played with a red King piece and go say hi. All should be fine from there, but you have to get there. Leave all your cases in hotel and we will collect later. Oh, and have fun I hear the sun is out."

"We will and thanks, by the way Carmichael will be coming out with me, he will not be staying."

"Tell him I am glad," and with that hung up.

"Hugues sends his love," I say, "and seems Kowlowski and Hogg are setting up New Order links for a possible takeover I guess in Russia as President knows nothing of the bonds. Enjoy breakfast we have new route out and this will be real decisions as we reach them sort of caper."

"Sounds right up my street," says Carmichael and it is a full forty-five minutes until we see a lift stop on 23 and look to come down. "Seems as if no one trusts anyone in that relationship," says Carmichael and pays for breakfast and calls the lift next to the one coming down. A lift arrives and we step in. as the doors close a hand juts in to make them open again and in walks a Japanese tourist and his wife, complete with camera and guides in hand.

We hear the lift from 23 stop next to us, and the doors open. We are able to see a flustered Boss Hogg exit although he does not see us. Then the Japanese tourist drops his guide and as he bows to pick it up stops the doors again from opening. He apologies and we smile and then push the button to the 21st floor. The tourist's wife nods her head and at last the doors to the lift close as I see the Serb hand Hogg his umbrella and then rush to the lift we are in hoping to get in. The Japanese man politely looks to stop the lift and push the open doors button, but Carmichael manages to slap his hand away and apologises as if mistake and the lift rises. At one point I thought the Serb recognised me, but we got off with the Japanese on the 19th floor and walked up to the 21st just in case.

In our room we decided to sit tight. Pack what we needed for the crossing to Germany and neatly packed our clothes away to be collected later. The whole procedure was done in silence and as if in military precision. As we both finished it was like one of those movies scenes where the heroes look to each other, lock and load their weapons and exit the room putting on sunglasses.

Walking down the hallway I see a cleaner exit a room and tut, I look at her and she complains how messy the guest is, "All money and no manners, Serbs!" I hold Carmichael's arm and stop him.

"I am sorry to hear, but would you mind if we saw as we are looking for a Serb, on the run, cannot say much as Interpol, I hope you understand, but without telling anyone can I have a look it may be our man?"

Carmichael looks at his watch and the maid happily lets me in. On the bed is a jacket and on the side folders that I open and see it is the Serb I saw earlier, well there would not be many in Switzerland.

"It's him," I said to Carmichael who nods, but behind the glasses I can feel his eyes questioning what am I doing? The maid freezes and makes the sign of a cross over herself and I reassure her he is not dangerous just online fraud.

I open the file and there it is, jackpot! A map of an area of land, a detailed geological survey saying huge oil deposits and in the file underneath the same, except the land survey show huge radioactive waste dumping ground in secret Russian file. I quickly take pictures on my photo and we exit with the maid. I hand her one hundred and fifty Swiss francs and say-to-say nothing. She smiles and is happy to as she wanders off we hear her saying that it serves the dirty Serb right. Counting her money she skips a little. It is the same as dollars and about £120 GBP.

Carmichael opens the lift doors and inside alone asks me, "What was all that about?"

"Seems Kowlowski and the Serb muscle are selling Yerno duff land and in the process making 500 million extra for themselves. Seems Yerno is looking at a big deal on the side as always and King Tiller's deal to be out trumped, but Yerno is not a diplomat, or a player. He is a crook from a crooked family that married the President of America's daughter and weaselled his way into a top position at the White House. It seems Kowlowski will foot all blame on Russian President, and have Serbs as fall guy if all goes wrong, and buy his position as head of New Order in Russia with the money and power. The land Yerno thinks he is buying is a nuclear waste site and there if no oil. His greed has ruled his head. Now he has the problem of replacing this five hundred million in bonds to make sure his massive oil deal worth he thinks the same amount a month. Once we hit the escape route we need to get this to Hugues and the Knights."

The lift doors open and as we walk out our Serb friend walks into the lift. As he passes me he is talking on the mobile. We walk out and then I sense he noticed me or thinks he has seen me before. The lift door closes as I see him look at me in a mirror on a column in the reception opposite lifts. He tries to exit but the doors close and I grab Carmichael who moves quickly with me back to the lifts by the lift Serb is in.

The Serb rushes out and into the reception then into the street. We get in the lift he left and then go to the first floor. We watch him return from the balcony animatedly talking on his mobile. He gets back in the lift and is violently pushing the lift buttons. The doors close and we see the lift numbers rising.

Calmly we walk out of the hotel, into a cab, and go round the square to the bank next door and walk into the bank. It is ten past one and the Mexican President is there.

Carmichael nods and walks to the bank manager to say into the room now and we all disappear. Sat in the room Carmichael opens up the suitcase he has. On top is his passport and toothbrush.

"I travel light. Now here is four hundred and ninety million dollars in bonds to be deposited into the account set up for the President. Please have counted and signed for then have the President the number for the bank and forward from the account in batches of ten payments of forty-eight million seven hundred and fifty thousand in ten transactions to an account in the Mexican President's new health and wellbeing account as if ten donors have given collectively the money. Then take two million five hundred thousand as your fee. All Ok with that gentlemen?"

"How can Mexico ever repay you?"

"Mr. President sir, just build the clinics and infrastructure that we will then also help support that would embarrass the POTUS as his hatred for the former President means he is desperate to scrap the care system in the US for anything named after him. We look to make America the world's worst health system and also help get rid of an idiot in charge. Tell no one, accept and in a few months Knights will travel to meet you to an opening and special event to announce the incredible works we are all doing together."

Carmichael looks at his watch as the Swiss banker weighs and has counted the bonds.

"Gentlemen, all seems to be satisfactory, if you would like to sign here Mr. President?" says the banker.

"Of course we have your confidence sir?" I ask and the banker looks at me, and smiles removing exactly two and a half million bonds into his own drawer, "Exactly, we are all happy," I say and then look to Carmichael who takes his case

177

with nothing but toothbrush and passport and motions it is time.

"Sir, please note that the Knights are proud to be working with Mexico as new ally for the curing of all known diseases worldwide. I believe this young lady will show us out," I say as an assistant in the corner was patiently waiting.

As we leave the President takes his acknowledgement slip and is speechless. Carmichael and I walk into an adjoining room where we see the Serbs in the foyer. They see us and start to make a way towards the room we go into. We walk in and through a door concealed behind a bookcase and then into a small room that opens another door into a room off the restaurant in our hotel. Sat in the room is another bank manager who then takes the ten million dollars of bonds and gives Carmichael his receipt and smiles. They exit with the bonds, we have the account number and now we need to get out of town.

I open my case and remove a burka. After the bankers have left I put it on and smile. Carmichael watches through the slightly open door to see Roskov and another Russian with other Serbs looking at everyone in the foyer.

"Roskov has joined the party," says Carmichael who is extremely calm. " He is by the lifts to the right. The exit to the left so what is your thinking?"

"I am the wife of a sultan, you are my personal bodyguard. We just walk out, but leave the cases, as they would look strange. That is my plan, we just walk out."

"You Invisibles like to keep things simple, well here goes nothing. Roskov is watching people in lift so your highness time to move."

We exit the room and into the foyer and head straight for the door. The Serbs see us and look at each other, then one goes to Roskov who sees alarm bells and rushes to the room where he sees the cases handed to us in Ghana. Running out of the room he tripped over the Serb and we were gone.

As we speed off to the Parc des Bastions I see Roskov exit and jump in a waiting car. Within seconds another car is tailing us.

"Shit! They must have access to CCTV in city," says Carmichael and I ask the driver to pull into a side turning last minute that he does and we skip under a bridge and I shout stop. The driver scared brakes and we are under bridge. Jumping out I remove burka and throw in taxi and then tell him to drive off and pick up another fare. Confused he does so and we hide behind a wheelie bin used for collecting rubbish in the park nearby. We hear the Russian cars trailing us whiz by as they pick up the taxi again on CCTV and are in hot pursuit. We still have to get to Parc des Bastions.

Carmichael takes off his jacket and tie and folds them to carry. I am ready just my clothing and we walk through the park as two lovers walking in the glorious sunshine. We manage to get to another taxi across the other side of the park and take it to Parc des Bastions.

At the Parc we find chess set with a Red King. I look round and see Nichols and Robbins walk past and we follow. It seems there has been a huge interest in us from loads of foreign secret services and we were marked so new exit is in motorhome with them to the German border.

As we exit the Park I see the Serbs running in and realise they caught up with the driver who said we were to be taken to this point. They do not see us as we get in the motorhome, but seeing Nichols the Serb for no reason opens fire. Robbins shoots the Serb dead. He turns to see Nichols is dead. Robbins lifts his lifeless body into the vehicle and then jumps in the front and drives.

I go to see if I can help not realising Nichols is shot badly to see he is dead. As we drive away there is no one else around and we pass Roskov as he pulls up to the park. I am distraught and cannot hold back the anger wanting to shout at Roskov, but Carmichael holds me down.

"It's OK, it's Ok. Schhh, let it go, now is not the time." I cry in Carmichael's arms as Robbins hits the steering wheel hard.

Driving for an hour we hit the border and without any hold up we are driving to Munich to our collection point. Sat in the seat I am numb. He wasn't supposed to die; Nichols was not supposed to die.

Pulling into the Sofitel Munich Bayerpost Hotel I see Hugues waiting in the reception. As we get out of the motorhome Robbins hands the keys to another agent and Nichols and the van are gone.

Hugues sees Robbins who cannot look him in the eye and Hugues hugs him, "It wasn't your fault, he was a great soldier, a great Knight." Robbins breaks free and straightens up as if to salute, but Hugues gives him some room keys and says, "Talk later, go rest, there is still much to be done."

Robbins walks to his room and Carmichael shakes Hugues hand and says that may be we should go somewhere more private. Hugues realises that even he has let his guard down, I realise here was the ex-head of the CIA and he really did care about all his men. Hugues hugs me and then gives me a room key, "I know he loved you," he says and as it is Hugues I seem to manage to pull myself together.

"I know sir, but this cannot wait. Nichols would of wanted it this way, and thank you, I loved him too as much as he loved you. We all lost someone today."

Sat in an alcove in an area off the bar Hugues gives both Carmichael and I a hot toddy. We look at each other and I start by getting my mobile out.

"Please sir take these, they are pictures of files in the dead Serb's room. He was the one that shot Nichols, Robbins dispatched him before we left." I am suddenly too emotional so Carmichael continues.

"Sir, it seems Yerno is getting duped. May be King Tiller knows as does Boss Hogg and this is a coup against him, but the money we intercepted was to be paid back to the Russians, and by that I mean Kowlowski who is the Leader of the Russian New Order. He would have had it as a deal with Americans for oil and confused the real secret deal with Tiller as the same. Yerno will pay the same amount from American funds we gather to Kowlowski to replace the money he stole in exchange for the oil rights to a huge piece of land."

"The land is a radioactive wasteland and worth nothing. Yerno would possibly never say anything as what he is doing could be seen as high treason, but also possibly is stealing from American Reserves to pay and also in our escape I feel we have uncovered the trail other heads of the New Order," I say.

"How?" asks Hugues.

"Well sir, in the taxi we realised the Russians were using the city CCTV to track us. We found a blind spot and then saw many other different nationals hunting us. We then used my mobile to hack into the sources of who was saying find us as not coming from known or Interpol."

"We saw that instructions were coming from these individuals and all lead back to second in command people as well as a few leaders copied into Roskov call out. Nichols died because these people acted together to find us so we deduce all New Order," says Carmichael.

Looking at the list Hugues raises an eyebrow as he looks back to us, "Three of these we identified yesterday from different sources, but how did you trace the other calls we never even monitored these?"

"I managed to send a tracer call to Roskov that is still working. He does not know it seems so the mobile is yours sir," I replied and Hugues calls two other agents to get it to the office to be updated to the main frame.

"Sir, may I ask a favour?" says Carmichael and Hugues nods.

"I have decided that, well decided that I am not going to instigate a change in my life, my appearance that is and.." stutters Carmichael.

"Carmichael my wife's sister used to be her brother, if you want to stay as you are I respect that and to be frank if this about the money, you keep it and use it how you wish, hell you can spend it all on helping other women trapped in men's bodies as a suggestion, but whatever you do I would like to have you on our side as a man or a woman. That clear enough for you?"

Both Carmichael and I stare at Hugues.

"Folks I was the Head of the C fucking IA and I saw most things. The bad I managed to sideline or get rid of, not all of it, nobodies perfect, but what you two and my two favourite sons did over the past two weeks has been incredible. We have new allies in Mexico for life, we have so far thwarted a corrupt deal with the Whitehouse Family, now we have the Intel on the Heads of the New Order and they have no idea, you cannot imagine how much you are appreciated. Listen I lost a son today. A man I would have been proud to of called a son in Nichols. He and his family will be well looked after and I am sure in time we will lose more good men, but Carmichael I want you to consider becoming a Knight of the Knight's Templar."

"He does sir," I reply and there is a tear in Carmichael's eye.

"Thank you sir I would be honoured."

183

"Good now tomorrow you will be looking after Robbins, he spent the past fifteen years with Nichols and he will need you too. Now I think you two should hit the sack and we will continue this tomorrow."

And with that Hugues gets up and shakes my hand then salutes Carmichael before exiting and followed by two new men.

"This is now completely surreal, I am only two weeks ago in Ghana ready to find a way to a sex change to embarrass our phoney President and now I have embarrassed him beyond my wildest dreams, screwed over his family, helped Mexico find health care for its poor and a become a backer for a show with a chorus of drag queens and all thanks to you."

"And you get to keep your dick," I laughed and so did Carmichael.

"Iain, think on what Hugues said, may be there will be ways to help other girls trapped in boys bodies or even help lost gay souls find refuge and a friend from something you do. Nichols would have been proud of you, he loved you I know and I am numb thinking he has gone, but would you do me a favour and do something in Nichols name?"

"That is a great idea and if ever you need to talk I am here."

"I know thanks."

Sat in my room here in Munich I look out of the window at the city lights and realise they never turn off. Nichols died, but his light and spirit will never go out as I will dedicate everything I do to the man I loved, sorry Reader, just realising he, another time OK, Reader, sorry. Night.

21

It was 10am and I had overslept. There was a knock at my door and as I got out of bed and put on the bathrobe I heard a voice call in, "Suzie, you OK in there?" I opened the door and there was Conchita Rodriquez smiling and she steps forward and gives me a huge hug. I was not expecting her at all.

"I heard about your man, heard he was good man and took bullet for you. Best not to think of this," she said and then walked into the room, but sad thing is she had said something and my thoughts went to Nichols.

"Of course I deliberately said it. Just want you to see pain never go away. But life it do go on."

I smiled as realised this was the morning after and started to find some clothes, "So how come you are here?"

"President flew home and I saw the Serbs then found out, wanted to see you OK and that big guy if he needed a shoulder to rest on?"

"Oh! Carmichael. Yes he is fine. So you are here for?" Conchita did not answer. "Have you had something to eat, feel I need to eat."

"Yes we eat, good idea. So I tell you. Big trouble in Russia as seems large amount of cash disappeared. We happy as seems there is to be shake up if not sorted and my film guy now wants to film there. I think he just says he is filming everywhere, gets money to go travel and see if possible, finds actresses daft enough to sleep with him and then moves on. In sixteen years he make two films, one he made shit, another he was able to bring money to film, did well had Johnny Travolta, he trades on that, but he did fuck all. So you think Carstairs wants to join us, you know big boy?"

"Carmichael, he is next door, why not knock on his door as I get dressed?"

"Good idea, he is not your man now? No? Too soon. OK I have a try, knock his door and be back in case he sleepy or if not come back you have to eat alone as we not eating either."

And with that Conchita exited the room. I heard her knocking on Carmichael's door and him answer and the sound of the door shut as she went inside. I had a quick shower, in and out and was about to leave as the door knocked again. I open to see a slightly flustered looking Carmichael who smiled and asked if I was OK? I smiled back, "Breakfast is waiting I guess?"

"Yes he was hungry for food," said a disillusioned Conchita.

Sat downstairs we see Robbins walk in. I stood and walked over to him. He hugged me and I could feel his loss. We stood for a few seconds righting ourselves and then he joined us for breakfast. Carmichael called the waitress and ordered another full English and she bought coffee for Robbins. He sipped it and apologised for oversleeping, but we could see he had not slept a wink.

A few minutes later as we ate without chatting another full English arrived and Robbins looked as if he couldn't eat.

"Eat it, you need your strength as today will be a tough day," said Carmichael.

"Yes of course," said Robbins. "I am to take Mike home it seems. Sorry Nichols, his first name was Mike. I am on the flight tonight and we touch down in Seattle tomorrow, yes from Seattle, and meeting his family. Mike and I went to school together, joined the agency together, served together and...."

"I know he loved you like a brother," I said.

"Did he say that?" he asked as if wanting to hear it was so.

"He said it to me too," said Carmichael. "Yes it was a weird conversation in Africa, he just said that he would do anything to protect me and that the same from his brother in arms, his brother he went on to say and told me how you two met and even you dated his sister once. Ended badly as she went off with a guy twice your age. She was four and fancied this guy who was eight and broke your heart."

"He told you that? Yes, and now I have to deliver his sister Jeanie his body and see his parents. They already know and to be honest after all the scrapes we had been in together surprised this didn't happen sooner. But should have been me."

"Hey, don't be stupid boy!" says Conchita, "eat that food, be strong, carry on, he would want it, no?"

"Yes, you are right," said Robbins and held back a tear and started eating all his food off the plate.

We all sat in the silence of the hotel, yes there ere people pushing past, music playing dull noise from speakers hidden, but we sat in silence. Suddenly Conchita stands and says to Robbins, "What time your flight?"

"Two hours got to go to airport."

"OK, come with me, I come to your room and help you get ready." And with this Conchita leads Robbins to the lift.

"Why is she here?" asks Carmichael.

"She is here with her producer guy and off to Russia to do another fake movie deal it seems."

"Fake?"

"Yes, seems the guy gets people thinking he will film in their country, they invite him over, put him up, pay for everything, introduce him to actresses and he abuses them then says he will be in touch. Different world film, Oh and she told us word was Russian in Russia looking for money that has been misplaced."

"She will be there for a few weeks and devouring men herself I expect. Listen going to check any messages for us at the desk." And with this I left to talk to the receptionist. In fact there was a note and told us to make sure we left before two and were expected to book into another hotel in Munich, the K + K Hotel am Harras. Seems that the arrival of everyone last night put up flags and we should expect a visit from the New Order so move on.

As I walked back to Carmichael my mind flitted to the message 'expect a visit from the New Order' and rushed to Carmichael. I showed him and asked if he thought Conchita turning up was more than a coincidence. We both suddenly thought, Robbins and dashed to the lifts.

He was on the floor above ours and I managed to pick the pocket of the housemaid master key for the rooms and we poised outside to open up carefully and see what was happening. We both knew the sound of the card releasing the lock would be heard and so did it, opened the door and let it stand as if shut. No one came and we could hear noise of a struggle. Quickly we stepped inside the room and could hear the noise from the bedroom. I must say Reader Robbins had a much nicer suite than me. Quietly we move to the bedroom door and upon looking in could see Conchita and Robbins having loud aggressive sex. Both seem to be so into the throws of ecstasy that we retreated quickly and found ourselves in the hallway. Carmichael started to laugh.

"Well looks as if she is helping him get ready."

"We better be ready too and also give Hugues a call and see if he has any info on Conchita." I flashed a smile at Carmichael and he held my hand at the lift.

"Are you OK?" he asked.

"Yes I am OK," I replied. "So you think you need to help me get ready?"

Carmichael smiled and hit the lift button, "Nah. I think you will be fine. But here if you need me anytime to talk."

Reader I packed and it seemed the grief of Nichols, realising my connection was so brief in consideration for what Robbins had been through, so I decided to focus on getting Roskov, he was my mission, he was going to get everything pent up inside me thinking of Nichols.

Packed and leaving as just had new carry on bag as everything was in case from Switzerland to this hotel then new and so did not take long. As I exited the room Carmichael too came out.

"Got your toothbrush?"

"Oh shit!" he said and went back into his room to get it. Returning he laughed and said that it was the only thing he had to pack and he forgot it.

We walked to the coffee shop off the reception and sat near an exit as well as had great view of all people inside and outside the hotel.

Drinking a fresh mint tea Carmichael noticed Hugues in reception and made himself seen. Hugues started to walk over then stopped. He turned to greet someone coming out of the lift. It was Conchita and she gave him a hug and whispered in his ear, then went out into a car where the film producer was tapping his watch.

Hugues walks over and sits with us. "You two are to be in London for the opening of that show with the Ladyboys from

Australia. Oh and Conchita has worked for me for years, I sent her, but seems she had an eye for Robbins. She said that she sat and helped him through some grief issues. So your mobile has been incredibly helpful, but time to talk will be in London and also when you get to next hotel book in and then take the lift to the basement where you will meet an old friend Carmichael and he will take you to jet that will fly you to London. You will be staying in the Savoy until further notice and something a friend of yours Suzie told Arthur to stay in the obvious place as those that seek you will never think to look there. He has friends there and you have wonderful suites and also we have helped with the first night party, as the whole event is to be at the Savoy. Don't worry Carmichael, you are still benefactor, but we paid for a few things too. As I say you two have given us a great service and being paid for what you did. Also Arthur has some messages for you in London Suzie, so enjoy your trip, I'll send best wishes to Robbins, you will all see each other again I am sure, but word is you have five minutes to get to the lift and basement before people arrive looking for you. I'll buy the mint teas. Go on go."

And with that ushered us off and we met Jimmy in the basement below. He opened the back of the van and as we climbed in there was another face sat who half stood, headroom allowing, and introduced himself.

"How do you do Iain, they call me Sir John."

I have to say I gave him a huge hug and he laughed, "Hang on Suzie I haven't had chance to shake this man's hand."

In the back of the van Sir John told me that the Serb threat was back and that he had decided to see what could be done. It seemed that he had a plan and once in London all would be revealed and not to worry.

"Jimmy will be joining us as well as it seems he needs a break from married life and I feel is acting a little fatherly over you. Did you know she killed me once Iain?"

"No sir. Obviously she was a lousy shot."

"Not at all. Perfect. But I have been watching and think I have a rouse for you that will confuse the Russians and you will enjoy, trust me, we are still on a little mission, but this one should be a lot of fun. How much further Jimmy?"

"Why have they fallen asleep from all your chatter?" Jimmy joked from the driver seat. "Be in hanger in ten."

"I do enjoy all this diplomatic service crap. It makes things so much easier, but also can be easier for people to track. So the Ruskies think we are transporting Guanabana that is being tested as cancer treatment.

"Oh and we have four more friends in London to catch up with. Jimmy and I will have you in the open and see what threat there is, you'll be safe, but as Suzie Johnson you have no links to Knights except some bird with this bloke who backed the show with Erin and boys. Anyone surfaces we can handle, but need to know Serbs are again in check."

"So who, I mean what old friends?"

Reader, Sir John looked at me and grinned, "Ben and Earl with Joseph and Chenguang. Seems Misbehavebadly shoot huge hit, they now know Margo was a stage name and all want to thank you for invite to show as just what the boys needed and you will be in on talks sending Joseph and Chenguang to Rio. Now feels like we are pulling into hanger."

The car suddenly stops, the back door opens and in a hanger by a plane Jimmy smiles, "Ladies and gentlemen, your chariot awaits."

22

I wake and find myself in a suite with twin beds with Carmichael. We are in the hotel and posing as wealthy backers behind Erin's show and today we get a sneak peek. Carmichael walks into the room, he is showered and laying out a stunning blue suit.

"Sorry to wake you, but must be still tough for you. I mean all the travel lately, your mission and well, must be tough. I was going to go for a stroll around Covent Garden. I was not meaning to disturb you."

"Iain, our cover is couple so if you do not mind waiting be nice to join you."

I jump up and get into the shower. The bathroom is luxurious, and then I see a stunning room off this and a balcony that over looks the Thames. We were in a suite in the Savoy. The sun was shinning and London looked as only London does, vibrant, friendly and a place anyone can call home. I think of my homeland. I then think if it is my homeland anymore as an Invisible I am everywhere but home.

"Listen, have I got a nice casual dress to wear," I shout to Carmichael.

"Already chosen," comes the reply and after a quick refresher shower I see Carmichael dressed and the most beautiful summer dress laid out on the bed with shoes and a handbag.

"You have thought of everything, are you styling me now?" I joked.

"Not entirely," smiled Carmichael, "you can choose your own underwear. I will see you in the foyer as want to see if we have any messages." And with that Iain walks over and kisses me on the cheek then exits.

There was a little note on the dress from Carmichael and it read:

'Little dress for my saviour and it should fit.
Well I can afford it as millionaire now XX'

I smiled and looked in the mirror at myself, and seeing Nichols stand behind me. I turn and it is just Iain's suit hanging in the closet. I found myself a little lost and then see another note on the mirror from Iain:

'It will never get easier, but remember
what love taught you and remember love'

I smiled and looked in the mirror at myself again and realised Nichols was safe in a place where all good CIA agents go, but now he is with the Knight's Templar looking out for us all. Under the message is a picture of Nichols laughing in a small frame. Carmichael was a good man and knew I had a new friend for life. I kissed my love's picture and decided on what underwear to put on. Dressed I left the room and walked to the lift.

As I exited the lift I saw Carmichael who was waiting walk towards me and give me a huge hug. All the staff watched and smiled. Our cover is a wealthy man and his girlfriend and we looked the part, but we were not acting, we do truly love each other, but in a brother sister kind of way.

"Come on darling let's take a walk," he said and the doorman opened the hotel door and we exited. The sun shone, doorman doffed his hat and we walked into the Strand.

The cars were buzzing, the city was buzzing, people from all over the world smiling at each other and Carmichael points to a bus and we see an advert for Erin and the Priscilla Drag Boys with guest artist Katie Raban. We both laughed and felt proud.

"That was incredibly generous of Erin, to give Katie a huge headline like that."

I looked at Carmichael and agreed and realised that people are wise, people are good, and you just give them a chance. We discussed the ethics of being Invisible and how strong this was a theme. Carmichael listened attentively as if he was studying for an exam.
"So in essence, we, Invisibles, see corruption, we see missions to help those that need help, and we save without recognition and we let the people see and it is up to them to change the world in which they live. That is all we can do."

"We give them the courage to make the change collectively, yes?" he asked.

"Yes," I replied as we wondered from Covent Garden and into Leicester Square.

"I want to buy you a suit!" I exclaimed at a startled Carmichael. "I mean I want to do something for you."

"You have done more than you will ever know," he replied and placed his arm around my shoulder, "I will always be here for you as your big brother."

"Not sister?" I joked and he smiled and looked away. "Sorry Iain, I didn't mean to make fun, I was.."

"No. Not at all. You made me realise, well the Priscilla Drag Boys helped, that I like being a man, I like feeling like a woman and if I really need to be a woman a dress and a bit of slap and hey presto, there you are. Come on feeling peckish, we have been wandering for two hours."

I looked at my watch and realised it was nearly midday. "OK then this way and no arguments." I walked us back to Covent Garden where we were in Hackett and bought Carmichael a stunning Prince of Wales check grey suit. He looked better than any actor who had played James Bond. I then asked for a pair of Loakes co-respondents, shoes folks, and was surprised at how inexpensive it was. Seem not many Englishmen over six foot five like Carmichael, so it was even on sale. We left with them for minor alterations before going to the Paul Smith shop.

In there Carmichael was in heaven. He was looking at all the colours and we both laughed at the style of drainpipe trousers that touch ankles as how to wear. We met an assistant called Adam who then had Carmichael measured and pulled out a few maroon and purple suits, then one bright red. We laughed as Carmichael would never of thought of a suit these colours if shopping back home, but this was England, the centre of fashion, oh you have Paris and Milan Reader, but they are more way out wacky designs for stick insects, men are dressed in London.

A suit in a beautiful deep purple chosen and shoes and socks, with trouser leg more mature than young guy style as we described it to Adam, and bought fun cufflinks that we took away with the socks. We were giggling as we exited and walked down into Covent Garden.

We found ourselves queuing to get into a burger bar called ShakeShack. We ordered then took our receipt to find a table in the outside where a beeper would inform us to collect our food. We even queued to find a seat. What is it with the British, they are always so polite and queue, chatting, no aggression and around them tourists from all over the world happy to queue, something they would never do at home. A little baby in a pushchair behind us starts to scream and the mum with baby and toddler seems stressed as she tries to juggle.

Carmichael looks back as a gorgeous black girl, called Vera, a waitress with an enormous smile says that she has a table for us. Carmichael looks to the Japanese couple behind and asks if they would not mind us letting the mum jump the queue and take the table. They gracious agreed and the husband helped lift the pushchair with Carmichael through the crowds to the vacant table. The mum was embarrassed and kept saying thank you and Carmichael just placed his hand on the crying babies head and smiled, "Please no worries, you are the most important person here. Being a parent is hard, but a mum in a crowd coping is tough. Please we are honoured to help a mother." The baby stops crying and the Japanese man laughs.

"I tell my wife we should of trained our children to cry in queues and get to front. You lovely man, lovely lady, we also love babies," and then he bowed and walked back to his wife in the queue.

Just as we are seated my buzzer goes off to get food and Vera rushes over to get it for us. The burgers arrive with really sweet homemade lemonade and all is delicious. The British showing us Americans how to do Hamburgers.

We sat and chatted and Carmichael asked where I got the phrase 'Because I can' as said did this job because I wanted to stand up for those that are unable to stand up for themselves. I told him about Willis and killing Sir John, how he managed to persuade me to become an Invisible and that as an Invisible we often work alone, but we are never alone. The Knights were Sir John's idea and he even gave credit in a story of another of his sayings, 'Collective Intelligence' to a filmmaker he met in Cannes one year.

That is why the Knights work in the way they do. Credit is given to all, as we could not achieve what we can without the other. Apparently this filmmaker was saying that even the runners are as important as the star of the film. Together, collectively, with everyone bringing their different talents, different cultures to work together we can produce anything. This was his Collective Intelligence and it resonated with Sir John.

"I like it," said Iain, "And we are apparently meeting Sir John at the opening night next week. I guess we better start to work on that as we need to make sure the press night is a huge success."

"I also think that Sir John has orchestrated us to be the couple behind the show to test out our abilities to remain Invisible, as this will be a global event with many senior politicians and stars coming. Pictures will be taken, press will interview and our faces cannot be seen by Kowlowski as he is still hunting for his money." Carmichael smiled at me and nodded in agreement.

"I will wear the purple suit as possibly folks will see the suit and not the man."

"Iain, you are male model look and feel the famous will want to drape themselves over you for photo opportunity. But why not be a great test." With that my mobile went and it was Arthur asking if we could pop into Parliament to meet at Knights offices there. He then text me instructions on how to use Jimmy's entrance, as he called it, and be unseen entering.

Carmichael stands and collects our tray and wrappers then walks them back to Vera who is laughing with another customer. He places his tray in her clearing up area and she sees him and says thank you.

"Do you like theatre, Vera?" he asked.

Quizzically Vera nodded yes and asked for her number and that next Thursday she would be guest of honour with three friends at the show's opening.

"Really?" Vera said in astonishment, "my mum used to be a singer in shows back in her home town in the day."

"Is she in London?" he asked.

"Yes, I live with her still and my sister."

"So will four tickets be enough? I mean you have been such a superb waitress; great smile and you are like it with everybody. Normally on night out how many of you go out?"

"Oh it's OK, there are seven of us.."

"OK you talked me into it, ten tickets so your seven plus mum and sister and another friend of mum or sister. I will pop by with tickets to show and after party tonight. Vera it has been a pleasure meeting you." And with that kissed her on her cheek and we walked off into the crowds.

"Seems the Invisible life may be just what you needed, but as a Knight Templar I feel you will excel best." I looked at him and he smiled. "Feels good doesn't it?" I asked.
"Yes, feels good," he replied and took my hand in his and squeezed it.

We walked back to the hotel and then jumped into a taxi on the Strand and headed off to Parliament. At the secret access point was a newspaper seller and he looked at me and winked. It was Jimmy.

"First time here so thought I would escort you. Did you delete text sent by Arthur? Yes. Good. Come on this way, hi Iain, looking dapper, this way." And with this we walked between two pillars and pushed the wall to enter a stairway down then along a corridor to another door, then up some steps and from between two other pillars in the main hall appeared wearing passes Jimmy had. We walked through the corridors and into a broom cupboard then into another secret door and were in the printing room of the Knight's office.

"Lucky you dressed as Bond, eh Carmichaels?" Jimmy laughed and we entered the room and were in the boardroom with Arthur as the others came back from lunch.

As everyone walks in and the room is full of buzz and atmosphere and in true Clara style she suddenly realises it is me she is talking to about her parents wedding anniversary. She lets out a scream and all turn and look.

"It's you! It's you!" Clara then hugs me and starts crying and then looks confused and steps back and looks at Arthur, "this is lady who organised surprise party for my parents." Clara looks at everyone dumbfounded and Chastity laughs and walks over and hugs Clara.

"Yes, we know."

"You all knew?" Clara asks and Chastity cannot stop laughing and everyone walks up and hugs Clara and then me.

Arthur smiling as everyone is in one corner of the room stands opposite, "Hello, hello folks. This is Iain and is a Knight Templar that will be working with us with the Mexicans as well as be travelling to Rio as Knight on new project."

"Rio?" says Carmichael confused. Suddenly in the doorway I see Jimmy and Sir John. Sir John has a folder in his hands and opens his arms and I waste no time in hugging him, and of course as we break hold Clara also moves in and hugs him.

"Hello Clara, how are your parents?"

"They had tea with the King in Palace and they invited me to go as well and visit, the King that is not my parents, but they also want to see me if I do go."

"That is wonderful Clara. Now folks if we can all gather round will explain new initiative and will need to organise press and publicity as well as some go to support in Rio. So let's get started."
Everyone gathers round the boardroom table and some sit whilst others stand. One thing Carmichael notices is that all the women sit and men are standing.

"Right, recently two of our team met with Joseph and Chenguang and they arrive today so we need to have everything ready for them. We will need places to stay, an office and will need access to laboratory and team there, we also need a place that is so romantic it will blow their socks off as they have not had a break in years as they fight to find cure for cancer. Now here is latest project in Brazil." Sir John lies out some pictures and maps and starts to explain.

"Tree Soursop or Guanabana has anti-carcinogenic properties and found in Brazil. To date in small treatments and tests held the extract from the Tree Soursop has shown positive results to cure cancer. There have been great results in twelve different cancers and helps regulate blood pressure.

It destroys cancerous cells as found in cancers like Lung, Colon, Prostrate, Breast and Pancreas. In fact it has shown it inhibits cancer cells growth ten thousand times better than chemo drugs, but the big plus and most exciting discovery is it only destroys affected cells, not the healthy ones."

Arthur's mobile rings and he listens then rushes to put on the TV in the room. It is live report on three high rise blocks caught fire and there have been many deaths. As all stand and watch in horror the local council, Conservative, start to shift blame from the previous administration, and what seems to be a directive from the Prime Minister, fault is being blamed on Arthur as all the fatal building regulation mistakes were made during his time in charge. Arthur is visibly moved and looks to his team in shock. Clara takes the TV control and turns it off.

I do not know why but I just jumped into action Reader. I do not know the history, do not know Arthur in previous carnation as Prime Minister, but he is now a good man and we need to act.

"Thanks Clara, right everyone this is what we do. Robert and Quetty you join me, and Jimmy as our inside eyes. Henry and Chastity if you lead a small team to find lab, office and deal with local officials in the area, and Clara you take a small team to find the honeymoon villa of your dreams for Joseph and Chenguang. OK everybody team up and let's get on this. Robert and Quetty if you wouldn't mind holding back with Jimmy and Sir John you're taking Arthur for a drink and organise picking up Guinevere as she may be being hassled by press. All OK? Yes? Great so why we all still standing still?"

"Thanks everyone, job in hand," says Arthur and I see Sir John chatting to Iain as everyone ushers out and each one shaking Arthur's hand.

"OK, Arthur we need to talk and call Guinevere as need to have her picked up. Iain has said he is more than happy to do so now and also Iain is using his money to pay for safe house for you and family so you can all lay low. As he says if he hires no one can trace funds to Knights or you."

Arthur shakes Iain's hand and makes a call to Guinevere, "Yes Iain will be on his way and Quetty has the address of new place already?" says Arthur, "It is the amazing flat opposite Houses of Parliament we loved in 'Matchpoint' that Woody Allen film. Seems Iain was already looking at it. Yes, just pack a few clothes and be ready to leave, also Sir John says to pack clothes and not take as we will collect and move later when house not being watched. Yes love you too."

Iain exits and Sir John whispers in his ear as he goes. Iain then stops and doubles back to hug me, "Thanks for a wonderful day." I smile as he exits with Jimmy via the print room.

"So what do you want?" asks Robert looking at me.

"According to my small knowledge PM is Head of New Order here and as big a racist as my POTUS so you and Quetty go together to ask for her help for Arthur. She has a problem with Quetty and while she feels in charge and on top see if there are any files or anyone working on exposing Arthur as at fault. She will not know we already are on this and think she has time to set him up. I hear she has been waiting a long time for this and that is our advantage and her Achilles heel."

Arthur's mobile rings, "Lancelot, yes it is dreadful, what do you know?" We all watch as Arthur listens and talks to Lancelot. Sir John looks concerned and walks to talk to Robert and Quetty.

"Guys, well especially you Quetty, you have been to the PM's office many times so you know all her staff. Do me a favour and look to see who is new that is suddenly working hard. They will be the ones she has building buckets of shit to throw at Arthur. Use secret camera to get images of them and then bring back to me. I will be with Arthur in the bar looking as if we are trying to dodge the bullet and look like headless chickens. Cause even further false sense of confidence in PM and come find us there. Always look really concerned even when we have a plan as I am sure there is something to be done, but if not we need to diffuse with what we have. Suzie, spot on again and timing superb. Just do not forget you also need to make sure you and Iain do not come up on the Russian radar."

Arthur finishes his call and Lancelot as the Leader of the Opposition is going to throw everything he has at the PM and her team as they have a dreadful record on helping those on the poverty line. He rang as wanted to say that he wished Arthur well and if he found anything would also tell us if helped his defence.

Quetty hugs Arthur. Then Robert shakes Arthur's hand and they exit with a pad and pen as if desperate for PM's help. The office phone rings and Arthur answers, "Ah, Prime

Minister, yes dreadful and of course for all concerned we need to look on helping each other as well as saving the parties face. I have sent Quetty and Robert to your office to lend support in getting to the bottom of things. Yes, the black girl. I appreciate that Prime Minister."

"Right, drinks at the bar and feel we need to look concerned to regroup and possibly look as next step," says Sir John.

"Can I ask something?" Both look at me and nod 'sure'. "Has the PM made plans to visit the site? May be that would be the first plan. And be seen trying to do what is right even if not good for you is what I would say. If they say it is a tragedy say it is a beyond a tragedy and we must take full responsibility, if they say during your time agree it was and you will do everything to find out why it happened. Agree to be seen taking responsibility and then we will see what does truly come up, but that should diffuse the press. It worked for one of our Presidents who asked if a despot was a friend he said he was a good friend, then asked if he was a good friend he said that he was his very best friend. Gave press nowhere to go."

"Lancelot is delving to so anything that can do us harm he will use, but will look to find anything that can help and not bury, but send to us. He is going there tonight."
"Arthur join him, show a united front," says Sir John.

"I am really taken aback to be honest. The works that caused the fire to become untenable; if I dismissed a call for works for safety and this caused the deaths as being reported I feel that I truly not sure I can feel I should be allowed to be free."

We looked at Arthur and already feel he has resigned himself that he is guilty.

"Come on old chap," says Sir John, "let's go to the bar and be seen being resigned to taking the full brunt of the blame. Suzie, use the office to sort out the seating and tickets for opening night event for the show as we will all be going and have a list of names for you to call and personal numbers in a file on the desk for you."

With that the two men exited and I was left to look at the list. The day had been thrown a curved ball, but the list had half of the world's leaders and top sports stars and film stars and if only a tenth of the names turn up this show will be set to be huge. What was I thinking calling from the Knights so after three hours I had filled the theatre and still had sixty seats for Iain's new friend Vera from ShakeShack and Erin has a few friends as well as the boys do too. We have an eight hundred-seat theatre packed with names and faces. The party was now all that was left to be confirmed.

Sat back Reader feeling happy with the way the opening night is going it was not long before more news on the tower fires. It seems during Arthur as PM it was discussed that the cladding on the buildings to make them more attractive to wealthy property owners nearby was dangerous. They were not removed and in fact more tower blocks were clad in this dangerous beautification.

Why did Arthur let his right wing council get away with such disgraceful disregard for the people he was meant to represent, but as news was breaking it was soon clear it was becoming worse for Arthur, and yet the Prime Minister still has yet to do anything. I wondered why, she was obviously behind leaked information implicating Arthur, but she never went after the Tory council. Why?

23

The news of the tower tragedy fills all the news channels and Arthur's face is everywhere. I was sat in the American Bar at the Savoy when Quetty popped in and came to join me. She handed me a very small file with just two photos and two names. These were the PM's new team to work on tower disaster.

"Seems Arthur allowed savings on cladding to go ahead and was aware of the danger, but did nothing. These two are from PM in the Home Office where they worked for PM when she was there under Arthur. There is nothing on them and all looks clean. I think Arthur is ready to make a move to resign from Knights as he does not want to bring shame to one thing he is so proud of." Quetty's head drops and I look at the file and an idea looms. One of those Invisible moments as I see Carmichael return and call him into the bar.

"Iain, looks bad for Arthur, how is Guinevere?"

"She is worried as she knows this will hit him bad. He made some duff decisions he made for the party and not the country. It seems in a brief conversation they had he remembers something of this."

"Quetty?" I said, "can you have Arthur join the Leader of the Opposition going to the towers. I have a gut feeling on these two and think you and me Iain should pop into the Home Office. Also what is Lancelot's number, can I have it?"

"Sure, but what are you thinking?"

I show Iain the file, two photos and a couple of names, "Is this all we have?" I nod at Carmichael, "perfect," and he smiles.

"What is up?" asks Quetty.

"At the CIA we call them cleaners, remember Pulp Fiction, The Wolf, Harvey Keitel, called in to clean up and hide all leads. These two are cleaners so there must be something they are cleaning up. Tell Arthur and Sir John we may have something. We will go in as opposition party members as they will not expect that."

"Quetty, Suzie is right, we have this," says Carmichael.

I call Lancelot and he answers. He is with Arthur. "Hello Lancelot, Suzie here we spoke earlier about the show next week, but need huge favour, Oh you are with Arthur now, well just going to call him and tell him to join you at the towers if that was OK with you? Yes, great, but real favour is can you organise me, and friend access to Home Office as part of your party team? Yes, I am listening, yes, yes… thank you, we will see them outside."

I look at Quetty, "Interesting, Lancelot got wind that there is to be clean up at Home Office tonight and they are trying to find out why, seems he was there to tell Arthur and need you to join them so can call you if we find anything. Iain, get your jeans and most worker-like jacket on we are moving files into the Home Office for the Opposition as a ruse to get us in. we only have an hour. Quetty, tell Sir John we will be at the Home Office and look forward to seeing him in the restaurant later for a bite to eat. Go on girl off you go and did the PM make you grovel earlier?"

"Oh yes she really enjoyed it," said Quetty.

"Well then you will be the bringer of the good tidings tomorrow to her door. Seriously go and give Lancelot a hug from me. Iain let's get changed."

And with that Quetty dashed out, Carmichael and I went upstairs and we managed to borrow two porters brown jackets from the Savoy and within forty-five minutes we met Eric from the Opposition Party who gave us large boxes to carry and marched us through the security gate holding up three passes for security saying he has ours as the boxes are heavy and would not want to put down and lift again. It was that simple. We were inside. We all walked up to the third floor and then Eric said that he was not sure what we were to do so Carmichael leapt into Seal mode.

"Eric, we need you to stay here and make sure no one seizes those files until we return."

"But they are empty boxes?" Eric said mystified.

"Well they won't be when we leave. Come on, we have some cleaners to meet." And with that Carmichael and I left Eric by a room holding large empty boxes.

The rooms and halls are all made of glass. You can literally see everyone and with the large atrium entrance we see our two cleaners enter. They ask for room 74 and are told it is on the fourth floor, but would need to be shown in. They said not to worry and rushed in.

Carmichael and I take to the internal; stairs as our goons waited in the lobby for the lift. We were on the fourth floor as the lift arrived downstairs for the PM's cleaners. Carmichael immediately found room 74 and picked the lock. As the lift doors opened the goons walked out and Carmichael was there to greet them.

"Are you the guys for room 74?" he asked.

"Yes, 74."

"Well we are here to help you as you know everyone has to be assisted. My colleague here has the door open for you."

I open the door and my hair covers my face. In the brown Savoy porter's jacket I could have been a boy for all they knew.

They walked straight to a filing cabinet and started to take out files, "Can we help gentlemen?" asked Carmichael.

"No, sensitive stuff has to be shredded, immediately."

"OK well I will turn this shredded on then and can assist as unless you have clearance to operate shredder under union law I cannot allow you to have clearance in case of emergency." Carmichael sounded as fake an English worker as Dick van Dyke from Mary Poppins.

"What's your name?" one goon asked menacingly.

"Burt," he replied. Priceless. Seems Carmichael had only one reference point as well for British and that was Burt from Mary Poppins.

"Right then, Burt," he said, "I will hand you files and you shred immediately. OK?"

"Certainly sir," he replies and motions me to move over by the shredder. I do so and duck down under the table. It seems they have forgotten about me in their haste to delete the paper files.

Carmichael handed me the files as he then replaced with files on the desk and as they got low I sneaked him more to shred from desks I could reach without being seen. The goons just handed the files to 'Burt' and he would switch like a magician from the ones to shred to the files I handed him. I gathered all the files and placed them on the floor out of site. We were lucky as there were only eight files and then the goons looked to ensure all shredded. Carmichael lifted the shredder off the floor and showed the pieces of shredded paper in the collection tray.

"Thanks, Burt," he said, "you just did your country a great service," and laughed as he and his colleague left. We heard them get into the lift and are met by a little man with a bunch of keys called Harold. Harold had been sent to open the office door and suddenly the goons after asking who Burt was realised something was up and rushed back to the room.

The door to 74 flew open and they rushed into the room. They saw a window open and even though we were on the fourth floor felt we must of jumped out of it and ran off in a panic, then one ran back, "Listen 'Harold, are you sure you don't know Burt?"

"May be he is new guy, but I was sent to open room," Harold replies.

The Goon looks to see shredded files and then looks round the room.

"Those bloody cleaners!" exclaimed Harold.

"What?" said the Goon.

"All bins are to be emptied at six and they obviously did not do this one."

The Goon smiled and then apologised to Harold for his gruffness and said that obviously Burt was the new guy and exited grinning that all was OK.

The great thing about being with a Navy Seal is within seconds they can hide and become Invisible. Yes Reader, Iain and I sat on the floor behind a chair in the shape of the chair and no one noticed. Both of us sat on four files each to help us sit on. Carmichael was actually visible as so tall but used the water drinks dispenser to conceal his top half. I saw everything between the chairs.

We managed to get out and drop files in boxes Eric was guarding. In the reception passed security as we did coming in and Carmichael told guy on door to tell Harold we were helping and that Burt would be back in ten. Guard just said,

"Whatever," and we made it to the car opposite waiting for us.

We got in the car and drove off with Carmichael and I looking at the files. Eric looked excited as if he was part of the secret service. Carmichael found a file and smiled. "Do you guys have paper back up for computer files on everything?"

"Yes, why?" asked Eric.

"Call Lancelot and say you have some great ammunition for tomorrow in Prime Minister's Question Time. Eric does so and then Carmichael shows me what he found in two different files. I rang Quetty and told her. She relayed this to Arthur and he walked to the press. I saw what happened on the news later that night.

Arthur walked alongside Lancelot, as if like a lamb to the slaughter towards the press.

"Friends, fellow residents. The tragedy here is beyond anything we have seen before. I have seen reports that the reason this happened was due to cut backs and not funding works when I was your Prime Minister. I stand here today a broken man as if this is true then I will expect to be held fully accountable. I ask my good friend the Leader of the Opposition to make it so that I do not escape prosecution if I am accountable. It has been a day since this tragic disaster and the Knights have already called teams of Guardians to come and work day and night looking after the survivors and helping the people come to terms with what has been an unforgiveable tragedy. I hope to return when I have more information as to the chain of events and call out to the local council, whom for reasons unknown to me, have not yet come to visit the site. Please my fellow countrymen, let us not look for retribution tonight for we should all be thinking of those that lost their homes and loved ones in this appalling fire. But mark my word, and if you doubt my word, then the word of a true man of the people, my good friend, the Leader of the Opposition, that if retribution is to be made that no one is safe from being accountable. I thank you all for being here at this time and I am happy to answer questions, but if I may suggest we all put that aside and see how we can help here right now those that have more pressing needs than ours."

And with that Lancelot shakes Arthur's hand and they walk among those that are homeless and those that still not sure if their loved ones are to be listed in the fatalities.

One woman crying in the crowd sits lost and Arthur walks to her. She stands crying and shouting at Arthur, "Why did you let this happen, Why?" and starts to hit Arthur's chest. Arthur holds her close and the woman capitulates and sobs in his arms. It was on every news channel on every station around the world who heard Arthur reply, "I have no answer, but can promise it not be allowed to happen again."

It was a dark sombre night as we met Sir John in the Ivy and to my surprise we met Hugues and Robbins as well.

"That was a shit storm, but you Brits never run from a fight do ya? I have so much respect for that Arthur guy of yours," said Hugues.

"He will be vindicated we are sure, but what is new with the Serb and Russians?" asked Sir John.

"Nothing, but we feel that Kowlowski is working alone, we now have built up a complete picture of all the Eastern Block New Order leaders and we feel that the deal being done was to discredit the President of Russia and an internal coup with Kowlowski taking the reigns. Have one more favour to ask Suzie, do you think you can have a private box at the theatre for a very special friend of mine, well he is now, to have as feel he may be helpful for us as well to stop what looks like the fastest rise of the New Order in Eastern Europe since Hitler. Even that moron we have in the White House has embarrassed us with his right wing friends recently, but his dementia is getting worse. Funny that a Jew like Yerno will be head of a Racist Right Wing Nazi movement. Yes it seems Yerno is making a move to line himself up as the idiot Fake President we have in office at the moment."

"So we have a box and be good to know what you would like us to do," I said and with that Hugues told us that the Serbs were in London and also that Kowlowski was meeting the PM in a special meeting.

"Also President's daughter and wife to Yerno is banging the Speaker of the House in order to keep him in line. Boss Hogg looks to be on his way out and could be the patsy for Yerno."

We all looked at each other and realised that the President's daughter and husband Yerno were making a coup within the White House to run America with a POTUS with dementia playing golf more than looking after business.

We sat and discussed plans and then a tired Carmichael and I returned home. Back at the hotel was another file as Chastity had run off the opening night guest list and the party guest list.

I see the manager looking at me and asking if I would like a coffee. Chastity had left details of an old Soho Nightclub was being looked at by developers and may be good to use as party venue before closed.

It was a superb idea and then manager returned with a lovely pot of tea. Well it was hot water and in the glass fresh mint. Fresh mint tea was just what the doctor ordered.

"Just to say next Wednesday the main riverside terrace and function suite is free, we would be more than happy to hosts the Knight's and your show party. I am sure we can theme the room and offer great deals on drinks and cocktails as room and theming on me. Just say, we here at the Savoy love the work that you do."

I looked at this man's face and his smile, he did not expect me to say yes although genuine in his offer.

"As manager of the hotel I will accept your generousity if you will allow me to hire the rooms available that night for our most special guests," I say.

The manager looks at me and smiles, "How many rooms?"

"All, that is suites as well as rooms, how many will there be?" I ask.

"I will check and we can pencil," he says as he walks off to see the main reservation bookings. Upon his return he smiles and sits beside me. "We are having a surprisingly quiet week, but I see the Saudi family have made provisional booking and believe they may be coming to show?"

"They have been invited and reply to their enquiry that the room has been settled, well the three they have asked for, and that all has been paid for compliments of the Knights. I see you have eleven rooms free and seven suites. I have an idea, pre theatre drinks here at the American Bar, all cars collect guests and escort to show, then all guests returned for party. What would it cost?"

"For everything?" he asked.

"Yes and also want to have photographers here that did your brochure and we will organise press together, so the hotel gets huge coverage," I said as I was on a role, this was going to be an incredible event, "I even think the King and Queen of Spain may come so they get the top room of the hotel," and then the manger cuts in.

"Well I must say, this is the best price negotiation ever. We give party and pre-show drinks for free. The terrace and ballroom suite free, drinks we do a deal at cost price, The rooms will be take two get one free and can have all drawn up for you tomorrow morning."

Then I notice Carmichael is standing by the table smiling, "I was worried something had happened to you," he said.

"Oh Iain, this is.."

"I am the hotel manager, it is a pleasure to meet you."

"Iain, we are throwing the first night party here and done the following deal, cost to give party and pre-show drinks for free. The terrace and ballroom suite free, drinks we do a deal at cost price, The rooms will be take two get one free and can have all drawn up for us tomorrow morning," I say excitedly.

Carmichael did not show any sign of emotion, he looked a little annoyed and there was a still pause in the air.

"Well, I feel your negotiation skills are crap, you could of done much better," he said, "call yourself a manager?"

The manager and I looked at each other slightly embarrassed and Carmichael holds up his hand and smiles, "Listen I totally understand, she is tough, but you should of played hardball, break her down, now Suzie let's not forget our Russian benefactor that shall remain nameless will be secretly footing the bill so here is the new deal; We take all the rooms and pay for them all with a five percent discount and a service charge in cash for staff to be shared equally the following morning of say £500 per head, no arguments. Then the drinks will be cost price plus a 25% mark up for hotel and hire of rooms accepted as free. Now will that come to less than £750,000 or close?"

"It could all be achieved for £500,000 and that would include staff tip, please say no more," said the manager.

"Blimey, as they say over this side of the pond, that was easy or was my negotiating bad?" laughed Carmichael.

"Spot on," I said laughing and then we ordered more mint tea to celebrate and the manager joined us with the concierge who we said we would pay to sort out cars and transportation from airports for guests and Carmichael said that it would not be on the house, except the Saudi Family must have the hotel Bentley.

"I am just so excited as the impromptu is always the best and we can have everything done by Monday for you to see. Shall we make the room look like something from a burlesque house and I have a friend who could bring cancan dancers, that the hotel will pay for so no arguments," smiled the manager. The concierge whispered in his ear and the manager smiled. "I will have the River Room for pre-theatre up to 150 people and then the Lancaster Ballroom for stage and show with some seating for about 400 and parlour rooms as well. That is new deal and feel that way you can keep any contentious heads of state from meeting each other."

"Well I am tired and so off to bed," said Carmichael, "I will see you in the morning gentlemen or tomorrow night as may be good to bring Erin and the cast to survey for ideas. Actually can we book dinner for say twenty for tomorrow night and be flexible on numbers?"

"Of course, sir."

"I am Iain and never been called sir, especially not by friends. Your name sir?"

"Sean," he replied and they shook hands as I stood and said in a husky voice, "Come on darling, time for bed."

And with this Carmichael and I disappeared into the lift and soon were in our room. We were like an old married couple and very much at ease with each other. It was plutonic and passionate, weird.

24

I awoke early, well I am here writing up the events in the journal Reader and it is 4am. I could not sleep. Carmichael is fast asleep in the bed and seems he would need a fire bell next to his head to wake him. I look over at the man in bed with me, and sadly could not sleep as Nichols is still on my mind.

This is my first journal Reader so forgive me for being a little erratic and possibly all over the place as things happen, but have faith you will be able to see all that is happening. The journals are an integral part of being an Invisible now and our way to inform the masses of things happening. We trust you as Readers will consume the information and digest to come out with a good conclusion. This new POTUS, his administration, his family are all crooked. There are a thousand missions we could run, but at present by highlighting this one we hope you read and make the right choice to remove them democratically.

Again the deals with an Invisible to save those that cannot be helped without some intervention or help a people see the wolves among their flock. I also realise my own mortality as I see my love Nichols face as he died. I see that the people we deal with are the people who feel all life worthless compared to their own ego and wealth.

I see on the first night guest list is Marco, yes Marco Di Marco, our friend of the family. I need to see why he is there and must chat to Jimmy. It is funny, but the main income for the family since becoming involved in Knight's business is their gambling revenues. Drugs have been mainly selling legally to clinics to help sufferers and medical supplies. Of course we know they must be doing some activities somewhere as a leopard cannot change it's spots, but on the whole they are enjoying meeting people in the open more than all the power and never being seen.

As things happen so quickly I have found it impossible to keep up with everything and it is true being busy helps you cope with loss. Just at 4:15am now and realise that moments do catch up with you. I see an email from Robbins and open it.

'Mt dearest Suzie, I have been having tough time losing Nichols and I am sure you have too. Things were rocky for him and want you to hear from me rather than read somewhere else as you need the truth and send as a true friend. We buried him as a hero in his hometown; our hometown, full military honours and the Knight's Templar made sure his family would never need for anything. The shit in the White House we at present have installed is cutting our own government compensation for service personnel. This is why I am proud to start to help bring them down with political coup of no violence. Anyway writing to let you know Nichols was married with two sons. I never told you and he did not have chance to tell you, but I want you to know things were never good in that marriage. He loved his boys, but his wife was no stranger from affairs herself and he always stayed true and forgave for the boys' sake. He told me that what he felt for you was greater than that bond with his sons and was going home to finally terminate his marriage. Just wanted you to know from me rather than by accident. I did not want you to feel you meant nothing. To Nichols you meant everything. I wanted to tell you face to face, but not been able to and things coming out in press feel you may see and just want you to know I tell you as I love you for making my closet friend know love before he died. I really do not wish to upset you, just want to tell you when next have chance like to take you out and tell you more about the man who happily took a bullet for you. I pledge to you, myself, the same devotion and promise to be there for you as he did. I want you to know my girlfriend and I love to meet as told her, and she is here writing this with me. You ever need a friend just call, Mr. and Mrs. Robbins, (if she will have me..she says yes) and then a heart emoji.'

I felt myself cry and knew that there was a back-story to Nichols and knew not what, but I am glad I now know and from a true friend. I emailed this back and told Robbins that I look forward to us enjoying a drink over looking Lake Como with his wife, as remember him saying something that he loved Lake Como.

I closed my laptop and looked back again at Carmichael. He lay asleep and I went into the bathroom and closed the door.

The tears I cry Reader are for the loss of a man I started to feel for and not for the betrayal, as did not feel anything other than true passion came from Nichols and I. I ran a bath and thought what would have happened had things not turned out as they did? Reader, this was I felt a new test to be an Invisible. We have a code to not place people we love in danger due to being around us and yet now wonder what will be my future; am I to spend the rest of my life alone?

I took off my clothes and got into the bath. It was luxurious and started to smile as I gave thanks for meeting Nichols, knowing that no matter what happens I had that at least.

Lying in the bath I started to relax and closed my eyes. I had been soaking for about five minutes when the bathroom door opened and a sleepy Carmichael shuffled in and started to pee in the toilet. I lay there not knowing what to do. He was oblivious to me in the bath, as if sleepwalking peeing and as he finished and turned he saw me.

"Oh, Jesus Christ! Sorry! I thought you must of popped out, the bed was empty and.. I am so sorry," he stammered.

"Just be a real man Iain, flush the loo and put the seat down." I laughed and he exited laughing too. Lying in the bath I felt a realisation of Nichols spirit had sent Carmichael in to remind me I am alive and I need to live on.

It is now 5:45am and finishing writing this part I see my laptop was open and as I touch the buttons the screen lit up and saw the email was still on the page. I looked at Carmichael who opened his eyes and looked at me. He had read it and that is why he thought I had gone for a walk.

"Sorry I read that, if it makes any sense, I had a feeling this was the case and also the one thing I can only say I know was true was Nichols loved you. Come to bed I need a cuddle, whether you do or not. Thanks to you it seems I am going to have to spend the rest of my life as a woman in a man's body having to stand to pee."

I laughed and got in and cuddled Carmichael whispering, "It is fine. I loved him no matter what and know he is with me always."

"I know, but remember that he would want me to remind you to carry on living and find love otherwise his death will be the worse for him."

I looked at Carmichael and realised the sincerity in his voice and that he probably had said this to the wives of a lot of his comrades lost in battles.

I gave him a squeeze, "Thanks, and trust me I hear your feminine side, plus I think we should have you in drag for the party," Carmichael stares at me as if to say 'what?' "I mean it will help me as well as it is what Nichols would of wanted."

"Bullshit," you just want to see me in a dress," he laughed and all I remember is falling asleep in this amazing giant's arms.

25 We did not leave the room until 11am. Carmichael was awake the whole time just stroking my hair and letting me sleep in his arms. Reader, I would love the moron in the White House oppressing transgender men and women just one round in a ring, he was never going to be man enough to survive one of their badges of courage. I want you all Reader to see that we are all different, many colours, many sexual orientations, many different outlooks and religions, we even support different football teams and types of sport, but we are all people. Please Reader never forget.

As I woke still in Carmichael's arms I saw he had not moved. His smile radiated warmth and he kissed my forehead and then slowly rose. Walking to the window he pulled open the curtain and let in the light. Standing there he saw the laptop and list and then looked back to me.

"I somehow remember doing a deal with the hotel last night."

"Me too, over mint teas, and also you saying how you were going to wear a dress at the party."

"My dear Suzie, in the words of my dear beloved grandmother, get your ass out of bed before I fuck you up good and proper! Real fiery woman Granny Carmichael. And as to the dress, we will see, now come on we also need to meet Jimmy."

I get up and walk to the bathroom to see my face in the mirror. Funny thing Reader as never again were Carmichael or me ever discussed the email or Nichols ever again.

As we dressed I put on my jacket and Carmichael walked over and opened up my jacket I had on. He took out a small pin badge and pinned it on the inside of the inside pocket.

"It was Nichols. He gave it to me to give to you as he died and carried him to the vehicle. I cleaned it and was waiting for the right moment. Keep it on you here next to your heart and remember he will be with you always."

I was incredibly strong, I showed no emotion other than smile and felt proud, I think I had found a way to deal with Nichols loss.

"Right, to work. We have a show and party as well as catch up and wonder if we are on anyone's radar? Here's to a fun day," I said and we exited.

In the reception a beautiful assistant manager handed us an envelope with all the first night party details, cost was less than money agreed, in fact half and was far less expensive than we thought.

On the way out of the hotel we handed the envelope back for safekeeping and Carmichael took a second online to transfer the exact funds. The Assistant Manager, Sergio, yes if I say beautiful young I am talking male Reader, stood open mouthed and kept shaking Carmichael's hand and can see the manager would be over the moon.

The Bentley pulls up and Sergio smiles, "It will take you where you are going."

We get in and soon are in the London traffic on our way to the theatre for the rehearsals. As we pull up we get out and see already the street is packed. It is hard to get in, let alone out and my Invisible Head starts to think escape routes.

We enter the theatre and there in a smart suit is Uncle Mike. He sees us and rushes over.

"Hello, hello," he gushes, "just trying on my first night suit, what do you think?"

"Uncle Mike you look great, but would you mind coming shopping with me later as we need to treat you. No ifs or buts. Listen we have done a little research and you are one of those guys that often goes without for others and I feel we would love to show you gratitude from Erin and the team. Are they in?"

"Everyday working and I have to say some of the numbers are just sensational. Katie has three solos and even written two songs for the guys. I mean I have never felt such a buzz in years, I am so proud I wish I could be up there with them, trust me you are going to get your investment back in spades, come on this way," and Uncle Mike leads us into main auditorium as Ellen is belting out a solo.

She sings a note that makes the hair on my arms stand on end and I look to Carmichael as she sings about the love for her mother and how her Dad told her musical theatre was full of homosexuals and she's never find a man to marry. Then follows on to say her father told her to be a hairdresser, the irony and we sat in the dark mesmerised. Then on come the boys all drag and the number is funny, but at the end we applaud and Carmichael stands.

"Formidabla, everyone formidab," says Carmichael in a camp, fake voice. He walks to the stage and Erin hugs him and the boys do too as he stands centre stage to say he has an announcement.

"Ladies and Gentlemen, and Uncle Mike, your promotions manager has now secured your first night party and guest list, but might I suggest I felt the song just performed was lacking something. I hope you don't mind?"

"I know, but what can we do? What do you suggest?" asks Erin.

"Uncle Mike, you are an ex-chourian, been in a few shows as an actor? Where are you during the show, when it is in full swing?"

"Well being um er, I guess helping out backstage and.." stammers Uncle Mike.

"Erin the song is about your dad and brilliant, but we need to see your dad's perspective so why not include Uncle Mike as some of the stereotypical characters missing when needed. I mean at the end when he meets all the boys in drag end with him not realising they are men."

"My God that is genius! I love it! Uncle Mike would you?" screams Erin.

"Also, the boys can you get quick change outfits so we see you as men with Uncle Mike and then come back as women at the end?"

"Sure, but we open in five days," says one of the boys.

"Oh for Shit's sake Laurence, we made nine costumes and put on a show with seven hours until lights up. I can help Marta with outfits and so can Barry," said Trevor the oldest of the Drag Queens.

"Shall we do each number quickly from start to finish and then see where we need Uncle Mike?" asks Carmichael.

"Great idea, and thank you Uncle Mike, what do we call you as need to call printer now to make sure you are in program before going to print," asks Erin.

"Uncle Mike?" he says sheepishly.

"Suzie can you get a quick shot of Uncle Mike on your phone and do a quick biog and let's all get to first places." Carmichael starts busying everyone then shouts, "Stop!"

Everyone stops and turns to look at Carmichael, "I am sorry as we came to tell you that this amazing woman in the stalls has not only arranged a who's who of people for the first night, but you have the Savoy ballroom and terrace for the first night party."

Everyone screams with delight and start shouting 'we love you Suzie' and blowing kisses as Erin holds up her hand and all look, "This is just too amazing so everybody we have five days

to completely rewrite the show and the world will be watching so absolutely no pressure," and Erin looks Katie, "and on top of that remember that fricking Katie is going to steal the show unless we are all on our best game."
Everyone turns to look at Katie and they start to applaud.

"Right, Carmichael, ass off the stage and come sit next to me, Uncle Mike has given me pads and pens so can we please see the show?" Everyone laughed as they looked at me in the stalls ordering Carmichael off the stage then started whooping and cheering 'Go Suzie, Go Suzie'.

Again Carmichael was a natural and just like the photo shoot he added touches here and there and gave solos to every member of the cast with them all as ensemble backing each other. Uncle Mike fitted in like a real pro and the songs had more meaning, it was as if Carmichael had just taken a great show to the show of the decade.

The end song, the finale is now completely hysterical as midway through number Uncle Mike realises that all the girls are boys and he sells it brilliantly. Carmichael leaps on stage choreographing and drags Uncle Mike off stage, as the number is the final showpiece for each singer to take his or her curtain call. I get a call on mobile from Carmichael backstage telling me to tell the lighting to get a follow spot ready on the top of the stairs centre stage.

Just as they are all about to sing there is a huge crash of noise and all turn, Carmichael shouts now and the follow spot comes on as Uncle Mike in full drag walks down the stairs and joins in the final chorus of the finale song entitled, 'We Are All People.'

The guys in the wings in the lighting and sound box and me are screaming and cheering, as it was just brilliant. Everybody hugs Uncle Mike and I can see him crying with joy. Uncle Mike had never experienced a spotlight moment or to feel part of the show and soon everyone was hugging and crying.

"Right, if you've finished arsing around Carmichael I think we need to get going, things to do." Carmichael rushed down the stairs towards me; he was on a real high and grabs his jacket and starts waving as we both leave. He stops and turns and shouts, "Uncle Mike, whatever you do, don't steal the show." And all laugh as we exit.

As we leave the building the streets are busy, but I look round as we are exposed. Apart from the stage door this was only way in and out. I looked around and Carmichael holds my hand, "Suzie, I know we need an escape route, but tonight we come back and have a dry run, OK?" I smiled and agreed and so we went to Notting Hill to meet Jimmy at Chastity's house. As we entered I saw Jimmy at the back of the lounge overlooking the garden as Arthur then obscured him.

"You made it great, listen we need to update and chat. Guest list done and got email about Savoy, but seems in a news item on an internet blogger channel Carmichael was seen as backer for show, well all the world's press want to be there and know what it is all about. We wanted you in the open to see who else appeared. It seems one of the Serb rebels working for Kowlowski came in last night and we have him under surveillance, Kowlowski we have invited as a guest for the show, but not the party as we have another plan for him. El Cid sends his best along with Sophia and apologies for not making it, but we are happy to say they intend to see the show in three weeks time. Anyway, it seems the deal you uncovered is a real hornet's nest. Jimmy do you want to show what you found from files Suzie seized?"

Arthur sat down and Jimmy walks to a laptop on the table linked to the TV and we all sit and watch.

"Well you were right, Suzie, this is a major coup being planned and it seems far bigger than we can cope with," starts Jimmy.

A Picture of Kowlowski is seen and he is seen angry with the Serbs and seems to be threatening someone who then hands Kowlowski a file; then a picture of Yerno walking out of the same building and getting into his car.

"They now believe each other and that both were duped and the bonds are missing. Both had a major row over both looking to double cross each other and then teamed up to catch those involved. Hugues has had his guy slip them false info and yesterday he was found dead, suicide, hung himself is verdict. They found his wife and daughter shot, is a bloodbath, and guess he was told confess or family dies. I fear he gave you guys up and then the bastard killed them, framing our guy as mentally unstable killing his family before hanging himself. They now know who you are, but Intel suggests only Carmichael recognised, Robbins, but he was eliminated, as they knew he was with me in Brussels. The other hit is out on a blonde with big tits. Sorry to say that is the actual wording. Now what we are asking is a big ask, but we cannot do this unless you agree. If all goes to plan we will curb all this on the opening night, but it means you both being exposed."

"Thanks Jimmy, guys your call and no one will mind you disappearing, in fact we have a flight sorted for you to Rio waiting," says Arthur.

"Tell me," I ask, "will we destroy another New Order cell if we stay?"

"Yes, we may do, but nothing is guaranteed," says Chastity and then looks scared to Arthur.

"I'm in, just get Suzie out they have no idea who she is," says Carmichael. I look at him and stand up and hug Jimmy.

"Listen Iain, I got you into this and I will be there to get you out. Jimmy what little aides have you for us?"

Before Carmichael can answer Jimmy says, "We have a bug on our Serbs and your phone will have a beep go off if they are within half a mile of you. We have people watching all movements, but nothing is guaranteed, as you know. I know you want to do this, but there is a huge risk."

"We just need to get everyone into the theatre, the show goes on and afterwards you both take a bow and go off to the box we have waiting for our special guests. Yes we have special guests that El Cid reached out to," says Arthur, "but we cannot let you know until you walk through the door as they cannot be compromised if something goes wrong. I am sorry, but all will be clear."

"From what we know Kowlowski is second in charge of Russia. He is dealing behind President's back we assume, although cannot be certain. Yerno and daughter pulling strings at

White House, now POTUS is, as far as we can ascertain, suffering dementia. The money we gave to the Mexicans was to be a slush fund for the New Order and there is a land deal on top of the deal Russian President did with King Tiller years ago El Cid put a stop to. I want to concentrate on the land deal so that will take my mind off the Serbs, and don't worry, I will tape my boobs down, I will be invisible." Arthur nods and leaves and so does Jimmy handing me a USB.

Standing in the room Carmichael looks at me and seems concerned. He looks at the file and then Chastity hands him a mint tea. He looks up as all is silent in the room and she leaves so that only Carmichael and I were left.

"So you get tea and I don't, is that how it is going to be?" I joked.

"Suzie," Carmichael looked at me as if worried for me.

"Yes Iain, Suzie is a big girl and if we pull this mission off we could save thousands of lives. I have seen what the New Order can do in Serbia; I have seen the anti-gay murders where killers walk free. This is in Europe as we start to see the rise of the New Order grow. I feel we should go back to the theatre and have a scout round at exit strategies as well as see if anyone watching. And just to let you know I promise I will not let anything happen to you."

It became dark and we arranged to meet Uncle Mike at the theatre, well he lived there Reader if you remember. He told us the box office door would be open and to walk straight through. The theatre looked closed, but door was unlocked as promised. I looked up to see an ancient security camera and then heard the door lock to the box office click. Uncle Mike was watching us enter.

Through the box office into a room behind and then into the auditorium and to a stairway marked private where we were met by Uncle Mike, "Hey, come on in, I have fish and chips for us if hungry?"

I must admit we had missed food most of the day so all sat in his kitchen at a big wooden table and odd chairs.

"One day I will get the money to do this place up and look to have rooms for those who seem lost in Soho. I mean to say, be a place where many young boys and girls who find themselves without a friend, homeless can get some safety, and if we are doing well give them work."

"Sounds like another magical Uncle Mike idea to me," Carmichael said.

"Would you show us around so we can get a feel for the place?" I asked.

"Sure, after supper. Well no one likes cold fish and chips," he says and we sit laughing and talking about Uncle Mike's failed career as a musical theatre star, looked at old photos and then a picture of him with his ex-wife who passed away with lung cancer. Just as she was dying she did a lottery ticket as a joke and they won about three million pounds. She made him buy the theatre that was totally run down for two, got the freehold from his old boss who also loved his wife and they spent her last days with plans of how they would transform the theatre back to it's glory days.

"Right food done, I've bored you with my stories, let me show you around," he says with a real excited bounce in his step.

There were sixteen rooms and the first floor was the green room and four dressing rooms. There were six large dressing rooms behind the stage as well. One the next two levels were a series of large rooms. Each could be a self-contained studio with double rooms and en suites. Uncle Mike showed us his wife's original drawings and had a tear in his eye. At the top was a huge dome that had a door out that let to a fire escape over the roofs to other houses. I looked at Carmichael and both clocked that this would be our escape route if needed. We walked back into the theatre and Uncle Mike started to laugh. We looked at him and joined in not knowing why we were laughing.

"Let's meet at Mark Powell's in Marshall Street to get you your opening night suit. Well I am sure your wife would of wanted you to look the part at the Savoy," says Carmichael.

"Sorry, we have spent an evening together and I still know nothing about you two. Not that I am prying, but the wife always said that people came into your life for a reason and you two have transformed mine. I am just glad you did and thank you for everything."

I gave Uncle Mike a hug and felt a true connection with this awesome man who lost his greatest love, but carries on helping others as he promised her and yet asks nothing for himself. This is what being a human being is really about.

Hands shook and we exit the street. I notice the street lights light up the area in pools of light and we walk in and out of the shadows back to the Savoy where Sergio opens the door to say all has been sorted with cars.

We went to bed and cuddled wide awake as we knew the next few days would be dangerous for us both, but we knew so many people were counting on us.

You see Reader our lives are crossed and we have destinies set that we follow, people come into our lives and we are who we are because that is the way we are. I do not know what I am saying, but to say the path for exposing the New Order is set in my timeline and I accept the mission so if I do die I want you to know that life carries on and others will fight for those that cannot fight for themselves.

Sat here writing the journal I realise that things escalate the minute we turn away. The British PM is as dictatorial as ever and her government are the worst for years on human rights of her own people. Throughout Europe smaller fractions trying to break the EU are teaming with leaders in waiting as the far right Nazi element tries to take hold. In Russia the second tier ready to dispose the leader so they can join far right New Order for their own public gain and in America it seems the White House leaderless as we have a POTUS who before dementia set in was the worst in history, we are being run secretly by right wing New Order group at the White House. Luckily all the in fighting for power is slowing them down.

News came in of a major catastrophe in a sweatshop in India as a group of workers and lead by courageous woman protecting the children from slavery conditions and abject poverty is captured as a radicalised Jihadist. It seems that she was about to expose the POTUS's daughter as having all her Made In USA line visible to the world. Seems nothing the President or his family make is actually made in USA. They have clothing flags, Made In the USA, made in India and sewn into all the goods that they manufacture in India.

Three children working fourteen-hour days for ten cents a day died when crates fell on them in cramped conditions. When a revolt was led by a young girl called Prisha, the army moved in and she and three others disappeared. Prisha has just surfaced to be placed on trial saying she was one of the Jihadist bombers that caused the children to die. Due to civil unrest to is to be moved and tried elsewhere, but no one knows where.

There is just not enough Invisibles to go to every mission and I remind myself to keep ear to the ground whilst avoiding the Russians and Serbs looking to grab Carmichael and me.

26

Sat in Covent Garden at the Snack Shack Carmichael is giving Vera ten tickets as promised. We are sat in the open and we realise easier to be found, but easier to be watched as around us the Knights Templar are close. Sometimes being seen helps you be invisible and harder to find. You see Reader if you look for your keys you never find them, and yet they often are right in front of your eyes.

After another amazing burger we walk to the theatre and see the signs are up, the posters up and even a queue for tickets. I also put a Save Soho logo on the poster as even Soho is at threat from the money-grabbing colleagues of the Prime Minister and her husband's friends.

Sat in the theatre watching the show rehearse for final tech run I see in the paper that the PM and her appalling response to the tragedy at the housing fires has made her even more unpopular. It seems this evil woman was side swiped by the Leader of the Opposition, Lancelot, as he had evidence that the fires were due to a report that was handled under her control at the Home Office, whilst Arthur was at the helm, and quashed by her. It seems her husband's investor friends were not wanting the housing made safe or done up as wanted condemned so they could buy and build luxury flats that no one will live in. Just for investment.

It also seemed that the buildings could have been made safe by spending a further fifty million by local council on the correct cladding, as one used was reason fire took hold. The council bragged a month before in the press about having two hundred and fifty million made in savings and gave all their wealthy landlords a huge rates rebate rather than make the homes of the poor safer or better living conditions.

What was most concerning is the PM has hidden low on this now and been flooding her Right Wing press with other news stories and sad to say my President's stupidity sort of takes over all the world's press. She is hiding for now, but would of loved to of seen her face when Quetty walked in with Arthur to hand her the files we had absconded from her men as copies from his files. Arthur acted confused and asked Quetty to point out the highly damaging correspondence to the PM to look at and that he of course would do what he could to quell the party uproar that had commenced.

Quetty was heard to of left the meeting, gone into a ladies toilet and screamed for a whole ten minutes out loud, loud enough for all the commons to of heard. When she returned she looked at Arthur and calmly said, "It's OK, I am alright now, but I am sorry, that was amazing. The look on her face as me, her most hated person to deal with, dealt the killer blow." Then let out another scream of 'Yes!' and walked to the desk and sat and did nothing, just trying to control her sheer joy.

Sat in the theatre I take the seat Kowlowski and his party will sit in and survey the exits. He will be unable to leave without making a nuisance of himself as sat in the middle of a row. Best seats in fact, and best seats for us to watch him.

Hughes tells me that his man in the White House has disappeared and seems Yerno is mounting a clean house sweep. But fear not as the man Hugues picked was a Boss Hogg man and as such free from Yerno scrutiny. He had disappeared and as of yet no one knew why.

I am tired and feeling thirsty, but more than that need to take a walk. Carmichael is now directing and tell them I will be back shortly. On the street London is alive. The buzz of Soho never diminishes. It has been hit as a place of sleaze and corruption as a foil to sell off to developers' prime land. As a red light district and den of iniquity it is neither. The sleaze is the politicians and developers trying to ruin this great community.

Walking passed Soho Radio I see Lenny Beige on air with Chris Sullivan ready to hit the decks. It is a great little Internet radio station with really eclectic sounds and chat. I listened in on my iPad the other day and now hooked. I pop in and leave four tickets to the opening night and they wave with thumbs up whilst on air. Lenny gave the show a shout out as well as Chris and seems I am doing my job.

I walk into a bar in Old Compton Street and seeing I am the only girl feel safe that I will not be hit on. A very camp young barman flashes a smile and asks what I would like and soon I am sat in the dark rear enjoying a mouthful of liquid goodness. I laugh as write this trying to be descriptive for you Reader and look to see in a gay bar describing being in a dark rear having a mouthful, then feel best next time say enjoyed a coke at a table to the back.

Just as I relax and unwind as things been pretty full on I see a Serb arrive with a tall gay man. I find out that the Serb has chatted up the man and they have come for a drink. I know him, the Serb that is. One of a team I hit that was looking for me, and the last face I saw in Serbia that caused me to destroy original journal.

"Oh, hello Rory, who's the friend?" the barman asks and Rory answers that it was none of his business and laughed. I was not seen and yet sat close to the outrageous flirting of Rory with the Serb. The Serb looked as if he was interested, but too butch to show in public he was gay that seemed to egg Rory on more.

Then I heard the show being mentioned and Rory saying that as one of London's leading drag queens he would be guest of honour. The Serb has a shoulder bag he places on the floor and it is open. I can see a file and temptation takes over. His back is to me and the seat behind becomes available. I quickly and without being seen take the seat.

Sliding my hand down I manage to slip the file out and open it without being noticed. I see the toilets are opposite and take it with me to look at. I have no idea how much time I have, but Rory has told the Serb to relax his friend will be over soon with the tickets. I have a momentary few minutes so act.

There is a queue; of course there is a queue. One queen is banging on a door shouting at the occupants to go do it elsewhere these are toilets not cottages. I had no idea what he meant until later, but queuing managed to photograph the papers and all relating to land and bank details. I had no idea what they were either, but decided to get back to the Serb and get his folder back in the bag.

I was too late and saw one of the Priscilla boys with Rory and shaking the Serb's hand. I see the young barman picking up glasses and tell him to clear my table and then hand the folder to the Serb asking if it was his as if he had just picked it off the floor. I exited and watched him trough the bar window do just this, and the Serb react scared as if it was highly sensitive and place it back in his bag. I managed to get to the corner and see the Priscilla Drag Boy walk back to the theatre and managed to bump into him asking if he had managed to get rid of his four tickets. He said that he had and an old friend called Rory was coming with his new Serb boyfriend and two others. I noted down the seat numbers and again often Reader things can happen by sheer coincidence. When something happens three times in a row with same person by coincidence then you know it is not.

Everyone is on stage and chatting and Carmichael sees me and comes to say it has been a fantastic day. "It really has," I said and told him of the chance encounter with the Serb. "We now at least know of two fractions to watch in the audience as well as need to check out the files I copied."

"Everyone, everyone, can I have your attention please? Thanks. Me and the little missus as I think the English Aussie phrase may be have to pop orf, my God this accent is awful," Carmichael laughs, "anyway tonight all of you at the Savoy for dinner and Uncle Mike is in charge so all names and numbers through him and Uncle Mike if you would call ahead to the hotel with the list, just tell Sean needs this and they will understand. And one last thing, boys just inspirational, every solo is worthy of a Tony, Katie, you are going to be a star, Erin you already are a star and will shine like the great you will be set to become, but folks make sure you are all on you're a game as Uncle Mike steals every time he is on stage.

Support each other and there is no bigger star than when you all are there together."

All cheers and hug each other as Carmichael and I disappear. "I am loving this creative streak. I think I will direct shows and style fashion shoots as my new under cover alter ego when needed for the Knights."

"Well let us hope after Wednesday night you get to direct many more shows," I reply and we both remember the streets are not safe and manage to jump in a taxi and get to the hotel.

I got a strange feeling from the cabbie as if he was not coincidently outside and free and nudged Carmichael when the cab driver asked where to?

"We are staying on the embankment so by the station would be great."

"Rightio," he said and off we went. I noticed the meter not running and then saw he had a bag like the Serb earlier. As he dropped us off I smiled and paid him five pounds, far too little for the fare.

"We live in this block here," I said and he looked at the building, "thanks and keep the change."

"Rightio," he said again.

"What's up?" asked Carmichael.

"Just follow," I said and walked briskly to the building and as if going to the basement saw the taxi drive off and then pulled Carmichael back through the side street to the Strand and whisked us both into the Savoy.

"What was all that about?" asked Carmichael.

"He managed to pull alongside as we hailed a cab, he never turned the meter on, wanted to know where we lived and then took a fiver and change for fare that cost us seven pounds last time. I think that if we watch that basement we find out how to follow back goons to where they are based."

Carmichael grinned and said, "I will call Hugues and address is here on my map showing ways to embankment."

As Carmichael walked off to phone Hugues I saw Sean walking over to me smiling. I stand to greet him and we exchange a warm embrace.

"Sean, how has the hotel world been?"

"Well, much better since you arrived. Owners are even coming back to oversee party as we have so many names and dignitaries they did not want to miss out," Sean laughs.

"Carmichael," I call to Iain looking around as he finishes his call and wave him over, "How many bosses?"

"Sorry?" asks Sean.

"How many owners in the party coming for our night?"

"Four, two and wives, to be honest one is in the doghouse so he is using the trip to make amends."

"Right, when they arrive tell them you will give them your four tickets as you feel you want to be here to make sure all goes well."

Sean looks at me as confused.

"I will have four tickets among the names for them to the show and then invites to the party, and why not have the wife make the toast for a successful show at the before show drinks?" Now Carmichael looked at me and laughed.

"Sean, you must swear to say you are giving up your tickets OK? No excuses as we will find out and time they should be more grateful of you, you are the Savoy for us. Plus when is your next night off?" asks Carmichael.

"Thursday, but"

"Give it up Sean, you know what incredible negotiators we are." And with this we all laugh as Carmichael looks at his watch, "I must redo the seating plan I guess and they will be listed as VIP until you furnish names. I will have Gerard Butler next to wife and have them all sat with Arthur and Saudi group. Come on Suzie, time to sort out stuff and Sean you and seven friends, eight in total, to Thursday night seats and also be ready to enjoy the Ivy on us as well."

"All on us of course and stop being thankful, just know we see you as shampoo...because you are worth it." I laugh and Sean and Carmichael raise eyebrows.

"Seems your comedy is as good as your negotiating," quips Carmichael and we all laugh.

"I will take care of the drinks bill," says Sean and Carmichael laughs.

"Now that is comedy genius! Well we never had anything," and Carmichael waves at the barman, "Sean has your tip."

The barman looks confused and Sean walks over and gives him a fiver from his pocket, "It's a long story, this is yours."
We can see that all the staff love Sean and his incredibly calm temperament and ease of not panicking make it a joy to work for him.

In the lift Carmichael looks at me seriously and becomes more alert to the floor numbers, and what may best be our exit.

"Hugues has said that Intel has placed the Serbs close by and we have to lay low for one more day. They managed to track the taxi and he led them to a garage in Mile End, wherever that is, and seems the Serbs are using as a base. Kowlowski has also been seen coming and going, but his whereabouts remain a mystery, as it appears the garage sits over mainline tube station exit point. They think there is a stairway from the garage to the platforms. This is why they have not turned up on CCTV cameras other than entering stations in West End."

The lift stops and we exit. Carmichael removes a small Berretta handgun and there is no one in the hallway. We move to our room and I follow Carmichael in. The room is spotless, too spotless I think and call the Knights from outside the room to come with bug detection kit. Robert arrives smiling forty-five minutes later.

"Hi, got it here, sorry only me in office so hope you know how to use it," he says.

I motion to Carmichael to chat about the show with Robert and soon they are doing what all men do; talk sport. I meanwhile sweep the whole room, twice. Nothing.

"Rooms seems clear," I say and Robert smiles.

"When I told Arthur he said to get there quick just in case, but it was the Savoy, their cleaners could make a completely white suite covered in red wine clean in an hour and no one would know the difference. Listen, I have to dash to meet Quetty as she wants new shoes for the first night."

"Robert, can I give you a tip? New shoes will most definitely blister her heel, toes or both so pop to chemist en route and buy Compeed plasters. Say nothing and when she starts to complain produce and be an even bigger knight than you already are. Well even guys have their uses," laughs Carmichael and looks to Robert.

"Compeed, OK got it."

As Robert exits Carmichael pulls out the seating plan. We start reorganising the seating and order room service as we work the night in our room.

27

It was the morning of the big night. I was so excited and sorted out flowers for all the cast as well as making sure that the bar is packed. I had all this done as Carmichael exits the bathroom.

"Need to make sure bar is packed for booze and how about roses for all the cast and have them arrive at seven to the theatre or have them there laid out for when they arrive? What do you think?" he asks.

I hold up my mobile and smile, "Done it."

Carmichael's mobile rings and it is Hugues. A short conversation then Carmichael looks at me as if to nod I am in agreement and hangs up.

"So what am I signed up for now?" I ask.

"Meeting Hugues on the roof, now."

"Sorry?" I ask, "what roof?"

"The Savoy of course," he smiles back and we exit the room and there on the roof in glorious sunshine sits Hugues having a coffee with Robbins.

Robbins stands and looks at me as I open my arms to hug him and whisper in his ear that I got the email and thanks.

"Guys we have a situation as night before last the body of a drag queen called Rory Fitzsimmons, better known as Stella

Goodthighs was found. He sang in shows and organised singers before giving up on the stage to take the spotlight in the world of drag. Now Suzie we know this was the guy your friend gave tickets to so expect Serbs. Do not stop them entering, we will have men posted to make sure they do not exit at anytime during or after the show, but we want you to have them follow you backstage to meet in the room we have for special delegation. Robbins will be backstage as stagehand and make sure you get in the room and direct the Serbs, who will be asking for you, to where you are. From there we can take over and the threat will truly be over. Now we have Intel that they will not be moving until the show from a Russian Agent that is talking to us from Kowlowski camp. We know the Intel is sound and we trust it, but enjoy the day and just be alert when in town."

"Hugues, they want us alive don't they? For the money?" I asked.

"Of course one reason is that, the other is that many of the people invited from diplomats and politicians are New Order and they all want to see the show and enjoy the party. Anything happen to you and they do not get their free cocktails and caviar, well, their lives would not be worth living. Seriously, be safe and trust me when I say we have your back. Now go enjoy what I hear will be an amazing show and take Robbins, he needs to blend in with the show as well as I feel would like to spend time with you guys. I fear I am boring him." Hugues smiles and nods to Robbins.

"Oh, if you insist sir," he laughs and shakes Hugues hand, "you'll be alright to…?"

"Find my way home alone, of course not! I have Phillips and Whistler waiting by the door. Tell them to call the car as you pass, I am going to finish my excellent coffee and enjoy this glorious view."

I looked back to see Hugues sipping his coffee completely relaxed and in his own space feeling content that he would take care of us.

The Knights Templar are now growing as many of the Guardians are becoming also Knights helping protect projects that may be at risk from corrupt officials overseas. Phillips and Whistler were both Seals and knew Carmichael. They stood to attention as he passed out of respect and Carmichael turned to shake both their hands and even hug them.

"Guys, that is one special person out there on the roof, take care of him won't you?"

"Yes sir." They replied.

"Oh, and my name is Iain, not sir and hope to work with you two soon on something fun."

We exited the hotel and walked to Trafalgar Square. Chatting and laughing a pigeons swooped to get at our snacks and then a huge seagull flew in trying to grab Robbins snack. It missed, but swooped in again to steal an ice cream from a little girl. She started to cry and Robbins rushed over as the mum, already laden with kids struggled to cope.

"It's OK, it's OK," said Robbins to the little girl and pulled out a wet wipe and cleaned her hand. "What did that silly seagull do? Did he just pinch your ice cream? Listen, shall we get you another?" and Robbins motioned to the ice cream seller for another ice cream and he rushed one over then refused to take Robbins money.

The mother struggling with a moody fourteen-year-old son bored being stuck with his mother and little sister shouted at the boy to stand still. She was at her wits end. "I'm sorry," she said.

"It's fine I have three myself back home. Hey you have a West Ham shirt on, you what they call a hammer?" I was impressed by Robbins knowledge of British soccer. "Back home I watch the soccer and are they not playing tonight? I have to work so going to miss the match?"

"Dunno, we have to wait for dad from his interview then go home." The boy seemed disillusioned and the mum was embarrassed and stressed.

" I am so sorry and thanks for your help, hope you have a better day," mum said.

"Impossible, a better day than you guys, with all you have organised secretly?" said Robbins as the mum looked confused. Robbins nodded at Carmichael and me and laughed, "I have to babysit these two."

"What is hubby interviewing for," I asked.

"Well yesterday he applied to be porter at Parliament and today as a driver for some banker, he used to chauffeur for lovely guy, but he died of a heart attack so we have had bit of a rough patch. Sorry don't mean to burden you just tough for everyone."

Robbins is on the phone, "Sorry listening to all that can you tell me what time hubby meeting you?"

"About ten minutes, why?"

"That would be amazing and bring forms or whatever and are you sure Henry, you can sort all that, see you at front of Portrait Gallery in half an hour." Then Robbins hangs up.

"Right, hubby used to driving Bentleys and Aston Martins?" Robbins asks.

"He loves cars and a brilliant mechanic, once they broke down outside Stockport and boss needed to make his plane, but my Harold fixed car and made plane for his boss. Sorry, who are you?"

"Robbins, Knight Templar. This is Suzie and another Knight Iain Carmichael. I have a job for hubby on one condition you spend the day as I have had a friend organise."

By now even Carmichael and I were confused. Suddenly a guy in badly fitting suit appears flustered and looking sad as meeting did not go well. "Oh there's Harold. How did it go? Oh this is Robbins, and Knights people."

"Hi," said Harold looking confused.

"Wife says you are driver and used to top motors and can fix if needed. Right. We want to offer you a job as special driver for the Knights. You will have a substantial salary, working part-time as not always need driver and good pension scheme. Car will come in twenty minutes for you to decide terms. Package as follows; salary £35,000 a year with bonuses and six weeks paid holiday. Have to attend fun outings with family and will receive second car for your wife to help with kids. Second part to agree is you will be driving heads of state, knights to functions and meeting, but today you must go with one of our drivers for the day and sign contracts and meet your fellow workers."

"Are you for real?" asked Harold in real cockney accent.

"We are the Knights Templar Harold, you will work for the Knights of the Round Table who work with us. We do things because we can. Plus this morning on the roof of a hotel close by this morning my boss told me to do something noble. You will meet my boss I am sure too." And then Carmichael notices a Bentley pull up in the road by the Portrait gallery and out steps Henry.

"Folks if you will follow me," says Robbins and Harold walks his son as Carmichael carries the little girl and mum and I push the pram.

"Hello Henry this is Harold, your new driver," says Robbins.

"Excellent, nice to meet you Harold. This is Fred and he will chat you through the job. I have a contract here for you to sign and you start on any day you wish after two weeks time, this being the summer holidays we need you refreshed and happy to start, so if my colleague has not told you of package yet, no, OK, then this is the first part, Fred will sort out your uniform, Hackett is Fred's favourite and I think Suzie can take the girls to a lovely boutique opposite whilst you get measured and fitted with you son. You must each get a suit to leave in. Suzie can you shop with mum to get the girls some outfits and all meet back at Hackett in one hour. Carmichael I feel you will assist the ladies and Robbins the gentlemen with Fred. Then in new outfits you will have family day out for the girls, it will be Madam Tussauds on us followed by the zoo. Then boys turn for treat will be lunch at West Ham stadium and a box from Arthur to watch the hammers play Manchester United. After match drinks in the bar with the team and then Fred will drive you all home. Yes Fred is also a hammers fan and happy to show you the ropes and has funds to pay for day. Right, Harold you want to take the job?" Henry holds out a pen to the dumbfounded Harold.

"Blimey Dad, sign before he disappears," says the son.

Harold signs and then Fred chips in, "Sorry, you will need passports, have you got passports?"

"Yes, back home, not on us," says mum.

"Good. They did the same to me when I joined," says Fred.

"Did what?" asks Harold.

"Well as you signed you are now officially a Knight with a paid holiday to start to show our gratitude to have you on board. In two days you four will be flying to Disney Resort for all expenses paid holiday for a fortnight. Two days later back on GMT you will arrive at Parliament and ask at reception for me, Henry from the Knights and I will get you sorted to work.

Fred will be happy, as we needed a replacement as he and the wife are off to a Mediterranean cruise and you will be his cover as we were short staffed. So all agreed I better get back to the commons as arranging drivers for the show." And with this Henry walks back towards Parliament and has a real step in his stride. Henry loved that, as did Robbins who kept grinning.

As we stand they Fred looks to Mum, "Listen let's get the pushchair in the boot and you three in the back with the Knights and Harold, you're up front with me."

Fred just took over and a tearful mum was just crying with joy. I held her hand as the kids stared out of the window excited and happy. Carmichael smiled at Robbins and said, "Well that'll take some topping." It broke the air and we all laughed.

"You a Spandau fan like my missus? Yes then lets get the day started,' says Fred and suddenly we are all singing 'Gold' and laughing as we pull up to Hacketts. As the boys exit to buy suits I see a nervous embarrassed mum look to me as there was no Primark and she was never been to a designer shop.

Carmichael lifts the little girl off her feet holding her in one arm, "Listen, I think I know just the colour for you two, trust me, and please lets have fun shopping." With that Carmichael strides into a boutique and Mum and I find ourselves standing outside I smile and we rush in after him.

"Ladies," Carmichael says, "this young lady needs transforming into a Princess and she would like the same for her mother, now that green is divine can we see you in that in a 10?" asks

Carmichael. The women of the shop rush round and mum stands there still blinded in the headlights.

"I am so sorry," whispered Carmichael, "I do not know your name."

"Beverley," came a timid reply, "and that is Ethel."

"Right Beverley, do exactly what I say and this will be such fun. Suzie, find a dress for tonight. Ladies we have come to shop can we please have some assistance?" screamed Carmichael and all the store assistants came over to help; to be honest they all fancied Carmichael.

We had an absolute ball and even bought clothes for the holiday; it was electric. Carmichael was as usual spot on for time and we met the boys as planned. Fred opened the boot and deposited the buys as well as the clothes exchanged for new dresses being worn. The girls looked gorgeous in summer dresses as the boys were suited and booted as they say. Carmichael handed Harold a packet of Compeed and told him that if the wife's new shoes started to pinch she will find instant relief with these. Out of the back Fred picked up his camera.

"Right I have my camera here so pics of the day on me." And with that photos of the family outside Hacketts and in outfits in Covent Garden then Fred looked to his watch and said that they would have to get going as time for Tussauds. Harold shook Robbins hand and a tear in his eye as Beverley pushed him aside to give Robbins a hug. She then hugged us, and then Fred who joked, "Alright Beverley, I'm going with you."

"See you sometime when you get back from Disneyland," I said as they all got in the Bentley. The kids screamed with excitement and we heard the CD playing Spandau Ballet 'Through The Barricades'.

"Blimey one o'clock, what now?" asked Robbins.

"ShakeShack," said Carmichael and marched off.

"What?" asked a confused Robbins.

Sat eating our burgers Robbins laughs and said better than home as he devoured his burger. We sat and chatted. We talked about Nichols and it helped Robbins as much as me. Seems Nichols widow had already moved on and took the severance given to her for the children's schooling and upkeep, found a new man, who he suspects she was seeing before, and the kids spend time at his with his family. Robbins reckons the money will all be gone in a couple of years and the kids will not get their school money. I was sad, as Nichols loved his kids it seemed.

"Can I set up a secret fund with you for the kids?" I asked and Carmichael also wanted to help.

"Well my girlfriend and I have already put some of our savings into an account so they should be OK."

"Sod OK!" retorted Carmichael, "our buddy would want you OK too. From the money from Ghana I will place two hundred and fifty thousand into the account and you make sure the money over goes to you and wife as well as making sure Nichols kids get a chance to life their lives. I have no kids so no arguments and no more talk. In fact double the amount and eat up."

There was a silence and then Robbins had a tear in his eye, "Iain, will accept, but from my friend the kids will know when time is right."

"That is up to you, but today we need to stay alive. Better do the transfer at hotel before show as may be dead and unable to later." Carmichael laughed and so did Robbins. Robbins looked to me and squeezed my hand, "Seal humour." It seems Robbins was also once a navy seal.

Lunch finished Robbins phone rang and it was Hugues. Robbins listened and nodded and smiled then hung up.

"Seems Hugues is impressed with new driver and thanked me. But I feel you out did me Iain for Nichols kids. Come on I need to walk these burgers off if I am to enjoy ice cream."

"Ice cream? Wow Robbins, you are living the dream," I remember joking as I walked off out of Covent Garden with these two giants. Not just big tall men, but giants of the heart.

Reader we all have the capacity to be giants, not just with money, but with kindness when needed.

As we walked in the beautiful sunshine of London my phone beeped. I looked and suddenly realised it was because a Serb was close. I looked to the boys who looked around. We popped into hikers store and the beep went again and then we saw two Serbs walking straight past the street. They just happened to be there and realised they were not looking for us; they knew where we would be when they wanted us later. Hugues was right, we were safe until after the show.

Robbins had managed to get a photo of them and so we knew their faces for later. The Serbs disappeared into a perfume shop and we walked on briskly to the Savoy. No point is chancing anything.

I smiled as we entered the hotel as to how Harold and family were getting on when in the front reception was Joseph and Chenguang. Ben and Earl were in their room and we all went for a cold drink at the bar.

Watching how in love Joseph and Chenguang were reminded me of Nichols and I then remembered they had no idea of the honeymoon they were to be having after the show in Rio. I enjoyed the secret and it was a perfect wind down to a special day.

28

Six o'clock and as, well Reader, as the now director of the show and backer, Carmichael and I were ready to meet staff before the parties. Sean had everyone lined up in the terrace rooms and even bar staffs were there. I saw Sergio and his team who smiled at me and gave me the thumbs up. Sean takes my hand and leads me into the room to introduce us.

"OK folks listen up. This is Suzie and Iain, to always to be referred to as Suzie and Iain. They want everyone on first name terms with them and I want all of you to know that you are all to receive a huge tip each in cash at the end of the night as I already have it. These are the most generous clients you will ever have here and make sure that whilst making sure every guest is happy make a point of asking them if there is anything you can get them if passing. So Iain and Suzie, is there anything you would like to say to the team before we start?"

"Sure, love to," I said. "Yep, I am Suzie and this other yank is Iain. We know it will be an incredible party and most guests will leave around an hour before the end possible, which is when if clearing out we want all staff that can stay to come have a drink with us after the party. On your breaks you will all be able to enjoy the food and we want you to enjoy the night. I have three photographers at the event tonight and they all have been told to get selfie shots of you with the stars if you want. Yes as well as if you want a mobile selfie I am sure it will be OK as I am asking all guests to tweet pictures of themselves at the party and show for publicity. Also all photos can be used for future publicity for the Savoy.

The show will run for two months and each of you will be able to book for free a pair of tickets for you and guest to go on us. If anyone is rude to you, if anyone does not behave in a correct manner, then let Iain know, no exceptions, you come first. We have a policy that look after your staff and let them look after your clients. Sean has been magnificent to us and we know that is because his bosses trust him to do his job and he in turn knows you will do yours. Also on breaks you may enjoy your food and drink with us in the party and have an area here where you can enjoy. Do not hound the stars, but if you want to meet someone just ask us or if they are close by say hello, they will love the attention and please note today you will show the world why you at the Savoy are the best staff in the world."

And with this everyone clapped and cheered then a moment of silence as Sean raised his hand, "So everyone knows what he or she is doing? Good and thank you guys for making me proud. Go on bugger off and get in place for guests here in twenty-five minutes," he says to suddenly be interrupted by two of the arsenal football team.

"Sorry we are early as I fretted about traffic and there was none."

"Oh my God you are.." started Iris a waitress.

"In need of a drink gentlemen?" interrupted Sean.

"That would be lovely and heard the speech so Iris can I get my first selfie with you as want to be first to tweet?"

Iris squealed with delight and after the picture told everyone to make way so she could take the players to the bar for a drink. Sean just looked at me rolled his eyes and laughed, "Iris, had to be Iris."

The guests arrive and so do the party of four from the hotel owners. I see them excited by being part of the event, the wives were really excited and started noting who was there, and Sean was able to gesture that he was fine giving up his tickets. Soon the four enter and immediately meet them as they entered the room.

"Ladies, thank you for coming, please order cocktails on us, and have to say they are all amazing as this is the best hotel in London, and gentlemen there is a wonderful selection of drinks as well as bottled lager. I am Suzie and over there is the show's backer and director Iain, and need anything at all the staff here, under the brilliant supervision of Sean, can make you feel right at home."

"We are home, my man here is one of the hotel's owners," says one of the trophy wives. I say trophy wives, as both men were little on conversation and businessmen more than party animals. But I have to say misjudged them as once they relaxed and were chatting to footballers and the Saudi family they relaxed and were amazing hosts. Never judge a book by its cover Reader.

Soon the whole gang were there and Arthur was introducing and being, well Arthur. Guinevere was just amazing as always and she and the ladies of the knights, laughing as I write this Reader, well they were like an immoveable force for good. They had the owners and wives laughing with stars of stage and screen. Carmichael was literally having everyone eat out of the palm of his hand. He kept watching staff look at certain stars and call them over and then ask the star to have a selfie, which they always agreed to. The photographer were told that we were never to be in a photo and in walks Sir John with Paulina, the model make up artist he mentioned in one of his journals. The photographer friend was there too and he was on fire shooting amazing pictures.

Sir John walked towards me and to be honest I wanted to ask where was Marjorie, but didn't have the nerve.

"Miss. Johnson, you look ravishing. May I introduce Paulina, Paulina this is Suzie. Sadly Marjorie could not make the party as she has taken on some Knight's work in a clinic in LA run by Wentworth and Dominic, friends who have set up an HIV call in centre. She sends her love and hopes to see you when you next get home."

"Hello Paulina, let me sort you out a cocktail and Sir John? American champagne?"

Suddenly Elaine arrives and sees Sir John, walking over she is laughing as she has sent Lancelot off to find her a gin and tonic. "Sir John, with the ladies I see. Where is Marjorie or is that a delicate question?"

"Hopefully not," laughed Sir John, "she is in LA, this is Paulina a model and make up artist supreme, and this is a show backer Miss. Suzie Johnson."

"What the girl that shot you?" she exclaims.

Paulina looks shocked and I reply with a smile, "Well I am glad that skeleton is out of the closet."

"Well tonight will be a triumph for me, talk about out of the closet, my man is neither homophobic or ever been shocked by gays, but he is really out of his comfort zone since a colleague announced he was gay then proceeded to get arrested for the most unexplainable acts. I fear he hopes his presence does not draw questions about it. I am loving him look uncomfortable as never knows who anyone is that is famous, so lets all enjoy," and starts to laugh as poor Lancelot finds his way over with drinks.

I excuse myself and make my way to the bar as curtain up tonight is eight and it is already five past seven. I must admit the show will be a shame to go to, as the party already is so good. I see a couple of footballers looking over at Lancelot. He was chatting to Sir John and after a brief chat it seems they are all fans of him and his leadership.

I call to the photographer to follow and soon the look on Elaine's face was the picture as one by one all the stars wanted to shake his hand and have selfie's. At the end of the night the person most photographed turned out to be Lancelot.

Henry came over to join and then asked if he could have a word with him. I said that they could use an area on the terrace and led them out. I stayed to ensure no prying eyes as felt this was about the New Order.

"Arthur was extremely grateful for the papers on the PM and her involvement in the tragedy at the towers. It seems that you hitting her with the fact she buried the report and cancelled works recommended at question time really helped Arthur. He still feels slightly to blame, but has unearthed more info that it was a consortium of investors led by the PM's husband that wanted to originally tear down the blocks and build luxury flats for their own profits. Seemed the council were in on it too, so may be more to fuel the fire she is trying to put out."

"In our moments looking for something to do Carmichael and I also accidently took another file from Work and Pensions Department. Seems the Minister in his report left out these facts that the PM and he concocted that also may be of use," and on a USB hand to Lancelot the information. "I had Arthur go through and check and would like you to have this. Basically, in a bid to bring down unemployment sick benefits there was a purge and tens of thousands were reclassified as fit to work. What the report reveals is that over four thousand of those men and women died with the last six months due to the stress and hardship they faced trying to get to a Job Centre."

Lancelot looked deeply concerned and clenched his fist in anger around the USB and then slipped it in his pocket, "That woman is just pure evil and hear she is working closely with that degenerate moron in the White House to sell him the National Heath Service. Thank you, thank you and thank Arthur. Tonight we enjoy and celebrate as tomorrow we give that shitty PM a kick in the arse!" And with this he walks back into the party and hugs his wife.

As we walk back in Elaine looks at us as if to say 'what did you do to my husband, I like it' and she returned to chat to the Saudi Prince about the work of Chagall.

"Right," shouts Carmichael, "can we get all staff with mobiles to line up from ballroom to main exit as cars and taxis are waiting and we do not want to hold up the show? My friends and guests please walk the isle of staff and we are looking for the best selfie's as you exit."

The staff all get exited and form two rows and soon Iris calls out, "Come on folks, I'm ready." Everyone laughs and as they exit everyone poses with staff and they hash tag the pictures so they are all on a feed that gets uploaded later on twitter and Facebook pages.

At first the owner looked horrified as Iris was there with the Royal family and she sees her boss, "Sir, can we have you with me and the Prince?" The Royal Saudi Prince laughs and beckons him over and soon all are getting in cabs and Bentleys and cars of all nomination, one hundred and twelve in all, and Sergio out does himself as he had arranged a huge police escort all the way to the theatre where huge crowds had assembled.

Iain and I walked into the West End and saw all the Priscilla Drag boys and Uncle Mike welcoming guests. They thought it would be fun and Ian hugs them and we disappear inside. I see Robbins on the desk distributing tickets and then in walks Kowlowski, with three Serbs, one the one I saw with Rory. I froze and then as they went to their seats Robbins nodded he had tagged them.

The show was going to start late as it took time to get all cars to the theatre door and unloaded. Carmichael takes to the stage and there is a thunderous applause as Uncle Mike introduces him. He raises his hands to quell the cheers and one of the drag queens walks past him and looks to the audience, "Don't cheer to much, the show isn't that great." As he exits Uncle Mike looks to Carmichael and smiles, "Give us a minute and I'll sort her out." Uncle Mike then exits and I realise again Carmichael brilliantly choreographed the whole thing.

"Your highnesses, Lords, Ladies, Knights and Gentlemen, as well as a few guests of non denomination. Apologies for slightly late start, but the Arsenal back four created an offside trap hard to beat, but we got there in the end. It is with huge pride that we not only present the Priscilla Boys from the land down under, and do not worry if you are not sure where that is, I am sure they will show you later," a huge cheer and laugh from audience.

"But tonight we not only bring you one of the brightest, most fabulous leading ladies, Erin Cornell ladies and gentlemen," more cheers, "but we introduce a rising new star, who has also written many of the original songs, and tonight will be the toast of the West End, Miss. Katie Raban," again everyone cheers as Uncle Mike pokes his head through the curtains.

"Don't build it up too much, we're bricking it back here," and laughter floods out from the audience as Uncle Mike smiles into the crowd.

"But mainly ladies and gentlemen it is with great honour we bring back to the stage the one and only Uncle Mike," the crowd give huge round of applause and Uncle Mike takes a bow then looks to Carmichael.

"Thank you, thank you," and in a stage whisper and audible aside to Carmichael, "get off the stage we want to get going," and he smiles and bows at the audience as Carmichael gets offstage.

The lights dim and the curtain rises, and within ten minutes the show is a huge hit. Erin hits notes that were scientifically impossible, Katie wows the audience, Uncle Mike makes them laugh and then the Priscilla boy bring empathy and tears stream as they sing a song about it is hard to be a woman when you are born a man.

After an hour on non-stop applause and performance the first act ends. Uncle Mike announces in a comedic way, "Right bar open, waitresses available just raise a hand, and gentlemen please aim straight when using the loos."

Then some of the Priscilla Boys come out in drag as waitresses and bottles of Prosecco and glasses and sell to everyone in the seats that did not want to get up. The buzz and energy was amazing. I watched as Kowlowski and friends did not move, they remembered Carmichael and me and where happy as they knew they would soon have their money.

Carmichael went backstage and told the performers how amazing they were and took time to ensure all stage crew were equally as magnificent. He returned to walk to the lighting and sound guys and patted them on the back telling them everything was wonderful. He laughed with them saying that at the party after we would all enjoy a drink.

All sat in the curtain rises for the second act and the applause is so long and loud Uncle Mike walks out on stage, "Alright, alright, stop taking the piss. As soon as we get this over with we can all hit the chippy, now settle down and behave."

Katie sings her Bond-like ballad and it is a complete showstopper. Erin and all the boys and stage crew come on stage in full view to applaud her. Katie turns as did not know they are they are there and starts to cry as Uncle Mike shouts, "Quick! Make up she's blubbing, oh and Erin, darling, follow that." All leave stage and Erin stands looking out at audience. There is a small laugh and she looks nervous, but what she did next was sing a song about never being good enough that took the audience from laughter to tears, to a standing ovation.

Comedy and tears follow as the boys all do their part and if it hadn't been for Uncle Mike, as a sort of improvised MC telling the audience to 'stop clapping as really now it was taking the piss' we would have been there for another hour.

As the audience exit for cars I see Robbins call me to the side of the stage with Carmichael and we notice our Serb friends stay seated and look to one another. Slowly they rose and walked to the stage and to the steps to the side. As the audience left, one by one they nipped up onto the stage to find us.

Robbins was there to give us a nod as to when to go through a certain door to a room for special guests Arthur had arranged. They watched the show out of sight from everyone.

"You guys with the backers, they went to the room up the stairs," said Robbins and then Kowlowski and his three Serb henchmen followed.

Carmichael and I entered the room and there was no one there. We looked at each other and thought we had made a mistake as Kowlowski entered and showed he was wearing a gun.

"I believe you two have my money," Kowlowski said to be interrupted in Russian by a voice that appeared from a side room. I will interpret as best I can Reader the gist.

"What money would that be, my friend?" In walked the Russian Prime Minister and completely threw Kowlowski.

Kowlowski looked around as a stunning blonde woman in a man's suit appeared and held out her hand, "Lucy Wilshaw and I believe the President was asking about what money, these two have your money?"

"Mr. President, we were in Africa looking to a special deal and these two conned us out of the money, my friends..." Kowlowski looking round cannot see the Serbs, "Mr. President, these two and two CIA agents stole five hundred million dollars in bonds in what was to be a sting that we were to bring to you in person, but in Africa we were ambushed."

"The President has been made aware and hopes that upon your return to Moscow you will be able to meet up and explain the money, and he knows that these two were never in Ghana as a good friend has explained they were with him in Brussels," said Lucy, "and according to your diary and records you were not in Africa either so the five hundred million does not exist and when we meet in Moscow all will be seen to be nothing missing. It seems that there is other amounts needed to be rectified and upon your return the President hopes you will be able to account for all."

"Mr. President. If those Serbs have been stealing I will personally get to the bottom of it."

"Mikalei, Mikalei, I am in a meeting here although no one knows I am here, but rumour has it an American has offered to pay to the money back, so I leave you to do the deal and I expect all to be sorted by the end of this week. Well Arthur, it is Arthur is it not?" says the President as Arthur appears.

"I trust you enjoyed the show Mr. President and on behalf of the Knights I do hope you can help curb the senseless attacks as agreed on the LGBT community. As for this meeting, never happened and the items we discussed will never be discussed again." With that Arthur shook the President's hand, Lucy translated and the President smiled then he placed his arm on Kowlowski's shoulder and walked him down to an obscured door that led through Uncle Mike's flat and out over the roof to waiting cars.

Arthur smiled and shook Carmichael's hand, "Serbs are no more, you young lady were correct in so many areas and yes that was the President of Russia, but let me be the first to say congratulations the show was incredible. Come on, let's get to the party, wife will kill me if we are delayed any longer."

"Thank you Arthur," I said and kissed him on the cheek.

"Tonight we enjoy all we have and the day after tomorrow we will reconvene and there is a bigger mission to be sorted.

It was surreal Reader. The show was the best thing ever and the party was totally lavish and nobody left until 2am when Sean and his team literally threw even the Saudi's out, to their rooms.

But the most poignant moment came when a tearful Priscilla Boy received a text and it was news breaking of Rory's death. Erin took to the raised Dias and helped up her drink and made the most moving speech. We stood there as with raised glass she dedicated the show to Soho. I will never forget her speech and today Reader, friends of the British PM and her husband is trying to sell off prime lands to developers for profit to kill the squares and community that is Soho. Stood with raised glass she gave a most moving speech.

"Dear friends and honoured guests as one of many of the shows performers I want to thank you all for coming. I thank our director and backer for making this show so much more than we could of wished, to a beautiful young American called Suzie who helped beyond our dreams and delivered us Katie. To Soho for delivering us all the amazing Uncle Mike. He steals the show and reminds us all that his wife's dream to keep the integrity of Soho, and opportunity for creatives and those that are lost as a beacon to come to, to those that live in Soho and fight for her against developers and false prophets allowing this part of the people's London from being sold out. To all the LGBT community, the creatives, the minorities, the lost and orphaned who make Soho a wonderful showcase for London and its diverse communities living together in her breast. Yes Soho is the breast and heartbeat of London. As a foreigner I feel at home in Soho and urge everyone to help fight the moronic change being forced upon the people by the gentry and rich. Soho has given us great characters. We lost the Prince of Soho, Bernie Katz, who could only have been moulded in Soho and today we lost the Queen of Soho in dear friend Rory. Our show is like a group of misfits that come together and produce something wonderful and tonight in the middle of London's theatreland we showed being different made the world a better place. So I do not toast the show, I do not ask you to toast, Rory or Bernie, I ask you to toast with me the heart of London and dedicate our show to Soho."

"To Soho," cries Lancelot and followed with cheers and applause from everyone there.

Lancelot and Arthur were literally in different corners of the room. Neither chatted to each other and all noticed there was a distance between them. Reader this was so that the New Order and the PM were reported that there was a rift between them. Truth is Arthur hand handed Lancelot another grenade to throw at the PM during Prime Minister's Question Time.

One of the owners of the hotel asked who Bernie Katz was and Erin smiled, "He managed for decades the Groucho Club. Was loved by everyone, abrupt and rude, but always really funny with it. Even the Big Issue sellers close by the club loved Bernie. You own a hotel just a short walk from the most vibrant area in London, do you not feel may be we need to save the area as something we should all be interested in?"

"We will make friends in the House of Lords aware and have folks from Save Soho some funds to fight," he said and then moved to the bar where his wife was enjoying selfies with stars.

"Don't worry Erin, he will be part of the developers or friends of developers trying to buy up property, but great speech. Can I get you some more prosecco?" asked Arthur.

Sat in the hotel in the aftermath of the party all the staff were looking at mobiles and all their pictures and I see a worn out Sean having a sneaky cup of tea. In fact he made tea for many of his staff and centre stage was Iris showing Erin all her pictures.

"I got one of me with all the stars, in fact every star here tonight," said Iris and Erin laughed as she said that she loved the picture of Iris and Katie. "Did you get any love?" Iris asked Erin.

Sean handing Erin another prosecco laughs and takes Iris's phone from her. Laughing as he looks at the picture then looks to Iris, "You are one of a kind Iris, you have everyone, but Erin."

"Who's Erin?" Iris asks.

"I am," said Erin.

"Well I haven't got one of you and me either Sean," Iris jokes, "but even though you are not a star you are a star to me, come on in you come, Erin can you take it?"

"Sure," says Erin and takes a picture.

Then after the picture was taken Iris asks Erin, "Did you get any good selfie's on your phone?"

"She never had time," says Sean.

"Oh I'm sorry," said Iris, "how come?"

"She was the star of the show!" exclaimed an exasperated Sean. Everyone in the room was watching and roared with laughter. Iris does a double take and without an ounce of shame hands Sean her phone, "Quick Sean, get me with Erin. I didn't know you were in the show, what do you do?"

"I sing a little," laughs Erin and in true Erin Cornell style hugs Iris and starts to laugh.

"Listen, Erin all the boys have gone out clubbing and Uncle Mike is back home safely tucked up in bed no doubt. But we have one suite for you so you do not have far to get to bed and a Knight turned up earlier and left clothes for you so that tomorrow afternoon you can use for all TV and Radio interviews."

Erin looks to Sean as if to say 'Really?' and he smiles and looks to Iris and gives her a hug. I looked to see everyone tired and lots to tidy, but suddenly a fresh team arrived and Sean shook their hands.

"OK folks, everyone into the bar for last drinks and I have organised a team to tidy up as you guys look too tired as I thought you would be. Come on folks before I change my mind and if you want to make a move please know that I am proud of all of you."

"We love you Sean," shouts the staff and we all made our way to the bar. Some sat in the bar and some hugged and left.

One stunning young waiter was smitten with Erin and when she went to bed the young lad disappeared too. My lasting memory going to bed was Sean's smiling face. Plus the Serbs really were no longer looking for me.

As I got into bed and relaxed feeling that things were good I thought about Lucy Wilshaw, who the hell was she? I thought about how I laughed and cried watching the show. Then thought about the millions and Kowlowski before I realised I was in bed alone.

Carmichael was missing. I panicked and grabbed my mobile. His mobile rang and he never answered. I started to worry as Kowlowski was left to sort out the millions and he had seen Carmichael. Kowlowski was vicious and I started to get dressed when the room phone rang. It was Carmichael.

I could hear loads of noise and it was Carmichael. He was out with the Priscilla boys and in full drag at a club under the arches. He was having the time of his life and said he had been calling me, but I never was answering. He was worried. He told me to look in the drawer in the bedside table and hung up.

I looked in the drawer to find a beautiful Breitling watch and a note saying thank you and that the watch represented thanks for the timing we met, for knowing that he has time always for me if ever I need him and being with me has been the best time of his life. I slept well.

29

I wake at 10am and slowly rise as I shower, dress and lastly put on my new watch before going downstairs. Today was a day of rest and tonight I was looking forward to a relaxed evening after checking the theatre. All the staff were coming in around 11am and collecting their tips from Carmichael. Sat watching out of sight as they come out of the office in shock and smiling.

I see Iris see me and she comes over and gives me a hug. Then motions to not move and rushes back into reception and I see Sergio looking tired off duty nod he knows where something is and together they both return with the papers.

"Morning Miss. Suzie," says Sergio, "the party was in such full swing we never read the reviews, but you have to see them, they are incredible."

Across the board the show was a massive hit. Erin was hailed as one of the West Ends greatest voices, as was Katie and the critics picked up on Erin's speech and stories ran of how developers were running one of London's greatest landmarks and calls to halt many projects in Soho. One story led 'Soho London's Heart was in need of love'.

I got a call from Arthur saying to visit the offices at twelve noon, if I was able as it was going to be a fun day. I looked at my watch and called Carmichael. He had stayed at the house with the boys and would be slowly getting back to the hotel to meet me at six at the theatre.

With great reviews and sat now in the bar with Erin reading the reviews I realise that doing something for others is amazing. It was 10:45 am and 7:45pm in Melbourne. I handed Erin my mobile and smiled, "It's your mum for you."

"Mum, oh my God mum, I miss you...the reviews they are phenomenal. Yes every one... phenomenal. Yes having breakfast with a backer called.. yes Suzie? What? OMG! Mum really, next week? I will find you somewhere to stay... The Savoy? What?"

I walked to reception and left them to chat and Erin read her mum the reviews. I had sorted out that her family will come see the show and stay at the Savoy, in fact Sean gave me a rate I could not refuse. Sergio walked over to me and looked to see who was about before hugging me.

"Miss. Suzie, everyone paid, everyone happy and everyone wants to say thank you. All drivers got tips from your guests and so I have left over from my budget £4,300. Would you like it in cash as Mr. sorry Iain gave me cash to pay everyone, or shall I give it to Iain or transfer to your bank?"

"Sergio you did an amazing job in a really short time so take you and your daughter, she is seven is she not? Take them to Disneyland or wherever you choose and say no more. But only on one condition."

"Of course name it, but I would rather hand you the money I feel that it would be wrong to take from such nice people."

"Sergio, take it to make up for all the not so nice people and with our thanks. Can you sort out a car for me to take me to the Houses of Commons?"

"Whenever you wish?"

"I will need it at half past eleven and thank you," and with this squeezed his hands like an old friend and went back to my suddenly dizzy blonde Erin.

Erin jumped up and hugged me, "My family and staying here, are you nuts?!" she screamed.

"Great reviews and the show is going to make a lot of money it seems with the theatre booked for six months and up to you for what after that. Listen, what did you think of Katie's reviews? Some gushed more about her than you."

"She was wonderful and my big song she wrote so I am so pleased for her. Listen you guys have taught me so much about doing things because we can and I am over the moon that when she hits the stratosphere as a megastar I can say I gave her her her first big break. Seriously though, some of the papers raved about the boys more too, seemed we all got amazing comments. That show and party last night was the greatest night of my life. In fact it took so much out of me feel as if I have just completed a three-month run in one night. You coming tonight as be nice to have a more sedate intimate celebration just the crew and cast. I was thinking of cooking and having us all have a quiet one where we are staying. You up for it?"

"I think Iain and I would love it. Oh is that the time, have to dash, see you later," I said as I saw Sergio signal car was ready.

I quickly dashed to my room and fetched my files I had and then next thing I know I am grinning and laughing at Sergio as there he is waiting for me with the Bentley.

"Only the best for you Suzie," he quips and off I drive down the Strand to Trafalgar Square and then towards Parliament in a beautiful Bentley.

Growing up in America we have Disney Princesses, but here in the UK you have real Princesses and I felt like one as I admired my watch realising for the first time it is from the Bentley range of Breitling. The driver pulls up at the main gates and opens the door. I step out to be greeted by a British Bobby. No guns, no tough talk, but a real gentleman.

"Morning Miss, are you here to see someone in particular?"
"Yes I am expected at the Knights Office for twelve."

Looking at his clipboard he smiled and said, "Ah yes, Miss. Suzie Johnson have you hear. Tobias?" he called to another young bobby, "will you escort Miss. Johnson to the Knight's Offices?"

"Yes Sarge," Tobias replied and then motioned for me to follow.

"Call me if you get lost Miss, it is his first day," and with that he went back to his hut and sipped on his mug of tea.

Tobias duly delivered me to the Knight's Office and to be sure had I to come again would have to ask directions as walking through the halls I was mesmerised by the beauty and stunning walls and tapestries and paintings, that the building itself overawed me. Tobias knocked on the door and opened it for me to enter and as I walked in there was Arthur in the boardroom with a rather stern looking woman not happy at all. It was the PM herself. I waited, but Robert asked me to join him in the printing room. As we entered I saw others giggling inside. They were all watching and listening to the PM losing her rag with Arthur, not at Arthur, just at everything.

"And this whole tower burning fiasco is another nightmare, of course that twat, a friend of yours no less, got files showing it was me at the Home Office deciding not to commit to making buildings safe, you of course get off scot-free!" she rants and all smile at me in the room.

"She's been in there twenty minutes," says Robert.

"What the fuck were you doing when Prime Minister? I mean you left me with this fucking Brexit shit to deal with, that you know cannot be dealt with as those twats that led the campaign have all fucked off as everything they promised was a lie, which we both knew, then there is my total arse of a Brexit Minister trying to showboat and making things worse as he hasn't got a clue! Then I have to go and again take shit from your friend the opposition and have nothing to steer him away from this tower deaths and just makes me look even worse.."

"OK Quetty, that'll be your cue," says Henry and Quetty leaves the room to interrupt the PM.

"Excuse me Prime Minister, but sir the report you wanted I have managed to find facts that will help as instructed for Prime Minister's Question Time." And Quetty places the file in front of Arthur. "I like your shoes Prime Minister," she says and exits closing the door.

"And what is this file might I ask, and why do you employ her kind so high up, you know that her sort are lesser intelligent that us?" says the PM and everyone looks at Quetty who is visibly angry and then smiles as if never heard saying under her breath, "Well we find out how stupid she is shortly." We all turn to the monitor again.

"Prime Minister, Quetty has one of the highest IQ's in this building and anyway she just may have saved you. Seems that the previous opposition government also had reviews on the same building and put them off to be reworked. Quetty feels that if you gave a speech like this one she prepared then you may just dodge completely the bullet."

Arthur hands the Prime Minister the file and walks to the window. "Prime Minister one word of advice I would say is that no matter what anyone says against you just smile, it looks as if you are listening, it looks as if you care and you will enjoying smiling more as you know it will piss the other person off who is trying to rile you. Quetty has a speech there saying that accepting blame is not the issue and that collectively the responsible thing in light of no one person responsible, but to collectively accept the tragedy and work together to make things better and safer moving forward. The plans you set out have been derided as we feel you were poorly advised and feel you should look to who came up with initial plan as they are first person we feel is after your job, go beyond the norm, take over hotels in the area and cost rates on hotels for all survivors still homeless and then set up a group to rehouse as quickly as possible. Quetty also has a list of empty homes that could be done up and we have the Guardians as a workforce ready to make habitable. In three weeks all could be sorted. Anyway time is ticking and wish you well today Prime Minister."

Arthur walks to open the inner door and then walks the Prime Minister to the main door and outside her aides walk her to the commons.

As soon as she leaves Arthur makes sure he is seem just looking out the window. Behind me Chastity calls Lancelot on her mobile and we all listen.

"Hello sir, the wicked witch has the parcel and time to loose a battle to win another." Chastity hangs up and all in the room high-five.

"Come on Suzie, Arthur wants a chat," and I follow Chastity into the boardroom and we are alone, just Arthur and I. Robert walks in with two mints teas and smiles at me before addressing Arthur, "Two mint teas Arthur and if you want more kettles full of hot water, we are all off to the gallery to watch, fantastic reviews for last night and we are all a little worse for wear, but congratulations and see you later." With that Robert exits and shuts the door as the others leave the office waving as they go.

"You have an amazing team Arthur."

"Yes, hand picked everyone of them, but not by me, I think you know by whom and how we arrive here today. I am sorry Suzie, but a bad day. I live not far from the towers and I feel I should of done more as PM. It is funny you fight to rise to the top, beat the opposition and then when you are there powerless as the civil servants run most of the country, cabinet runs policies you decide how they want to and therefore often master of nothing, but the guy to take the bullet. Now, I am a crusading Knight, a hero and yet placed in this position by pure accident and receive all the praise and plaudits that should be given to you and all the other Invisibles. If it wasn't for Sir John and Jimmy none of this would of happened, the new fascist rising in place unopposed and you adding with others in the network still making changes I only ever dreamed about."

"I believe Sir John once told the story of GJ Isaac, a great Invisible man who did so much and died without a fanfare, and yet attributed all his success to the people for once seeing being wise and without the help of good men like you it was all pointless. Invisibles can only do what they do if there is assistance from good men like you are today. Collective Intelligence. Now you wanted to see me? What gives? You about to tell me of your defying love for me and want to leave Guinevere for me?"

"Good God No! I mean, you're joking; of course, sorry I am running on sixty percent today. Hugues called to see when you could pop to New York as we need some Intel. Listen I feel you should have a rest personally so it can wait."

"Hugues is a good man too, he would only ask if he felt he had to. What is up?"

"We have a report that Kowlowski and the President of the United States are far more connected than we first thought. It seems Yerno was keen to do a duff deal to appease Kowlowski. Our informants see Yerno amazing funds to make sure Kowlowski gets the five hundred million and a further five hundred million as a sweetener. Now why Yerno would save Kowlowski who is already under the bus we do not know. You would be Emma Beauchamp again and have access to the Pentagon as a British strategist on a trade embargo mission. We need to find out all their links and as quickly as possible."

"Arthur, who is Lucy Wilshaw? We met her with the Russian President last night; she is British, MI6 or what? If it is OK for me to ask?"

"Lucy is an Invisible like you. You did not know? I forget you often never know each other for safety as, I feel I should not of said, but she will be meeting you tonight for a drink as she has some info also we need to follow up on with Kowlowski. Listen, let's cheer ourselves up watching Prime Minister's Question Time."

We sat there watching the television and sipping our mint tea while the sun shone in through the windows of Parliament. I enjoyed the quiet and relax to be honest, but what followed Reader truly made my heart pump and I felt ecstatic.

The Prime Minister is taking a bashing from Lancelot, the odds are stacked against her and Lancelot is going for the political kill. The country majority hate the PM as she is useless and yet continues. After another attack from Lancelot she stands and literally just stands and waits for the house to quieten. Raising a hand she smiles and places

Quetty's report in front of her then delivers line for line on how all the country should take responsibility, that we should not fight in a crisis, but come together, all the time building herself up with confidence as she sees she has the mass of MP's in what she feels will become a career defining moment. She starts to talk passionately and with regal mannerisms and then lets Lancelot have it, "My dear colleagues on both side of the house we have been truly looking into how such a disaster could of happened and yes much was on our watch, my predecessor did not act as swiftly as he should of and the opposition government, not then run by my learned friend opposite also did nothing as they too were conflicted with the dilemma of what to do with the towers and in fact it was their government that made the decision to place cladding on the towers to making them look better to view for the wealthier neighbours surrounding, but they had no idea that they were so dangerous. None of us did, but I do not want a witch-hunt, no for no one wins and certainly not the people surviving the towers or those that lost their lives. I want a combined effort seeking 'which' way best forward to prevent such tragedy, 'which' way forward to securing safer homes for all and call on the whole house to join me in choosing the right way forward for those people above all else." Huge cheers come from both sides of the house and Lancelot stands and the PM gives way.

"Prime Minister, I concur and at last feel you have finally come forward after doing nothing for too long. My party fully supports this initiative and look forward to helping the people as they always come before party with my party."

The PM smiles as she feels his remark stains her image and remembers to smile. "I have a plan worked on tirelessly here to propose that we take housing available, have the Guardians make ready as new homes and in the meantime take over local hotels to house the people."

A massive round of applause and there is huge cheers and shouts from both sides of the house. Lancelot once again rises from his seat and a smug PM gives way. She feels completely safe, in her fortress, impregnable, but Lancelot smiles and the whole chamber quiets after the Speaker of the House announce him to speak.

"I am truly overwhelmed by the generosity shown by the government and something not seen in a long time," and soon the government faithful start to heckle and mock Lancelot. I see Arthur lean forward to watch more intently the TV as Lancelot looks around and up to the gallery then turn and smile.

"Prime Minister, you have finally put the people first and look forward to helping the housing you suggest in the report in front of you being made ready, and I am sure they are local not two hundred miles away as previously suggested." More jeers and the PM stands and hands Lancelot a copy of the plan. This is unprecedented and Lancelot takes and reads then looks up, "Well jeer me all you like, but I have to say this looks very promising and seems that the housing selected here would be perfect for the situation, and in this season of goodwill, on this point I would like to congratulate the Prime Minister and her team on this report." Cheers ring out and even the opposition front bench stand and applaud the PM. It is scenes never seen.

"Come on my friend, now, come on, give it to her," says an excited Arthur. I look and he smiles at me, "I love being in politics, well being involved," he grins.

"Prime Minister, now that we have an agreement on this may you please devote your attention to another distressing matter that we have to deal with?" Lancelot leans on the dispatch box and looks back at his party members and gives them a little wink, as to them he is losing dreadfully to the opposition. The PM waves, in a manner you would expect from the Queen.

"I have here a report omitted from your unemployment figures that are most distressing. It would appear in light of your newfound 'put the people first' mode your Minister for Works and Pensions does not feel the same. It came to our attention that a constituent in Devon recently recovered from cancer, cannot have much needed operation to her knees due to have to wait until cancer drugs flush from her system, is called to a 'works assessment'. Yes, and after struggling to get the forty miles on public transport is meet by the government's assessment team to go through a hundred and fifty page form to fill in, during the filling in of report she has a medical and all is stopped as it appears that on top of all her other ailments she has had a mini stroke. Now members of the house, yes I am about to get to the point, it appears that after the assessment, seeing this lady incapacitated, cannot walk without crutches, told she has just had a minor stroke receives a letter through the post saying she is fit to work. She has to sign on costing her expense as she already is on the poverty line that means spending money to sign each Friday she cannot use to feed herself. Oh, and also she is still grieving the recent loss of her father she was looking after.

But if she does not turn up she cannot appeal. Now to the point, this is not an isolated case as your Minister is well aware of. It seems tens of thousands of people were taken off the ESA sick benefits in a move to shift numbers. In the past six months four thousand of these people have died, will the Prime Minister give us her reaction to this, tell us why the report was left out, and what she intends to do about this putting the people first not herself and Ministers?"

As Lancelot sits the chamber surges into a wave of cheers and jeers at a beleaguered PM. The camera pans onto her face. Not smiling, seething and her true colours grabbing towards the Minister who holds his hands up as not his fault and she stands.

The Prime Minister stands as if a woman in stocks having rotten fruit pelted at her and the Speaker shouts above the din for 'Order'. The noise is deafening and the Government Party MP's look as horrified as the opposition at the news. Holding up her hand as before an opposition backbencher shouts out, "What's the matter Prime Minister, want to leave the room?" and everyone laughs as the Speaker once again cries for 'Order'.

"I thank my learned friend and without the full facts in front of me this is an emotive point that I will look into."

Lancelot stands and handing the seating PM over the dispatch box the damning file, "Prime Minster in looking to follow your suit of transparency and working together, please have this copy, it is a terrifying read and highlights that this is a government that has no care for the people that it is elected to govern!" The chamber goes wild and the Speaker calls to an end Prime Minister's Question Time. The opposition exit cheering as they have trounced the government, made the PM look horrendous and after placing herself on a pedestal the PM exits with ministers furious and lets her anger show.

Soon Quetty and everyone re-enter the offices laughing and cheering when Arthur motions to calm them down. The telephone rings and Arthur answers, "Knight's Office, yes Prime Minister, I agree I watched. Quetty's piece was a triumph though and it seems all are off the hook on the towers, but... yes Prime Minister, but where did he get the leak on the unemployment figures. Exactly, I was literally so proud of your speech delivered perfectly and yet then all undone by that bumbling idiot... yes he will pay for it I am sure. Would you like something on him for help with..... I am sure we can help and I am always happy to assist a former and valued colleague. Why thank you Prime Minister, of course Prime Minister, talk soon." Arthur hangs up and motions all to the Boardroom.

As the last Knight enters and shuts the door Arthur congratulates them on a very productive day, "We must now surge ahead without delay having the Guardians prepped and ready to make good in three weeks all the properties on that list and the Prime Minister has given me the go ahead to get it going asap. Get a statement out that Prime Minister immediately acts to help the people of the tower tragedy and Guardians amassing an army to win the war against poverty on the Government's instructions."

Arthur looks incredibly pleased with himself, "I am about to scream folks so please excuse me as I take Suzie to lunch and then will be with my wife after that. Chastity, can you take the lead as we do not want there to be a link to you Quetty as you are innocent of everything about to happen. I tell you Suzie we should be writing 'Game of Cards', TV show is far paler in comparison. Everyone good, right, come on Suzie I am starving off to a friend's new venture in Acton. Henry, you need me be at Tailor Made. Come on Suzie keep up you need to get me out of here. Print room exit I think best," and with this Arthur and I are dashing out of the Houses of Parliament into a cab and off to Acton.

30

Sat in Tailor Made, a well-designed, funky spot you would expect to find in the West End Arthur and I blend in as just everyone else and look at the menu. Andrew is in the kitchen and his brother Michael is sat at his laptop working on something for another event. Andrew steps out and sees Arthur.

"You came back, Michael, put the laptop down we have friends with us," says Andrew as Michael looks up as if he was literally miles away starts apologising and looks at the waitress who is already giving us menus and water.

"Andrew, Michael, this is a good friend of mine and the wife will be joining us later, sorry this is Suzie."

Both were incredibly gracious and were Greek heritage and both made me laugh. It was just such a great spot to visit. We both ordered the Salad Nicoise and I had a lovely glass of red wine, a large red wine, and Arthur had a white. It was so laid back and unpretentious and a Greek restaurant that loved creativity.

Arthur handed me a USB and told me on it were the details of the young Indian girl taken from the dispute with the POTUS daughter's business. Seems that Kowlowski was building his own little empire and using the Serbs as muscle to sort out things that needed attention. The young girl, who was twenty, had also allegedly stumbled upon a file in the office where she picketed that was very sensitive to the President's daughter and Yerno. In fact it is rumoured to be the blueprint for much of the family wealth and how they rose to infamy and where their fortune came from. The girls name is Prisha, and she was abducted and removed to safe house that was thought to be in Middle East.

It was explained that the Knight's Templar had not managed to gain access to the inner circle since the money being lost in Ghana, but hoped an Invisible could make way to find out where the girl is. Now we know what we know from Lucy, you met last night, whom was caught by the President in Moscow trying to save her, but it was too late and she gained clemency as President had no idea of New Order or Kowlowski's movements.

When she was caught one of the President's highest Ministers, a Minister working undercover that the President has never met, called to say that he should contact me. I listened then looked at Arthur.

"Have you met this mysterious Minister?"

Arthur smiled and answered, "I believe he is close to Sir John. Listen Suzie I am sorry to ask, but we need this girl to help stop a new East West Cold War that would happen and give the New Order a great cover to work under. How's your salad?"

"Sorry, what, oh the salad is great, sorry just taking it in and yes I am of course happy to travel," I said. "Would tomorrow night be good?"

"That would be awesome as you American's say," joked Arthur who then stood and smiled as Guinevere entered, " Darling please tell me you did not buy in the auction?"

"Sit down you idiot," she laughed, "Suzie, sorry to of left you with him alone, hope he wasn't too much of a bore?" Guinevere as always had a way of calming even the roughest of seas so an entrance and a glass of wine ordered she told us that she had bought a stunning desk that was once owned by Winston Churchill and was for Arthur to write his memoires at. "Mind you I will have to edit so Reader's do not fall asleep," she joked.

Arthur's mobile beeped and he looked at message to see the PM had made the Leader of the Council resign as it appears they had two hundred and fifty million in funds and could of easily carried out the work needed when first discussed three years ago, but it was for the poor so not high on a Tory council to do list. Arthur hung his head in shame and Guinevere lifted his face in his hands and kissed him.

I left them to go see the desk while I caught a tube into Piccadilly and meet Carmichael who seemed to be buzzing about some sponsorship deal for the show. He literally saw me and ran towards me and lifted me off the ground swinging me around.

"Put me down, what is this amazing news, you are dragging up full time?" I laughed and Carmichael could not stop hugging me.

"Come on inside Uncle Mike is waiting as told him would not say a thing until you got here." And we rushed into the theatre past a queue to the box office and up into Uncle Mike's flat and rooms.

Uncle Mike is making a bacon sandwich, big over here in the UK and the smell is incredible. I thought Uncle Mike was Jewish, but turns out he was or is, but loves bacon sandwiches as his only sin, well only sin he would admit to.

"Right she is here now will you please tell me your news before you have a heart attack. He has been pacing up and down and driving me mad." Uncle Mike looks at me as we both watch Carmichael try to compose himself.

"Right let me start by saying that I have had projections on the box office and six months as we sell out that will net me a profit of nearly twenty million. I had no idea theatre if goes well was so financially rewarding. The Saudi's also loved the show and one of the Princes joined us last night and seems he likes boys more than girls and interested in investing in future shows and in exchange he has a secret base here in Soho. Now I realise this is all subject to you Uncle Mike, but I have a plan that I feel you may agree to and be in keeping with your wife's wishes."

"Can you pass the ketchup?" asked Uncle Mike as if unmoved.

Un-deflated Carmichael continued and held both of our hands, "Right this is proposal as we are all linked to the show and theatre as all want the same. Now I have made twenty million means with each of us third backers I want to draw up contract and back date so you all benefit."

"You what?" exclaims Uncle Mike, "so you saying you will split money profits, that would mean each having earn six million, are you for real?"

"Iain, I don't expect anything and..."

"Suzie, none of this would of happened without you and know that you have no earner at present so I would feel happier if you were financially secure. Listen Uncle Mike, cannot go into what has happened between me and this amazing woman, but last night as you slept Soho partied, well I did with the boys and also Katie, and in chatting to everyone we met they were over the moon that Uncle Mike had a hit; you have helped nearly everybody we met." Carmichael hugged Uncle Mike and said that there is more.

"Katie was looking backstage and found in a desk by the stage door these old drawings and I realised they were by your wife. This was her dream and so try not to interrupt and I will explain the plan."

I look at a stunned Uncle Mike who was motionless and looking at his bacon sandwich I took it from his hand before he dropped it and offered him a tissue as seeing the plans had bought a tear to his eye.

"OK Uncle Mike here goes. We have the second entrance opened up at the back out of sight of public and also your flat is accessed via stage door. The rear green room will become a garage for two cars and a lift in the side to take you to the new penthouse suite at the top. The rooms below rented to stars of shows as well as a second apartment for you Uncle Mike. The theatre to have a complete makeover and in the basement we build a dance studio rehearsal room, and recording studio next door. The building to the side is also free to buy and we develop that as further accommodation for rentals or stars depending on show. All revenues are yours

Uncle Mike. Penthouse will be for the use of the Prince and he will pay for all refurbs and buildings as his donation to do up the theatre to these plans by your wife. So after this show ends the theatre will be closed for a year to refurbish with the Guardians in and out and you can choose all designs for your flat and rooms. The theatre to be multi venue as can be a cabaret diner as your wife saw with easy transformation or theatre as is. We would loose a few seats as we extend bars and new stalls dance floor, this was the boys' idea and Prince loved, that the audience can come see a show and then stalls exit, seating and floor disappear down and a dance floor would cover from under stage move out on hydraulic lifts. So to end we are all joint owners of this show, the Prince has a lifetime lease on penthouse built and upon his death resort back to being owned by theatre freeholder, Prince pays for years major refurb, and we buy the property next door for three million to be owned by you Uncle Mike and manage. Figures as such subject to stars of show benefitting from profits to be worked out. So Uncle Mike what do you think?"

"You're an idiot," he says with deadpan face and looks at me, "he's a nice idiot though and I still do not understand half of what you have said, but I really liked the bit where Erin and guys get bonuses."

I hug Uncle Mike and we note it is now nearly six and the performers are starting to come in.

"OK, let's agree to this. In six months time we take five million each and that would leave five million. There are seven boys, Katie and Erin so how about we give each performer £250,000 bonus at end of show as many want to buy flats in Ibiza and a nest egg to take worries of being unemployed off

304

their to do lists. And the remaining funds treat the theatre staff by paying them a years pay whilst we are closed, we have a staff bill from box office to stage door and crew heads that only come to eleven each paid £45,000 to then come back so we do not lose them is then meaning we have two million contingency to help any lost youngster on the run from home, rehabilitation from addictions and employ them to run our new bars and coffee shops also in the plans helping them find new starts. Extra funds we leave for you to use as you see falls in line with what your wife would of wanted. What do you say?"

"Yes of course your Pratt!" and Uncle Mike hugs Carmichael, "but can we tell the gang tonight?"

"Yes you can," said Carmichael to Uncle Mike.

"I am flying out tomorrow so tonight let's do the Ivy? Yes?" and I looked at Carmichael's confused face.

"Do you have to?" he asked. I nodded yes, as I was to be invisible again and for fun Iain called all the cast and crew into the stalls and sent Uncle Mike on stage. He then sat at the rear with me and Uncle Mike told them all the plan and even the box office were confused. In fact all turned to look at us and then wanted us to confirm.

"Uncle Mike is a legend as we all know and we made him equal partner, he has decided to proceed as discussed so end of run all off to find place in Ibiza for many, and to the front of house staff you of course can get another job while theatre is dark without affecting pay from us it is up to you. We see you all as family and the versatility of theatre and cabaret venue with full dining and dancing facilities means this theatre will be here for a long time."

One of the boys stood and asked if his money could go to a fund in the name of his friend Rory. I looked at Carmichael and then Uncle Mike spoke up from the stage, "We celebrate Soho, we celebrated how Soho is the heart of London and so I propose that we organise a Soho Mardi Gras in connection with Pride, and we will fund in Rory and dear friend Bernie Katz's name. We can plan whilst running the show so the final show will accumulate with the last week being the nucleus for the Prince and Queen of Soho Mardi Gras."

Everyone hugged and cheered and then Erin raised her hand, "Right you ugly miserable bastards, get your slap on we have a show to do, right boss?"

Erin looked straight at Carmichael and he smiled, "Right, so audience here in an hour now go get ready and Uncle Mike can you have a suggestion box at back door for all to be able to post ideas for the Mardi Gras? Great, and thank you all and will be watching, go on hurry up don't want the audience to arrive and sit in wet seats where you lot have been crying all over them."

They all went backstage and Katie walked up to Iain and kissed his cheek then looked at me, "You don't mind me trying to steal him from you do you Suzie?"

"Think you are woman enough?" I joked.

"Well we both know he is," Katie quipped and ran down the isles to the stage and disappears backstage.

"Will you be in danger?" he asked me.

"Of course not. Just need to meet a friend in New York," I kissed Iain on the cheek, "and anyway I think I have lost you to a star of the stage."

The box office lady is called Delores. She was an ex-working girl and Uncle Mike and his wife took her in, as she was not wanted anymore. "Can I have a moment sir?" Delores asked.

"Iain, call me Iain and sure Delores."

"Well I do not think you know what you have done. Mike and Philomena were two crazy kids in love and managed to put on a show and buy this, as it was destined to be scrapped. How they got the money for the show was selling his beloved Aston Martin car and she sold her house in Clapham. In the years leading up to Philomena's bad health they took in lost causes like me and even Ernie the stage door man was a prize fighter left for dead at his last bare knuckle fight. Just if there is ever anything I can do that can help him please I want you to ask me. Really, I may have been a tart, but you can trust me."

"Delores I know we can trust you and you already have been huge part of this change. Listen make sure that you get that little cottage in Brighton or a nice flat you wanted and not to spend it on anyone else, but you. I know you help out a couple of girls on street as it is, yes I know, so can you do me a favour, if you think they will respect Uncle Mike have them move into the rooms with you in Uncle Mike's and you need two new trainee box office girls do you not?" I asked.

Suddenly another girl appears and it is one of the girls we had been discussing, "Delores, oh I am sorry," she says as did not expect to see us.

"Thanks Delores and may be now would be a good time to find that new staff. Come on in young lady, I am Iain and this is Suzie. Lovely to meet you and Delores thank you." And with that we left the theatre.

"Not planning on going back to States then?" I asked Carmichael.

"I think I will in time. I like it here. May be when the show ends take Katie on a trip to see my old hometown and hopefully that idiot in the White House will be no more. Sense will of taken over the country and we will start to get America back on track to being a country to be proud of."

"Looking forward to New York and have a friend I need to catch up with. I have a mission and suddenly I have a new part to this mission I think will fit nicely." Carmichael looked at me and thought at what I just said before placing his arm round me and we walked to Chinatown and ended up sat in Leicester Square just people watching.

31

Sat in business class on the flight to New York I laugh as I think of the stories I read in Sir John's journals and reflect how my life has changed. I am not sat scared or worried about the new mission, which is still in part about the previous missions, but feeling energised that I am making a difference.

A stunning hostess comes to my booth and asks if everything is OK and I smile saying that life could not be better. As she walked away I thought of Marjorie and Sir John and then to the house in New York; Greenwich Village here I come. I turned in my seat to get comfortable and felt something dig into my chest, it was Nichols pin. Reality strikes and I remember that time is precious. Readers do not waste today, help someone, a stranger or friend and do something for no other reason than you can.

Touch down, customs, taxi and then the house. I have arrived and the warm welcome from Tasha there with her son made me realise that little things matter.

It was lunch and a very flustered Mrs. Hudson enters and looks at me with a wry smile and walks to the kitchen, "Come help me unpack," she cries as she walks away.

Tasha and I look at each other only to hear her son say in an all-knowing voice, "You guys better get moving." We laugh as he then turns to turn on his PlayStation.

In the kitchen we are emptying the groceries and Tasha suddenly stops and laughs about something that happened at work as she was broadcasting a link from the studio to Yankee Stadium when Tasha spotted Ernie and had him called over on screen.

"It was hilarious as Ernie and I chatted and discussed this Yankee team compared to previous and even had Floyd, the young gay lad he works with, talk about he season so far. The studio lapped it up and Floyd and Ernie will be regular spots commenting on how the season is going and helping sort out all ground staff as an everyman's section for the show. They even are paying them to do their own interviews with fans and me in the studio. I was complimented on my knowledge of not just the team players, but all the staff as well, got some serious brownie points there, and they loved your man too."

"Ernie on TV? Oh my heavens whatever next? Don't tell him you told me he is getting extra money, let's see what he says, alright?" Mrs. Hudson laughs and tuts, and then stops in her tracks and turns to me, "Suzie I have placed a yoga mats out for you in the downstairs so you can enjoy garden at same time in case it rains."

"Thanks Eveangelina," I say and the door opens and in walks a blissfully happy Julius and Marielle.

"Hey, mum Julius saw dad on TV, they are all talking about it in the bar. My mobile has not stopped."

"Seems Tasha has made him a TV star so get used to it the network loved it." Mrs. Hudson tuts and nods her head as she opens a bottle of wine and starts to pour some glasses. "I feel we should at least drink to this, my daft old Ernie a TV star, who would of thought it?"

My mobile rings and it is Hugues and he has heard that after our beloved idiot of a POTUS childish speech at the United Nations the British PM was to be giving a talk the following day, but she had a dinner meeting with her hubby and associates the night before and wanted to see if I can find anything out. He hangs up and the doorbell rings, I shout that I'll go to the Ernie appreciation society forming in the kitchen and open the door to see Lucy Wilshaw standing there smiling.

"Heard you'd be here and going to need your help tonight, if you're free?" And with that walks into the house. Lucy was a very positive character, she exuded charm and grace, but was able to say what she wanted and you would say yes not knowing exactly what the question was.

"Does the UK PM know your face?" she asks.

"No, I have been invisible in regards to her, why?"

"I have got you a job as a waitress at a private dinner tonight where she and her husband are meeting a group of British based financiers that are plotting something and just like to know what? Oh by the way I am MI6 and the Russians know I am as we trade information to each other that both want, but won't hurt either of us. I am here trying to find out more about the Yerno deal I believe you may know something about. It's OK Arthur told me to see if you knew anything and I guessed that was his way of saying you did."

"Silver service waiting?" I asked as still on the backfoot.

""No plated and just pouring wine. Seems that the guys meeting are behind Brexit and we still do not know why, as well as want to know their involvement in the New Order. Have you got a white blouse and short black skirt? If not I bought you something in this bag. Hope blouse is big enough; I only got a quick hello at the show in London and remembered you were a girl with an ample bust. Easy way to stay invisible I guess, they always looking down instead of your face. By the way I was recruited from being an Invisible so ask me anything you want to confirm or call Arthur, but we need to be at the address on the card in two hours."

My mobile rings and it is Arthur, "Suzie, really sorry almost forgot to ring. We have Lucy you met with the Russian…. She is already there isn't she? OK. Listen we need to know whether the Intel from that dinner is harmless nonsense or New Order business. Even the German New Order is using a new Nazi party to hide behind. We need to be able to sort out whom to watch. Also Yerno is in New York and looking to meet Kowlowski, but is unaware Kowlowski is at this moment chatting like a canary to his President back home. Tomorrow will send you invite to President's daughter's event and see if you can ascertain anything useful. Sorry, just been hammering on, how was the flight, all good?"

"Yes, everything fine and Lucy is going to be fun to work with I am sure. Can I bring her to the event with me if she is free?"

"Of course will have it done courier tickets now to be there first thing tomorrow morning. Night." And with that Arthur hung up.

"Well it seems I am your waitress and you are my extra for an event with the POTUS daughter and Yerno tomorrow night, I will go get changed, but first come to the kitchen." Lucy follows me to be met by Mrs. Hudson and clan. "Folks, this is a good friend from London, Lucy. Introduce yourselves and please give her a glass of wine." I leave the kitchen to get changed.

As I come down there is another knock at the door and I open to see Big Tony. I give him the biggest hug as Ernie enters at the same time. Big Tony does a double take at Ernie as he strolls in, "Hey Buddy, you're the guy on TV aren't you? Yankee Stadium?"

"We did meet before, but now I am the guy on TV, name's Ernie, Big Tony yes? You going to another concert together?"

"No, I am to drive the ladies to a function," replies Big Tony.

"Lovely, well got to face the wife, is she in the kitchen? No worries I am sure I will find her." And with that Ernie goes into the kitchen to load squeals from all inside. The door reopens and out comes Lucy who looks at Tony who offers his hand.

"Tony, Hugues asked me to drive you ladies to work tonight and sit close by."

Lucy looks at Tony and smiles, "Hi, Lucy, and thanks for the lift in advance."

"Well with Manhattan traffic may be we had better get going?" said Tony and with that we were in the car and driving to the East Side of Manhattan.

Tony dropped us at the end of the block and we walked along the sidewalk and into the building. There seemed to be a lot of security. Our bags were checked and Lucy had her shirt and skimpy knickers dragged out by a burly security guard who then went bright red and Lucy packed them back in the bag and asked where she could change. The guards showed us to a green room for staff and once in there Lucy smiled as at the bottom of the bag was her small camera and glasses she used to record unnoticed. I had a pin that recorded sound and video and into the room we went where we grabbed trays of drinks and offered them round.

The barman was Pete and he looked as if he was not sure who we were and I managed to kiss him on the cheek and offer my hand saying 'Lucy and I am Suzie, agency sent us last minute' to which he seemed to feel was fine and carried on without another word.

In the kitchen I got acquainted with the chef and saw Lucy return in a very tight white shirt, busting at the front and a wonderbra that was built on the theory of how to launch rockets or missiles. To say the evening was going to go by with no one looking at her face was an understatement.

Pete motioned to us as we entered the room that he had trays of drinks to hand out and so we dutifully deployed ourselves in the room serving and recording conversations as we stood patiently for the clients to grab a refill. It was funny as I was standing next to this one beadily eyed little man, one would describe as 'Toady' looking when all of a sudden the British PM joins his group. It was her husband. Seems he was hosting the party.

His company had rented out the whole of the penthouse that helps the wealthy avoid paying tax due to loopholes the government provides. Yes Reader, once again from the little councillor in your village to top office corruption is inevitable unless you the people monitor it as they grow.

Lucy has an empty tray and passes me to say that there may be a complication and so I follow her to the bar. Pete is off to get ice and Lucy divulges what she has learnt.

"These are all top British businessmen that have backed the Brexit campaign, some vacuum guy who has made over a hundred and twenty three million on the exchange rate as bought Euros the day before. This group were behind the phoney bus campaign and even paid the ministers handsomely behind the false campaign to take the UK out of Europe. Now here is a spanner in the works we have another guest coming, Yerno."

I looked at Lucy and then around the room as Pete re-entered. I was nowhere near an exit and had met Yerno when in the CIA. Lucy placed her hand on mine and just said, "If he does speak to you affect a deep southern accent, it turns him on and he'll forget everything." At that moment in walks Yerno and many of the room look to greet him and it was then that I saw him.

Standing in the shadows in a distant corner was one of Kowlowski's henchmen who Yerno acknowledged. I made my way to offer him a drink and to gain his attention gently came up from behind and tugged at his jacket. He turned abruptly and seeing me apologised and helped himself to a vodka martini. As I walked away Yerno grabbing a vodka martini from my tray walked over smiling to greet the Russian. Yerno was forcing a smile and you could tell he was nervous.

Lucy joined me at the bar, "I wonder what those two are talking about?" As she motioned towards Yerno and the Russian I smiled and told her how as I tugged his jacket to offer him a drink I placed a bug on his arm. Lucy grinned and looked at me with renewed admiration and then down at her cleavage, "Nice one. Well none of these perverts will remember my face and if the vacuum creep pinches my backside one more time I will knock him out."

"May be over dinner we can sort him out, let's see how it plays," I say and then the PM's creepy little hubby calls everyone in to dine. The room next door opens and everyone walks into a dinning table fit for kings and all exit the main reception. Lucy and I collect glasses and return them to the bar. Pete smiles and decides to make a pass at Lucy and she grabs a bottle of wine asking if we should stay in the main room serving drinks whilst waitresses do food? Pete looked as if we were only here for reception and then I added, "At least we will be here to the end of the night and all be able to go home together."

Pete smiled and gave me a red as well as a white and said that if we needed anything else, and he emphasized, 'anything else', not to hesitate to ask.

So there we were stood in the room with some of the biggest crooks as we saw them chatting freely about their fraudulent successes and laughing. Yerno on the other hand seemed perplexed and unable to relax. Sat next to the Russian I heard the Russian say that his comrades back home eliminated the girl at the factory in India for his wife and she was in the middle east. They were going to deal with her so there would be no further problems with Yerno's wives luxury goods business.

The girl was called Prisha, and she was to be a personal mission I wanted to help, but now with the Russian Mafia she could be anywhere in the middle east. Only thing keeping her alive is she writes home to her family saying she is overseeing a new factory as promotion. Still no idea if this is her writing or if she is actually dead.

After a boisterous meal where the guests became more and more drunk the PM's husband stood to make a speech.

"Gentlemen, gentlemen, your attention please as we have great news to depart. As you know when we started to orchestrate Brexit we had no idea it would prove to be so successful. Apologises from our other investors for not being able to join us, but from the New Order, brilliantly run by my wonderful wife, the fund where we asked those interested in investing raised three hundred billion pounds and from the exchange rate of pound to euro plummeting all of you have just earned two billion each and that included the fifteen billion fee to the New Order as agreed."

Everyone clapped and knocked cutlery on the table like some medieval banquet as the PM's hubby continued.

"Each of you has today had these funds deposited into your offshore accounts we run for you so there will be once again no tax to be paid. My firm of course has deducted a small fee and all in all gentlemen, and my good lady wife, should conclude that business is now concluded and we all have reason to cheer."

The room is ecstatic and dessert is served and throughout the whole of this sensitive speech nobody noticed Lucy and I in the room. We looked at each other and then the door opened as the PM's hubby rang a little bell and in walked waiters with dessert as Lucy and I exited with empty bottles. Pete was outside with brandy bottles for us to pour at the table with him.

Lucy went to the vacuum creep and on form he pinched her bum. She over reacted causing everyone to see and look his way. He looked totally embarrassed then grinned and I followed up by spilling brandy on his trousers and as he stood somehow a candle on the table fell and his crutch was on fire. Lucy managed to throw water on the fire and both of us pushed him to the floor as if putting the fire out, but punching him hard between the legs.

There was a silence as Pete rushed over to help him up and all looked, but Lucy and I were already by the door to exit. The Russian stood pointing and laughing as the vacuum guy doubled in pain, "Hey Englander, I guess we call you Jerry Lee Lewis, eh? Great Balls Of Fire!" and the Russian started to laugh, as did the others and the vacuum guy in pain nodded OK, funny joke and was escorted to the men's room.

The PM was ready to leave and started to make her excuses and shaking hands, as she did not want her presence known. Her hubby was already two sheets to the wind as they say, and she whispered in his ear and left. We however were stuck as Pete asked if we would run the bar while he dealt with vacuum guy who had severe burns to his... well it would appear the fire missed both his legs.

One by one the guests left and handing Lucy and I huge tips. These guys were crooks, but also really generous. We noticed the PM's hubby with Yerno and the Russian in a corner having a full on debate and then departing as if they did not know each other.

Soon all had left and the waitresses lined up to be paid; one hundred dollars each and then they collected their coats. The chef walked off annoyed as no one complimented his work and suddenly the room was clear and just the staff and Lucy and I in the room. All looked dejected as they opulence and obscene wastage reflected on their hard lives.

"OK, is everyone here?" I started and all looked at me as if to say who is she? Pete walked back into the room and looked to see bar done and a hundred dollar tip he received. Looking at the tip he noted twelve staff including kitchen looking at him with envy.

"Eight dollars each guys?" he joked and Lucy looked at me and smiled.
"Well we got tips to add to your one hundred," says Lucy and looked to me counting money.

"One second, one second," I said. "Right if we add the one hundred already scored by Pete and add that to what we received from the perverts tonight it comes to..."

"Two hundred and fifty dollars," joked a waitress, "these types never tip."

"Actually no, not two hundred and fifty, you are right, actually it is one thousand four hundred, each!" I grinned holding up the money and all looked at each other and squealed.

Lucy and I handed out the cash and as we left found the two valet boys about to leave. They looked dejected as saw all the staffs leave with their tips.

"How did you do guys tonight?" asked Lucy.

"Thirty bucks to share…" said one dejectedly.

"Plus add the fourteen hundred from us that makes one thousand four hundred and fifteen dollars each," says Lucy and together we hand them our share.

The boys offer to buy us drinks and at first refuse to take the money, but we told them we were from the agency and were already well paid. They ran off to catch up with some of the other staff heading to a bar downtown.

"Well, I saw your ears prick up when they mentioned the Indian girl," says Lucy.

"She came on my radar a month ago as Kowlowski and his mob were doing a favour for Yerno. His wife was shipping Made in USA clothing tags to actually get sewn in into garments made in India in sweatshops. Prisha saw the corruption and tried to speak out, but was stopped by the factory owners and then disappeared, as scandal was never exposed. I have had feelers out, but now hear she is in Middle East and sending letters home so must hold out some hope."

"Let's get out of here as want to hear tapes of what Yerno and Russian were discussing." Lucy looped her arm in mine and we walked to the house in Greenwich Village. I was staying in one of the coach house flats at the rear so could come and go unnoticed.

Sat in the kitchen area with a glass of red we listened as the Russian divulged that Yerno must find the five hundred million by end of week and also how he would also help him finally bump off the Indian, meaning Prisha, she was alive and in a jail in a district in the Yemen. Yerno then says that he has the money sorted as he has transferred two hundred and fifty million for public housing towards a new luxury harbour development and the pre-sales means we can meet the money by end of week and look forward to the return of his share of one point six billion dollars from oil deal and then the five hundred repaid as well as harbour deal done leaving him at least six billion dollars to pocket.

Later on the tape was the PM's hubby discussing how his property deal in West London ruined due to fire of towers and also happy to invest in new harbours with Yerno, but also divulged how Arthur had caused huge disruption with the Knights by exposing councils and the vacuum guy had made a fortune putting dodgy appliances into tower that they had to cover up. Conversation changed after Arthur mentioned to the wall with Mexico and how knights taking money from prisons had drained finance to use inmates as slave labour. Also how unemployment figures were starting to embarrass the POTUS as his policies started to fail.

The PM's hubby laughed and say what his wife did with her employment and pensions minister as they transferred many people claiming benefits as ill health back onto required to look for jobs as shift in numbers looked good, and then he says as laughing four thousand dies from the stress so the numbers went down of those claiming and we reaped the rewards.

We noted the names of the New Order members from the evening and were placed on a monitored list with the knights. Watching the news we saw a huge party in London for save Soho and Erin attacking the PM saying that when she returns questions must be asked why she voted to keep section 28 prohibiting local authorities to promote or acknowledge homosexuality and there was a mocking competition of who was the best Prime Minister with drag queens taking part playing the PM. In the end there was no winner as all contestants ruled out, as none were butch enough.

We then saw news of POTUS bragging on twitter how he was to build more new homes for the people than anyone has ever done. With what we learned of funds being stolen I decided to listen to the tapes again and found a section we had missed.

The Russian stated that he has more investors from the New Order in buying up condos owned in the POTUS and Yerno's range of new buildings. There was also talk of funding new golf courses. I remembered one of the POTUS idiot sons mentioning that most of the money to fund the golf courses came from Russians, but only now linked these investments to money laundering and embezzlement.

This was something I realised would make the next part of clean up possible and also rang Arthur as noticed it was now

2am and in London Arthur would be up. We had a chat and he said that we should get out of New York and meet in West Country as visiting a Guardians Help Farm.

I noted Lucy flagging and in true Invisible style we both blackout as so tired and woke this morning in bed together. As I woke I saw a message from Arthur, he had Prisha's location and was wanting to help as he looked up the meaning of the name and it means 'beloved'. One of my favourite words. Looking over my shoulder Lucy places her hand on my shoulder and says that she would love to help.

She was off to Russia first and then wanted to meet in one week later to discuss a plan she had. We sat having a coffee and realised that the extra news of POTUS pre-President activities proved him to be part of a huge fraudulent scheme in getting his buildings built.

We booked flights and grabbed a taxi together to the airports to fly out of America. Me to London and then drive to southwest and Lucy has a flight to Moscow as she flies in as British diplomat, but has already a meeting on a farm with the Russian President, who has struck up an unusual alliance with Hugues as they look to fight the New Order together.

Relaxing in first class flying back to UK my thoughts remain with Prisha and my fears I will not arrive in time, plus why are they keeping her alive? Is it just a hols on Yerno and his wife to make sure they come through with the money?

32

As I walk out of Heathrow I grab a taxi to the car park where my drive is waiting for me. I am not sure what I have waiting as Guinevere apparently sorted out the rental. I collect the envelope and remove the keys to see the key fob of a Range Rover. I smile and see note handwritten by Guinevere saying that I should enjoy the drive.

Soon I am on the M4 and then turn off to follow the old route to the southwest and take the old A303. I had intended to make Stonehenge and enjoy a cuppa as the sun sets before driving on to Exeter where I am to meet a Knight.

En route I stop and offer a lift to a young student studying at Exeter University. We stop off and I buy us lunch and then manage to buy a thermos and have the café make us tea and fill the thermos for later. I then notice in the back of the car is a wicker picnic basket and it is full of wine and sandwiches. It seems our Guinevere is one truly resourceful woman.

My new travelling partner, Tiegan, and I enjoyed chats about sports and how she hopes to work in sports field somewhere, but for now she just wants to live and travel. She was coming back from a festival where she had had a great time and even met someone who could be the love of her life, well until lightning strikes again she laughed.

It was eight thirty as we passed the sign to Stonehenge and drove into the car park. The sun was soon to set and we took the picnic basket and thermos and set with the monument and the setting sun between us. Both refusing to take photos, as both believed the moment should be now and a memory, not another photo that never captures the emotion.

At eleven I was dropping Tiegan off at her digs and found myself at my digs, which was a new farm bought by the Guardians to be a new wildlife sanctuary and also centre for visitors with over seventy-two fields left for the wildlife. I book myself in and stand looking out over the barns and fields waiting for tomorrow and meeting Knight for talks on what to do next.

I had a message the next morning from Quetty saying she had been delayed, but would be with me early evening. I decided to have a coffee and wandered into Exeter. Sat in the Boston Tea Party, Dan the manager was laughing with a member of staff as Emma waltzed by and smiled saying hello. I ordered a steamer, which is hot milk.

Sat in the corner with headphones on I listened to more of the tapes we had made from the party held by the British PM's husband and in particular could not believe what was on there as listened to more of what Yerno divulged.

Yerno discusses how King Tiller has his oil fields also funded from money he has purloined from charitable funds for poor housing. Also had taken huge shares from prison profits to fund another dubious scheme for his empire. There was nearly five hundred million in an account that does not exist that Yerno had intercepted. The tone of smugness of Yerno's voice as he laughed how he would lift the money without Tiller knowing and when Tiller found out there was nothing he could do, as all was illegal so will be flummoxed to find where it went. It was stealing money already stolen.

Kowlowski's man decides to brag how using the New Order base in Eastern Europe he found out who had laundered money through the new POTUS and his family thanks to Yerno, and that Kowlowski has all the deeds and ownerships of the shares in the buildings and golf clubs and would be happy to sell back at a loss, but a huge gain to himself and his personal empire. Kowlowski was using this power over Yerno and it seems the President was compliant, as he never wants anything to get back about his tax frauds or dodgy dealings.

I sit and think how can we use this as I get a call that just says International Caller ID. I answer. It is Lucy.

"Hi, just calling in to see you are safe? I am in Moscow and Kowlowski being held on a short rope as it seems he has information on President and the two are as crooked as each other. We need any leverage we can get to shift power back to President so Kowlowski and his New Order are side-lined. Russia was all about bumping off opponents, but sadly without the Iron Curtain to hide behind the public side of things make anything to do with a high profile figure like Kowlowski more delicate to deal with."

"I think I have just what you need, but we need to set up meetings where Yerno and Kowlowski are free to meet," I said as I feel that we can kill two birds with one stone. "Sending this to you in an hour and hopefully if the Russian President wants to use as a power move with the POTUS it could be beneficial to thwart the New Order."

"Sounds sexy," replied Lucy, "chat soon got to go." And with that the call was over. My thoughts returned to Prisha.

Wandering back through Exeter to the car I saw the people rushing by, ignoring the Big Issue sellers and those unfortunates homeless sat in doorways even at 4pm. I thought of how Sir John and his journals had inspired me and yet making a change often is not what happens, just a shift in power to help a few.

Back at the farm waiting for me is Quetty; as always full of life and also free from work in a way so ready to party. We have an early dinner at the farm's restaurant and head into Exeter nightlife.

We have a few drinks in a few pubs and then realise it is nearly eleven so fancy taking in a nightclub. Well we enter this one club Fever, when I say club, like nothing I have ever encountered. Quetty described it as a school youth club disco for eighteen to twenty year olds who buy cheap drinks, get drunk, throw up and pass out. To be invisible would be impossible as Quetty and I stood out like sore thumbs. We avoided the advances of a bouncer and made our way back to the farm where the bar stayed open late for clientele and there was an ex-marine, Roddy, a Guardian running the bar, who was fascinating and we had a final nightcap and headed to our rooms.

I am sat here at my laptop Readers and writing up events as well as finishing off an idea for Lucy in Russia. I copy Arthur and El Cid into the email and send. I think what I have proposed should break up the New Order in Russia and Eastern Block for a while at least as we remove their access to money.

It is funny Reader, when you free up your mind and literally think laterally just how clear you can clean up a mess without complication. Keep It Simple.

Arthur pings back an email and has a huge emoji thumbs up and so does one from El Cid with a message that Sophia sends her love. Then a message from Arthur comes again saying that he has an idea how to get Saudi's involved and there is a knock on my door. It is Quetty.

"Can't sleep, and can see you up to your usual brainstorming, but can I help?"

"Of course Quetty, be grateful as once a very wise man talked to me about Collective Intelligence, and it has stood me in good stead ever since."

We sat up with madcap ideas and laughed as one was taken on as the plan by both El Cid and Arthur, followed by an email from Lucy saying that the games afoot, she was a huge Sherlock fan too, and that she has convinced the Russian President to have a meeting in Geneva at the G10 summit.

Quetty looked at me, and her eyes lit up as she realised how we were about to bring together two men at loggerheads, and have them work together. Then a fun email came in from Lucy with smile emoji's all over it. It read:

Yerno not the father of all his children as one from inseminated sperm from her father, the others were from Yerno's sperm, but they never have sex as she had been her father's sex slave and slept with everyone he needed to do business with. She hates sex, Yerno gets none and explains why he is such a miserable bastard. But, and this is a Big But Reader, it seems she is having sex with the Leader of the House to ensure all Republicans do as they are told and back the POTUS. What the money grabbing, spineless little man does not realise is that Yerno and his wife run the President who is now completely under doctors for dementia.

Then a PS at the foot of the email saying that she has located Prisha. She is alive, but on trial for adultery and expected to be executed under the laws of the land. It seems Kowlowski had her promoted to a big job overseas and so no one saw as a ruse to kill her, kept her alive and in contact with family and now found sleeping with a married man, all false no doubt, and after trial could be stoned to death.

Geneva was in three days and trial in five. Now we had prison and details we could try to find a way to sort. I suddenly went from adulation to feeling very down and Quetty hugging me we fell asleep only to be woken from a knock on my door by Roddy. He had kept us some breakfast, as it was 11am.

We dressed quickly, met in the restaurant and the delightful Roddy served us what they call a full English. Bloody hell Reader! I literally ate the lot then found getting up and walking difficult. Do the Brits eat this every morning and even though I could eat no more saw that there was one more slice of bacon and Quetty and I finished that off having half each.

I phoned Arthur to say Quetty and I would drive back today and he said that Guinevere and Sophia were hoping to take us out for lunch tomorrow. Things were happening Reader; things were about to go into action. As we discussed on the drive to London Quetty squeezed my hand and said that she never tires of being a Knight and that whatever happens she would always be there for me.

Sat next to this powerful, beautiful, and Amazonian of a woman I suddenly felt secure and safe. We listened to the Notting Hill Sound Machine's new album and laughed as we sang along. Covers and the band is a mixture of people each time so constantly changing. Pulling into a service station for fuel we saw kids in the back of their parent's car looking bored. We parked by them and saw that their iPads had run out of power. Quetty ran into the petrol station as I filled up and returned to give the parents a cigarette power adaptor with two leads for iPads. When they looked confused she just said, "Please a pleasure from the Knights to you."

I paid the petrol and we set off leaving a completely confused set of parents and two smiling kids waving from the back seat as they excitedly turned on their games.

33

Sat back in Chastity's house in Notting Hill I felt relaxed and was not expecting anyone, but there was a knock at the door. I have no idea why, but I answered it cautiously noticing the security chain was on. I thought strange as thought alone, but how come the chain was on?

"One second," I said through the door to hear a voice come back immediately to say, "Open up, it's not as if I haven't seen you naked."

I recognised the voice and to my pure joy as I opened the door there stood Mr. Carmichael and his soon to be Mrs. Carmichael, the fabulous Katie Raban flashing her engagement ring. Both looked beaming as we all just stood in the doorway.

"Well you going to invite us in," asked Katie as I jumped outside and hugged them both to hear the door shut behind me. We all looked and then I started to laugh as realised I had no key. Carmichael smiled after hugging me, well he actually lifted me off the ground, and took out his little leather wallet with skeleton keys and re-opened the door. "Old habits, well luckily for you," he smiled and we all walked into the house.

"So getting married? I am so pleased for you both, any dates?" I asked.

"Day by day as sadly when we cast Katie in the show she and Erin became superstars. I am the sad guy, arm candy at best, on the red carpet. Erin and Katie have a small tour of Europe and then possible have a couple of weeks to fit in a wedding and honeymoon." Iain beamed pure joy as he told of how hard life was being the backstage Johnny in their romance.

"I owe everything to you Suzie," said Katie. "You gave me my break, got this one to meet me and we fell in love from the get go, show was a hit due to your promotion, even the boys have their show being produced for TV next month with their Manager come Producer, my future hubby behind them."

"Well I feel it would of happened whether we came along or not, but let's talk about this tour and how you put up with this one always dressing you better than you can yourself." Katie hugged me and laughed as we walked into the lounge.

"Listen, I will put the kettle on, and Chastity told me there was cake in the fridge, you two get all the talk about me and my annoying traits out the way and we can catch up on you Suzie." With this Iain walked into the kitchen.

Katie was just the same bundle of energy as before and after ten minutes of her suddenly remembering something that happened and telling me funny story, she would suddenly remember another and finally Carmichael walks back into the room with a tray of tea and cakes.

"Right, Suzie thanks for the ten minute break, this woman can talk, but I love her for it. Not a day goes by when I do not thank whomever for meeting you in Ghana. Yes Katie you have had ten minutes without breathing and now time to hear Suzie's stories." Carmichael holds up his hand and Katie gives a sheepishly loving grin back and hugs him on the settee.

"Well, have been back in States..."

"Made yourself into a great waitress I hear? You forget I am still Knight's Templar. In fact this also why I am here," said Carmichael.

I had hardly started to talk and already was taken aback.

"Katie and I are to join you in Geneva, she is singing with Erin, Erin sends her love and cannot wait to see you," says Carmichael interrupted by Katie.

"And the boys say hello."

"Yes, so you are not so invisible at the moment, but hopefully making you visible in Geneva will help make you invisible elsewhere. Anyway, more on that later, we thought we should pop out, shop or go for a meal or both."

"So in reality," I said, "you two have come to buy me a dress for Katie and Erin's concert in Geneva and hope I take us to Covent Garden so you can both have burgers without feeling guilty."

"I have to hand it to you Iain, she's good." Katie laughed and then eating a cake stopped to look at me, "Well tuck in, I am not going to eat these without an accomplice."

Sat in the cab on our way to the West End it was a joy seeing these two, and so much in love. I looked out the window watching the people race by and wondered if I would slow down to have others view me with someone. Then without noticing Iain lent forward and slid his finger behind my lapel to feel Nichols pin.

"We are also meeting another friend today, well you are to meet his family," and with this Carmichael sits back in the middle between Katie and I and holds both our hands.

As we pull up to Covent Garden I see Robbins with his wife and two children and another woman. We exit the car and Robbins hugs me tightly.

"Suzie, it is so good to see you." I can see Robbins is truly emotional and nervous as he turns to the children and women.

"Ladies," he says, " I have great pleasure in finally introducing you to Suzie, Suzie this is my wife I married upon returning from our last escapade, Chelsea, this is Suzie."

I hug her and she is just lovely and starts to say that Robbins talks about me a lot. I turn to see the other woman standing nervously with a tear in her eye. I instinctively walk towards her and we hug. She squeezes me tightly and laughs to hide her tears, "Hi, I am Jeanie."

"Mike's sister?" as I say this she looks to me, and then the boys. "So which one is Mike Nichols junior?" I ask.

"That will be me ma'am and this is my little brother Cody." Both held out their hands to be shaken and I reply shaking theirs and without a moment I found myself scooping them into my arms and start crying.

"Are you OK miss?" asked Cody.

"I am sorry boys, but you are just like your father in every way."

"In what way?" asked Cody.

"Well, he was handsome, a gentleman, like you two and most of all a true hero. I think before we get all caught up I have a confession to make."

They all looked at me as wondering what I was going to say.

"You see this is Iain and Katie and they bought you guys here as an excuse for them to have the best burgers in town."

"That's dumb, but if it helps be happy to be their excuse as I am hungry," says Mike.

Jeanie hugs me again and we walk arm in arm to Covent Garden and see Vera at ShakeShack who waves excitedly and screams, "You two back again, well you did say you would yesterday."

"Yesterday guys? Honestly?" laughs Robbins.

"Well there is a great gym nearby," says Carmichael.

"But I bet you're not members," laughed Robbins.

We ordered sat and ate to both boys saying that they were the best burgers ever, and if ever Iain and Katie needed an excuse to come again they would be willing to help out. Jeanie just squeezed my hand.

"This is the best day ever," I said and Robbins took my hand and said, "Well I am coming with you to Geneva with the

Knights and then the girls are staying here in London until I get back."

"Where you staying?" I asked.

"A small hotel in Bayswater, is that right honey, Bayswater?" asked Chelsea.

"Yes darling."

"Well I feel plans are changing and Iain can you call Sean?" Carmichael looked at me and grinned.

Carmichael started to call Sean and I got on the phone to Guinevere, "Guinevere, yes, good to hear your voice too. Would you please get Jimmy to call me on this number? And tonight you free to join us all for a meal? Yes bring Arthur if you have too, we understand. I know it will be fun."

"What is going on?" asked Chelsea.

"Sorry darling forgot, this is Suzie so no idea, but sit back and let's see what unfolds," says Robbins.

Carmichael returns to the table, "All done."

"What is all done?" asked Chelsea.

My phone rings and it is Jimmy, "Hello, oh Jimmy, just a favour short notice. Need to know can you accommodate young newly weds, two boys, and a sister in Venice and then sort out a house on Lake Como with servants and all the trimmings within next three days? Yes, in the name of Robbins Love you thanks and see you soon."

"What is all done?" asked Chelsea.

"Well I guess you are off on a trip," says Robbins.

"Yes, thank you sir and happy to go. Can you call him now?" says Carmichael who was on the other phone.

"OK Chelsea, here goes, my part is as follows, you and Robbins here will be at the Savoy in the honeymoon suite for the next three nights, Jeanie and the boys have suites too, Sean is waiting and all paid for, literally all expenses paid. You see your husband here is a real hero and does much to keep many safe and we thought time to return favour. Plus as your daddy boys was a real hero too, you also get treats. Then I guess Suzie has organised flights to Venice and staying there a week, before a week in a luxury villa on Lake Como for a belated honeymoon." Carmichael smiles and Robbins smiles and then says that he has sadly the Geneva job and as he does his mobile rings.

"Yes sir, but are you sure, it is very generous, a jet? Sir, I cannot thank... I will sir and yes thank you." A bemused Robbins looks at Carmichael.

"Yes I am going to Geneva with Katie so you are excused."

"I forgot flights!" I said and immediately Robbins in tears holds up his hand saying that Hugues has given him access to use the Knight's Templar jet.

"What is going on?" asked Chelsea.

"Chelsea, you must know that your husband saved our lives as did your brother Jeanie. So you are to enjoy the very best of London, Venice then relax in Lake Como. Oh and for three days the boys and Jeanie will dump you at Lake Como to go visit Portofino for a few days as our friend has a friend who is giving you his yacht to explore coast, plus great beaches to relax at. Great now we are all up to speed I can see two boys that must come with us shopping for suits and ladies that need to buy new wardrobes for the trip. Hugues asked if you would put on your Knight's Templar card with a twenty-five ceiling," I laughed.

"Twenty-five what?" asks Chelsea.

"Do not worry about a thing Chelsea, you are going shopping without limits, what you cannot take we will ship home for you. But if we can all raise our cups and toast with this scrumptious lemonade to missing friend, brother, father and hero, to Mike Nichols, we miss you Buddy." A tear comes into Carmichael's eye and we all sit silently reflecting when in true fashion Katie breaks the silence.

"Well, I do not know about you, but these two have done all the talking and I heard that there was shopping to do, so what do you say Ladies? Shall we break this guys card?"

"We can help," says Mike Junior.

"Jeanie, do not be shy, OK have a plan everybody, if boys we can get Auntie Jeanie and Auntie Chelsea to buy at least five new outfits and all that goes with it, shoes etc., and my man here will be a great guide, Robbins, you will come with me and buy suits for you and the boys, and once everyone is shopped out we will go one shop more to Hamleys, what do you say?" said Katie in triumph.

"We love you Auntie Katie and Auntie Suzie," and the boys rush to hug us.

With tears in my eyes we leave to go shopping and I see Henry walking towards us, "Henry, hello?"

"Hi, oh Hi boys. Right, can I have your old hotel keys as Guinevere has asked me to collect all your things with Chastity and move to Savoy, and we are all having a barbeque at Guinevere's tonight to celebrate meeting your new wife and honouring this beautiful lady and her nephews."

"Who is he?" asks a still confused Chelsea.

"Another Knight we can trust," says Robbins as he hands over the keys to their hotel in Bayswater.

After a truly fun day shopping with Carmichael totally winning over the ladies we walked Robbins and family back to the Savoy. We are greeted by Sean, and soon as they all squeal with delight at their suites I bid my farewell and made for a room with Uncle Mike. It already had transformed greatly and even asked Uncle Mike and Delores to join me in going to Guinevere's barbeque. She was happy to accommodate and I wanted to help the two of them get out from the renovations and a night off.

At Guinevere's Arthur was as usual being told off for trying to eat the desserts, as well as being told to stay away from cooking as last time the food was badly burnt. On barbeque duty was Robert who was a dab hand at cooking and Quetty by his side making sauces. Then in walked Chenguang and Joseph. They were radiant and we all caught up about the Brazil trip. It took Joseph three days to slow down from working mode, then they had an amazing ten days honeymoon period, and now Joseph says that he enjoyed it so much he cannot get back into work mode.

I loved the look on Chenguang's face as he said this as she then mentioned the amazing results they are working with on the Guanabana. The minute she mentioned the name Joseph immediately could not wait to talk of the results of how the anti-carcinogenic properties work and I shared a glance with Chenguang as she beamed with pride, as well as proved Joseph was already fully back into work.

In a quiet moment with Arthur he told me that I was to join Lucy in Geneva and plans had been made as I had requested. Arthur also told me that there was also another back up plan in waiting should things go wrong. He never said what, but I felt it was an Invisible plan not a Knights.

We found ourselves in Arthur's study and a Skype call came in from Hugues and he was hoping I would be there.

"Suzie, you look lovely," he said and then went on to inform me that the Intel of information from the party had proven hugely beneficial.

"Yerno is moving five hundred million dollars from an arms sale and making out they did a bombing attack on an ISIS stronghold, but in the true tradition of this POTUS fake news, they were using an old attack footage making out it was new. The cost of the bombs dropped was nearly five hundred million from a company owned by the POTUS family in shares and so a payment to Yerno for this was not a big deal, but as nothing had to be paid for they could steal the money. It seems the whole deal was concocted in another meeting after the dinner party in New York and Kowlowski's man still wearing the bug. Your bug Suzie and even better is we then found out the money Yerno is to give to the Russians is going to buy land that has been radioactive for the past twenty years. Worthless, Yet the info Priceless!." Hugues laughs and I ask if I may throw in another idea? Hugues agrees and I asked if I could bring in Lucy to help. All present agreed and I managed to have her join the conversation and she was at a dinner where the Russian Prime Minister was attending.

"Hi Lucy, listen seems I am running an idea past guys here and wonder if you can get the Russian PM on board too?" Now this Reader is quite unbelievable, but true and out of nowhere the Russian PM is joining us in the Skype as I pitch the idea.

"Evening Prime Minister," I said and after all say hello I continue. "Kowlowski is still trying to muster the New Order in Russia and has another deal to get the money he misplaced back in situ and scupper all chance to have him removed. But with all the allegations of Russian involvement in American election etc. and really not bothered what happened as feel this is my plan. We get Yerno to meet to hand over personally to Kowlowski the money in Geneva as believe both will be there. We intervene at the meeting and explain to Yerno that

341

he has used American money to buy worthless land. You sir, will also be there incognito from Russia and suggest you use this to disgrace Kowlowski and his followers and have him step down. You then make him hand over all the real estate deeds he has owning majority of POTUS dodgy company deals and you sir can have them to do as you please. We will then use the deal gone bad to turn Yerno to help us route out the New Order in USA as well as severely haemorrhage New Order funds in Europe and UK. I do not expect Kowlowski to last long once his crime bosses have realised he has lost all their money and Yerno will be handcuffed to creating no more danger to the USA."

I watch as Lucy is translating this all to the Russian Prime Minister and Hugues smiles as he sees the PM nod and in poor English, as he refuses to speak any other language other than Russian, say "I look forward to Geneva." He then nods his heads turns from the call and exits.

"Talk later, and again inspired Suzie, inspired," says Hugues as he clicks off and Arthur looks to me and starts to laugh out loud as the study door opens and in walks Guinevere.

"Oh there you are, come on Suzie the Robbins are all here now and I am sure you need rescuing, and I need my wine waiter back," she says as Arthur attentively realises she means him and we enter back into the soiree.

I manage to have a chat with Mike junior and I ask Nichol's sister where their mother was? It seems she is now taking all Nichol's money and with new man going on a world trip without the boys. A tear came to her eye and I told her not to worry as I feel she and the boys will be better off and provided for.

Jeanie was such a lovely person and told me how she was always ill when Mike was overseas or away, not just as she worried he may be at risk, but because the boys were left with her and the wife was nowhere to be found. Nichols had been living a lie for his sons and had told her he had met someone, but would tell her when he returned. As you know he never returned alive and so much was not known. She then squeezed my arm and kissed me on the cheek before whispering, "He sounded happy and Robbins seems to have hinted it was you. I hope that was true as I wanted my brother to be happy."

"I loved him, albeit brief," I said, "but I want you to have something I wear everyday and feel that one day his boys should have."

I removed Nichol's pin and placed it on Jeanie's lapel and saw Robbins watching us. He smiled and Jeanie and I hugged and the rest of the night was an evening of joy. Nothing happened, Guinevere joked at Arthur's expense and Uncle Mike got a little drunk and told Arthur he never voted for him to which Guinevere laughed that she hadn't either.

Oh, and one other piece of useless information that was circulated was Yerno never has sex with his wife, but she was having an affair with the Leader of the House and that CNN had run a report.

34

Sat on the plane with all of the Geneva party I manage to travel alone with Carmichael as not to be seen. I am even wearing my mole with my favourite identity. That of sexy business entrepreneur off to trade shows, with her Bellissima Gel nails and also main rep for UK and Europe. I love being Emma Beauchamp as discovered here real identity on Facebook and she is just the most wonderful person. Every time I am Emma it makes me feel really warm and happy inside.

Through customs and off to our hotel Carmichaels and I stop off for a drink at the Hotel Le Richemond, that has wonderful views overlooking the lake. Not that we were staying there, but Kowlowski and his entourage were and we just made sure they were all there.

Kowlowski managed to sidestep the chop in London and is already feeling he is above any chance of being deposed as the next Prime Minister as head of the Russian New Order. We see Yerno is booked into the hotel too. Carmichael decides to have fun and in a risky move contacts Kowlowski's man as if from Yerno stating that the meeting should take place in Le Bar at the hotel in the rear of the terrace garden area. The goon nods and goes to tell Kowlowski. Carmichael then manages to spot Yerno has a man dealing with things at the main desk and intercepts him saying, in the worst Russian accent ever performed, that Kowlowski wanted to meet in Le Bar at the hotel in the rear of the terrace garden area. He even got both to agree to meet around 10am the next day and can only assume that both parties called each other to agree and it was done.

We went off to our hotel, the Hotel President Wilson, and settled in for the night and kept a low profile. Early night and with Hugues and Russian Prime Minister ready to descend and disappear for the meeting tomorrow Carmichael and I enjoyed watching Logan on the TV in our room.

Now Reader as a woman, Hugh Jackman films have always been enjoyable to the eye, but have to say one of the best films seen in a long time. We sat in silence together loving the brutal action dispersed with emotional and beautifully acted scenes as Logan discovers family and loss. I slept thinking of seeing Lucy also tomorrow and thinking, which one of us would win in a fight for a night with Hugh Jackman? I set alarms for seven and we were asleep I guess by eleven that night.

It was now 8:30am and Carmichael and I were already in the Le Bar at the hotel and have made sure a secluded section of the garden terrace is kept clear and had staff make even more secluded moving a few hedge style barriers. In fact a table for twelve to sit around set up and told security would need second access so one person could arrive and leave without being seen.

Now Reader, this would seem a strange request in most places, but this is Switzerland. The Swiss would be happy to accommodate the requests of anyone, literally anyone, as long as they are paid.

Hugues arrives and has a huge smile on his face walking towards us he cannot wait to tell us that all is in place and two extra guests will be coming. It seems El Cid is making an appearance so the POTUS knows we know his crooked dealings with the Russians, as well as letting the Russian PM know we know more openly.

It is amazing how time lingers, but we see Kowlowski men surveying the lobby and bar, then ask to see the terrace area and literally bump into Yerno's men. It was a little keystone cops and then a spaghetti western standoff. Then in walks Conchita Rodriquez and her Producer friend. I am wearing a wide brimmed hat and would look conspicuous, but the brim hides my face. However Carmichael moves to the exclusive menswear shop off the reception and watches through the window. I smile as he stands motionless and looks like another shop mannequin in the store.

Hugues has already disappeared and as no one is looking for him or expecting him he actually walked past the Russians who had no idea who he was. I look to the clock over the reception to see the minute hand click to twelve to read 10am. And on the dot both Yerno and Kowlowski enter and rush to the terrace.

Conchita looks to see and then looks round as her Producer friend has appeared. She has obviously no idea this was happening and is there by coincidence. I see her look round and then her Producer friend tell her to go see the lake as he has business and he walks to the terrace. I watch a dumbfounded Conchita and as she stands there alone, a little perplexed, I manage to sidle up next to her and say hi.

She spins round shocked and then says nothing, as she knows something is about to go down.

"We had no idea your Producer friend was involved, but somehow I feel you will need a new boss or cover after today," I say and we walk in to meet Carmichael.

"I am confused," she says and then sees Carmichael.

"Just a routine little sting to make sure that the shift in power does not happen," says Carmichael.

"Go have a coffee and we will fill you in later," I said, but Conchita smiled and says, "No, one better, I have the idiot bugged twenty-four seven, so we can listen, but how did this happen without me knowing?"

"I think you may be now a pawn and exposed, so would you allow me to have the Knights Templar look after you for a few weeks?" asked Carmichael.

I get a message on my mobile that Hugues and Russian PM in place and message back hold and turn on earpieces to channel seven. I get a thumbs up emoji from Hugues, which never ceases to make me smile, and Conchita turns on her bug that she placed on her man seconds before he entered the terrace.

"So we are all here?" we hear the Producer say. "I have organised in the usual manner for deal to be done via bank in Cyprus as always."

"I have transferred the money already in good faith, but have a little job for your men to deal with as a way of sealing the deal. The Indian girl in Yemen, she must die, as wife is annoyed at bad press she got."

"Be a pleasure and we have an idea that she is arrested for adultery and therefore death by stoning." Kowlowski relished in the telling of this. "So my friend, the account number?" asked Kowlowski.

"I have it here in my pocket," says Yerno and I hear Hugues say, 'gentlemen shall we?' And then a commotion as from a secret path enters Hugues, El Cid and Russian PM.

"I think Mikalei this is one deal too many. No please Mr. Yerno, do not get up. I am shocked by this too and Mr. President I was not aware you would be here either."

"Happy to be just passing sir and feel it is in both our national security to nip this in the bud. If I may Prime Minister," says El Cid and sits at the table as security take the weapons of Yerno and Kowlowski's men.

"Yerno, I dislike you, you dislike me, but you and your father-in-law are the worst administration of crooks America has ever seen, no do not interrupt and I would like that bank account detail by the way. You see Kowlowski here has sold you hectares of radioactive land. The money you were handing over would have financed a coup in Russia so that your beloved right wing New Order would of taken charge. America would have been at threat and Russia is better off, although we have had our differences the Prime Minister and I, in his hands."

"I agree," says the Russian PM, which he has translated. "It seems you have used the Cyprus banks a few times too many Mikalei and now to save your own skin all will be transferred to me. All the POTUS properties and investments made and shares owed by your gangster colleagues. I have a plane waiting to have you fly back with me and make sure all is done. Mr. President, or El Cid as I believe you are now known, I am five hundred million dollars short so may be the money should come to Russia?"

"I feel that we have negotiated you have all the POTUS shares in his golf clubs on American soil as payment enough, they are not totally worthless, but I feel Yerno we will have you back to the White House and can explain what has happened to your father-in-law and we will let this slide. You will need to explain that to save yourself from treason you will have a year to complete and make good tax returns for you, your wife and all members of the POTUS family, especially the POTUS as how a man can claim to be a businessman and file a few dollars short of a billion dollars as a tax loss in a year should make interesting reading."

The Russian PM laughs as translated and jokes, "Kakoh iiiytep," and the translator looks to El Cid and says, "What a buffoon." All laugh and Yerno hands over to El Cid the account number.

"What about my fee?" asks the Producer who everyone had forgotten was sat there.

The Russian PM offers to take him to Russia, but El Cid says that he has a man ready to take care of him. El Cid hands Hugues the account number and shakes the Russian PM's hand. "Let's meet later at a conference and throw surprise joint meeting as I feel you still owe me one last favour." They exit and I see Hugues signal to me to and point to the bar where a confused King Tiller is standing. I have a waiter say that there is someone waiting to meet him on the terrace.

Tiller walks in to see Yerno and Hugues sat with the Producer. Confused he sits and after a few pleasantries is bought up to speed. You see Tiller is also a corporate crook as far as I am concerned, but would not place his country at risk. He wants Yerno sent to the chair and then explains what will happen as per the wishes of El Cid.

Tiller agrees as the monopoly Yerno and wife have on the POTUS been straining even his patience. All agreed that the POTUS was a moron, but this move gave Tiller active role to run the President and his idiot savant, as the Vice President was referred to, would be oblivious also to the shift in power.

The five hundred million would be ploughed into housing for the poorest people in America and that once this had been done the file would be closed. Tiller looked uneasy and agreed before in an awkward and embarrassed silence departed from the table taking Yerno.

Sat at the table were the Producer and Hugues. Hugues looked at him and smiled. Before nodding to his men who then stood either side of the Producer.

"Sir, you will be safe in America, do not worry, but you will be helping us with all dodgy deals you have done for Yerno the POTUS, his daughter and once all done released to live a quiet life in the south of Italy where friends of ours will ensure no harm comes to you as long as you never raise your head above the pulpit again. I think we are clear. Gentlemen I think our friend is ready to fly home, make sure he gets there."

The guards lift him up and he is walked out of the back area. Hugues appears in the lobby and smiles a huge grin. He sees Conchita who looks worried.

"Conchita, you will need a new employer, and may be some time to relax. Your old boss did not collect his three million dollar fee, which was earned in the interest and feel you should have it as that bug he is wearing was of great assistance. Then when you are relaxed and feeling ready I would like you to be a Knights Templar. Good, enough said and will transfer the money tomorrow. Suzie again thanks as brilliant idea and El Cid will be the cover you need for where you are going and wish you well. Carmichael, I leave you to buy the ladies a drink." And with that Hugues walked off with his security men and Yerno's men who also were repatriated to be Knights, but reporting from the White House.

As we had a drink in the main bar we watched Tiller screaming down the phone at someone back home, "We need to sort that moron and his family out now!" He hangs up and marches angrily out of the hotel and then walks straight back in as a driver arrives rushing after him like 'Manuel from Fawlty Towers' and Tiller follows truly annoyed.

Conchita sits quietly and I place my hand on hers, "It is obvious you knew nothing of this and seems that the Producer was washing money through Cyprus for some time and was how the Russians funded the POTUS. Hugues knows you are innocent and we believed you, to be honest the look on your face would have been an Oscar winner if played by an actress, but we could see you were knocked off your stride. Come on you have some money and go have a break, a nice break and put down some roots, nice place to return to."

"And you, where do you lay your head, your place?" she asked.

"Well, looking at returning to LA as far away from the POTUS that is within my beloved America. Come on let's enjoy the lake views and forget everything for now." I realised that I could not stop thinking about Prisha. I was scared as this time an Invisible and with no back up, Lucy was joining me, but we were at the mercy of our own wits.

35

I am on a train to the airport and meeting Lucy. We fly to Yemen and then have a car drive to a prison on the outskirts in a backwater area with little interference from anyone outside. The court and the main jail are linked via an underground tunnel and executions are done in the marketplace. This was to be a difficult extraction and as we drive away from the airport a message arrives that three women are to be executed on the same day. I find out it will be stoning.

Now the person to be executed is buried up to the neck with just the head above ground. It will happen in the prison, but many men are invited to throw stones. Direct hits to the head until pronounced dead.

Even though the Saudi government are at war with Yemen, they have spies and influence and Lucy and I are new team on the death squad, as they are known. We have to take the women and bury them and then dig them out to burn their bodies in furnaces in the jail.

We pull up to our safe house outside the city park the car in an underground garage. In the house are two women also risking all to save loved ones and this has been done before. We are shown a trailer that is an optical illusion as it has a huge false bottom. There are two of them and three bodies of girls taken from the morgue who died from road accidents ready to be placed inside.

In the barrows are shovels, three body bags as women are fitted into bags so they cannot fight to make the burying them harder and then have a white cotton hood placed over their heads as the men throwing the rocks see the blood soak the bag and officials see no reason why they should see the faces of the victims.

After a day of looking at routes in and out of the prison it seems we only have one way in and one out. The tunnel to the court is not practical or possible. All will be dependent on the men walking around in superior mood and letting the women do the work beneath them.

I hear from the new Prince of Saudi Arabia, who is trying to reform slowly his country as women are allowed to drive. Others in his entourage feel it is a mistake as women are too stupid to know how to drive. This ignorance and misogyny is exactly why our plan has a hope.

We have to get into the prison and dig the holes. We need to then get the dead bodies in and bagged and into the holes whilst those sentenced to death are hidden to escape in a three-minute window.

As dawn breaks the next day Lucy and I in full hijab with our colleague have papers sorted by the Saudi Prince with a local lawyer friend in the city as the death squad. We are stopped at the prison entrance and papers checked. Lucy is fluent as is our helper in the language and I realise I speak nothing. For I act like dumb stupid woman and the men make fun of me as I keep going the wrong way and Lucy pushes me back into the van and we enter towing our trailer behind us.

We find out that it will now be tomorrow that the girls are to be executed, as there is a talk about something went wrong in

America and they want to get rid of any connection between them and the girl.

It is baking hot in the execution square where the holes are to be dug and we set to work. Lucy is taken to meet the women to be executed to measure them for how deep to dig the holes. Sadly, there is no chance to let the women know that we were trying to help them escape.

With the holes dug we suddenly realised that one of the girls we had that was already dead was only five foot tall. How could we of overlooked this. We are ushered out of the Prison. We leave the trolley in the hold and as we exit we start to realise that this was to be a highly risky mission.

That night before I could not eat. I drank bottled water and took a few vitamins whilst our friend prays and cries in her room. We stay in our hijabs and realise we cannot relax for a second as if the guards suspect us in any way we will be joining the girls about to be killed.

That was one of the longest nights I think I have ever encountered. I slept in parts, but when awake Lucy and I went through our plans. If all went to plan we would have three women saved and onto a helicopter flying in undercover to pick us up.

It was now 7am and we heard the sound of prayers and drove to the prison where we were ushered in without hold up. It seems this was to be a private execution and only a few local officials and guards in to throw the stones.

Suddenly at 8am we hear the door to the room we are preparing the body bags open as keys turn on the other side. It was two hours early. In walked three drugged women with a male guard and led to us. The main door shut and locked again there we were with the guard waiting for us to fill the women into the bags. He shouted in Arabic and suddenly we realised they was no way we could switch the bodies. My heart raced.

In the background was the trailer with our three dead women. The guard opened the first bag ready to place a victim inside, but he stopped and started to throw in large rocks and sand. He then turned and winked at me, "I heard one is only five foot. Hurry up ladies we have a show to put on." It was Sir John. He had managed to get himself into the prison a few weeks ago and was how we knew Prisha was still alive.

We pulled the dead bodies into the body bags and zipped them up and then placed the white cotton hoods on their heads. We heard the keys to the door to the execution yard turn and the three scared and confused girls were told to hide behind the trailer and two got in the false bottom. Then we realised that we did not have enough room to hide the third.

The door opened and Sir John shouted for the other guard to get back. He carried the short girl that now weighed a ton to the first hole and dropped her in and instructed the girl helping to fill in the hole. Lucy and I dragged the other two girls and the men with stones started to cheer and joke with each other as to who would get the killer blow.

Once all buried Sir John stayed on the yard by the heads and we were made to watch from the side.

Lots were drawn and the men drew numbers to see who threw first. It was just so sickening. Some had bribed officials to be given the chance to be there to kill the girls.

The first stones are thrown and glance the head, blood is drawn and we stand there stoically watching and then one stone makes a direct hit and the head inside the bag is crushed. Sir John stops the throwing of stones and feels the neck and nods affirming that this person is dead. He picks up a large stone and crushes it down on the head of the person deemed killed. Blood splatters and all cheer.

As each head is hit and confirmed dead Sir John throws a huge stone to confirm dead. I had no idea why he did this except as we dug the bodies out of the holes watched by the men hanging around having a cigarette there was literally no heads left. Sir John helped pull the bodies free and we each dragged blood soaked bodies to the preparation cell. One other guard showing more than a little interest came into the room as we lit the oven to burn the bodies. He wanted to see the girls' faces to ensure Prisha was there and dead. Sir John pulls off the hood to reveal a mess of blood and smashed bones. It was enough to make him throw up and rush out.

The fires started Sir John helped throw the bodies onto the fire and threw on petrol to ensure they burned fast. We then look round to see a terrified Prisha and Sir John says that she must be brave and be home soon. He lay her down in the trailer and laid a canvas over her and then gently lay the shovels and blood soaked body bags on top so it looked as if that was all in the trailer.

He then pulled the trailer to the outside and hitched it to the van and he got in with us as Lucy drove. We got to the gates and Sir John jumped out and ordered us out of the prison. The guards looked as if to inspect and Sir John held up the blood-drenched body bag and offered it to the guard who recoiled and shouted to have the gates opened.

As we drove off I looked back at the prison and see Sir John walk back in. Had he not been there all would have been over. We never knew a guard would be there, but it seems we were now out of the prison. Twenty minutes later we are in the safe house garage and the girls crying and distraught are taken into the house and given showers.

Prisha walks in and is still in a trance. Lucy takes her hand and the girl helping knew one of the other girls. That night we sat terrified we would be discovered, then at one in the morning there is a knock at our door. Lucy looks to me and we hide all the girls in a bedroom. I open the door and there stands Sir John. I cannot tell you how long I hugged him once inside, but I could not of been happier to see him again.

"OK ladies grab your things we need to move now. It seems as you saw the prisoners they want to make sure there are no witnesses and you are to be arrested. They are looking for you in town as gave them a false address for you so we need to be at these coordinates in half an hour.

Sir John then starts to set incendiary devices in the kitchen and brings in three more bodies from the morgue. "I need to set fire to this house and have your bodies found as they are a very lazy country and will just accept you are dead. What makes it even more bizarre as they have no pictures of what you look like, and in the lounge need to leave in this little fireproof box your prison passes. Just in case others taken in as they cover their tracks.

We all get into Sir John's seven seater, and off we drive away from the house. We see in the distance on the road to the house a pair of cars headlights and Sir John flips a switch and the whole house we were in is in flames. Up over a hill and into a flat piece of land Sir John turns off the car lights and turns on a beacon that the helicopter locks onto. In silent mode it lands just one hundred yards away and we run to get on.

We are in the helicopter and in the air, we are flying to safety and although written up for you Reader as it happened it was a really tense situation. Landing in Dubai we are then placed onto a jet and flown to the UK.

I am sat on the plane holding Prisha's hand and we all sit in silence. Sir John sits in his chair with his eyes closed and then smiles as he hears we are now over Europe. He looks back towards me and smiles.

Landing at RAF Northolt we enter the country under the cover of night and all of us taken to a house in Chiswick and each have a room and I sit with Sir John at the main table having a mint tea. We do not say anything. We never need to say anything. In the silence, in a look, everything is said.

36

I am sat in Parliament in the Knight's offices and Lucy is already on her way to the airport in her well deserved break, looking to sunning herself tomorrow in the Maldives. I will miss her, but there is the matter of Prisha to settle up.

She has given a report to why she was removed from India and it appears the President's daughter was having sweatshops make her luxury clothes and then had them sewn in Made is USA tags to all the products. Prisha had let word get out from the factory that three children had died and that one was killed by an order from the President's daughter as she was forced to check a loom that had stuck holding up production. She was there and forced the child to move an obstruction and the child fell into the machine as she removed the obstacle and was killed. The first daughter, as she likes to be called, ordered that every worker be deducted a day's wage for the hold up on production.

A complete report with photos of the made in USA tags in India were sent to King Tiller and he was even more aggrieved as he watches this failed POTUS falling down around him.

King Tiller wanted to get into power thinking the crook he helped win the election would be an easily controlled moron he knew he was. Sadly, it seems the POTUS and his family have embedded their corrupt fingers into the White House and are hanging on for all the gold they can steal. Fake news to bogus stories it seems like an idiot in charge, whilst behind the fool stands the commanders in chief, corruption has no boundaries and US soldiers lives at risk as he warmongers and his family sell enemy weapons. Never in the history of America has there been such a dreadful President or administration and Tiller cannot see how to remove himself from the fallout and go down in history as the worst administration ever.

We watched a report of reporters showing Tiller entering the White House and that an announcement imminent. Arthur smiled and then saw news move to show Sophia entering the Houses of Parliament.

"Yes, we have a guest, folks, oh and Sophia will be going as an Ambassador for the Knights to Rio as the work Joseph had initiated has born remarkable results. It seems the Guanabana has remarkable results on cancer cells and kills the cancer cells only, healthy cells do indeed remain untouched, fighting 10,000 times better than chemo drugs. Chemo kills all cells and is why most patients die. Sophia is here to join me at the Guildhall tonight to discuss how new health plans and in a well-positioned speech destroy the POTUS new health reforms.

We have also more news to be had as we have a new ally in the White House who will be made an honorary Knight and be asked to accompany Sophia on a fact finding tour of Europe and South America. In fact my friends this will be the biggest kick to the corrupt American White Supremacists in the White House. We shall have them try to align as well as wish us dead." And then Arthur smiles.

"Quetty, would you ask the PM if she would like to join us for a tea and meet Sophia?"

"She is on a flight to Brussels sir for the Brexit talks," says Quetty.

"I know. Invite her anyway as if just happened. I am sure you can enjoy the task Quetty?"

"Of course Arthur, I will be delighted." And with this Quetty smiles and leaves to visit the PM's offices.

"And Robert, how about you and Henry going to the main hall and walking Sophia here for tea?"

"With pleasure Arthur," says Robert and the two scurry away like schoolboys.

Quetty returns and from her expression the message was conveyed and met with much irritation by the PM. She was furious as she was not there as head of state and that the Knights have again made her look out of step and they are on the world political stage whilst she is dealing with a cause that she does not believe in, but she knows Brexit will be the biggest launch for the New Order in the world. She is just furious that no one will know of her power.

You see Reader the government you have here in the UK does not care about anything than being in power. We have the same in America.

All this bunch of crooks care about is power, they do nothing to help, and they just blame the opposition or others and never take responsibility. The power they use to line their pockets only and you see food banks and poverty everywhere, yet listen to their fakery and grubby opportunist nonsense the people are told that they represent the middle classes and even the poor want to be classed as middle class.

Readers here in UK look to what they do, not what they say they do, look to not see that the opposition would be worse because they say so. Change is coming throughout the world and only the people can make sure that the right wing New Order is not the future. Look to the politician that does and does not say that it is them having to deal with the mistakes of those that came before them. Sorry seem to be rambling Reader, but we cannot change the world, but you can.

Sophia arrives and she is radiant and has a friend. My mouth almost hits the floor; it is the first lady. She is stunning and looks radiant. Very reserved and humble when first you say hello.

"Why Suzie, hello, so nice to see you here. This is our latest member of the Knights and we have decided she shall be known as Joan as in Joan of Arc. What do you think?" quizzed Sophia in a coyish manner.

"Welcome Joan to the Knights, a noble cause and I trust you will enjoy working with us," I replied and then for no reason I can fathom I gave a little curtsy and Joan laughed.

"You mock me, but I am here for some of that irreverent humour. Believe me we need it where I come from?" replied Joan.

"So Joan are you ready for your first official trip? I trust that you can make the time?" asked Arthur.

"Please may I be candid?" asked Joan and then to her credit she told us all how she had been a virtual prisoner in America and that she had not been as husband and wife with the POTUS for many years, in fact just after their son was born. She even joked that the son was not his and somehow we felt she was not joking.

In walked Elaine and Guinevere, "Ladies we were meant to be here before you arrived, but no matter we are here now and reckon a trip to the bar would not go amiss and be good to have the press get wind of our plans and prep everything for tonight," said Elaine.

"I am known as Guinevere and wife to Arthur and this is Lancelot's wife Elaine, and these two handsome young men are Henry and Robert, and over here I see Quetty and Chastity, and the others you will meet informally as the weeks go on. You are happy to be known as Joan?"

"I am happy, no delighted to be Joan, and be in all your good company," replied Joan and Quetty walked over to her and hugged her. Then in walked a handsome security guard for Joan and she looked coyly away. This was her lover I reckon and he was assigned to be her personal secret service.

"Hello, I am Suzie, and your name?" He looked at me then Joan and seemed totally fazed, as he was never meant to speak or be seen. "If you are to be assigned to travel with the Knights may I be so bold as to say that we call you Gawain, one of the most noblest Knights of King Arthur. I feel that we should ask Hugues to pull some strings and have Gawain transferred from the secret service to be a Knight and be on hand to travel with the ladies at all times, that is if he feels he would like to?" I was enjoying a mischievous moment and the young man stood forward and looked at me and Arthur and then Joan.

"I have read much about the work you do and heard of your deeds. It would be a great honour to become Gawain you say, and it is a pleasure to meet you all."

"Well Gawain, I guess I shall have El Cid make a few calls and it shall be done," said Sophia.

"I feel if you offer to pay his salary thus making costs to my husband less he will agree it in a second," laughed Joan.

"So Arthur, what have you planned for these ladies of the Round Table," I asked.

"Yes Suzie, what indeed. Well I will need you to first go on a trip through Europe to meet some of the new hospitals and see some of the new businesses and communities started by the Guardians, as well as be there to make announcements on successes. You will also be asked to fly to Rio to inspect the amazing cancer research work Joseph has now initiated with the folks there, as well as I feel with the Princes and their African charities we are involved in, accompany them to make great donations on our behalf. I want you to be the flagship of all Ambassadors and bring peace and joy to everywhere you visit."

"Will I be travelling all year?" asked Joan to a silent room and we all looked at Arthur. "For I feel I would love to dedicate as much time travelling to help as you need," she continued.

"I think we ladies are going to be having lots of travels and working abroad for the people, but I think that we should have that drink in the bar and really get to know each other," and with this Guinevere took charge and all the ladies left for the bar and as they walked down the corridors you could hear the gasps from the MP's and staff.

Stood in the offices alone with Arthur he walk to me and gave me a huge hug, "You are to fly back to LA and take a month off. I have a plan for Prisha and will have her join a group of businessmen from India and Pakistan that have come together to produce quality clothes from new designers where the clothes are made in factories here, not sweatshops, and good wages paid. Prisha will oversee and we already managed to get her family over here too. She will blend in and start a new life. The company they have named as Mesheme.com and already looking to take on the giants that use less ethical practices. But she is safe and tonight will be reunited with her family...all fifteen of them."

"How is Sir John?"

"Oh he is back in Italy seeing to Kowlowski's new associates Marco has set up give him every opportunity to sort out exactly all the deals done for the POTUS. He has asked that you join Joan and Sophia with my wife to go to Lake Como where you will be guests staying with Robbins and his family, give you a chance to spend a few days relaxing with Nichols sons. I heard Nichols wife has already run off with some army boy and blow all the money they received as severance at a casino in Vegas. Whilst in a drunken stupor she signed the guardianship of the boys to Jeanie and the papers need to be delivered as Jeanie does not know yet. Hugues has organised

366

that Nichols remains paid every month as a Knight Templar into Jeanie's bank account and felt that should she need a hand then possibly you may offer to help?"

I looked at Arthur and a tear ran down my face.

"Well, time for all that later, better join the others for a drink and celebrate another successful mission as well as a real coup for us as now the POTUS is in a real pickle. His wife with her lover travelling the world doing great deeds he will want to be visibly seen to be supporting, his daughter and her erstwhile husband having to leave the White House to make sure they manage to sell off most of what they own to settle their huge debts that will be coming, and of course Tiller will be in the White House running things we reckon and this corrupt President will soon be seeing himself side-lined and berated for all the damage he has already caused. You see Suzie often we need a bad man, a fake like this POTUS to come to power to see all the problems we have that we have ignored. I feel that after this Presidency the American people will not be so stupid to allow such a cretin back in power. Plus the New Order not only in America, but here in Europe and the Eastern block has been severely thwarted by what you have achieved. Why even a Saudi Prince is now trying to reform his country. Some days are just great days and today Suzie is truly a great day. Gin and tonic or glass of bubbles?"

"Bubbles," I replied and we walked arm in arm through the corridors of power in Great Britain to the bar where Joan was already laughing freely and with great joy as Quetty was making her laugh.

I looked at Quetty and she raised her glass, "Such a shame the PM could not be here to join us." Everyone laughed and I thought of how infuriated she must be seeing once again herself in the middle of a shit storm whilst her predecessor and his team enjoy a life of wonder.

"Aunty Jeanie wants to know if you are joining us for a swim Aunty Suzie?"

Yes Reader I am in Lake Como and this was Mike Nichols junior asking me if I would come swimming with him.

37

Jeanie and I have become good friends and Robbins and Chelsea are with us having the time of their lives. As I wander down to the poolside I hear laughter and see El Cid in the pool with the boys as his own daughters sun themselves on loungers chatting with Chelsea. Sophia is with Jeanie in the kitchen and Robbins is tending the bar. I see Joan on a lounger in a beautiful costume having Gawain in his trunks rub suntan lotion into her back.

El Cid throws a football to the lads and it hits Gawain in the back. He turns and I see for the first time his chiselled body. No wonder Joan was smiling.

"Come on Gawain, you and me take on the boys at water football? What do you say?" asked El Cid.

"They look pretty good sir, do you think we dare?" joked Gawain.

"Yes, water football, let's play water football," shouted the boys even though neither had a clue what is was. I just think El Cid was having a great time with the boys.

As I sit here in the bar area outside in the villa I reflect on my time as an Invisible. Of Sir John and of all the people I have encountered and helped, but mainly write this journal Reader to help you see what I see from being close to the power.

Robbins joins me and seems coyish and explains that Chelsea and he were on off as a relationship for years and that all his affairs away happened when he was not with her. It was Nichols death that made him realise she was his glue. He told me how Nichols had told him to stand up and be the man he always knew he was proud to call his brother and marry Chelsea; that one of them should get the right girl. He laughed and thanked me for the wonderful trip, and that the honeymoon to looking after Mike Jnr and Cody with Jeanie was an honour, and I realised that Robbins and I will always share a common love for a man that did what was right, as he saw it. In a way he saved us both and his boys will remind us of the great man he was.

America is in turmoil, worst Presidency ever and we have to put it right. If they will not impeach then we need to go to the ballot and ensure he is voted out, vote so hard that he feels like he has been kicked out of the country. In the UK they have to see the government they have are also only there, as they want the power, the abuse of it they have already succumbed to the seduction of the New Order and ultimate power. The people must see the light and use their vote to make right the wrongs their politicians and friends are making.

I have a week here, a week in Venice meeting Ana and Vesna with Jimmy and his new wife, and then home to stay in Malibu with Tasha a regular house guest and decide what to do next, but for the time being I need to rest. I want to find time to see what I want from life. I now find myself wealthy enough to retire and have properties of my own that I somehow inherited. As far as new missions are concerned I am not sure. I need time for me and possibly spend more time helping Jeanie.

But for now, I leave you this journal, as I know at least one thing; I am now completely invisible again.